PUPPY LOVE
BY JEFF ERNO

Seattle, WA

Published by Fanny Press
PO Box 95462
Seattle, WA 98145

Cover design by Sabrina Sun

Contact: info@fannypress.com

ISBN: 978-1-60381-433-1 (Paper)
ISBN: 978-1-60381-463-8 (Cloth)

to Brad, with all my love,
pup

1

"Why are you shivering? It's seventy degrees." I looked up sheepishly at the tall jock standing beside me and shrugged my shoulders in answer to his question, then quickly looked back towards the ground at my feet, shivering again. "You sick?" he asked. I shook my head.

I knew who he was. His name was Matt, and I'd admired him from afar for the past four years of high school. He had been in many of my classes over the years, yet I doubted that he could even identify me by name. We were standing together at a bus stop, and I was waiting for a bus that would transport me downtown to the community college for my morning class. I was not sure why Matt was there this morning because I'd always noticed him driving around in his own sports car. As if reading my mind, he said to me, "Yeah, sucks havin to catch this stupid bus, but I'm having my car detailed today. I get to pick it up at one o'clock." He was trying to make small talk with me, and I wanted more than anything to be able to respond to him, but when I opened my mouth to respond, nothing would come out. Again I shivered and looked away. I wondered what he must have been thinking about me. He probably thought I was a total nerd...a complete geek.

It was a relief when I finally heard the bus pull up, and as I looked up Matt had already bounded the steps and was paying his fare. I climbed in behind him and looked around for a seat. The bus was nearly empty so I headed towards the back and sat alone; Matt grabbed a seat somewhere in the midsection of the bus, and I settled in as I heard the gears of the bus roar and we headed towards the downtown district. I opened my backpack then and pulled out a copy of *Harry Potter and the Goblet of Fire*. It was not unusual for a

college-aged guy like me to be reading this children's book—
it seemed the entire planet was in the process of devouring
this latest installment of the boy wizard saga. It was my third
time reading the book, for I was a bit obsessed with the tales.
I pushed my glasses up on my nose and scrunched down
comfortably in the seat as I dove into chapter seventeen.

The bus came to a stop to let on more passengers. I knew
that we had three more stops before we reached the college,
so I didn't even bother to look up. A group of rowdy
teenagers got on. From high school I'd learned how to easily
tune out the background noise when I was reading or
studying, so I paid little attention. I felt pressure against my
back as someone must have settled in and pushed their feet
up against the seat behind me. Reflexively I turned to glance
behind me and saw it was Devin Baker, a high school senior
who took a cooperative tech class at the college. He was a
regular on the bus, and I had the misfortune of frequently
sharing space with him on public transit.

"What are you looking at, fag?" he sneered. I quickly
looked back down into the pages of my book, not saying
anything. "Hey, I'm talkin to you, geek! What the fuck you
looking at?"

"Nothing," I squeaked. "I—" His hand instantly connected
with the back of my head.

"Shut the fuck up and turn around, faggot." I instantly
obeyed him, rubbing the back of my head to try to wipe away
the sting of his slap. I dove back into my novel, trying to
ignore Devin and his friend who were making obscene
gestures out the window to pedestrians that we passed. By
the time we reached the college, I was nearly through with
my chapter, and I remained in my seat reading quickly to get
to the final paragraph. It was best if I waited to exit the bus
until Devin and his friend were long gone, anyways. At last
the bus was nearly empty and I marked my page, closing the
hardcover book and tucking it under my arm. I swung my

backpack around my shoulder as I headed down the aisle and descended the steps.

Looking at the ground in front of me, I walked briskly down the sidewalk towards the science building, which was where my first class was being held. All of a sudden, as if out of nowhere, I felt a powerful blow connect with my back, right between the shoulder blades. Gasping, I was hurled forward and lost my balance, landing face down on the pavement with my book flying ahead of me about ten feet. I heard laughter. It was Devin and his friend. "Watch where you're walkin fag!" yelled Devin, "then maybe people won't run into you!" I lay there quietly, praying they would just leave. I would have gotten my wish but Devin's friend Kyle caught sight of my Harry Potter book.

"Hey Dev, look at this! It's Harry Potter. The fag boy is reading a kiddy book." They both laughed as Kyle tossed the book over to Kevin. I got up to a kneeling position.

"Please... uh, please give it back," I implored. The two boys looked down at me, grinning, and then back at one another, as if they both had the same idea simultaneously. It was Devin who spoke.

"If you want it fag, crawl over here and get it." I looked up at him, wide-eyed, and suddenly became aware that there were other people walking by who surely would notice me crawling across the pavement. But then again, I really had no choice. It wasn't like I could overpower these two bullies to get my book back. So I placed my hands flat on the ground in front of me and crawled towards him. He backed up as I got closer to him and both boys were laughing hysterically. "You look like a fuckin dog! If you want it, DOGboy, sit up and beg for it!"

I felt my face getting red. "Please Devin," I asked meekly, "Please just give me back my book." Just then I felt another startling blow as Kyle's foot connected with my gut.

"You heard him faggot! He said BEG...like the dog you are!" I doubled over in pain, tears now coming into my eyes,

3

blurring my vision. I forced myself to sit upright as quickly as possible and they both were staring down at me smirking. I pulled my arms up against my chest, holding my wrists in a limp position as if to imitate a dog who was begging. I stared up at Devin who busted out laughing. "Here doggy...you want your bone?" He held the book out to me and quickly I reached up for it. He snatched it back from me and tossed it to Kyle. "All you gotta do now is catch it, fag! That shouldn't be hard, should it? Uh-oh...I just remembered something...FAGS CAN'T CATCH!" They laughed, tossing my book back and forth over my head as I jumped up trying to catch it each time.

Their taunts continued and I was starting to get really worried, knowing I was going to be late for class. I was getting so frustrated and was in so much pain from the kick to my abs that I was openly crying. This seemed to do nothing but fuel the passions of my tormentors. They continued to call me names and insult me as they worked me into a frenzy. Finally out of frustration and pure exhaustion I dropped down to my knees and buried my hands in my face. I was sobbing now, but my weakness did not provoke any sympathy from the bullies. They met my cries with more ridicule and Kyle sneered at me, "Here faggot, you want your sissy book back? He pulled back his arm and swung the book full force into my face, connecting with my nose and knocking my glasses off, shattering them." I felt the blood erupt from my nose as searing pain shot through my skull.

Just then I heard another voice. I had then fallen prostrate on the ground, but I heard the familiar voice of the jock I'd encountered earlier. It was Matt. By this time there really were no other people around. The sidewalks had emptied as students made their way into their morning classes. "What the FUCK is goin on here?!" Matt demanded.

The bullies laughed, thinking they had recruited another participant for their "fag" bashing session. "This faggot here wasn't watching where he was walkin. We're teachin him to pay closer attention," said Devin.

"Oh, is that so?" asked Matt smugly. "I hate it when people are inconsiderate like that. But you know what I do when someone is in my way? I MOVE them," he said. I looked up right as Matt's fist connected with Devin's chin. "Like that!" Devin was taken by surprise and was forced backwards by the powerful blow. I heard the thud of Matt's knuckles as they cracked against Devin's jaw. Devin was on the ground in an instant. Almost immediately, Matt turned to face the other bully. Kyle was at least six inches shorter than Matt, and he stared at him, sort of the way a deer who is caught in the beams of oncoming headlights.

"Hey man..." Kyle said, holding his hands up as he faced Matt. "We don't want any shit. We were just having fun. That's all!" He was backing away from Matt.

"Get the fuck outta here now! Both of you!!" yelled Matt. Devin scrambled to his feet, rubbing his jaw. They ran towards the science building together. Matt watched them disappear before he approached me. Then he squatted down beside me. "Hey, are you okay?" He put his arm around me and pulled me into him. "We better get you over to the emergency room."

I shook my head violently, still unable to talk. "No" I finally managed. "I'll be otay." I could hardly talk, my nose bleeding profusely.

"Yes!" he said, and scooped me up in his arms. I did not really remember much after that until I woke up in a hospital bed. Matt was standing beside me, along with my sister Kathie. My nose had been bandaged and I could breathe only through my mouth. I felt excruciating pain shoot through my head as I tried focusing on the visitors beside me.

"Hey Petey!" it was Kathie. "Petey, you're awake." She grabbed my hand. "I'm so sorry about what happened to you babe. But it's okay. You're safe now."

"Hey little guy," it was Matt speaking. "You got yourself a bad concussion. And your nose is broke. It's a good thing I didn't listen to you when you refused to go to the hospital." I stared up at him, hardly believing what I was hearing. Why would this jock guy take me to the hospital? Why would he care?

"Your car...?" I began to ask, remembering that he was supposed to pick it up.

"Oh, yeah," he laughed, "Don't worry about my car. I can get that later." A doctor then approached, leaning down over me. He introduced himself and shined a bright penlight into each of my eyes, pulling my lids back with his fingers. I was so groggy and still sort of confused. He continued to examine me and spoke to my sister as he did so. I was not paying attention to his words though. I reached out my hand, grabbing towards Matt. He looked down at me and met my hand with his, squeezing it.

I was in the hospital for only a few hours before they released me, instructing my sister how to care for me. I was not allowed to go back to sleep for the next several hours, which seemed impossible. All I wanted to do was sleep, especially with the pain killers they'd pumped into me. My sister drove Matt over to the dealership to pick up his car while I sat alone in her backseat. The two of them kept trying to talk to me to keep me awake. Before getting out of her car, Matt handed Kathie a piece of paper that had his name and phone number on it. He asked her to call him and let him know how I was doing. She promised to do so, and then drove me back home.

Kathie and I shared an apartment together. We were the only immediate family that each other had. Our parents had both died two years prior, during my sophomore year of high school. Kathie was four years older than me, and had her own apartment already. She allowed me to move in with her while I finished out high school. After which, I then decided to attend community college for a couple years before going to university. Neither of us really was excited about the possibility that we might be separated some day.

* * *

My name is Peter Drinkell, but I grew up being referred to affectionately as "Petey." It became apparent by the time I was in the second grade that I was cursed with shortness. As a toddler I was a slight child, like so many other babies, but even after the other kids my age started to grow, it seemed I always lagged behind. By the time I reached puberty it was obvious that I would not grow much taller than 5'2." When I walked down the aisle to receive my diploma, I weighed in at a mere 106 pounds.

When I was twelve years old, my mother took me to the optometrist to get my first pair of glasses. For the longest time I was too humiliated to wear them. My peers already seized every opportunity to ridicule me, so why should I give them yet another weapon to use against me? However, once I realized how much better I could see with the glasses, I started wearing them more and more frequently. Eventually it really didn't matter much that the others sometimes called me "Four eyes" and other such childish put-downs; really, the glasses seemed to suit me. I guess I was sort of a geeky kid anyhow, might as well be smart-looking too.

It was not really that I was friendless and a total outcast in my school. I pretty much kept to myself and was always rather shy. There just always seems to be a clique of people, in any school, who seek out the most vulnerable students to victimize. A lot of my female classmates found me a bit endearing, actually, possibly because I was little. Most of the jocks didn't really even realize that I existed. My biggest problem was dealing with losers like Devin Baker, guys who really didn't have much about themselves for which to be proud so they boosted their own egos by torturing people who were smaller than themselves.

That night after my beating, my sister and I stayed up into the wee hours of the morning playing trivial pursuit. She made us a pot of coffee and kept me occupied so that I would not get too drowsy. When I was released from the ER, I was instructed not to sleep for twelve hours, so that meant we wouldn't be going to bed until three in the morning. I told Kathie to go ahead and zonk out, but it was pointless.

During our game, I kept losing concentration, and I'm sure that Kathie was concerned that my distraction was due to the concussion. In reality, though, my mind kept drifting back over the events of the day. I kept seeing Matt's face as I had first seen it when I woke up in the hospital. He was staring down at me, smiling affectionately. I remembered him scooping me up into his embrace when he carried me away from the campus. I guess he had hailed down a car, one of the other college students, and they drove me to the hospital. By that time I was out of it, so I wasn't even sure who it was.

Matt had called around eight o'clock to see how I was doing, but Kathie was the one who talked to him. I was sort of relieved actually, 'cause I'm not even sure what I'd have said to him. It was like when he was standing next to me at the bus stop, I could not come up with any intelligent words to say to him. God, I hated that feeling! It was so embarrassing to know that this really cool person must see me as being a complete numbskull.

Matt was everything that I was not. He was tall, 6'2," had an athletic build, light brown short hair, and a stunning smile. It seemed he excelled in just about every sport. During high school, he had been a pitcher on our school's baseball team, he was wide receiver on the football team, and he ran track. He played basketball for one year but for some reason dropped out of it, which was rather surprising to me because of his height. He was the sort of guy that wimpy dudes like me totally emulated. He always had a girlfriend, always was popular, and seemed to be born with a silver spoon in his mouth. It was not that Matt Porter was overly nice either. I mean, he had an obvious air of confidence about him that sometimes made him seem rather cocky. This cockiness was the one factor about him that made me the most self conscious when I was around him. He just seemed to be so superior to me...he made me feel like I was his subordinate or something.

I think that Matt knew in his own mind that he was superior to a lot of other people. It's not that he was prejudiced or conceited, just that he knew he had his act together. He knew that other people had a tendency to idolize him, and for good reason. This wasn't something that he gloated about, but merely something he accepted as a fact. Maybe he just was one of those guys who was a born leader. He had it within himself to be the head of the pack, number one at everything he did. He was the junior and senior class president of the student council, went all state in baseball and track, was in all the advanced classes in middle and high school, maintained a nearly perfect GPA. He just was the sheer embodiment of perfection to me.

So when my twelve hours of forced insomnia were up, I finally headed for the softness of my waiting bed, but I found myself unable to drift off to sleep in spite of my tiredness. I doubt it was the caffeine that was keeping me awake--more likely my own rapidly-beating heart, as I lay there ruminating on the images of Matt in my mind. He was like a super hero to me, having swooped down upon my enemies, grinding them under the powerful justice of his vengeful wrath. He then carried me to safety, cradled in his protective and mighty arms. I could feel my small body pressing against him, as I relived the rescue over and over in my mind.

When I awoke in the morning I blushed, realizing there was a sticky wet spot in the front of my briefs and on the bed sheets. I checked to make sure my door was locked before I stripped the bedding and headed for the shower. Already I could hear Kathie puttering in the kitchen, obviously preparing breakfast. Generally I did the cooking, but perhaps today she was allowing me to sleep in a bit. After my shower and my stop in the laundry room, I joined Kathie in the kitchen.

"Hey Petey...wasn't sure you'd be getting up this early. Don't you want to take a day from classes after yesterday?"

I rubbed my hair with the towel that hung from around my neck, "I don't know, I already missed all my classes from yesterday. Do you think I should cut class again today?"

"Well, honey, it's not really like cutting class. You were assaulted!"

I shrugged, "Well, I don't even know if I want to ride that bus again today. What if Devin is on it again?" Just then the phone rang. Kathie looked at me puzzled, probably wondering who was calling so early in the morning, "Hello?" she said. "Oh hi, good morning...No, he is up. He seems to be doing fine other than a couple of shiners.... Okay yeah, here he is..." Kathie handed me the phone, mouthing the word "Matt" as I took the receiver from her.

I hesitated, wondering what I could possibly say to him, "Uhhh, hello?"

"Hey guy! How's your head?"

"Oh...well, umm...it doesn't hurt so much any more. I have a black eye though."

"Figured you would. Hey, you aren't going to class today are you?"

"Well... I don't know. I mean, I should probably go cause I don't wanna get too far behind. But—"

"You wanna ride with me?" he asked, "I mean so that you don't have to worry about those bullies?"

"Ummm, no, really; I don't want to put you out..."

"I'll be there at nine o'clock to pick you up. You aren't putting me out or else I wouldn't have offered. Plus, we need to file a report about this at the police station too. These punks aren't gonna get away with this. We aren't gonna let em."

When I hung up the phone, I looked up at Kathie, panic-stricken, "He's uhhh...he's gonna come over here!" I ran into my bedroom despite Kathie's cries for me to return to eat my breakfast and started whipping clothes out of my closet. I stepped in front of the mirror and was aghast at my own face, badly bruised and sporting two black eyes. The one shiner was not nearly as pronounced as the other one, but I had to admit, I looked pathetic. Maybe I should just skip class today after all. I mean, I did look and feel like total shit. But then I thought of the prospect of riding alone to campus with Matt. I pulled a tee shirt over my head and jumped into my jeans.

It was just a couple minutes past nine when I heard the rap on the front door. Kathie was closest and went over to let in our guest. Matt smiled at her as she invited him in. He glanced over towards me and his jaw dropped. He cracked into a big wide grin, almost laughing, "Oh my god! You really do have a couple of shiners. You know what you remind me of?" I looked down at my feet, embarrassed, shaking my head. "You ever see the Little Rascals?" he asked. "You look like that little dog on there...Petey!" He busted out laughing and so did Kathie. "And that's even your name!"

I felt my face getting red, but as I looked up to meet his gaze, I saw such kindness in his eyes. "I'm jus' messin w' ya, you know?" He stepped over to me and put his arm around my shoulder, pulling me into him. "Just am glad you're all right."

Before we left, Matt asked Kathie for copies of the discharge paperwork from the hospital. He said that we would need them when we filed the police report. Kathie offered to take off work to go with us, but he assured her that her presence wasn't going to be needed because she did not witness the crime or anything. We were going to wait and go to the station after Matt's first class, he told me. Neither one of us had a second hour class scheduled that day, so it would be perfect timing.

When we got into the car, I turned to Matt: "Can I ask you something...sir?" He looked over at me, puzzled, probably surprised that I called him that, but did not correct me.

"Shoot," he said, giving me the go-ahead to fire my question to him.

"How did you get me over to the hospital? I mean, your car was in the garage."

"Oh, well I knew my girlfriend Tracy was probably in the parking lot. She actually would have picked me up for a ride yesterday morning, but she had some kind of appointment just before class. She was in the lot when I ran over there with you, though, and took us up to the hospital."

I felt a very sinking feeling in my chest. Of course Matt had a girlfriend. He always had a girlfriend, and why wouldn't he? A guy like him probably had all kinds of girls begging to go out with him. "Oh, well, will you tell her thanks for me?"

"Sure, Petey," he grinned at me, still enjoying the L'il Rascals joke, I'm sure. "Turns out, my girlfriend knows your sister," he said. "Guess they are pretty close friends."

It suddenly dawned on me, his girlfriend must be Tracy Mansfield. She and my sister had been best friends for the past ten years, at least. I could not stand Tracy and did not understand what my sister even saw in her. This was pretty wild; talk about a small world.

"So how long have you two been goin out?" I asked.

"Oh, just about a month, actually." That explained why I did not know about it, since Tracy's presence had been scarce as of late. That must have been how they got a hold of my sister from the hospital. Tracy would have recognized me and known to call her. It was weird that Kathie hadn't said anything to me about it yesterday, though.

When we got to the campus Matt gave me instructions to meet him back at the car after first hour. He walked with me to my first class, obviously aware that I would be skittish after what had happened the previous day. I was embarrassed by all the stares of the passers-by.

It felt weird in class. I could not really focus clearly on what was going on, not without my glasses. The professor at the front of the classroom was just a blur to me. It would be at least a couple of weeks before I'd be able to come up with the money to get a replacement pair. My only income was from a part time job I had at a bookstore two or three nights a week. My college tuition was being paid by a PELL grant, and my sister's income paid for our living expenses.

After class, I headed briskly towards the parking lot, squinting to see Matt's car. He was already there, and alongside him was Tracy. As I approached, she turned over towards me, and without a word turned and walked away. She did not even kiss him goodbye! God, what kind of a girlfriend was she?

Matt clicked the remote to unlock my door and told me to hop in. He got in behind the wheel and peeled out of the lot quickly. I could feel the tension, obviously from the words he'd just shared with Tracy. I glanced over at him, and eventually his face softened, "Don't be nervous about the police station," he instructed me. "I'll do most of the talking."

"Yes, sir," I said to him as we drove down the street.

* * *

I didn't have any more problems with Devin or Kyle after that. They were charged with assault, and a personal protection order was issued that barred them from having any contact with me. This meant that they could no longer ride the bus, because if they were to come within a five hundred feet radius of me, they would be in violation of the order. They also obviously took pains to avoid me on campus as well. Although they were minors, since they were both seventeen, they were charged as adults. I did not have to testify against them in court either, because they simply pled guilty. The best thing, though, was that they even had to pay for my replacement pair of glasses.

After the incident was over, it was quite awhile before I actually had contact with Matt again. I found out from Kathie that there was some sort of a history with Matt that involved her. Apparently she and Tracy had both been attracted to him. Kathie confided her feelings to Tracy, who then went after Matt behind Kathie's back. Next thing Kathie knew, Tracy and Matt were dating, and that was pretty much the end of their ten year friendship. I assumed that the argument that Tracy had with Matt on the day that he drove me to the police station was related to that whole situation. Tracy did not want Matt to have anything to do with me for fear that it would ultimately involve him with Kathie. The whole situation was rather twisted, and frankly I did not want to be a part of the madness.

Thus it made perfect sense to me that Matt would distance himself from me and from Kathie both, and he did precisely that. My feelings for him were still those of hero-worship, however; he would always be my knight in shining armor.

It wasn't until about two months later that I finally encountered Matt again. I was walking back to our apartment one day from the corner market, carrying a bag of groceries when I saw Matt coming towards me. He was walking a small dog- just a puppy actually. The dog was white and had bandit-style markings around his eyes, just like the L'il Rascals dog he had compared me to. I stopped in my tracks, grinning down at the dog.

"Hey guy!" Matt called to me. "See my new pup? I just got him from the Humane Society yesterday." I set my grocery bag down on the curb and knelt to pet the puppy. "Guess what I named him?" Matt beamed.

I looked up at him. "Petey?" I asked. Matt nodded and laughed heartily.

"I could not resist him. Can you believe how much he looks like the original Petey? What a coincidence to find a dog like that after what happened." I nodded to him, continuing to pet the puppy. "So how you doing? Havin any more problems with bullies?"

"No sir," I said, "None at all. I never even see those guys any more."

"Well you let me know if you have any problems with anyone. I'll take care of 'em for ya." I smiled up at him, never doubting his sincerity for a second.

"I can't believe how nice you are to me sir," I said, still kneeling at his feet petting Petey. "I mean most people would have just let those guys finish me off."

"Well in case you haven't noticed, I'm not most guys," Matt informed me.

"I noticed...really I did," I said to him, though this time not having the courage to look up at him. I continued to stare down at the pup. My heart raced as I knelt there in front of Matt, petting his dog. I wondered if he even had an inkling of what I was feeling towards him. Before I could worry about it any longer, though, he interrupted my thoughts.

"You should come over some time and visit us. I think the pup likes you. Maybe it's cause he sees a resemblance."

"Very funny!" I laughed. "But sure, I'd love to come over some time...if I can catch you when you aren't with Tracy, that is."

"Oh," he said, "don't worry about Tracy. I don't even see her that much."

"Really?" I asked, "Well maybe I will stop by this week sometime then. Do you live on Fourteenth Street?"

"Yeah, remember, I showed you?" I nodded. "Come over tomorrow afternoon. I'm home alone."

My heart was beating about ninety miles a minute as I rushed home. I could not believe that Matt had invited me to his house. And what was more, was that he made a point to tell me he would be home alone! I wondered why. I did not even fully understand the feelings that I had for Matt at this point. I mean, it was obvious that he was not some sort of a fairy. I often questioned my own sexual identity, especially when I had wet dreams about jocks like Matt, but I was certain that he was not in the same category as me. Even if he were, he definitely would not be interested in some little twerp like me, anyhow.

That night when I went to bed, I lay there thinking again of Matt, and our encounter on the sidewalk. I thought of how I had felt kneeling there in front of him. It just felt right I guess. It was so odd. Why would it feel "right" to me to be kneeling in front of someone? It was not like I was some sort of slave or an inferior of some sort to other people. This was a free country, after all—wasn't it? But as I lay there thinking of him, I remembered when I glanced up at him. He seemed to tower over me. That was when I found myself quickly looking back down to the ground, or to the dog I was petting. I guess I did feel inferior to him somehow. Probably it was because he had rescued me from the beating. Maybe it was because he was this really popular jock and I just envied him. Maybe it was because I had been bullied so much that I just was used to thinking that way about other guys, especially guys who were really masculine.

If that were the case, though, then why did I not feel inferior to the bullies like Devin Baker? He was nothing to me— just a piece of low-life trash. There was something within Matt that I identified as being genuinely superior. My heart was racing again, and I even felt the redness in my cheeks. I must have been embarrassing myself. It really wasn't right for a guy to be so obsessed with another guy like that. Maybe it was true what Devin said about me. Maybe I truly was a fag.

I got up out of bed and stood in front of the mirror. It was a full length mirror that was mounted on the outside of my closet door. I stared at myself. God, I had a puny body. I was only wearing boxer briefs and I saw the bulge— still rock hard from my thoughts of Matt. I wanted to see myself as he saw me. I stared at my reflection and took in the very narrow shoulders, the tiny waist. I saw my own big brown eyes staring back at myself. Instinctively, I lowered myself into a crouching position, ultimately kneeling there in front of the mirror. I was kneeling just as I had done earlier that day before Matt, on the public sidewalk. This is what he saw when he looked down at me. He saw a weaker person, one who was servile and submissive in appearance. He saw a quiet and shy boyish-looking guy who needed protection. No wonder he never corrected me when I addressed him as "Sir."

I wondered now, however, why he had invited me to his house. Why would he open the door of his life to the likes of me? My pulse again raced and I reflexively groped myself. I knelt there then and continued to touch my crotch as I thought of him. I pulled down the elastic waistband of my briefs and began to stroke. Kneeling there, I envisioned him before me and continued until I reached climax.

2

It was not surprising to me that Matt's family had such a nice home. It seemed that he always had the best of everything and always was the best at everything. He was hot-looking, athletic, smart, and obviously came from a family that was not hurting for money. I had ridden my bike over to his house, but I was unsure where to park it. I pedaled over to the side of the garage and left it there leaning against a tree. Then I tentatively looked towards the house.

I couldn't go in there. There was no way I could go through with this, even though it was all I had thought about for the past twenty four hours. What would I say to him; how would I act in his presence, totally on his turf? Why would he even want me there in the first place? He must have just invited me to be polite. Probably he'd given it no further thought since yesterday afternoon and would be shocked that I even showed up. It was probably best if I just went back home. If he did happen to question me about it later I could make up an excuse, say that maybe I forgot because I had a lot of studying to do.

I remained rooted in my tracks for a few moments and then turned back towards my bike. I took a step back away from the house, and just as I did so, I heard a noise behind me. It was the front door. "About time you got here." It was Matt.

"Oh, hi Matt" I squeaked out. "I wasn't even sure you were home."

"Huh? Oh, did you knock? If so, I didn't even hear you. Well come on in."

There was no turning back now, and I swung around and headed for the door. I felt so awkward just then as I made eye contact with my hero. Matt was wearing Umbro shorts and a beater shirt, basketball sneakers, and a cap. I made every effort to appear casual, as if I did not even notice him. I doubt that my efforts were successful, for I could feel every fiber of my being wanting to take him in. I wanted to drink in this image of my jock hero and savor every glimpse.

Matt let me pass him through the entryway, and I was immediately greeted by my namesake, Petey the dog. "Hi pup!" I said cheerfully as I dropped down to pet him. He excitedly wagged his tail as I showed him bunches of affection. "Awe, did you miss me? Good boy! You're my good pup! Yeaaaah!" I petted him incessantly, and he wriggled around frantically as if he just could not get enough.

"I told you he likes you," said Matt. We both were laughing. After a bit, Matt invited me to the kitchen where he got me a soda. I was not even sure what I was expected to do at his house. I'd never just hung out with a jock before. I kept waiting for him to reveal some sort of agenda he had planned for my visit, but it did not seem to be forthcoming.

"So Matt, can I ask you something?"

He laughed at me, "I don't know why you always ask for permission to ask a question. Go ahead, ask away."

"Why am I here? I mean, why did you invite me over?"

He looked down at me. I was sitting at his kitchen table and he was sitting on the countertop with his legs dangling over the edge. "You are so silly sometimes, guy. Haven't you ever heard of friendship? I mean, friends invite their friends over for visits all the time. It's no big deal. We are just chillin...why you gotta analyze shit so much?"

"I'm sorry," I offered.

"Don't be sorry." It was like a command. I felt I should then apologize for apologizing, but instead I just shrugged, letting it go. "Why don't we go up to my bedroom. I'll show you around the house and you can see where I work out." I smiled up at him and stood up as he leapt from the counter, leading me quickly up the stairs. He gave me a quick tour of his huge home and finally we made it to his bedroom.

It was amazing to me, being probably larger in terms of square feet than our entire apartment. "Here's my gym." He pointed to this enormous weight training system. It must have been a solo flex or something like that. Visions of him stretched out on the weight bench pumping iron flashed quickly through my head. "You like it?" he asked.

I nodded.

"I knew you'd like it," he stated matter-of-factly. "I bet there are a lot of things I know about what you like and don't like."

I turned and looked up at him, surprised by this sudden candid statement. "Why do you say that, sir?" I asked.

"Why do you call me sir?" he countered.

"Ummm...I don't really know. I guess just out of respect."

"But you are the same age as me. You don't have to show respect to me by calling me 'Sir.' I think you do it for an entirely different reason. Am I right?"

"I don't know what you mean, s—, um, Matt."

"I mean I think that you're surprised that I want to be your friend because of the way you feel about me. I think that you consider me out of your league, so to speak. You think that I'm above you or something. Superior, maybe."

I looked down at my feet. "Why would you think that I'd feel like that? Do you think you are superior to me?"

"I know who I am," he replied. "I don't go around trying to be superior to anyone. I'm just me, and I do whatever feels right to me. I'm not gonna tell you things about myself that you already know. It's up to you to tell me."

My heart was beating fast again. I was shocked by what I was hearing from him. Could it be that he actually did understand how I felt about him? Could it be that was what this invitation to his house was all about? "Okay, it's true.... I do think that."

"You do think what?" he asked, forcing me to verbalize what I was thinking.

"I do think you are —" I stammered.

"I am what?"

"Superior?"

"Is that a question?" he grinned.

I shook my head. "No, I do think you are superior...Sir."

"Sit down," he motioned me towards the bed. Unable to even conceive of doing anything other than exactly what he told me to do, I obeyed him and sat down on the edge of the bed. He stood in front of me, looking down. "What is it about me that makes you feel inferior to me?"

Apart from a direct order from him to look up at him, I don't think that anything on earth could have torn my eyes from the ground at which I was then staring. "I don't know. It's just something that I feel. It doesn't even make sense to me, sir. I mean... well, it was like yesterday. When I saw you...with Petey, and when I knelt down to pet him. I felt something."

"You felt that it was right. You felt it was your place to be kneeling in front of me," he stated.

I nodded, surprised that he phrased it so accurately. "And I'm scared of that feeling," I admitted.

"So why are you scared?" he prodded.

I looked over to the opposite wall, still avoiding his eye contact. "I don't know what it means. I don't know what it means about...me." I felt tears welling up in my eyes. This was such a difficult admission for me. "Does it mean that I'm a fag or something?"

He then laughed, but not viciously. It was a rather gentle and compassionate chuckle. "You shouldn't worry so much about stuff like that, little guy. I mean 'fag' is just a label. You are who you are."

"Well do you think that I'm a fag?" I asked.

"I think you're a chill dude. I don't care about what other people think. And even if you are a fag, why would you think that it's a bad thing?"

"Well, you're not a fag, sir. You have a girlfriend. You're this popular jock. I know you are not a homo."

He looked at me then so tenderly. It was as if he were a parent that was instructing a small child. "I'm not about to allow myself to be labeled as a 'faggot,' cause that just isn't me. I'm not at all the faggy type. You can see that. You know what I'm like. But that doesn't mean that even if you are a fag yourself, that it is a bad thing. I am me, and you are you. We both are awesome peeps, so why you down on yourself so much, Pup?"

I wished right then that I could tell him what I really was thinking. I wished that I could tell him honestly how much I loved him and how I thought of him constantly. I fantasized about being around him, being within the inner circle of his friends. I wanted to open up and confide these feelings to him. Instead I just said, "It's true. You ARE a chill dude."

Matt walked over to his entertainment center and pulled out a drawer of cds. "What kinda music you into, Pup?" he asked. I looked up at him and shrugged again.

"I pretty much like any kind sir. I like whatever you like."

"Good answer," he grinned. "But you know, it's okay for you to like whatever you want. You don't have to have the same opinions as me. Doesn't mean that you are right though." He laughed. He popped in an NSYNC cd which surprised me actually. I would not have guessed he was into boy bands. "I bet this is the type of music you like, huh?" he asked.

I nodded, realizing he'd chosen the music for me, based upon what he thought I'd be into. "Yeah, I like those guys, but I like lots of music actually."

"Me too," he said, "Jus' depends on my mood." He then sat down in a desk chair which he'd pulled out towards the center of the room. I stared at him as he kicked back, his

23

long legs sprawled out in front of him. He pushed himself backwards casually, swiveling in the chair somewhat. Then he clasped his hands behind his head. I was totally in awe, unable to pull my gaze away from him, for he appeared to be placing himself on display before me. It was as if a voice inside me was screaming for me to drop to my knees in front of him right then, to kneel between his legs. I didn't move though, but just sat there sort of mesmerized.

He too was looking at me, but was definitely not nervous and fidgety as was I. His lips sort of curled into a cocky sort of grin, as he sat there observing me. "What do you want to do?" he asked.

I felt myself blushing, "Um, I don't know...whatever you want," I answered.

"I don't think you really understand the question. I already know that you will do whatever I want, but what is it that you want for me to want you to do?" If I had not been so nervous I would have laughed at the complexity of the question. He paused and then rephrased, "If I were to give you an order right now to do something, what would you want that order to be?"

I was getting really frightened at that point. This just did not even seem real to me. Maybe he was just toying with me, trying to get me to admit things to him so that he could use them against me. Maybe it was just a game he was playing, a sort of bullying. But then I already knew that was not the case. Matt did not have any desire to bully me; he was the one who saved me from the bullies. "I um..." I started to stammer.

He continued to stare at me, by sheer force of his will, imploring me to go on with my statement. "I want you to tell me to touch you...sir."

His face got serious. "No you don't. That is not what you want at all. Say what you REALLY want." He almost appeared angry in the delivery of the command. "Say it!"

Tears were again in my eyes, as I struggled to find a way to form the words which would convey my deepest desires. "I... I...I want you to let me touch you when you are ... when you are...naked...sir."

"Well you are getting closer," he laughed. "Okay, I'm gonna tell you what you want. Then you are gonna tell me if I am right or wrong, all right?" I nodded, tears now streaming down my cheeks. "You want me to tell you to drop to your knees, to crawl over here between my legs, and to suck my cock."

I did not look away from him. I don't think I would have been able to had I tried, for he was staring directly into my eyes. I nodded. "What?" he asked me. "Don't just nod to me, say it!"

I gulped, and opened my mouth to speak. Eventually I forced myself to verbalize, saying only two words. They were the most important two words I have ever spoken in my life.

"Yes, sir."

I sat there on the bed, disbelieving the admission I had just made, waiting to hear what Matt had to say next. He was right, I did want for him to order me to my knees. I did want to touch him...with my hands, my mouth...to feel him in me and on me. But far more than this, I simply wanted to be with him. I wanted to please him somehow.

For all of these years I had been confused about my feelings towards men. I worried about and pondered my own identity, not knowing how to label myself. I'd try telling myself that those labels did not matter. I'd try to explain away the feelings that I'd had all this time, saying that it was merely a phase or that I was just shy and inexperienced with girls. None of that was true, though, and at this moment I knew it with such remarkable clarity that it was like an epiphany.

When Matt asked me what I wanted, I already knew at the core of my being that I would never, ever be satisfied or content with myself until I had the courage to admit the truth. I did want him, and I wanted him to want me, more than anything else in the world.

It was ironic though, for it made no sense to me why he would want me at all in the first place. When we had first really encountered one another those two months ago at the bus stop, he must have seen the weakling that I was. Then when he stepped in to save me from my abusers, he certainly must have seen how pathetically vulnerable I was. He must have viewed me as being inarticulate and a bit of a bumbling idiot for all of the times I tripped over my own tongue when he so much as spoke to me.

So my desire for him to want me was truly unreasonable. The likelihood of this ever becoming reality to me was practically nil. I had a better shot at the lottery. Yet, as all these thoughts raced through my mind, Matt continued to look at me, never flinching for a second. He exuded confidence and self-certainty as he comfortably reclined in his chair.

"I'm not gonna order you to suck my cock...not now. But I want you to come over here next to me." His voice had softened, he was being quite gentle, which sort of shocked me. "Come on," he encouraged me; it was like he was calling his dog.

I did not know whether he expected me to crawl to him, as he had previously indicated, or if I was supposed to stand. As if reading my mind, he held out his hand to me, and I stood, stepping over to him. "Now kneel down, pup. Sit here beside me." The tears had returned as I dropped to my knees, clinging to his legs. I rested my head against his thigh, and he made himself comfortable in the seat. He then cupped my chin in his hand and pulled my head back to look up at him. "Is this better? Is this where you belong?"

Through my tear-filled eyes I stared up at him, beginning to nod, but ultimately stopping myself. "Yes sir. It is much better." He pulled me closer to him, as I slid my legs up next to the chair's casters. This allowed me to rest my head in his lap. He did not discourage me or push me away, nor did he act in any way that was forceful or aggressive. He instead allowed me to get comfortable in my position. He allowed me to drink in the security of his embrace, to feel the strength of his dominance. He sat and I knelt. It was just right. It was totally right.

"You know, I have thought of you a lot these past few weeks," he said. "Since the bashing, I mean." I lay there with my head in his lap listening to him. "I knew from that first time I spoke to you, that you would eventually be here, in exactly this position."

"Kneeling at your feet?" I asked.

"Isn't that what you wanted all along? Haven't you thought of it too?"

"Yes sir," I answered. "I thought of it all the time. But I never thought you would ever want me. You have a girlfriend. You are not a fag."

"No, I'm not a fag, you're right about that. It's just not who I am. I already told you that, but it doesn't mean I don't like to do things with guys, though. You shouldn't be so down on yourself, either. I don't like that. I already told you how I felt about you. You're a chill dude. If I can say that about you, then you ought to be able to accept that it's true." He again pulled my chin back so that I was looking up at him. "You understand?"

"Yes sir," I said. I wrapped my arms around his waist, not yet certain he would even allow me this privilege, but he did nothing to dissuade me. In fact he slid down a bit in the chair so that I could pull myself up right next to him. I felt so secure and protected in this position. I felt the warmth of his body, and could smell the cleanliness of him. My heart was pounding rapidly and I felt myself becoming aroused as I held onto him, never wanting to let go.

Maybe it was the desperate way that I clung to him; maybe it was just being close to another person; maybe it was seeing the overpowering need that I had to submit to him— whatever the reason, Matt too was becoming aroused. I felt how hard he was as I pressed my body against him. His groin was just below my chin as I knelt there, pressing my cheek against his abdomen, firmly clinging to his waist. His hardness excited me and frightened me, but I could not pull myself away.

Matt placed his hands on my shoulders, gently pushing my upper body backwards. I remained in the kneeling position in front of him and sat down upon my own heels. I was then staring up at him, my pulse racing so quickly that I could hear my heartbeat in my own head. I reached in front of myself, down to my own groin, groping myself, sort of in the same fashion that a preschool boy grabs himself when he has to go to the bathroom really badly.

"No!" Matt instructed me, looking down at me authoritatively. "Don't touch yourself." I pulled my hand away quickly, being unable to do anything but obey him. I continued to look up into his face, wanting more than anything to allow my gaze to traverse down his body, wanting to see with my own eyes what I had just felt against my body. I wanted to see it, to touch it. But I could not pull my eyes away from his face. "Touch me instead."

At this point I could feel myself trembling. It was just like at the bus stop; I was shivering. Why did I have to do this every time I was nervous? His voice was so calm, so gentle and soothing, "Don't be afraid. Don't ever be afraid of me. Do you understand? Do you realize I will never, ever hurt you, pup?"

I nodded to him, "Yes sir." Maybe it was because I believed him so earnestly that I did in fact stop trembling. I allowed myself then to move my eyes down his body, down to his shoulders. They were so much broader than my own. I thought of the noticeable contrast between him and me. The structure of my own body was so slight compared to his. He had an athletic, toned body. His biceps were defined, as was his chest. I could see the outline of his pecs beneath the tight fitting beater shirt.

Matt was one of those jocks who maintained a very toned body. He was probably never overweight a day in his life. Had he not worked out and been so active with sports and fitness, he would have probably been scrawny like me, though a lot taller. He appeared slender and in perfect shape, muscular but not bulky. He reached to his waistband then and grasped the bottom of his shirt. He smoothly pulled it up over his head, grabbing his cap in the process as he pulled the shirt off, and then quickly replaced the cap on his head with one hand and discarding the beater on the floor with his other.

He must have noticed the quick intake of breath, sort of a short gasping sound, that I made as I first observed him shirtless. I could feel how hard I was myself, and wanted to grab myself again instinctively. But I instead placed my hands against his calves. I did this more to help resist the urge to touch myself rather than to demonstrate any sort of affection towards him. In so doing though, I felt the muscles in his legs, as he sat there before me in that kingly position, as if presiding on a throne.

His abdomen was very smooth and cut, not really a full eight pack, but definitely a six. His upper body was clearly v-shaped; he possessed the body I'd always dreamt of having for myself. He was the only person that existed in the world at this moment. He was the only thing that mattered to me, and my heart pounded in my chest as if compelling me to proceed to please him. I pressed my palms against his calves then more firmly and moved them slightly, glancing up at his face to seek his approval.

He made no objection with his expression, and so I moved my hands slowly up his legs, beyond his knees and into his thighs. He spread his legs apart slightly more than they were already, as if to indicate to me that everything was okay, but I hesitated before I reached the bottom of his shorts. I saw the outline then of his hard cock in his Umbros. It was as if I were frozen in time as I stared at the bulge, wanting with every fiber of my being to proceed, yet not knowing what to do.

Matt must have known that I would encounter this trepidation, for he was not in the least surprised by my hesitation. He seemed to be guiding me so gently, teaching me to embrace the things that I had previously denied about myself, or had simply ignored. "Go ahead, pup. Touch it." I think I again made that little gasping sound at that point, and he gently grabbed a hold of my right wrist with his left hand. His grip was firm but not crushing. "Relax..." he chided me. "Just be calm. This *is* what you want, isn't it?" I thought it ironic then at that moment that he'd point that out to me, for within my mind I thought I was doing this only because it was what he wanted. I thought that it was to serve and to obey him, yet he seemed to understand that it was really more for my own self that I submitted to him. It was perhaps validating to me, perhaps rewarding at some level.

He moved my hand slowly into his crotch, allowing my fingertips to brush against the outline of his cock. After making that initial contact, he held my hand there gently, and as I moved my fingers against the fabric to actually feel it, he released my wrist. It was like teaching a child to ride a bike, perhaps. Once I got to a certain point, he removed himself, allowing me to go it alone. Never before in my entire life had I felt of another man's private parts, not even another boy's . I was too shy in high school. I never had a close male friend that I experimented with or masturbated with. I did not even look at pornography.

Other than myself and the images I'd been exposed to in my sex education classes at high school, I had had no exposure to male arousal. The only person to which I could compare Matt was myself. Sure, I'd seen the guys in the locker room, but had always been very deliberate in my effort to look down at the ground when we were changing, or to dash in and out of the shower as quickly as possible, not wanting to ever stare at or look too closely at any of the other guys. Even if I'd had the courage to observe them more closely, it was unlikely that I'd have seen an actual hardon.

Matt was obviously much more endowed than I was, and really this was not surprising. His entire body was larger than mine. He was taller than me, his appendages were longer, and the structure of his body literally dwarfed my own. So it should not have surprised me that his cock was so much larger than mine, but I don't suppose that logic mattered much at that point. I felt so much smaller than him right then. I mean, literally all of me felt smaller, not just my penis. As I saw my hand moving across the fabric of his shorts, I was aware of the tiny-ness of my hand. I compared it to his hand, and compared my small wrist to his much thicker one. I knelt there feeling so little, and for the first time in my life, I actually enjoyed the feeling. I actually loved feeling so much smaller than this man I idolized.

It was warm—very warm. All the times I'd stroked myself, never had I noticed just how warm the groin area was compared to the rest of the body. His cock especially as it had continued to grow, and was now stretching the fabric of his Umbros— it was not just warm, it was literally *hot*. I wrapped my fingers around it, feeling the firmness of it, the veins in it, the heat. This did not even seem real to me! It was too awesome an event for me to encounter, I thought I might faint!

As I stared at his crotch and at the cock I had my fingers around, I felt so compelled to look up at him. I did so slowly, scanning his entire body as I moved my eyes upwards. When I reached his face, he was staring down at me. He looked content, though was not particularly smiling. He just had an expression on his face that seemed to indicate approval. I interpreted it to mean that he knew the scene was right. He knew that this was what was supposed to be happening.

"Pup, this is what you have wanted, isn't it? Tell me it's true." He was looking me in the eye.

"Yes sir...it is so true." My voice had seemed to have risen at least an octave higher than its normal range, and my words were spoken shakily, almost fearfully. It felt to me as if someone else's voice had been temporarily assigned to my body.

"Take your hand away," he ordered. "Put your hands on your legs, but don't touch your dick." I obeyed him without hesitation. He then used his firmly planted feet to push his chair back slightly, probably about a foot-and-a-half back from where he was originally positioned. "Take my shoes off." I looked down at his feet. They must have been at least size twelve. My own shoe size was 7 ½. I fumbled with his laces for a minute, untying them each one at a time. He then picked his heel up off the ground slightly and I grasped a hold of the shoe and pulled it off, first the right, then the left. I set them down next to me and looked back up at his face.

He then pushed his chair back even a bit further, by perhaps about the same distance as his first move, and replanted his feet on the ground in front of him. I remained in my kneeling position where I was, now three feet from him. He placed his hands on the armrests of the chair and pushed himself upwards, standing before me. He seemed to tower over me, and I knew I was going to begin shaking again. I expected him to step towards me or to order me to move closer, but he did not. Instead, he grabbed the waistband of his Umbros and pulled them down, exposing himself completely to me.

I watched as his knee bent and he pulled his leg upwards while pulling the shorts down, stepping out of them, one leg at a time. He tossed them on top of his shoes, and then stood in front of me, naked except for his socks and baseball cap. My mouth was open apparently, staring up at him in awe. Never had I seen a sight like this before. He displayed himself to me there, standing before me— the embodiment of perfection, the epitome of masculinity.

He only stood for about ten seconds and then sat back down in the chair smoothly. His cock was rock hard now, jutting out in front of him. It must have been about three inches longer than my own six inch penis. The cockhead also was very full, like the cap of a big mushroom. I was amazed by the thickness of his shaft too, even though I had just been touching it. To see it then for the first time was astonishing. His pubic hair was light brown, like the hair on his head, and it was not real thick. I was again overcome with emotion as I took in the sight of him, seeing him sitting there in front of me. I was again shaking.

This time, he did nothing to calm me, as it appeared his focus had begun to change. He seemed less concerned with me and more with his own pleasure. He wrapped his own fingers around the base of his shaft and stroked up and down a few times. He did this slowly and I knelt there in awe watching him. "Do you want to taste it, pup?" He grinned at me as he said this, again becoming aware of my presence, and seeming to revel in the worshipful obsession I was demonstrating.

I opened my mouth to attempt answering him. I could not even speak though, but instead moved myself closer to him. I crawled on my knees, without removing my hands from my thighs, shifting my body to inch closer to him. I was gasping as if trying to breathe, being more excited and aroused than I ever had been in my life. I finally managed to squeak my reply, "Yes...yes, Sir!"

He slid down in the chair so that his butt was on the edge of the seat. He was leaning back, his shoulders against the backrest of the chair. He was still gripping his shaft with his right hand, and he moved it outwards, away from his body and towards my face. Now I was merely inches from him, and I slid closer so that I was almost touching his cock with my lips. "Open your mouth."

Carefully I obeyed him, so uncertain of what to expect. I did not know what it would feel like to have him inside of my mouth. I did not know about the taste. I could smell him then, a much different scent than I had expected actually. Did I smell like that down there in my private parts? He was clean, for sure, yet it was a powerfully masculine odor, with sort of a slight muskiness to it. I opened my mouth, not real wide at first, but enough to slip his cockhead into my lips. I tilted my head forward and closed my eyes as I felt it touch my lips for the first time. I also felt his left hand against the back of my head.

He was not pressing against my head, but was gently touching my hair. He demonstrated no dominance over me at that moment, allowing me to feel him for the first time. It was not merely the first time for me to take him inside of me, but it was also my first time of ever tasting a man's cock period. I pressed my tongue against the underside of his shaft; it was just below the tip of his cockhead. I had to open my mouth wider as I took more of him in me. It felt so *hard* in my mouth!!! It was hard yet also smooth at the same time. It was about two inches into my mouth when I pressed my lips down around it, like it was a pacifier in my mouth.

My heart was pounding! I was trembling, and I felt the gentle touch of his hand, stroking the back of my hair. I didn't know what was happening to me: I was moaning while still having his hard cock just inside of my mouth. I grabbed a hold of Matt's calves again, gripping them firmly as I moaned real loudly, yet it came out muffled, for my mouth was clamped around his shaft. A chill shot through my body as my own cock erupted inside of my pants. I attempted to pull back my head instinctively, trying to remove myself from his cock, but at this point I could feel his grip on my head; he held me in place!

He moved his hand to the right side of my face as he grabbed the left side with his other hand. He had my head in both hands then but was not squeezing me or even being particularly forceful. The only force I had noticed was at that one point when I'd tried pulling back. Even then he was not aggressive, but simply applied resistance. I got the message. I knew my job was not done.

"Suck," he said calmly, offering no further instruction. I obeyed. I began to suck on his cock like it really was an enormous pacifier in my mouth. For some reason, I knew that I had to be so careful not to touch him with my teeth, so I concentrated on applying pressure from my tongue while pushing my lips down past my teeth so that they slid against the shaft as I sucked. I moved my head to take in more of him, while also sucking, pressing my tongue against his flesh.

There really was no describable taste to compare it to. It reminded me of sucking a thumb. It was just skin in my mouth. The sensory stimulation came from the feel of his grip, from the smell of his crotch, from the sounds of his movements and his voice. I opened my eyes then as I sucked, seeing him up close like that for the first time, having nothing to focus upon but his abdomen and his pubes. I sucked hard!

As I slid further down on his shaft, I realized that I needed to slide up and down on him. I knew that I had to stroke him with my mouth the same way that I had often stroked myself with my hand. I pulled back while continuing to suck. He allowed me to do so, realizing I was making no attempt to pull away from him, but was wanting to bob on his shaft. I was only taking in about three inches of him as I slid back and forth. His grip on my head was a bit firmer, but he still allowed me control. He was not pumping me.

"Deeper," he said. I wondered if it would always be like this, if he would always give me instruction in the form of one-word commands. I was compelled to obey him though, wanting to please him, and also wanting to have more of him in me. On the down stroke I pushed myself further onto his shaft, trying to take in more. I was succeeding, but felt his cockhead jabbing into the back of my throat. I opened my jaw wider when he was in me deeper, but I was afraid I was going to start choking. I did not want to gag on him!

On the next down-stroke, he pressed against the back of my head, urging me to take more. I concentrated hard on not gagging and thrust my throat onto his cock. Instantly I wretched! I was reflexively gagging, in the same way that occurs when you shove your finger down your throat to make yourself vomit. I suppressed the gag reflex as best I could though, as Matt quickly pulled me back, but not releasing me entirely from his cock. He never pulled out of my mouth, just out of my throat.

"Relax!" he said, "You have to control your gag reflex. You only can do that by relaxing your throat." Finally he was giving me some advice! There were tears in my eyes, though they were not from emotion. My eyes had watered when I was gagging. He again tightened his grip and gently guided me back down his shaft. I kept my eyes open, wanting to see how close I could get to the base of his shaft, wanting to get my nose all the way to his pubes.

He was in me deeper now on this thrust, and I bobbed back upwards on his shaft as I applied pressure with my tongue. He was allowing me to slide up almost to the very underside of his cockhead on each up-stroke, but as I continued, he shortened that distance with each thrust. I could tell what was happening. He was getting himself deeper into me and not allowing me to pull out as far. He was using my mouth like a jack off toy. He had still not taken full control of the situation though, was still not forcing me. Instead he was guiding me to do what felt good to him.

"Oh yeah!" he said. I was surprised that he was verbalizing something other than a command. "I knew you wanted this jock cock in your mouth, didn't you boy? I knew you wanted to be on your knees serving me!!"

I had not gone completely soft after having come myself and was now again rock hard in my pants. I wanted to grope myself so badly! His words to me were compelling me to suck him harder. I was aroused more than ever before. "Suck it! Suck my cock, fag. Be what you were born to be, a hole for my cock!" His grip was tightening on my head. On the downward stroke he held me firmly and I felt the base of his cock spasm against my tongue. It was his semen firing into his cum tube. He was about to dump.

He jerked me quickly backwards, pulling me all the way off his cock. I almost fell over onto my back, but my eyes remained glued to his shiny rock hard, pumping cock. He had quickly gripped the base of his shaft again with his right hand as he moaned real loudly. He cupped his left hand around his cockhead and thrust his hips forward, "Unnngghhh!!!!" he drained himself, shooting cum into his own palm! It shot out through his fingers and dripped down onto the floor. His body spasmed as he drained himself, half laughing, half moaning as he did so.

Matt then threw his head back and leaned all the way back in his chair, gasping for breath and obviously relishing the ecstasy of his orgasm. I knelt there in front of him as he reclined, his eyes briefly shut. He opened them. "Oh god!" he was still breathing so heavily, "Pup, you did a good job! You did a real good job!!" He held his hand out to me as he leaned forward in his chair. "Come and taste it. Come taste your reward." I then did crawl over to him, looking up in his face. He was smiling at me, and I smiled back, so thankful for his approval.

I did not take my eyes off from him as I licked his hand, lapping up what I'd just sucked from his body.

3

Probably the most important aspect of what happened that day, the day of my very first sexual experience with another person, was the way that Matt treated me afterwards. When Matt stood up and put his shorts back on, I was almost immediately flooded with feelings of regret and confusion. I had an urge to bolt out of the house as fast as I could. I looked down at myself and my crotch was soaked with my own semen, I could taste Matt's load on my tongue still, and I was all sticky and dirty from my own sweat and tears. I crawled over to the bed and leaned against it, pulled my knees up to my chest and hugged them. So it was true; everything I'd been accused of for all these years was totally true. The remarks of Devin Baker and his friends were not just bullying. Apparently they had seen in me what I was unwilling to admit about myself. I was a total low-life faggot.

Yet while I was so bewildered with these feelings of guilt and shame, at the same time I felt as if what had just happened was absolutely right. When Matt, during the heat of orgasmic pleasure, had called out to me, saying I was a fag and was born to be his cum hole, I knew he was totally correct. But then only moments before that, he had assured me I was a "chill dude." He had told me not to be down on myself. In fact, he'd given me a direct order in that regard. But how could he regard me as being such a cool person on the one hand, and a faggot cum hole on the other? How could I be of any value to anyone when I was so worthless?

Maybe that was where I did have value, though. Maybe serving a superior man such as Matt was the only worthwhile contribution I'd ever make in life. Maybe in order to have any sense of worth at all, I'd have to kneel before and serve dominant men such as Matt. I was nothing on my own—altogether incomplete. I buried my face in my hands then, not really crying, but just wanting all these thoughts and images to go away. I wanted to shut out all this horrible confusion.

Matt was suddenly beside me, sitting on the bed. I reached over and wrapped my arms around his leg, kissing his calf just below the knee. At this point I did begin to cry, and I clung to him so fiercely. He pulled me up onto the bed then, wrapping his arms around me. "Why are you crying pup? What is wrong?"

For some reason I was beginning to think of Matt as being this omniscient person who knew and understood everything about me. It was so easy to forget that he was only human and could not read minds. Maybe he would misinterpret my emotion. Maybe he would think I regretted pleasing him. Maybe he would think I was just an overly-emotional pussy. I tried to stop myself from displaying the emotion, to dry up my tears and to come up with some excuse for why I was acting like this. But all I was able to do was to melt into his embrace as my crying turned into something more like sobs.

He held me so protectively then, allowing me to express the overwhelming emotion that was within me. And very soothingly he spoke to me, "Pup, I know that what you just did was something you enjoyed. It was something that you *needed*. I could see it in your eyes. I could see and feel your hunger for it! And now you're confused about why you did it. You are wondering what this means. You maybe think it makes you some sort of a bad person for enjoying it as much as you did. Am I right?"

I squeezed him as tightly as I could. "Yes." He gently pushed me back from his chest so that he could look me in the eye.

"Well you are *not* a bad person. You are an awesome person...a chill dude, remember? It's just we each have a role in life, I guess. We each have a different identity, different characteristics that make us who we are. Some of us are dominant— 'superior,' as you say— and others are submissive. That doesn't mean that you are any better or any worse than anyone else. It just means you are you, just like I am me."

"But sir, you even said it yourself. You said I was just a fag, just a hole for your cum."

"Well what about that statement was untrue?" he asked. "Sexually this is very accurate. You were here to serve me, right? That is your role; it is who you are. But it doesn't mean that as a *person* you are nothing. It means that when you kneel to serve me, you are mine to use as I wish. And really, you want it that way, don't you?"

I nodded. "Yes sir... I'm sorry." I was wiping my eyes with the palms of my hands. "I am acting like a baby."

"Nah..." he said, "You're acting like who you are—my pup. And it's cool." He pulled me back into his embrace and I wrapped my arms around his chest again. I felt his strength, his protectiveness. Oh god, I loved him so much.

* * *

I left Matt's house with dry clothes. He had given me a pair of his boxers and some shorts to wear home. I used a duffle bag of his to tote home my soaked briefs and khakis. Pedaling away from my house I felt such an incredible feeling of euphoria. It was like being on cloud nine. The feeling was absolutely surreal. I was still in shock, amazed that Matt had ever been interested in me in any way. I was even more amazed that he had allowed me to be intimate with him. Before I even got back home I was wanting to turn around and head back to him. I did not think I would be able to bear being away from him, not after he had lovingly held me the way that he had.

I began to think about doing things with Matt that went far beyond what we had just done together. I fantasized about him kissing me, passionately kissing me. I fantasized about him being on top of me, being inside of me—and not just my mouth. That was so scary to me, though; I both wanted it and feared it simultaneously. What would it feel like to have someone enter you that way? I thought maybe it would be painful. Maybe I would not be able to withstand the pain and would cry. I would disappoint him so badly if I did that. But then again, what was the likelihood that he would ever do something like that with me in the first place? After all, he *wasn't* a fag. He had stated that very clearly.

How long was it going to be before I saw him again? I did not think I could wait a whole day to see him. It was strange, because I had not thought to ask him before I left when we would be together again. He had not mentioned it either. He did not give me his number, and come to think of it, he never had. When he rescued me from my assailants two months ago, he had given Kathie a piece of paper that had his number on it, but I had never seen it. Maybe that meant I should not call him. Had he wanted me to call him, he'd have told me to do so. This meant that I was going to have to wait for him to call me. What if he never did?! What if he had just wanted to get his rocks off and that was all? What if this was just some sort of a game he was playing to see if I would actually fall for him?

God, I drove myself crazy with this nonsensical thinking! If he was only using me and wanted nothing more to do with me, surely he would not have held me afterward, and he definitely wouldn't have loaned me clothing and a duffle bag. Why did I always have to worry the way that I did? Why did I fret about things that most people would not even think of?

I knew what I'd do! I would ask Kathie if she still had Matt's number. I'd have to come up with some excuse, and I'd definitely have to sound casual about it. Then if he did not call me soon, I could call him. But wait! I couldn't call him if he did not call me. That would make me seem like I was pathetic. I'd seem like such a loser who wanted him so much that I couldn't even wait for him to call me. I did want him that much though. Should I let him see how much I wanted him? Should I let him see how much I wanted him to want me?

When I walked through the door of our apartment I made a deliberate effort to head briskly towards the bedroom. I did not want Kathie to ask me where I had gotten the pair of shorts I was wearing. If she saw me at all, she definitely would notice the shorts. They hung down far past my knees, and I had the drawstring cord on the waist cinched really tight to keep them from falling. She did hear me come in though and called hello from the kitchen. As I headed down the hallway, she told me dinner would be ready in a minute. I wanted to shout back to her that I had just eaten, thinking of Matt's cum, but instead I just grinned to myself and dashed into my bedroom.

When I came out to the kitchen she had a big spaghetti dinner set out on the table. "Wow, Kathie. This isn't like you to cook a big meal. What's the occasion?"

"Hmm, there really isn't one," she said. "I just wanted to cook for you for a change. Then I was getting worried though, cause you hadn't come home. Where have you been?"

I hesitated a moment before answering, and in a split second decided it best I tell her the truth. There was nothing wrong with me visiting a friend, right? "I was over at Matt's house."

"Matt?" she asked.

"Yeah, Matt Porter. Remember the guy you used to have the hots for. The one who took me to the hospital."

Her face got instantly red. "Well I didn't have the hots for him...*obviously*! If I did, then maybe I would have at least remembered who he was."

"Then why are you so defensive about it?" I asked.

"I'm *not!*" she snapped back. "Plus he already has a girlfriend. Tracy."

"Well I think he is too good for that bitch!" I surprised myself by my own vindictive words. I quickly added, "I mean after the way she dumped you as her friend after all those years."

"Yeah, I know, but I think it's probably for the best. I am better off without friends like that."

"What do you think Matt even sees in her?" I asked. "I mean he doesn't really even seem to think she is all that great. He never talks about her or says anything good about her. Why is he even with her?"

"How would you know what he says about her? It's not like you have ever spent any time with him, other than your visit today, that is."

"Well maybe we will spend more time together after today. I think he is starting to become my friend. And his dog likes me too. He even named it after me."

"That's cool! Just be careful, Petey. I don't want you to get really attached to him and then have him hurt you."

"Matt or the dog?" I asked sarcastically. "Like how could some other guy hurt me anyways? That doesn't even make sense."

"It's just that I know you Petey. You're very sensitive. Sometimes those jocks like Matt can be really thoughtless and downright mean. Trust me; I know."

"Don't worry, I *know* he will never hurt me." I remembered his promise to me, *Don't be afraid. Don't ever be afraid of me. Do you understand? Do you realize I will never, ever hurt you, pup?* "Did you already forget what he did for me...how he saved me?"

"No, I didn't forget. Guess I'm just being overly protective again. I'm glad he's your friend; really I am." She smiled at me sincerely. "Pass the garlic bread, please."

I insisted on doing the dishes after dinner and then headed to my room to do some studying. I was in the middle of writing a term paper on disassociate personality disorder for my abnormal psychology class. I'd already completed my

43

rough draft and had most of my research done. I sat down at my computer to begin typing the body of text. After about forty five minutes, I had gotten about four pages of typing done and realized that I needed to look up a source for my bibliography. I minimized my word processing document and logged onto my online account. I located my search engine and typed in a keyword. As the computer opened the matches to websites that related to the keyword, I was interrupted by an instant message.

It was from MattJock82. "Yo pup" My heart skipped a beat, realizing it must be Matt sending me a message!

Ptboy1982: how did you get my screen name, sir?

MattJock82: wasn't hard. Profile search

Oh my god! This was freaky. I just left Matt's house two hours ago and here he was already with me in my own bedroom. I guess I shouldn't have worried so much about him never calling me.

Ptboy1982: thank you for today...for everything

MattJock82: welcome. What did ur sis say bout the shorts?

Ptboy1982: lol she did not see them. I changed soon as I got home. When should I bring them back to you?

MattJock82: don't worry bout it, I'm not. I know I'll get em eventually

Damn. I was wanting him to give me a time, so I'd know when I'd see him again.

Ptboy1982: Well, I have to work tomorrow after classes. Do you want me to drop em off after I'm done with work?

I waited for about three minutes, staring at my screen, willing his response to be affirmative. I was getting antsy. Why wasn't he answering right away?! I clicked back on my search results and started scrolling down until I found the site I was looking for. I clicked onto it and waited for it to open. I highlighted the resource information and copied it, then opened back up my word processing document and pasted the reference into my bibliography. When I returned to my online homepage, he still had not responded.

I waited a minute or so more, wondering if I should retype my question. Then I went back to my search engine and typed in the name of our local newspaper. I went to their online news page and selected the sports section. I then went into the archives and typed in "Matt Porter." Several matches came up, not surprisingly. Finally I was interrupted by his instant message.

MattJock82: nah, I have sumthin to do tomorrow night

Ptboy1982: do you know when I will see you again sir?

Oh god, I should not have asked that! Fuck. I was tapping my foot nervously against the floor, worrying about how he was going to respond to my question. Again he was taking a long time to respond. I hated this. I hated the waiting! I clicked on one of the links in my search results. It was an article about some game he had pitched a no hitter. There was a photo of him pitching. I right-clicked it to see the enlarged version of the photo. God he was hot! I was getting hard just from the picture. I left clicked the photo then and saved it.

MattJock82: I'll call u when I wanna see u again. Just be a good pup and wait for me.

Ptboy1982: yes sir... I found a pic of u online sir

Mattjock82: oh really? Where?

Ptboy1982: it's a sports pic...you are pitching. I found it from the paper's archives.

MattJock82: lol. U looking at it now pup?

Ptboy1982: yes sir

MattJock82: u hard?

Ptboy1982: yes sir

MattJock82: good boy. Don't touch yourself tho

Ptboy1982: okay sir, I won't

MattJock82: I don't want you to cum again until u see me next. That's an order.

I sat there staring at my screen, not really believing what I was seeing. Why would he order me about something like that? My face was getting red; I could feel it. I wasn't angry at all, just a little embarrassed in spite of myself. I was thinking about Matt visualizing me masturbating. He had not even seen me naked yet.

MattJock82: do you understand?

Ptboy1982: yes sir. I will obey you

MattJock82: good boy. Gtg talk later

I clicked on the icon to add him to my buddy list, my heart pounding. His name appeared on my list in parentheses, indicating he had already logged off. I closed the instant message screen and stared at his picture. I became aware that I was in fact very much aroused. It sucked that I was so turned on right now and could not even do anything about it.

Then I started thinking. How will Matt know if I cum or if I don't cum? It's not like he has a hidden camera or something in my bedroom. I reached down to my crotch and groped myself, all the while staring at his picture. I unzipped my pants. He looked so incredible in his uniform. I remembered him as he was earlier that day—shirtless. I remembered how he looked as I knelt in front of him. I was throbbing so hard. I pulled the elastic down on my briefs, exposing myself. I started to stroke as I continued to look at his pic.

Oh god...he was so awesome. I wished he had told me when I'd see him again. I wanted him so bad! I was getting closer to the point of orgasm, continuing to stroke. I looked as his pic, staring him in the eye, *I don't want you to cum again until I see you again. That's an order*. I removed my hand. It felt like he was here with me now. I then suddenly realized something else. He was certainly going to ask me if I had obeyed him or not. He was going to look me in the eye and ask me point blank if I had cum or not. I would have to then lie to him. If I continued what I was doing right at this moment, I'd have to ultimately lie to Matt. No! I couldn't do it. I knew I'd never be able to lie to him. Not now. Not after what had happened earlier today. Not after I had served him and obeyed him. Not after I realized just how much I loved him.

I zipped up my pants and returned to my term paper.

* * *

When I woke up the following morning, I was very much aroused. I immediately thought of Matt. Generally whenever I was so hard like this upon waking, I would jack myself off before I even rolled out of bed. I reached down to grope myself, primarily out of reflex and then remembered Matt's orders to me. Well, actually, all he had said was that I was not allowed to cum. He never said I could not be aroused or could not touch myself; but then, that would be so frustrating to stroke myself and to get really close to orgasm but not be able to completely follow through.

It struck me all of a sudden as being so silly. Why was I allowing some other guy dictate to me what I could and could not do? In many ways this went against what I always believed about people. I had always felt sort of smug in my belief that I valued equality. I thought of myself as being this great defender of civil rights, yet here I was now subjecting myself to a form of self-imposed slavery. Why was I so willing to allow myself to be treated like that? Wasn't it rather abusive of Matt to give me orders and to arrogantly expect that I obey him unquestioningly? What did he think it was about himself that gave him the right to dominate me in that way?

Then again, why was I so rock hard right now as I thought about these things? Why did I melt into this totally submissive pussy whenever I was around him? Well, actually, I guess I was a bit of a pussy all of the time anyhow. I just felt even smaller and weaker when I was around him. It was so ironic really, for one would think that these feelings of inferiority and weakness would make me feel horrible about myself. On the contrary, though, for the first time ever, I actually felt good about being the way I was. I felt as if it just was the right thing for me.

I must be schitzo or something. God! I kept going back and forth in my thinking about these things. I kept talking myself into and out of acceptance for my own feelings. Finally I threw back my covers and stumbled over to my computer desk. I decided to check email before I started getting ready to begin my day. Maybe there was something there from Matt. My heart beat a little faster as I logged on, waiting for my mailbox to open. Quickly I scrolled down through my mail listing, disappointed not to have received anything at all from Matt. I didn't bother to read my spam or to even delete it. I just closed the mailbox and opened the picture of Matt that I had saved.

When I looked at the picture, it was like I was seeing it for the first time. Although I had viewed it repeatedly just hours before, I was seeing it now anew. I zoomed in to enlarge the area of his face, studying his eyes. I saw such confidence, such focus. I tried to imagine what he was thinking as he prepared to deliver the pitch. I wondered what his opponent—the batter—was thinking as he faced off against Matt. I was again throbbing, and reached down to my crotch to again squeeze myself. I was starting to leak pre-cum. Uh-oh! I hope that the pre-cum did not constitute a violation of Matt's order. Quickly I closed his photo and logged off of the computer.

I then made my bed and headed for the shower. I showered really quickly and used much cooler water than I was normally comfortable using. I truly did not want to disobey Matt, even if it did somewhat seem silly to me. I was starting to wonder if maybe he was testing me. Maybe he gave me this command to see if I would just blow it off or would lie to him. I bet he realized that he'd be able to tell if I were lying. I already knew that to lie to him would be impossible for me, and I wondered if he realized the same thing.

Classes that day were extremely tedious, and I was glad to be done with them when the morning was finally over. I had not ridden the bus to college that day, but instead had taken my bike. I only did this on the days that I had to work, and only weather-permitting. I hopped on my bike and pedaled towards the parking lot. I rode around a bit, looking for Matt's car, and suddenly I spotted it. My pulse raced as I felt the excitement rising within me. I rode closer to it, heading directly towards his bumper when I noticed he was sitting in the car. He had a passenger with him. Fuck! It was Tracy. Quickly I changed direction and headed back out of the parking lot.

Why was this bothering me so much, I wondered. I already knew he had a girlfriend. It was not like it should be some big surprise for me to see them together. But just two days ago he had told me that he hardly ever saw her any more. After the time we spent together yesterday, I guess I was hoping he'd have even less of an incentive to see her again. That was wishful thinking on my part, I supposed.

I tried hard not to think of Matt any more as I made my way to work. This was a little like trying not to think of a pink elephant: the more I told myself not to worry about it, the more I did exactly that. I was starting to realize just how obsessive I actually was. How pathetic! I forced myself to stay busy at work, in fact, impressing my boss significantly as I got an entire shipment checked in, catalogued, and stocked in half the length of time that it normally would take. I was trying so desperately to distract myself from thoughts of Matt.

About twenty minutes before the end of my shift, I was behind the counter performing some mandatory cleaning responsibilities when I heard the front door open. I looked up, expecting to see one of our regular customers. It was Matt! I stood there frozen, holding a roll of trash bags in my hand. He acted very casual— nonchalant— as he approached me. "Hey Pete, what's up?" he said. "Where's your boss?"

"Um, oh... I think he is in his office. We aren't all that busy the last hour or so."

"So have you been following my order? The one I gave you last night online?"

I nodded to him vigorously. "Oh, yes sir. But I almost slipped up this morning."

"What do you mean, you *almost* slipped up? Did you cum or didn't you?" He had cautiously lowered his voice but was very firm in the way he asked the question.

"Well," I whispered, "I started to um...to..."

"Jack off?" he finished.

"Yeah. Well, that and I was sort of...leaking a little."

"But you didn't shoot?" he asked.

"No sir," I looked him right in the eye although I felt strongly I should be looking down at the ground. I wanted though for him to see how honest I was being.

"Good boy." He said. "You guys got the new *Sports Illustrated* yet?"

I stepped out behind the counter and took him over to the magazine rack. "It's right here, sir." I picked it up and handed it to him. He did not thank me, but turned to head back to the counter. I quickly stepped back to my place behind the register and rang up his transaction.

After paying me, he said, "Keep the change. I will see you Saturday. Be over to my house at three in the afternoon." I looked up at him wide eyed. "You got it?" he asked? "And my order still stands...even though you have seen me. Don't shoot until I give you permission."

"Yes, sir. I'll be there at three, and I will do as you say." After he left I smiled to myself. I was so excited.

* * *

It was only Wednesday when Matt had visited me in the bookstore, so I had to go almost three more full days without ejaculation. The entire situation was particularly challenging for me because whenever I thought about the fact that I was obeying Matt, I would start to get hard. Then I'd want to jack off more than ever. I wondered what would happen if I had a wet dream like I sometimes did. That would be awful because I would be disobeying him, even though I would not be doing so deliberately. I wondered what I could do to protect myself from this happening. I had an idea! Before I went to bed Thursday night, I tied a string around the base of my penis. I cinched it securely but not too tight. If I started to get hard, I was definitely gonna feel it. In fact, I don't think I would be able to actually get fully hard with it on...it would hurt too badly. Then I put on a pair of tight briefs and a pair of sleep pants over them. Sure enough, that night I did wake up starting to feel aroused. I think it was the pain in my dick that caused me to wake up, though, and I instinctively reached down to my crotch, suddenly remembering what was causing the sensation. I relaxed myself then, lying very still. My erection started to subside and the pain went away. I grabbed a hold of the spare pillow in my bed and curled up around it, falling back asleep.

I used this same self imposed chastity device all of the next day and night and even kept it on until Saturday afternoon. I hoped that Matt did not consider it to be cheating, so I was wondering if I should even mention it to him. But I realized that I'd have no choice. There was no way I could lie to him, not even if it were a lie of omission. He might actually commend me, though, because I had gone to a greater length to obey him. I guess I'd just have to wait and see.

Saturday morning was so incredibly long. I had gotten up early, too excited to sleep. I made a huge breakfast for Kathie and me, ham and cheese omelets. After we ate I did a considerable amount of stressing over what I should wear

51

when I went over to Matt's. I wondered if he gave his own wardrobe as much thought as I gave mine. Of course I did not have the type of cool clothes that he did, but still I wanted to look the way I'd expect for him to want me to look.

As I studied myself in the mirror, I wondered if I should ditch these stupid glasses. Maybe I should use some of the money I'd saved to get a pair of contacts. Then maybe he would not see me as such a geek. But he never indicated to me that he considered me geekish. Perhaps I should ask him what his opinion was. He would probably think I was just being stupid. He probably didn't give a shit one way or the other, so long as I showed up to suck his cock.

I elected to wear a pair of long-legged athletic pants. They were the kind that are sort of a nylon material, with a double stripe running down the side. I put on a tee shirt and a b-cap. I wore my Van's boarder shoes too. I wanted to look sort of pseudo-jockish for him. I wondered if he would see me as being sort of a miniature emulation of himself--I didn't really even think about the fact that I was still wearing a pair of really tight briefs under the sports pants. Probably he wouldn't see them anyways because he never even saw me naked the first time I was with him.

I left my apartment at two o'clock. This was dumb, really, because it took no where near an hour to get to his house. I ended up having to ride around for almost thirty minutes before I actually headed for his place. I had his duffle bag with me, containing his laundered clothing he'd loaned me. Also, I was smart enough to bring a spare set of clothes for myself in case I might need them again later. At about ten to three, I rode my bike up his drive. What the hell, I could not wait any longer! After parking my bike against the garage as before, I dallied in the yard for a bit. I suddenly was overcome by that same exact feeling of nervousness I'd had the previous Monday when I had been here for the first time.

I inhaled deeply then, and marched up the steps. Timidly I rang the door bell, and stood perfectly still as I waited for a response. I looked down at my feet nervously and was debating ringing a second time when finally I heard a sound from the other side of the door. It was footsteps. Finally the door swung open and I looked up to see Matt standing in front of me. This time he was already shirtless and was wearing a pair of athletic pants similar to my own. He didn't have shoes on though, just crew socks.

"Hey kiddo!" he said, beaming down at me. He was practically laughing. "You are dressed like me," he said.

I felt my face getting red. "I'm sorry," I said, hanging my head.

"Don't be silly! You look cute. Of course you do, if you are dressed like me, right?" I looked up at him and smiled, nodding. He led me into the house, and I of course was soon greeted by little Petey. Setting down the duffle bag, I picked him up in my arms and held him as I petted him with my free hand. He was so cute and loveable.

"Did you eat, pup? Matt asked.

I shook my head. "No sir, not since breakfast. I made omelets for Kathie and me."

"Oh? Do you like to cook?"

"Yeah, I do. I like it a lot actually."

"Well, I'm gonna get us a pizza, okay? What kind do you like?"

"Um...well, I like anything sir. I like whatever you like."

He laughed again. "Good answer, but it is okay for you to have your own opinions about the food you like, pup. Do you like ham and pineapple? Hawaiian pizza."

"Yeah. I mean, yes sir. I like that kind a lot."

"Cool," he said, and walked over to the phone to order. I set Petey down on the floor and he jumped back up against my legs, immediately begging me to pick him back up. It was cool how eager he was for my attention. I thought about how Matt always called me pup. I wonder if he thought the way I

53

craved his attention was cool. I hoped so. I didn't want to be annoying to him.

"Let's chill in the living room while we wait for the pizza...'kay?"

I followed him into the room, knowing my verbal affirmation was not necessary. Of course anything that he decided was okay. He had one of these absolutely huge television sets. It was mounted on the wall like a movie screen--it was one of those thin screened ones. He plopped down in a blonde recliner, and I just stood nearby, not sure where to sit. "Sit down pup," he said. I crouched down next to him then and slid over in front of his chair, positioning myself so that I was between his legs. He spread them apart and let me rest my back against his chair while sitting between his legs. He picked up the remote and turned on the television, seeming to not even be thinking about my presence. I thought it was interesting that there were so many other places to sit— a huge sectional sofa, a couple more chairs, and a love seat, yet he did not correct me when I chose to sit on the floor at his feet.

I pulled my knees up to my chest and hugged them, wanting really badly to reach over to touch his leg. I did not want to do anything like that without his permission, though, so I just sat there quietly. He flipped through the channels, surfing them carelessly. Occasionally he'd stop on a channel that seemed to have any sort of action. He paused at all the sporting events. I doubt that he at this point was wanting to get engrossed in any program, though, for he just seemed to be entertaining himself to pass time. He brushed his knee against my shoulder suddenly, for which I was extremely relieved, taking it as an indication that it was okay for me to touch him. I moved my hand down to rub it against his calf.

"Turn around," he said in a tone that was quiet matter-of-fact. I immediately complied, shifting myself into a kneeling position as I turned to face him. "Did you obey my orders and not cum this week?" he asked, delivering the question in a manner that seemed extremely authoritative to me.

"Yes sir," I replied. "I obeyed you. I didn't cum, sir."

"There is a 'but' in your voice. You obeyed me but... what? Did you have a wet dream or something?"

"Um, no sir. It' just um..."

"Just what?"

"It's just that I was afraid I might have one. I have had them before... about you, sir."

"Nothin wrong with that. My pup is supposed to have dreams about me. But so if you did not cum then what are you all worried about?"

"Well, sir. I thought I was going to cum maybe, if I dreamt about you, so I tied something around myself. I mean around my dick. It was a string."

"You didn't tie it too tight did you?"

"No sir, just snug. Only so if I got hard I would feel it, so that it would hurt a little. That way I would not get totally hard, and wouldn't cum."

He smiled as he looked down at me. "Good boy. That was good thinking."

"Really?" I asked, smiling myself then. "I was worried you'd think I was cheating or something."

"Nah. You did what you had to do to obey me. If you had cum this week, even in your sleep, I'd have been very disappointed. When I give you an order, I expect it to be obeyed. You did a good job. You were a good pup." Suddenly I felt like Petey, his dog, after having been given praise for remembering not to go potty in the house. Probably if I'd had a tail, I would've then been wagging it. "You're gonna cum today pup, but not till I tell you, and this time its not gonna be in your pants. You understand?"

"Yes sir," I said as I looked up at him, sitting there comfortably in the recliner, shirtless and relaxed. Whenever he sat like that it seemed to me like he was a king on a throne. It was no wonder I felt so compelled to kneel before him. My heart was beating a little faster, as I came to realize that he planned to see me naked. I lay my head down in his lap then, and waited quietly for the pizza delivery.

When the doorbell finally rang, Matt reached over to the end table which was next to his chair and picked up his wallet, pulling out a twenty. He handed it to me, "Go pay the pizza boy," he said. "Tell him to keep the change." I stood up and quickly headed for the door. When I returned, I wasn't sure if we were going to remain in the living room or go elsewhere so I stood next to Matt's chair, awaiting instruction. He reached over and took the pizza box from me, placing it on the armrest of his recliner. "Kneel down again, pup," he said, and I immediately complied. Matt then opened the lid of the pizza box, releasing aroma and steam, suddenly causing me to realize just how hungry I had become.

"Want a bite?" he asked. I looked up at him and was unable to keep myself from grinning. Today he was wearing no baseball cap and no shirt. I wanted a bite of him, not the pizza. So badly I then wanted to reach up and run my fingers across his chest. It was so smooth and hairless, his pecs being clearly defined. "Open," he ordered me.

I knelt there in front of him then, my mouth open and he dropped a piece of ham onto my tongue. I chewed it up slowly in front of him. "Thank you, sir," I said, as he stuffed a big wedge of the pizza slice into his mouth, biting it off while I watched. I opened my mouth again, and he held out this same piece to me and I bit off a much smaller bite than his and chewed while I watched him doing the same. "Take your shirt off," he told me. I did not stand, but merely leaned back a bit and reached down to the tail of my shirt and pulled it up over my head. I hesitated a bit before peeling it completely off--this would be the first time he saw me this exposed.

He looked down at me in a manner which seemed to be approving, as he continued to eat his pizza. He

56

intermittently offered me bites off of his slice, though he never gave me one of my own. Matt was relaxed, with his legs spread apart and kicked out in front of him. He was becoming engrossed in a television program as he sat there feeding himself. "Now take off your sneaks," he said without looking at me. I leaned back to sit down on my butt and pulled my legs into an Indian style position, pulling each shoe off and placing it next to his chair. I then returned to my former kneeling position in front of him and silently watched him, amazed that I was so privileged to even be with him in the first place.

After we had devoured three pieces of pizza, he moved the box over to the end table and used his thumb and index finger to wipe the excess sauce from the corners of his lips. He then looked down at me and held out his finger as if pointing to me. I opened my mouth as he slid it in past my lips, and I licked his finger clean. Then he did the same with his thumb. I stared up at him while he had his finger against my tongue, and he looked back at me. He was not smiling, nor did he appear to disapprove in any way. He just acted as if everything were as it should be. I sucked his finger much more than was necessary to clean it of the sauce, and he made no protest.

When he pulled his thumb out of my mouth, he suddenly picked up the remote and clicked off the television, standing up in front of me without explanation. He stepped around me, and I looked up, wondering if I was supposed to get up and follow him or to wait. "Come on," he said, "Goin upstairs."

I stood up to follow him and reached down to pick up my shoes and shirt. "Leave em there. You won't be needin' em," he instructed. Obediently I left my clothes on the floor and followed him up to his bedroom. When we got inside, Matt closed the door behind us and told me he had to take a piss. I nodded and sat down on the bed, thinking he was going to go to the bathroom. He had his own private bath right off his huge bedroom. "Come on," he said, and I looked up at him puzzled. "I said I have to take a piss. Come with me." I stood back up then, not at all sure why he wanted me to come with him while he pissed. He walked over to the bathroom and I followed closely behind him. When we were both in the small room together he told me to sit down. I thought he meant on the floor, so I dropped down to a crouching position and started to sit on the ground. "No...sit on the toilet," he said.

After I was seated on the toilet lid, I looked up to see Matt's face. He was staring down at me. "Now pull down my pants and take out my cock." I looked up at him wide-eyed. Suddenly it occurred to me what was possibly about to happen. Was he planning on pissing inside of my mouth? I was getting nervous, and fumbled around with the drawstring on his wind pants. I did not want him to piss in my mouth. I idolized him— worshipped him, in fact— but that was not something I would ever have even conceived of doing. Why would *anyone* in their right mind let somebody else piss in their mouth?

"Sir?" I said.

He stared down at me. "Take it out boy. Take out my cock like I told you."

I was shaking now, just like before, but this time I was not so much trembling out of excited nervousness as I was out of sheer fear. Why was he doing this to me? "Sir, please..." my voice was cracking, for I was on the verge of tears.

"Pup," he said calmly. "You have to start learning to trust me. I said 'take it out,' now do as I say." I finally managed to loosen his waistband and pull down the wind pants to expose his now flaccid cock. It was far different looking than when I had seen it Monday, having been fully erect at that time. Still it was an awesome sight for me to see, as I faced it, sitting mere inches from his crotch. At that point I wanted nothing more than to again take it into my mouth and make it get hard, just as it had been the time before, yet I was still shaking and still terrified of what was in store for me. "Pup, I do not make many promises. Eventually you will realize this about me, because I don't feel that I'm obligated to promise people things. I do the things I want to do, and am a decent guy, and that should be enough. But every once in awhile I do make a promise, and when I do, it's for a damn good reason. Do you remember that I promised you something when you were here last time?"

I looked up into his eyes. I now again was crying. Damn it!! Why did I have to get emotional all the time? "Yes sir, I remember."

"What was it? What did I promise you?"

"You said, 'Don't be afraid. Don't ever be afraid of me. I will never, ever hurt you, pup?"

"That's right," he said, "So why are you shaking and crying then?"

"I— I—" I started crying hard then, trying to go on with my sentence, "I don't think I can do it sir."

Matt then crouched down to face me at eye level, as I had buried my head in my hands. He grabbed my wrists gently and pulled them from my face, forcing me to look at him. "Did I tell you that you had to do something? I told you to pull down my pants and to take out my cock; did I tell you to do anything else?"

"No.." I cried.

"Kneel down," he said. I slid off the toilet seat and knelt next to his feet. "Now turn and face the toilet, and pick up the lid." I did as he said, replacing the toilet seat into the masculine upright position. Matt tucked the waistband of his pants comfortably under his ball sac then and positioned himself with his feet apart, standing in front of the toilet. He looked to me like any other man about to take a piss alone in his bathroom, except I knew that he was not alone, for I was there watching. "Watch me piss boy!"

I then knelt there and watched as a steady stream of piss shot out his penis. It became more forceful as he began to enthusiastically drain his bladder. I stared at the stream, watching intently...mesmerized. I did not look away from his cock until the last droplets of piss squirted from his dick. There are always trailers of liquid to drain from the shaft after the full-force stream has subsided. He shook his dick, getting all the wetness off his cockhead.

I stared up at him. I looked at his freshly drained cock and then shifted my gaze to scan his body, seeing all of him as he towered over me. He was everything to me. Why had I been so afraid? Why had I feared him so? I continued to stare up at him. He was so incredibly hot standing there shirtless with his cock exposed to me.

"You were not ready for more than this, but you eventually will be. You just need to relax and let me worry about what I'm gonna give you and when. Do you understand, pup?"

"Yes sir."

Matt tucked his cock back into his pants and pulled me up off my knees. He held me there with one hand on each of my shoulders and looked down into my eyes. As I stared back at him I wanted to say to him how very sorry that I was for freaking out. I wanted to tell him it was wrong for me to have not trusted him. I wanted to somehow be able to turn back time three minutes and to simply obey him without question. I said nothing though, for I sensed that this was not the time for words. It felt again like I was so very small as I knelt there in front of him.

"Stand up," he instructed me. I did so and he again placed his hands on my shoulders, moving his fingers down the sides of my arms and then over onto my chest. I felt shivers bolt through my body as his fingertips glided across my smooth, flat chest. I continued to look up at him but his eyes no longer met mine. He was scanning my body as he touched me so gently.

"Take off your pants for me, pup." His voice was almost a whisper as he continued to touch me. Still staring at him, I reached down and pulled the waistband of my pants down below my buttocks. He allowed me the space I needed to bend forward slightly in order to pull the pants down further. I pulled my knees upwards, one at a time and slid the pant legs down to my ankles, then stepped out of them completely. I now stood there in front of him wearing only the tight pair of briefs and my white crew socks. Matt's hands moved around to my shoulders and then slowly down my back. He actually had to lean forward a bit in order to reach down far enough to grab the cheeks of my buttocks. He pulled me closer to him, wrapping his arms completely around me.

He shifted his body around, taking me with him, so that my back was against the sink. Grabbing the top of my legs, just below my butt cheeks, he picked me up and stepped forward so that I was pressed right against the counter. He gently released me so I was sitting there in front of him, my legs dangling down from the counter, not touching the floor. I looked into his face, and he was at this point staring directly into my eyes. My heart was once again beating out of control and I felt the trembling, though certainly not of fear this time. It was a return of that over-excited feeling I'd experienced when I submitted to Matt earlier that week.

I put my hands against his body, mimicking the gentle way he had just touched me. I felt his hard, perfectly defined pecs with my small palms. I cupped them in my hands and rubbed so gently with my fingers. He tilted his head forward, bringing it closer to my own as we continued to look into one another's eyes. How I then wanted to express to him how deeply I loved him! How I then wanted to be as close to him as humanly possible! I moved my head closer to his, again copying the gestures he himself was doing. I slid my hands around his body, embracing him as he moved in closer to my lips with his own. Finally they were touching and he grabbed my head in both his hands, covering my mouth completely with his. My eyes closed as I felt the warmth of his body pressing against my own, and cautiously I pressed myself into him— my mouth, my torso, all of me— wanting to be connected with him.

Never before had I been kissed, and the feeling was so brand new to me. I was so aroused as I felt his lips against my own, tasted his breath, felt his tongue. He was opening his mouth slightly and I did the same, allowing him entry. I allowed him all of me then, melting into his embrace, feeling the strength of his far more powerful arms holding me next to him. Instinctively, I wrapped my legs around his waist, pulling my body into a position where we were pressed right against one another. He moved his hands again down below my buttocks and leaned backwards slightly, pulling me up off of the counter. I tightened my legs around his waist as he stepped backwards, all the while still kissing me repeatedly.

He turned with me in his arms and stepped away from the counter and back towards the door. He carried me then into the bedroom, walking slowly and carefully, continuing to press his lips against my own as I clung trustingly to his shoulders. I was so hard inside my briefs as he placed me on the bed, leaning over me. As he released me I wanted to immediately go for his waistband again, to expose him; to make it possible for me to see him and to taste him and to serve him as I so craved to do. I grabbed for him, but he stepped backwards, grinning down at me. He surveyed my body, taking in my smoothness, the tiny-ness of it, I assumed. He must have noticed such contrast from his own superior jock body. "Don't cum," he said as he slid his hand down to touch the bulge in my briefs. He cupped my ball sac in his hand, massaging it gently as my fully erect cock throbbed, begging for release against the tight fabric. He made no movement to free it though, and I dared not do so myself. I just lay there, my hands at my side as he touched me; I stared at him, totally amazed, taking in quick and excited breaths. Oh god! I wanted him so badly!

"Sir!" I whimpered... "Oh god, it's gonna make me—"

"Don't cum!" he repeated, now running his fingers up and down my shaft. Stroking it through the fabric of my briefs.

I reached towards him, trying to grab him the same way that he was touching me. But his reach was far longer than mine, and he used his free hand to gently push me back onto the bed. He grinned at me broadly as I looked up into his face, "Oh please sir...please!"

"What?" he asked teasingly, "What do you want pup?"

"Sir, please...please I want to—"

"What do you want, pup?" he repeated.

"I want— I want— I want to suck you. Please!"

His face became more serious as he stared down at me, still stroking my bulge with his fingers. It almost appeared to me that he did not really even hear what I had just said. I was begging him to let me suck him, and he did not even seem to hear me! "Why?" he asked, "Why do you want to suck me?"

Oh god, how could I say the words? How could I express to him all that I felt? How could I show him how badly I wanted to please him, to serve him, to — *belong to him?* I wanted to belong to him? Oh god yes! Yes, I wanted that more than anything. I wanted not just to be a pup to him, but to be *his* pup, just as Petey the real dog was his. "Because, sir... because..."

"Say it, pup! Say what you want. Tell me!"

"Because I want to show you how much I ... *need* you! Because I want to serve you. Because I want to *belong* to you!"

He moved his hand away from my crotch and stepped back from the bed, still in full view of me as I stared at him. I saw how hard he was! I saw it right through his pants. I let out a gasping sound as I had done the first time we were together. "Show me how much you want it, pup. Prove it to me!"

I leaned forward and twisted my body, reaching for him, using my feet to push my body in his direction. I rolled over onto my stomach as I stared up at him, yearning to do for him what I had done only once before. I wanted to re-experience it. I wanted him inside my mouth as he had been previously that week. I wanted to again feel his hands holding my head, to smell him, hear his moans, taste him. I wanted all of this so badly that I was nearly ready to cry. I wanted it so badly I would even beg for it!

"Please sir! I want it so bad...you've gotta believe me, sir! Please!!" I must have been staring up at him so wide-eyed. I wondered if I reminded him of his puppy, with that pleading look of desire on my face. He seemed amused as he stared down at me, still making no indication to me that he intended on affording me the privilege of serving him again.

He backed up even further. I had to be closer to him! I pushed myself up on the bed so that I was in a kneeling position right on the very edge of the bed. I pressed my hands against the mattress as I pulled one leg in front of me and stepped down to the floor, all the while staring imploringly at Matt. I dropped back onto my knees in front of him then, instantly resuming my position of servitude. My voice was almost breathless then, high pitched and whiney as I asked him one more time, "Please sir, may I please serve you?" There was so much emotion coursing through me, I felt my eyes tearing up. I was not about to cry from frustration or fear, not even from sadness. I was simply overcome with the overwhelming emotion as I poured out my desires to my hero.

"I want to do everything possible to please you, sir. You have been all I've thought of these past five days. You are so much like a dream to me, that you do not even seem true, but here I am now kneeling before you. Please sir, let me do it for you, not myself. Let me do it to make you happy, to bring pleasure to you. Please let me do it so that I can show you how very much you mean to me! Please sir, I'm begging you with my whole heart. Please!"

Finally he reached down and began to pull down his pants. His movements were slow and deliberate as he revealed to me the part of him I most longed to see. He tucked the waistband neatly under his ball sac and displayed his rock hard erection to me. It stood there as if at attention, while I stared in sheer amazement. Looking down at me he said only one word, "Come."

I crawled to him.

This time he was not seated, but was instead towering over me. It felt right, even more so than the first time I submitted to him. My face moved towards his crotch as he grabbed a hold of my head. He was not violent in any way but was far more forceful than he had been previously. He made it clear to me that he was in control and did so with a certain degree of reservation as if to show me that he had no intention of hurting me. I relaxed myself, wanting him to feel no resistance from me, wanting him to feel as if I were his tool to use as he chose. It was true what I'd said, I wanted to do this for him, not myself.

"Don't cum this time, pup." His order was matter-of-fact, delivered with the assumption that I somehow had the means of controlling whether or not I ejaculated. He was the one who made the decision about when, where, and how I came. I simply was learning how to obey. I was learning how to execute his orders without question.

I'm still unable to accurately describe the thrill that overwhelms me every time I kneel to serve. There is a sensation of ecstatic fulfillment the moment that rock hard flesh makes contact with my mouth. It is both smooth and hard as it fills me. As I wrap my lips and tongue around it, I'm literally transported to a mental state of security and self validation. I knelt there then and took him into myself, wanting to be one with him, wanting to be totally his.

There must have been a connection, some wavelength of communication between us that he tapped into, for it felt to me that he desired just as badly to be one with me. He slid into me smoothly yet forcefully, not even allowing me the time to get comfortable with having him in my mouth like he had done during our first encounter. He went all the way in, and surprisingly to me, I did not gag or reject his entry in any way. I opened myself to him, becoming a hole for his pleasure as I relaxed and let him have full control. I did, however, respond according to my nature. I began to suck, applying pressure from my tongue and lips, yet realizing that I did this only as a means of following his lead. I was only being given what he allowed me. None of him was mine to take; he was his own gift to me.

Momentarily he moaned. It was as if I were not even in the room with him. He was focused upon the sensations of his own body. I craved so badly to be used by him as his instrument of self-pleasure. He was fully aware that I already was capable of taking the entirety of him in my mouth. I was learning already to relax to the point of suppressing my gag reflex which allowed for a smooth entry into the back of my throat. This was where he drove himself, finding that tightness for himself that was obviously satisfying to him. I deliberately kept my eyes open as he pulled me into himself. I inhaled the scent of him while I saw only him and his body in front of me. He throbbed inside of me, and I responded with movement from my tongue and lips across the hardness of his shaft that was pressing against them.

He remained in me for a few seconds gyrating his hips slightly as he enjoyed my warmth. I did not want him out of me. I did not even think of my own need to breathe. I thought only of him and of how this must feel to him. He pulled me back in a movement that was so gentle and loving, allowing me to stare up at him while I held the head of his cock just inside my lips. He slowly pulled me completely off of him, and finally I gasped for air, suddenly realizing that it was necessary to inhale.

He pulled his pants down the rest of the way then and stepped out of them, tossing them aside. Now he was standing there in front of me completely exposed. "Do you know what is about to happen, pup?" he asked. I stared up at him, looking at his face, and nodded my head. "I'm going to give you my load. This time it is going to come right from me. Are you ready for this?"

"Yes sir," I gasped, rather surprised that he even would need to ask. Certainly it was not necessary for him to get my opinion as to my readiness, for he seemed to understand these things about me even more than I did myself. I think, though, that he was preparing me then, making me aware of his intention. It wasn't that he was seeking my permission, merely a statement about what he was about to do.

He stepped back into position and again grabbed my head. His feet were planted firmly on either side of my kneeling body as he towered over me. He slid in, again relishing the sensation. He did not bury himself so deep this time though, but pulled part way out almost immediately. Then he drove himself in again, holding onto my head all the while. He went deeper with his second thrust, then proceeded to the third. He got faster as he continued to thrust, pumping himself in and out of me, ultimately ramming my throat fiercely with his cock. I was not afraid or even that uncomfortable. I willed myself not to think of my own feelings but to instead focus on pleasing him. I was so hard myself, but did not allow my hands to go anywhere near my own crotch. I wanted to obey his orders and to refrain from cumming.

The movement was so quick as he thrust into me that I found it impossible to look up at him. I instead focused upon his abdomen and his pubic region. I resigned myself to forming a mental image of him towering over me, rocking back and forth into my mouth and throat. I was excited myself, feeling rather surreal at that moment. It did not even seem possible that this could be me kneeling here before this man of my dreams, taking him into myself.

"Suck it, fag!"—he began to verbalize the reality of his superiority. Earlier, when I knelt to watch him piss, he had not made any effort to demonstrate that he was superior; but now it simply was apparent. This reality needed no demonstration: It just was fact. I felt small. I felt less than him. I felt I was in the place where I needed to be. At this point his thrusts were no longer as long, he was not pulling out very far but was instead keeping himself buried. I quickly was learning how important it was to breathe quickly when my throat was clear, and to do it through my nose. I was salivating tremendously and his cock was slick with my spit. As often as possible I'd gulp to remove the excess.

This apparently was the point when I became only a hole to him. He became lost in himself and began to go for broke, ramming into me with fierceness and without mercy. It was ironic that only minutes before I had cried before him in the bathroom, afraid of his piss, but I knelt here now content, knowing that I was being used as his tool. As before, I felt his grip tighten when the cum shot into his shaft. I knew the eruption was only seconds away, and I moved my head forward. It was not necessary, though, for his hands were pushing me down all the way. He thrust all the way into me then, being completely buried, balls deep. And then I felt it for the first time! The pump!

He groaned in pleasure as he finally reached his goal. I felt both the grip of his hands on my head and the literal pulsing of his shaft against my tongue. The cum was firing up his cock. Instantly I felt it in my throat but could taste nothing. His grip was so intense that it was like his arms were made of iron. Truly, at this point I'd have had no choice about taking the load, regardless of what I felt. The pumping went on and on... two, three, four, five...I counted each pulse against my tongue. By the fourth pump I tasted his cum. It was backing up into my mouth as I gulped madly. He was making sounds I'd never before heard from a human being. Oh god, I was sucking him dry!

"Take it, fag! Swallow my load!" It was an unnecessary order, yet his verbalization was thrilling to me. I remained all the way down on his shaft, until he was totally drained. I wanted to remain there even longer, yet he pulled me back.

"Oh my god!" he said. "Good boy! Good pup!!" He was gasping for breath himself. He quickly bent over and pulled me up, sliding his hands under the pits of my arms. He pushed me backwards onto the bed, flat on my back, and tore down my briefs savagely. I was rock hard then, and lay there completely out of breath. I was so very aroused that it did not even occur to me that this was the very first time that I had ever been exposed this way to Matt. He reached towards my groin, wrapping his fingers around my cock, making that flesh-to-flesh contact with me for the very first time.

"Don't cum boy! Not until I say." He looked directly into my eyes as he slid his hand back and forth on my cock. I was far smaller than him without question, but proportionate to my body, I was endowed respectably. I grabbed for his hand, wanting so much to participate, to guide him as he stroked me; but he used his free hand to grab my wrist. He released my cock then, momentarily and grabbed my other wrist with his right hand. He pushed my arms up over my head as he leaned over me. I was helpless as he pinned my arms flat against the mattress. "Grab a hold of the headboard!" He ordered, stretching my arms far above my head. I obeyed him unquestioningly. "Don't let go for any reason. Do you understand?"

"Yes sir," I squeaked, as I lay there stretched out beneath him. He then released my wrists and moved back instantly to my cock. As he once again grasped my shaft, I felt myself fast approaching the indescribable moment of no return. "Oh god, Sir! Oh God!! I'm gonna—"

"Don't cum, boy!" He commanded. His voice rang with authority, forcing me to somehow hold back the ensuing eruption. I was on the verge of tears as he continued to stroke me. It was a fabulous mixture of erotic pleasure and cruel torture as he brought me right to the brink of orgasm but sadistically denied me release. "Who decides when you cum, boy?" he sneered.

I stared up at him, wanting more than anything to pull my hands free from the headboard and grab myself in order to take control of my own body. Instead I looked into his eyes and said the only words possible, "You do, sir. You do!"

He continued to stroke me, starting and stopping at his own whim. He caused me to arch my back and to push my feet madly against the mattress, squirming beneath him, wanting to bring this to its climactic conclusion. "Please sir!" I begged, "Please let me shoot!"

"No! No, boy. You don't cum until I say so! I decide when you shoot. I ordered you not to cum five days ago, and you obeyed me. You *had* to. You had to do what I said. Isn't that right, boy?"

"Yes, Sir!" I screamed, as I gasped for breath, willing myself to obey him still.

His hand was wrapped tightly around my shaft as he renewed his effort to jack me. He stroked it calmly but gradually increased in his speed. I lay there squirming and sweating beneath him, praying he would soon allow me release. He got faster and faster with his strokes, staring directly into my eyes as he did so. "Okay boy, do you want to shoot for me? Do you want to fire your load?"

"Yes Sir! Oh god, please!!"

"Do it!" he commanded, "Shoot it for me...NOW!"

It was like a cannon firing as my body literally shook and trembled. I blasted my load clear up past my naval, onto my chest and even into my face. Over and over I shot, half laughing and half crying as I stared up at this man I loved with my whole heart.

Puppy Love

Yes, I loved him. I loved him more than anything in the world.

4

When I got home from Matt's house that evening, I discovered that Kathie was not there. She had apparently stopped in earlier and left me a note on the kitchen table. She had a date! I was happy for her, thinking to myself that if she only felt half of the euphoria that I was experiencing with my devotion to Matt, she would be one happy camper. It was like I had this urge to smile all the time, possibly skip, jump, shout, dance, sing— I just wanted to express how deeply I loved him. I wanted to shout it right out loud, in fact. I guess this is the feeling they are talking about when they say you are on cloud nine. I think I was at least on cloud ten or eleven, though.

Before I'd left Matt's bedroom, he had again given me some very specific instructions. I was to come home and at some point in the evening log onto my computer and email him. He wanted a complete listing of my work and school schedules for the next two weeks. He also said that if possible I was to tell him what hours Kathie would be working so that he'd know the times that I was completely alone. His orders regarding ejaculation remained in place; I was still not to cum under any circumstances without his permission. This order did not bother me even slightly, although I had to admit that I could easily have gone into my bedroom right then and beat off, thinking about my hero. It had only been an hour since he made me shoot my load and I was already raring to go a second round. But it also thrilled me to know that I was obeying him and that I was giving control of my body to him.

Maybe if I had given more thought to this, I'd have concluded that I was giving him nothing. Perhaps he was merely taking what he wanted...which was me. Even if this were the case, it still would have been exciting to me, for the thought of him wanting *me* was almost unbelievable. I had not yet reached that point of realization, though, that my submissiveness to Matt was ultimately my decision. Yes, he took what he wanted, but there always would be the reality that I could walk away at any point. Had I actually pondered this reality, I might have been even more excited; it meant that my submissiveness was a sort of gift that I was giving. When I made the decision to belong to him (or perhaps made the decision to *accept* that I belonged to him) I was giving up a part of my own free will as the ultimate expression of trust.

During these first few encounters with Matt, I was so fearful. I thought that I was starting to understand my own needs to be dominated, yet these very needs scared me. A lot of the time I obeyed him simply because I was afraid not to. I was terrified of losing him, of disappointing him, of driving him away. I was afraid that he would become bored of me or find someone cuter or stronger or smarter. I wanted him to go a little faster with me. I wanted to experience much more with him, because if I did not continue to advance and learn to serve him better, he may decide that he was tired of me.

If I'd been able to step into Matt's mind during that time, perhaps I'd have seen that he knew the thoughts and feelings I was experiencing. We were the same age, and yet he was a mentor to me. He seemed to be guiding me along this path of discovery and trust-building. He was placing a net of security beneath me as he constantly reassured me of what a good boy I was. Even his criticisms were gentle and loving — guiding me towards compliance to his will.

During that second sexual encounter with Matt, though, I had started to experience something that was about to blossom within me. This experience was a very deep desire to please him at all cost. It was rather the opposite of the fearful feeling that I had previously known. The desire was simply to belong to him and to make him happy. I had not yet come to understand that ultimately I would respond to him in a very automatic way. Eventually I would not even think about how desperately I wanted his approval; I'd serve him simply for the sake of serving. I'd do what he said just because.

It was okay for me at that point to admit that I "belonged" to Matt; but had anyone stated to me that he "owned" me, I honestly think I would have freaked. I did not feel it was right for one person to claim ownership of another. I didn't even think that it was possible. Not only that, but I would probably have gone on to defend this belief by saying that if a person were to allow himself to be "owned," he had serious self-esteem problems. I'd have considered ownership to be unethical and even would have equated it to slavery.

This was such a time of transition for me. I was facing some dramatic realizations about myself and was beginning to open my mind up more to some viewpoints which would previously have been unthinkable. The irony was that for so long I had rather prided myself on being tolerant and open-minded. Throughout my high school years, I had blatantly defended liberalism in my civics and sociology classes. I had viewed my stance on political issues as being noble. Admittedly, I was too shy to be much of a crusader for justice, but I had a certain degree of confidence that I had everything figured out. I knew right from wrong.

The attitudes I then had were neither wrong nor even necessarily naïve. They were, however, limiting, for I had not yet taken the logical step towards understanding that true liberalism means allowing *all* viewpoints a voice. What a person decided was right for himself was ultimately only his business, so long as it was not behavior that endangered or hurt other people. Eventually, I came to the conclusion that if tolerance is forced, it actually is intolerant. If a person were to be genuinely happy and content with their position as "owned property," then why would it ever be acceptable for me to tell him otherwise?

Until I reached this level of understanding, though, I could not even begin to think of myself in these terms. At this stage, all I knew was that I was desperately and hopelessly in love with this absolutely wonderful person. In his presence I felt safe, protected, and secure. He had not said that he loved me in return, but it was something I felt inside of me. I wanted to obey him and belong to him, and in a way I wanted for him to belong to me. I wanted to be his pup, and for him to be my— I didn't even know. I wanted him to be my *what*? My mentor? My master? My boyfriend? I guess I just had to say that I wanted him to be mine...period. Maybe the label did not matter so much. Maybe it was something I was yet to discover. Maybe it was up to Matt to tell me what and who he was, and how I should view him.

I placed my duffle bag down on a kitchen chair and walked over to the refrigerator. I pulled open the door and removed a can of Diet Coke, a fruit cup, and a package of cheese slices. I then made myself a cheese sandwich and wrote down Kathie's work schedule, which was posted on a corkboard next to the fridge. I carried my plate of food and the schedule with me into my bedroom. When I walked in, I faced the same familiar sight which I saw every single time I entered that room. There was a gigantic poster hanging above my bed of Harry Potter flying on his broomstick, reaching for the golden snitch. In some ways, I felt akin to Harry right then, for in his tales he faced a new world of reality. He discovered within himself some amazing things that he previously had not even known existed. He learned that he was very different from those who grew up around him, but was a part of something much larger than himself, a group of similar people who seemed to transcend normalcy.

I sat down at my computer and took a bite of my sandwich. I'd eaten that pizza a couple hours previously but was still famished. Maybe the passionate level of intimacy

I'd shared with Matt had sparked my hunger. I logged onto my computer then and waited for the connection to complete. Soon I was typing my email to Matt, just as he had ordered. I included the outline of my class schedule, my work schedule, and Kathie's work schedule. I also added a note on the bottom.

Sir, thank you so much for today. Still I am overcome with emotion when I remember what we did together...what you did to me and what u allowed me to do for you. When I was putting together this schedule for you, as you had instructed, I noticed that I am free and alone in the house on Monday night, as Kathie is scheduled to work late. I wondered if you would consider allowing me to make you dinner that evening? Please let me know, whenever it is convenient for you.

Your pup
Pete

After sending the email, I then did the one thing that I'd done at least two hundred times before that week. I pulled up Matt's picture from my archives and simply stared at it. I had by this time memorized every detail of this photo, every line, every color. Man, I wished he had not given me the order about not cumming. I was so hard again. I sighed as I clicked off my computer, shoving the last bite of my sandwich in my mouth. Maybe I'd lie down for a bitand wait for Kathie to return. I wanted to get the details of her date.

I curled up on my bed and quickly dozed off, not waking until four hours later to complete darkness. I rolled over on my bed and flipped on the light switch, noticing that it was almost midnight. Geesh, I must have been exhausted to have napped that long. I stumbled out of my bedroom and into the hallway, making my way through the darkness to the bathroom. I relieved myself and then went to get a drink from the kitchen. Just as I was pulling out a bottle of water, I heard Kathie's keys in the lock. She tumbled in a couple of seconds later, obviously feeling the effect of some alcohol she had consumed.

"Hi Petey!" she greeted me. I looked over to her, laughing.

"Well it looks like you had a good time," I said.

"Oh I did! God, I met this wonderful new guy. His name is Carter--he is a customer down at the store. He asked me out yesterday. I couldn't even believe it! He is so cute. Well... we went roller-blading this afternoon, and then he took me out to dinner and a movie. He is such a romantic!"

"That's cool," I said, "I'm so happy for you. Tell me about him. How old? What does he do for a living? What's he look like?"

"Hmm..." she said, clearing her throat as she threw her purse down on the sofa and kicked off her shoes. "He's black," she stated in a matter-of-fact manner. "Oh, I guess that should not have been the first thing I told you about him," she corrected herself. "He is a wonderful, adorable, passionate, intelligent, successful man, and he happens to be black. He's twenty-four." I smiled at her, totally relating to her euphoria. "He works for a law firm just down the street from the store. He is currently a paralegal but is also going to law school. He is athletic, political... a non-smoker." She laughed at her own words.

"He sounds perfect," I responded. "So you are going to see him again?"

"Yeah, we are going out Tuesday night. There is a street fair in midtown."

"Cool," I said. "Bring him by the bookstore if you want, so I can meet him."

"Sure...if he wants to, that is. I'm sure he will, though. He is basically agreeable to about anything."

"So did you do anything with him?" I asked, as I plopped down in a living room chair.

"Yeah, I went roller-blading and to a movie with him, silly!"

"You know what I mean," I laughed. "Did you do the nasty?"

"Like I'd share those kinds of details with my *baby* brother."

"Shut up!" I said. "It's no big deal. Like do you think that I don't know you have had sex before? I'm not a little kid any more, you know."

"I know," she said, "but you always will be my baby brother. Carter is very much a gentleman. We kissed, but nothing more. I like that he is taking it slow. I'm not really into doing it on the first date."

"Me neither," I laughed.

She busted up laughing. "Yeah, you are so experienced, aren't you?"

"Maybe you'd be surprised!" I retorted, getting up then to flip on the television.

"Well maybe sometime you will share some details with me, but for now, I'm going to bed. I have to get up early tomorrow. Good night, honey."

"Night," I said, as I scanned the room for the television remote. I still could catch the last half hour of *Saturday Night Live*. This week's episode turned out to be really lame, and so I surfed through the channels for a bit. I settled on a Solo Flex infomercial. This was entertaining for awhile, but only made me think of Matt. So I decided to ditch the tv watching idea, and went back to my bedroom to check email. If I was lucky, Matt would have read my email and sent a response.

My heart leapt as I spotted his screen name in my email list. I quickly scrolled down and double clicked it with my cursor. His response to my previous email read like this:

Pup, got ur email. Good boy. Yeah, dinner on Monday sounds cool. Be at home Sunday morning too. Am stopping by.

Matt

Oh my god! Sunday morning...that was only in a few hours! Here I thought I'd be lucky if I got to see him Monday night as I requested, but he was paying me a visit *today*. But then almost instantly, worry swept over me. I wondered why he needed to see me so soon. Had I done something wrong? Maybe it was just the opposite, though. Maybe he liked our session so much yesterday that he was coming back for more. But he never would do that, not with Kathie being home. Then I remembered, Kathie said she had to be up early in the morning. That's right. She would be working.

I probably should have gone back to bed at that point, but I was too keyed up. I went to the POGO game section online and amused myself for awhile with Word Womp! until finally I was bored enough that I simply signed off. Finally, I took off my clothes and crawled into bed. I grabbed a novel that I was reading. It was one of Anne Rice's Vampire Chronicles. After about an hour my eyelids started getting heavy and the sentences were making no sense to me, so I put down my glasses and my book, flipped off the light and dozed into restful sleep.

It was daylight when I awoke, and I could hear a pounding sound. What was that noise? I was trying to focus, to bring myself to a state of alertness. Suddenly it dawned on me...someone was at the front door! It must be Matt. I jumped up out of bed wearing only my boxer briefs and dashed for the door. It did not even occur to me to get dressed. I pulled the door open quickly, hoping I was not too late, and stood face to face with my hero. There he was, in the flesh. He looked at me, raising his eyebrows, "Glad to see you are ready for me, pup," he said, referencing my state of undress.

Instantly I became embarrassed, feeling my face redden. "Oh god! I'm sorry sir. I just woke up when you knocked on the door. Let me go get dressed."

"Don't bother," he said, stepping through the doorway. "I'm not gonna stay long. I brought you a gift."

"You did?" I asked, astonished. "Why are you giving me a gift sir?" I smiled up at him.

"Cause you're my pup. Can't I give a gift to my pup if I wanna?" I looked down to his hands to see him clutching a plastic Radio Shack bag.

"Well come on in sir...please." I closed the door behind him and felt completely naked standing there in his presence. He was casual, wearing a b-cap, basketball shorts, tee shirt, and sneaks. His usual attire, actually. He walked past me, seeming to pay no attention to my near nudity and pulled up a chair at our kitchen table.

"Come sit down, pup." It seemed to me like this suddenly had become his apartment and I was the guest. I responded to his invitation and pulled out a chair for myself, first offering him a beverage. He refused, and instead directed his attention to the package on the table in front of him — my gift. He pulled the plastic bag away and revealed a box which appeared to contain a new cell phone. Was he actually giving me a cell phone? I'd never had the money to get one myself and definitely did not want to commit to a monthly payment. I didn't make all that much cash from my part time job, to begin with. "Here," he said, pushing the box towards me, "This phone has already been activated and I already have the number programmed into my own phone."

"Sir," I stammered, "I— I—I can't really accept this."

"Why not?" he asked, in a tone that was very direct.

"Well, because, Sir. It's too expensive. And plus I can't afford to maintain a cell phone plan."

"Wouldn't be much of a gift if you had to maintain it. I will maintain it. Just don't be making a bunch of outrageous calls. 'Sides, it is more of a gift for me than it is for you. I want to be able to get a hold of my pup whenever I need him."

"Oh. Okay, sir. Well... thank you! Still I don't think though that you should have to pay for any of my calls. If I make any, I will pay you for them, okay?"

"We'll see," he said, pushing his chair back and standing up. "I gotta head out though. Am headed for the gym. What time is dinner tomorrow night?"

"You decide, sir. And is there anything special you like to eat?"

"Anything my pup makes for me will be special," he smiled, "I'll be here at six-thirty." He then leaned forward and kissed me on the lips. It was just a gentle loving kiss, not at all passionate. I felt like I should swoon in his presence. Silly me, I was just being melodramatic. He made me that way, though.

As soon as Matt left I rushed into the bedroom, grabbing my crotch. I was so hard! I fell back on the bed and groped myself, wanting more than anything to start stroking. I did not do it though, instead I grabbed a hold of the pillow beside me and squeezed it tightly. He must really love me! He must love me so much!! He gave me a gift. He kissed me again on the lips! I rolled over on top of the pillow and squirmed around excitedly. It was gonna be a long day-and-a-half, waiting to see him again.

* * *

Monday morning I took the bus to school, for I knew that I'd need to stop and get some groceries for my big dinner that evening. The night before I prepared the dessert, a homemade marbleized chocolate cheesecake, and I was going to pick up the fresh raspberries for topping when I got my other groceries. I'd debated on preparing an entirely vegetarian meal, although I quickly dismissed that thinking it very un-Mattlike. I could make some really killer fish entrees and some excellent stir frys. But I wanted this to be a really special meal. Dare I prepare a prime rib? That would be a bit much for the two of us and rather costly. I decided to go with poultry. I would make a chicken parmesan and serve it with vegetable primavera, homemade dinner rolls, and a

Caesar salad. When I got out of my last class around noon, I hit the ATM machine in the college canteen and then waited for the bus which was due in about five minutes.

While I was waiting, I noticed that there was some sort of commotion going on over by the campus library. There were picketers of some sort who were staging a protest. It piqued my curiosity, but I did not want to leave the bus stop for fear of missing my ride. One of my classmates, James Caulfield, then appeared beside me. We often rode the same bus, as he lived on the same side of the city as me. "Hey James, do you know what all of those protesters are doing?"

"Yeah, it is some fag thing," he said. "I guess one of the buildings was vandalized last night. A gay student union or some shit. Now all the gay rights people are all in a tizzy."

"Oh," I said, trying to act casual. This was the first time since I'd been with Matt that it dawned on me that I actually could be classified as one of "them." "I wonder how come somebody did that. What did they do to the building?"

"Oh I guess they just broke in and trashed the place. Whoever it was seemed to hate fags or something cause they wrote all kinds of shit all over the walls and stuff. I can't believe you didn't hear about it already. It's all everyone has been talkin about."

"Well, I've been kind of preoccupied," I explained, "a busy morning. So what is the point of the protest then? The vandalism is over with; what good's it gonna do to protest now?"

"Maybe they think it might happen again. Guess they want something to be done about it. I don't know, go ask the fags." He shrugged just as the bus pulled up. I didn't allow myself to give the matter much more thought as I found a seat on the bus, for I wanted to stay focused upon my evening with Matt. The previous two times we had been together, Matt had hosted me at his house. This was the first time our visit would be on my turf. I just wanted so much for everything to be exactly right.

83

I got off the bus one stop earlier than I normally did, for that was where the grocery store was located. This meant I'd have to walk about three blocks up to my apartment. It shouldn't be bad though because I did not really need more than one or two bags of stuff. I had withdrawn fifty bucks from my savings account, and hopefully that would be enough to get everything I needed. It was kind of exciting pushing the shopping cart around, for I constantly thought of the fact that I was not shopping for myself, but for Matt. I wanted so badly to do something really special for him tonight. I wanted to show him that I could take care of him in some small way. He took care of me by protecting me and by saving me from my bullies; I wanted to now make an attempt to return the favor somehow. I knew it was only a feeble gesture on my part, but I must at least try.

After making my way through the produce section, up and down the grocery aisles, and finally hitting the meat department, I headed for the check lanes. Just as I rounded the corner of the last aisle an end-cap display caught my eye. It was an entire gondola of stuffed animals— dogs to be precise. Each dog was about four inches tall and had a clearly visible name tag on its collar. I quickly scanned them, looking for a black and white pup, one that would resemble Matt's Petey. There was one there! Believe it or not, there was a little stuffed pup that looked remarkably like Petey. I picked it up and looked at the tag. It said "Scamper," which I thought was totally stupid. This pup looked nothing like a 'Scamper.' Well, maybe I could fix that. I noticed that the lettering had not been carved into the metal tag but was merely printed on a clear adhesive strip. I checked the price tag. The pup was $6.98. I quickly looked through my grocery cart and mentally added my purchases. I'd so far spent about forty dollars. So with the sales tax, I'd have just enough to get the Petey replica. Perfect! I headed for the checkout.

When I got back to the apartment I found a note from Kathie. She stated that she had to work that evening until eight, but not to worry: she was going out with Carter afterwards. "Don't wait up for me," she said. It was the motherly instinct in her, I think. She knew I'd have a long day on Tuesday. That was one of the days I had classes and work both. Every since our parents had passed away, Kathie had sort of assumed the roles of both mother and father for me. I owed her so much. I just prayed that everything was working out well with her and Carter. From everything she said, he was a really cool guy. They must truly be hitting it off, for she'd earlier told me that her next date with Carter was not until Tuesday.

After unpacking the groceries, I began my preparations for the evening's meal. I still had almost four hours before my special guest arrived. I needed to marinate the chicken breasts for about an hour anyhow, before I breaded them. I dove into my tasks of meal preparation and when everything was fully underway, I went into my bedroom and peeled off my tee shirt. What was I going to wear tonight? Well, I couldn't start freaking about that yet; I had too much else to do. I slid into my computer chair then and opened up a new word processing document. Reaching into one of the desk drawers, I pulled out a packet of clear letter labels. I pushed my chair back, grabbed the stuffed dog off from the bed behind me and carefully peeled off the 'Scamper' label from his tag. Then I grabbed a ruler from the desk drawer and measured the tag. What should I print on the new tag? Should it be 'Pup' or 'Petey'?

I played around with some different fonts for a bit and ended up deciding on the word 'Pup.' I sort of liked that it would be more generic. Then if anyone saw the stuffed pup, they would think nothing of it. It would be my secret gift to Matt. After printing the decal on a sheet of clear labels, I then carefully used scissors to cut out the new name tag. I then carefully peeled it off from the label sheet and attached it to the metal tag which was hanging from the pup's collar. It was perfect. My new label actually looked even better than the factory produced 'scamper' label that was previously on the tag.

By the time I returned to the kitchen to check the pasta, I realized that I still had two hours remaining until the six thirty deadline. I removed the pasta from the stove and placed it in the sink to cool, and then headed for the bathroom. I spent a good forty five minutes showering and grooming myself, wanting every inch of me to be perfectly ready for Matt. I had no idea whether or not he'd choose to again be intimate with me, but just in case, I didn't want to take any chances. Wrapping a towel around myself I then headed back into the kitchen and began dicing vegetables for the primavera. I also checked the bread dough and saw that it had risen as desired, and then proceeded to punch it back down and formed small balls in the shape of dinner rolls. I placed them on a cookie sheet to re-rise and covered them with a towel. I then breaded the chicken and placed it into a glass baking dish, liberally covering it with the tomato sauce that was simmering on the stovetop. Voila! Everything was going fantastic.

I checked my watch and saw I had a little over an hour remaining. I headed back to the bedroom and flung open my closet. This was the worst part! No matter what I decided to wear, I knew I would ultimately regret it. As I was rifling through my closet it suddenly dawned on me: what if Matt did not take this whole evening as seriously as I did? Well, actually, of course he would not! He acted so casual about it yesterday. To him this was just a couple of buds getting together for dinner. Maybe he expected me to throw in a frozen pizza and kick back in front of the tube. I would be so embarrassed if he showed up dressed really casually and I had decked myself all out. Then on the other hand, what if he did dress nicer and I looked like a scum bag? I wondered if I should call him. No! that would be disastrous. What would I even say?

After twenty five minutes of deliberation I finally opted to simply wear khakis and a dress shirt. It was a safe compromise between casual and dressy. I put a small and simple gold chain around my neck and doused myself with Eternity cologne. As usual, my hair looked like a freakin mop. I gelled it and spent a good fifteen minutes in front of the mirror. Oh my god! The time! I rushed back into the kitchen and checked the chicken. It was doing fine...another five or ten minutes. I tossed the vegetables and pasta together in a skillet and placed them on a burner to simmer. Then I set about to set the table.

The timer for the chicken was going off just as I was arranging the linen napkins at each place setting. I rushed over and used a potholder to remove the baking dish from the oven, then reset the temperature and put in the dinner rolls. It was now six-fifteen. Quickly, I dove into the fridge and pulled out the romaine and endive lettuce and began tossing the salad. I grabbed the cruet of dressing and doused the lettuce leaves and tossed it all together hurriedly. I placed the salad in the middle of the table. Then I set about to prepare each of our plates, dishing up much larger portions for Matt. I cursed myself for not thinking to ask Kathie to pick up a bottle of wine for me, for I was not old enough to buy alcohol. Instead, I poured us each a glass of sparkling white juice.

When the timer went off for the dinner rolls, I removed them and placed them in a basket lined with linen napkins. I set the basket on the table. Now everything was ready. Chicken, vegetables, dinner rolls, salad, table was set, dessert was in the fridge. All that was missing was my guest. It was twenty-eight minutes past six. Oh my god! What if he changed his mind or forgot? What if he was running late? I should not have prepared our plates until he arrived. I was such an idiot!

Just as I was berating myself for these actions, I heard the knock on the door. Oh no! Now I was more panicked than I had been when I thought he might not show up. I raced over to the mirror in the hallway and checked my appearance. Man, I looked like such a nerd. What if I just don't answer the door? What if he doesn't like anything I've done? I was actually shaking at this point. He knocked again. Somehow I pulled myself together and nervously headed for the door. Taking a very deep breath, I pulled the door open widely and tried to look as nonchalant as possible.

There he was, as perfect as ever. He was wearing a polo shirt and khakis, maybe having thought the same as I about dressing semi-casual. He looked and smelled wonderful, and I stepped aside to let him in the doorway. "I brought a bottle of wine," he said, handing over the package he was holding.

"Thank you," I said, taking the wine from him. He leaned in and kissed me gently. "Smells wonderful in here, pup."

"Thanks...so do you," I smiled up at him. "Come on in. Everything is ready." I motioned towards the table, and then headed into the kitchen. I pulled out two more wine glasses and quickly used them to replace the juice which was already on the table. I then grabbed the juice bottle from the wine server and replaced it with Matt's bottle of real wine. I placed it on the table along with a corkscrew.

"Wow, this is fantastic pup," Matt commented. "You must have worked on this for a long time."

I shrugged, trying to appear casual. "Wanted it to be nice for you, sir."

"Well, it's very nice, but you don't have to go out of your way to impress me. Just be you, that's all." He had the most sincere and loving look on his face as he smiled over at me. All of my anxiety from the entire stressful day seemed to suddenly vanish, as I became captivated by him.

Matt took a sip from his water glass as I finally sat down. "Thank you, sir. Thanks for saying that, and for coming tonight. I never really got to show you my gratitude for when you saved me...from Devin and Kyle, I mean."

"Oh? Well seems to me you have shown me quite a bit of gratitude already. Pretty soon you can show me some more." His eyes locked with mine, and I became aware of the implication that he was making. It was so hot when he dropped these foreshadowing remarks like that. Like the last time we were together and early on he informed me that I would be cumming that day, but did not say when or how.

I picked up my knife and fork, looking away from him quickly. I had to suppress a smile, and so I focused my attention on my plate. "Do you like pasta?" I asked, wondering if my change of subject was too obvious.

"Love it, pup. It's my favorite actually." I was relieved. "What is the meat? Veal or chicken?"

"Chicken sir. I don't cook veal."

"Should have known," he laughed. "Can't bear to think of those baby cows getting murdered, huh?"

I laughed. "Actually, I'm practically a vegetarian myself. Only once in awhile I eat meat. Didn't think you would be that way yourself though. You seem like a meat eater."

"Well, you already know I eat meat. We had pizza with meat the other day, and you didn't seem to mind the ham."

"Doubt I would mind anything, sir, so long as it was you feeding it to me."

"Good answer," he said, shoving a forkful of chicken in his mouth. "Very good," he said, with his mouth still full.

I smiled in spite of myself. He was so cute when he was eating. Well, maybe not actually cute. He just was...Matt. He was awesome. I was glad to be sitting at the table for otherwise my erection would be obvious to him. I moved my napkin into my lap self consciously.

"How often do you go to the gym, sir?" I was trying to find conversation that was appropriate, realizing suddenly that we were so very different. I hoped we were not so different that he eventually would conclude we had nothing in common.

"Oh, probably three or four times a week. I'll take you with me sometime. Would you like that?"

"Well, yeah!...or I mean, yes sir." He laughed at me and my self-correction. "I'd like that very much. Would you like a dinner roll sir? They're homemade."

"Thanks," he said taking the basket from me. "How did you learn to cook like this?"

"Well, Kathie has always been so busy. For quite awhile she was working two jobs when I first moved in with her. I felt I should at least do this much for her; she shouldn't have to worry about cooking after working so much, ya know."

"That's cool. You're a considerate pup. See, that's what I like about you. You always think of other people. Good that you and Kathie have each other, too."

"She has a new boyfriend now. His name is Carter. They are going on their second date tonight."

"You think he's cute?" Matt asked.

"I don't know sir," I blushed, "I haven't ever seen him. I'm not used to hearing guys call other guys 'cute'."

"Not used to suckin dick either, pup, but you've done just fine with that." I couldn't believe he just said that! I gulped down a big bite of chicken. "You want some wine?" he asked.

"Yes please, but maybe only just a small amount. I am not used to drinking, either. Last year I had two glasses of champagne after graduation, and I ended up passed out. I guess I'm what you'd call a lightweight."

"Yeah, in more ways than one," he interjected. "Maybe I'll just get you drunk and take advantage of you. No, wait. I don't need to get you drunk to do that. Do I?"

"No Sir, no you don't." I wanted to reach over and grab his hand then. I wanted to tell him to forget about dinner and get right on to dessert...and I didn't mean the raspberry cheesecake. Instead I just stared at him, astonished by the sheer beauty of him. His masculinity and strength seemed to ooze from him. He dripped with self confidence and was so incredibly handsome. I probably should have pinched myself right then, just as an assurance that this was not another one of my crazy dreams.

When it was finally time to serve dessert, I was not sure how I'd have the room to eat any more. I hated that feeling of fullness just after a meal. It made me think I was so fat. In spite of myself, I got up from the table and headed into the kitchen to slice the cheesecake. I was surprised when I noticed that Matt was right behind me, carrying our plates. "Oh, I'm sorry, sir. I should have cleared the table."

"Not a problem," he said as he set the plates down on the counter. He stepped behind me and wrapped his arms around me. I held the knife out in front of me, pausing my task of cutting the cake. Matt leaned into me and kissed the back of my neck. I did not know whether to place the knife down and turn to kiss him, or to go on as if he were not even there. He then reached out and gently grabbed my wrist, guiding it down to the countertop where I obediently released the knife. "We don't have to have dessert just yet," he informed me. At this point I did slowly turn around and looked up into his eyes.

I was surprised to be already feeling the effects of my half-glass of wine. I was not so much intoxicated as I was relaxed. My skin seemed more sensitive as Matt ran his fingers up and down my shoulders and arms. "Take me to your bedroom, pup," he told me. I grabbed his hand and led the way.

My heart was pounding rapidly as I led him down the hall and into my bedroom. This was the first time he'd ever entered this, my private domain. As I walked through the door I saw the stuffed puppy on the bed. I let go of his hand and leapt over to grab the pup. Quickly I held it behind my back, turning to face him. "Sir, I have a gift for you now."

"You do?" he said in a voice that was partial laughter, "What was dinner? I thought that was already a pretty nice gift."

"Thanks, sir, but this is a gift you can take with you. Something to remind you of me and of what you mean to me." I pulled my arm out from behind my back and handed over the miniature stuffed Petey.

He busted up laughing. "Man, Petey is everywhere! Now I have three of 'em. A dog puppy, a boy puppy, and a stuffed puppy. Thanks pup." He stepped over to me again, once more wrapping his strong arms around me. I melted within his embrace instantly. As I clung to him I felt myself getting so hard. I wanted so badly to once again serve him, to drop to my knees for the third time in one week and be the servant to his needs that I felt I must have been born to be! This time, though, he did not seem to want this of me. Instead he pressed against me and backed me onto my own bed. Mine was not a big four-poster bed like his, but simply a twin without even a headboard. He gently pushed me backwards, placing his palm in the center of my chest. I yielded to his guidance, and lay back submissively on the bed beneath him.

I was very excited, not unlike the previous two encounters I'd shared with Matt, but this time there was something strangely different. I did not have the sense of overwhelming fear that I had had before. Perhaps the effects of the wine had relaxed me enough that I did not think the fearful and fretful thoughts to which I usually was a slave. Or perhaps I simply was trusting Matt a little more each time. Probably it was a combination of both factors; nonetheless, it felt so comforting to be with him, in his presence and under his control, and not to be terrified. I lay back on the bed beneath him, stretching myself out, wanting to offer every part of me to Matt, my hero, the only man I'd ever loved.

Leaning over me, he reached down and unbuttoned the top button of my shirt. I was tempted to assist him, to proceed myself to the second button. I looked into his eyes, though, and knew that I should simply lie there and allow him to do with me what he chose. Very slowly, he then advanced to the second, then the third, then the fourth buttons. When he had successfully completed this mission, I then automatically arched my back as he pulled the shirt from the back, un-tucking it from my khakis. He slid his hands then across my smooth chest and up onto my shoulders, pushing his fingers beneath the fabric of my shirt. In a very smooth movement he pushed down the sleeves of my shirt exposing my shoulders entirely. Finally, he grabbed each of the cuffs of my shirt and pulled as I pulled back my arms towards my body, removing them entirely from the shirtsleeves. I then leaned forward as he pulled the shirt from beneath me.

This seemed an unusual turn of events, for me to now be lying here in front of him, shirtless, while he stood there totally clothed. Even during our last encounter when I'd stripped to my underwear for him, I had already seen him exposed to me when we were in the bathroom. He then moved his hands down to my waist and undid my belt loop, then the button on my pants. He unzipped me.

My breathing was becoming more rapid as I grew more and more excited, though still not afraid. Still I trusted him with all of my heart. He backed up slightly, reaching down to pull off my shoes. He then grabbed my pant legs. I pulled my legs up for him and again arched my back so he could smoothly and easily remove them. Now here I lay, naked but for my socks and boxer briefs, stretched out on my bed staring up at him. He smiled at me, seeming to take in the sight of me. I wondered what his thoughts were during those few seconds. Was he aware of how very much he controlled me? Was he aware that I would do literally anything for him, simply because of who he was and because of how I felt about him? Did he know that I truly belonged to him at this point?

"Do you have any lotion, pup?" His voice was gentle and calm. I wondered if he planned to give me a massage. I nodded to him and pointed to my bedside stand. I thought briefly at that moment that he may find it peculiar that I kept a bottle of hand lotion beside my bed, but he acted as if it was completely normal, and he leaned over to open the drawer and remove it. He placed the bottle beside me on the bed and then moved his hands to the waistband of my briefs. "Let's get these off of you, pup." He pulled them down as I pressed my hips forward to raise my butt slightly from the bed. Almost instantly I was then naked before him. "For being such a little guy, you have a pretty good sized cock." He made this remark as a statement of fact, and I was unsure of how to respond. Should I thank him, deny it, agree with him? I simply looked at him, though, saying nothing.

I was so hard then as I lay there exposed to him. Part of me wanted to jump up from that bed right then and drop down to my knees in front of him. Another part wanted to go on with whatever he was about to do to me. I was so torn, wanting mostly to serve him, but also wanting to experience the pleasure of his loving touch. "I'm going to ask you some questions, pup, okay? And you are going to answer me honestly."

I looked into his eyes and nodded. "Yes sir," my response was nearly a whisper.

"Have you ever messed around with another guy... I mean other than me?" I shook my head as I continued to stare at him. "Okay, well I know you have jacked off before; I have the hand lotion to prove it." He smiled at me after glancing over to the lotion beside me. "When you jack off, what is it that you fantasize about?"

"Um, I don't know sir. It's hard to describe."

"No it's not," he corrected me, "Do you think about guys or girls, clothed or unclothed? Do you think about sucking dick, getting sucked? Do you fantasize about being fucked?"

"Well all those things, sir," I confessed, "except I haven't really fantasized about girls for a long time. I mean I used to try thinking about them on purpose. I wanted to see if it would...you know...turn me on."

"Did it?"

"No," I said honestly.

He did not look surprised. "Okay, well when you jack off, do you ever put anything into your butt? I mean like your finger?"

I was a bit shocked by the question. "No sir...why would I do that?!"

"Well, if you were fantasizing about being fucked, I thought you might jack off like that. Doesn't matter one way or the other. Just was wondering."

"Sir, do you want to fuck me?"

He looked down at me, staring me right into the eyes. "Pup, I am *going* to fuck you. It's just a question of when. I want to make sure you are ready. And I think you want me do it, too. Don't you?"

I nodded. "Yes sir. But I'm a little scared of it."

"It's okay," he said reassuringly. "I would not expect for you not to be scared, especially with it being your first time ever. But you do remember what I promised you, don't you?"

"You'll never hurt me, sir."

"That's right." He then picked up the lotion. "Hold out your hand, pup." I did as he said, holding my right hand up to him as he squeezed some lotion into it. "Now rub some of this onto your cock, just like you are alone, jacking off." That was the first statement I'd ever heard him make that I thought was totally absurd. How could I ever think of myself as being alone when I was in the same room with him? "Close your eyes," he said. "Pretend you are alone jacking off. Do it."

I obeyed him, squeezing my eyes shut, as I started to lube up my cock. I slid my hand back and forth on my already hard shaft, being very nervous and very much aware that he was there watching me. "Think of something that turns you on. Anything, pup. Think only of that, and describe to me what you're thinking."

95

"I'm thinking of you, sir," I said honestly. "I'm thinking of Saturday with you."

"Okay, what specifically?" I continued to stroke myself as I lay there, eyes tightly shut.

"I'm thinking of you carrying me out of the bathroom. I'm thinking of you kissing me. It was so hot the way you kissed me. I never have been kissed like that before sir. I never even knew what it felt like." I was stroking harder. "I'm thinking of your body pressing against mine, you pinned me underneath you. I felt so small, so ...um...overpowered."

"You are small," he said quietly. "You are very small, and you are very much overpowered when you're with me, but you like that. Don't you?"

"Yes, sir," I confessed. "I like that very much. It makes me feel safe. It makes me feel protected."

"Why, pup? Why does it make you feel safe?"

I continued to stroke myself, becoming more and more turned on. "I feel so safe when I am with you sir. I feel safe because..."

"Because why? Why do you feel safe pup? Say it!"

"Because, sir...because I know I belong to you!"

"That's right!" he said, "You totally belong to me, don't you?" I felt his face against mine, his lips brushing against my lips. I dared not open my eyes, but I responded by kissing him back. My mouth opened slightly as his tongue entered me. Then as he was kissing me, ever so gently I felt his hand down between my legs. He pressed his finger against my hole. I continued to stroke myself, willing myself to trust him, to not be afraid.

As he continued to kiss me, I continued to stroke myself, and he continued to slide his finger into me. Gradually he entered me deeper and deeper. He was moving his finger in and out. It was smooth. It did not hurt at all. In fact, it was an incredible sensation. He seemed to be pressing himself against some place inside of me that I did not even know existed. I was literally throbbing now, and very close to orgasm.

He pumped his finger in and out of me as he pulled his lips away from mine. "Open your eyes!" he commanded.

I obeyed and stared directly at him as he towered over me, fucking me with his finger. "Shoot for me pup...shoot your load!" Almost instantly I released the tense muscles in my groin and blasted a huge load from my cock. He shoved his finger deep into me, as far as it would go; I felt it moving inside me! It was like he was forcing the cum right out of me. He was fucking out my load from me using his finger.

"Oh god! Oh God!!! AAAHHHH!!" I was screaming as I blasted jet after jet of cum all over myself. It shot far up into the air, some hitting my face, soaking the bedding beside my head. He was laughing, as he stared back into my eyes.

"Good boy!! Good pup!! Did that feel good?"

I gasped for air, "Oh...Oh yes sir! Yes SIR!"

5

There was an article in Tuesday's paper about the protest that had been staged the previous day. Apparently the gay student union office had indeed been vandalized on Thursday of the week prior, but the school's administration offered little response. Many of the gay and lesbian students felt that not enough was being done to protect them. Some felt that the school's president should have made a public statement of condemnation and should have given assurances that steps were being taken to identify and punish the perpetrators.

What made matters worse was that this was the third such act of vandalism that had specifically targeted gays. The community college offered only one dormitory for on-campus housing, the entryway of which had been spray-painted during the previous month. The graffiti bore a very graphic anti-gay sentiment and was then quickly painted over within a day or two. The other incident was in the campus library, where several of the books in the gay interest section had been destroyed. The books had been replaced without comment.

What finally sparked the fires of protest was a rather off-the-cuff remark by a member of the school faculty, Professor Bryant. He had told one of his classes that if the gay rights people did not constantly draw so much attention to themselves and try forcing their agenda on everyone else, then maybe they would not be the victims of such attacks. When this quote was eventually reported to the gay student union, pretty much all hell broke loose.

Personally, I was not too bothered by Bryant's remark because I had grown accustomed to hearing those kinds of comments. Plus, I was not exactly impressed with him as an instructor. He taught mathematics classes, yet somehow always seemed to find a way to work in his personal political viewpoints into the class curriculum. He was a lousy teacher. Why should I worry about the opinions of some moron like that, I thought.

The one effect that the entire controversy did have on me, though, was that it made me aware that there was a gay student union. Since I had never really thought of myself as being gay before, it had not interested me to ever seek out or become involved in any kind of group such as this. And now the organization was rallying for the participation and cooperation of all students, both gay and straight, to respond to these "acts of hatred." They were having a meeting in the Student Services Center auditorium on Thursday night and had tacked up flyers everywhere around campus. I actually was debating as to whether or not I wanted to attend this meeting, mainly out of curiosity. I thought maybe I could go to it and just sort of blend in, without having to worry about somehow being labeled. After all, there were likely to be several straight people in attendance.

My pondering on this matter did not occupy nearly as many of my thoughts as did Matt, however. During my classes that day, I kept drifting off mentally, thinking about him and about what he had done to me the night before. I was so pleased with the way the evening had gone, even prior to our intimacy. He genuinely seemed to have enjoyed the dinner and acted truly appreciative of my efforts to impress him. When he left my apartment he had reminded me of the standing orders that were in place regarding my restriction on ejaculation, and he also told me to make sure I kept my phone charged and with me at all times. I did not question his orders, but found this peculiar because never once had he called me since he gave it to me. I'd have thought he'd have at least given me a quick call to test it out, see if it was working, or to make sure that I knew how to properly operate it. It was kind of exciting to me to know that I was always only a phone call away from Matt at any given moment, 24/7.

My last class of the day finished in the early afternoon, and I headed out to the bike rack to retrieve my bicycle. I should have enough time to make it to work with about ten minutes to spare. This was my usual routine—I almost always worked Tuesday evenings. When I got to work, I stored my back pack in the closet of the employee break room and went to log myself in on the daily time sheet. I then headed out into the store to locate my boss and to find out if he had any specific instructions for me that day. As I rounded the corner, I looked up and noticed someone coming through the front door of the store. It was Devin Baker. Both he and I knew that he was not allowed in the store, at least not while I was working, for it was a direct violation of my personal protection order. I froze in my tracks, wondering if I should inform my boss about his presence, call the police, or simply ignore him.

Quickly I turned away before Devin saw me and headed back into the employee lounge. I reached into my pocket then and removed my cell phone. God, I wanted to talk to Matt so badly! I suddenly realized, though, that Matt had not given me his cell number. He had only told me that he'd programmed my number into his phone, not vice-versa. I paced the room a bit, being completely alone at the time. I looked back down at my phone then and decided to call Kathie. When she answered, she knew instantly by my voice that something was wrong. I told her about Devin being in the store. She asked me if I'd told Mr. Bartlett, my boss, and I informed her I had not, that I had not even seen him yet. She told me to just wait where I was and that she would call back the store and ask to speak to him and then inform him of the situation. By this time I was actually shaking.

Man, this whole thing really pissed me off. Why was I allowing myself to be so intimidated? Had anyone asked me only a couple days before how I was doing after the bashing,

I'd have dismissed their concern and considered the whole thing a non-issue in my life. Yet here I was now cowering alone in a back room to avoid even being seen by my former tormentor. It had actually been nearly three months since I had last seen Devin, and outside of the courtroom, this was the only time I'd ever seen him since he'd beaten me up. I had not realized that his presence would ever affect me this way, and to be honest I was not even exactly sure why it was freaking me out as much as it was. It wasn't like he could actually do anything to me here while I was at work. Even if he had gotten verbally abusive towards me, he wouldn't get away with it for long. So why was I being such a big baby about this whole thing?

I was startled when Mr. Bartlett finally walked into the room. "You all right, Pete?" he asked.

"Um...yes sir. I'm sorry..."

"Hey, sit down," he said, "You look like you're pretty shook up."

"No, sir. I mean, I'm okay. I'm sorry about this ... uh... situation, sir. I mean...um..."

"Don't be sorry. I know that guy out there messed with ya pretty bad a couple months ago. I remember your black eyes and broken nose. Don't worry though, he's gone now. I kicked him out."

"Oh...well, thank you, sir. I don't even know why...um...why I got so freaked about it, or...um...upset about it, sir. It's not like he can do anything to me here."

"Yeah, I know, but still he is not even allowed around you period. I told him if he ever comes back I'm callin' the cops. I don't think you will have anything to worry about after this."

"Thank you sir. Is there anything you want me to do today...special, I mean?"

"Well, why don't you work in the back for awhile unpacking the delivery that came in this morning. I'll have Mandy work the front counter until you are more calmed down and relaxed. Okay?"

"Okay. Thanks." He put his hand on my shoulder reassuringly.

The remainder of my shift was uneventful, and just prior to the close of the day Kathie finally walked into the store with her new boyfriend Carter. "How was the street fair?" I asked, after a brief introduction.

"Oh it's pretty cool. Are you going down there after work?" Kathie asked.

"No, I doubt it. I have some stuff to do at home. I've got to read like forty-eight pages for my psychology class."

"Fun!" said Carter. He appeared to be everything that Kathie had said he was. He was a few inches taller than her, not quite Matt's height. He dressed nicely, kind of casual-sporty. I noticed right off that he had incredible biceps too. He was very masculine. I was so happy that Kathie had found such a decent boyfriend.

"Kathie tells me you are a paralegal, Carter," I said. "How is law school going?"

"Oh, it's goin'," he answered. "Lot of work. I work at really great firm, though; I'm lucky to have all the support I do."

"That's great. What kind of law are you interested in?"

"I'm gonna be a prosecutor," he said. "That reminds me, I hear that you had an unwanted visitor today. You really should report that to the DA's office. That is a probation violation, I'm sure."

"Yeah, I know," I answered, "But I don't so much care about whether or not he gets into trouble. I just want him to stay away from me."

"Well, sounds like you are a much better person than he is. I don't think I'd be so forgiving of someone who had beaten me like he did to you."

Kathie then jumped in, changing the subject, "You want to grab a bite to eat with us when you get out? You still can make it home in plenty of time to get your reading done."

"Oh...well, I don't think you guys want your little brother tagging along on your date," I laughed.

"Don't be silly," said Carter, "Just so you don't try to get between us at any critical moments." They both laughed as he leaned to kiss her affectionately.

"God!" I said. "Okay, I guess someone has to referee for you two."

"Cool, we will just browse for a few minutes until you're ready. Okay?"

I finished up my clean-up chores while the two of them roamed through the store. Then after I checked with my supervisor, I logged out on my time sheet and found the happy couple in the paperback fiction section. "Ready," I said.

Carter and Kathie took me to a little Italian restaurant that was walking distance from the bookstore. They sat together on one side of a booth and I sat opposite them. I took up just a fraction of my seat, and they were both scrunched together, voluntarily, across the table from me. We were chatting casually, when suddenly I heard this odd buzzing sound. I'd never heard the sound before but it seemed to be coming from my clothing. Then I realized what it was. It was the cell phone!

I reached down and pulled the phone from my pocket and in the display screen in all capital letters was the word MATT. My heart skipped a beat as I fumbled to find the correct button to push, hurrying to answer his call. "Hello?" I did not even think about the fact that Kathie and Carter were right there staring at me.

"Hey pup! Where are ya?"

"I'm with Kathie and Carter...her boyfriend. We are over at Vinnie's Italian Restaurant. Down on Washington Street. They're taking me out to eat."

"Cool. When you gonna be done?"

"We just ordered. Where are you, s— Matt?"

"Over by the campus. Did you just get there or are you about done?" he rephrased his question.

"We just ordered. Do you want to come over here?"
Quickly I looked over at Kathie to see if it was all right. She
looked at me approvingly, and I was relieved.

"Yeah, maybe I could.... Sure. Are you sure it's okay that I
horn in on your plans with your sis?"

"Of course. It wasn't 'plans' anyways. We just are getting
a pizza."

" kay...see ya in ten." He clicked off the call, and I looked
up at Kathie.

"I hope it's okay," I said.

"Of course it's okay," said Carter, "We ordered extra large,
remember?"

"Matt is the guy who rescued Petey, took him to the
hospital that day he was attacked. He's a really decent guy, it
seems. Since then he and Pete have become pretty close
friends. Haven't you Petey?"

"Yeah...really close."

I was nervous while waiting for Matt to arrive yet very
excited that I'd be seeing him again. This would be the very
first time we had ever been together in public, at least since
we had developed an intimate relationship. Every single
time that he contacted me, though, it was a major surprise to
me. I still was disbelieving of the fact that there was really
anything about me that he would find attractive to himself.
Yet just since Saturday I had talked to him at least once each
day, and we had "been together" twice. I wondered what the
reason was for him calling me tonight. It seemed so odd to
me that he was spending so much time with me; it seemed
that it would leave very little time for Tracy. But then he was
the one who told me that he was not seeing her all that much
any more. I wondered if Kathie ever heard anything from
her.

Matt was wearing basketball shorts, a tee shirt, and a
baseball cap when he arrived- my quintessential jock hero. I
slid over to make room for him, wanting more than anything
for him to kiss me right on the lips in front of God and

everyone, but he gave no indication to either me nor our dining partners that he had any interest in me whatsoever other than friendship. In fact, he did not even touch me. Our pizza arrived just moments after Matt sat down, and as we dove into it, Matt and Carter had begun a rather serious conversation about some sports team. I knew nothing of what they were saying, but sat there politely and quietly, barely touching my pizza. As soon as I noticed Matt had finished his first slice of pizza, I reached over quickly and served him a second. Even in this setting, it seemed only natural for me to serve him and to tend to his needs. Nobody seemed to really notice that I was doting.

Finally Kathie mentioned to Matt about the encounter I'd earlier had, when Devin Baker came into the bookstore. Matt paused and looked down at me. "You should have called the cops, Petey. Don't let jerks like that intimidate you." I looked down at my lap, feeling embarrassed that Kathie had even said anything to Matt about it.

"You ride your bike to work?" Matt asked me.

"Yes, it's still locked up over by the store. I can ride it home though. I do it all the time, cause there are plenty of streetlights."

"Nah, I'll give you a ride home tonight," he said. "If it's locked up, it'll be all right til morning. I can take you back to get it then. I'll pick you up on my way to class."

"Okay," I said, knowing better than to question him.

After we had finished eating, Kathie and Carter gracefully said goodbye to us. It was obvious that they wanted to get on with their date— alone. I was not real sad to see them go, for it meant that Matt and I were alone together. Carter had paid the restaurant tab on his way out, upon his insistence, and Matt moved over across the table from me, sitting where the two of them had been.

"Pup," he said to me, suddenly becoming very serious, "Why'd you get all freaked when you saw Baker today?"

106

Again I looked down, but he reached across the table and pushed my chin up with his fingers, forcing me to look him in the eye. "Well, sir...I really don't know. I mean...um... I mean it just sort of scared me. I didn't think that he even bothered me any more, but this was the first time I had seen him since..."

"Well you did the right thing by calling someone, pup. You ended up getting him out of there and you showed him that you weren't gonna let him get away with breaking the rules of the PPO. So you're chill. You did right. Okay?"

"Yes sir."

"I'm gonna give you my cell number too. But you only are to ever call it if it is an absolute emergency. You understand?"

I nodded. "Yes sir."

"You know what that means, right? It means if you start getting all worried and freakin about some stupid shit, don't call me. Only call me if you are in danger or feel threatened, or something like that. You understand the difference?"

"Yes sir, I understand," I assured him.

"Give me your phone." I handed him the cell phone, and he punched a bunch of buttons, apparently adding his number to my call list. "Now if you do ever have to call me, just press the down arrow button and it takes you to your phone book. Then select my name by pressing the green button. It is the only name in your phone list right now. You can add others easy enough, though."

"I know sir. I read the instructions. Thank you. Thank you for giving me your number. Can I ask you something though sir?"

"Hit me," he said.

"Well, what if I had called you today, I mean when Devin was at the store. Would that have been an emergency?"

"Did you feel threatened or in danger?"

"Well, yeah...sorta. I mean, I knew he could not hurt me, but I panicked."

"Yes, you could have called me then."

"Well what would be an example of a reason I should not call you, sir?"

"If you miss me or if you are horny, or if you are just freaking because you have not heard from me in awhile. Those reasons are not acceptable to call. You wait for me to call you. Got it?"

"Yes sir," I said, looking him directly in the eye. "I promise."

"Good boy."

I did not ask Matt where we were going when we got in his car, and I did not mention anything to him about my psychology reading. Actually, I had grossly exaggerated the situation to Kathie and Carter, as I'd already completed most of the reading. I just did not want to seem like a total loser, passing up the street fair to go home for no apparent reason.

I sat quietly beside Matt in the car, feeling no need to make idle conversation. It seemed for some reason that this was one of those times when just being together was enough. We did not have to always be talking. I did not question him when he drove out of the city and eventually all the bright lights and noises were far behind us. He drove for nearly fifteen minutes before he turned off the highway to head down a county road of some sort, one I'd never been on before. He turned again, this time even further away from the bustle of civilization. We probably were about forty miles out of the city at this point. It was interesting, because I did not even once question him about where he was taking me. I was developing such a level of trust in him that it really did not matter to me what he decided to do. All that mattered was that we were together.

"My parents own a cabin out here," he finally informed me, "in case you were wondering."

"Oh, I guess I just trust that you know where you are going sir," I said lightheartedly. "I've never been out this way before."

"Well, during the summer we usually have the cabin rented out for the most part. We do sometimes spend some time here when it's vacant. It's right on the water, a perfect place to vacation. Usually it sits empty this time of year, though, but it makes a nice get-away place. When we get there, you need to call your house and leave a message on your answering machine for your sister. Tell her you are with me and will be spending the night. That way she won't worry. In the morning I'll take you back to the store for your bike."

"Yes, sir," I said.

Matt finally turned again onto a very narrow road. It was paved but wound through a wooded area. I realized that the road actually was a very long driveway. Apparently we were at the cabin. A thought suddenly crossed my mind as we were pulling up to the front of the building. I did not even have so much as a change of clothes with me. All I had was my backpack, which contained only my textbooks. Maybe Matt was going to take me home in time to get changed before class in the morning.

"My plan was going to be to bring you here this weekend. Then, as sort of a last-minute thing, I decided I didn't want to wait that long. I brought you some clothes for tomorrow too. They are in the trunk."

"You did?" I was surprised, "It seems like you had it planned out after all, if you even brought me clothes."

"Nah," he said, "I'm just always prepared. Must be the boy scout in me." I laughed at his remark, thinking he was anything but the boy scout type.

It really was too dark to see much when we got out of the car, and Matt retrieved his duffle bag from the trunk. I slung my back pack over my shoulder and followed him cautiously up the path to the front steps. He slid his key into the lock and shoved the door open, reaching inside to flip on an outside light. I looked around me and saw a beautifully landscaped yard, complete with a gazebo and an enormous, well-tended flower garden. Obviously the Porters paid handsomely to have this place maintained, and I definitely would not have categorized it as a "cabin." The house itself appeared to be larger than any my family had ever owned.

It always amazed me when affluent people would trivialize the extent of their property. This place was a beautiful house on the lake, not a cabin by any stretch of the imagination. As Matt was driving me up the driveway, I was expecting to see a tiny, two-bedroom log home, not this sprawling, picturesque abode that I was now seeing before me.

When we got inside, Matt did not bother to show me around. Instead he just led me down a hallway, and I followed him into a big master bedroom. He flipped a light switch which turned on a single bedside lamp, and tossed his duffle bag on top of a large dresser that was against one of the walls. Within the room there was a huge king-sized bed, the dresser, a desk and chair, two high back chairs placed on either side of a small glassed-top table, and a rather large entertainment center. There also was a walk-in closet and a full-sized bathroom off from the bedroom.

There we were, then, alone, and out in the middle of nowhere. As I set my backpack down, resting it against the desk, I looked over at Matt and became aware that he was simply standing there in the middle of the room staring at me. "Strip off all your clothes and lie on the bed, pup. Now."

It was a very sudden and drastic change in his demeanor, for only moments before he had been talking to me, making me feel as if we just a couple of guys hanging out together. Now all of a sudden it was apparent to me that I was not here as his equal for a carefree evening of male bonding. He obviously had been anticipating something far different all along. I almost reminded him then that he'd wanted me to call home, but I somehow knew it was not really appropriate for me to even speak at this point.

I simply obeyed.

Matt stood there nearly expressionless as he watched me strip off my clothing. He did not move from his position even slightly, making no effort to assist me undressing as he had done so romantically the night before. When I was down to simply my briefs and socks, I looked up at him, as if to see if I had gone far enough. His expression told me that when he had said "all of your clothing" he had actually meant all.

When I was finally completely naked, I climbed up on the bed and lay down on my back. "Don't move," he then told me, and he left the room. He returned in less than a minute, carrying a large bath towel. He walked over to the bed and spread out the towel, placing it on the edge of the mattress. Then he said to me, "Move over here so your butt is on the towel and your legs are hanging over the edge of the bed."

I obeyed.

I looked up at him then, wondering what he was about to do to me, but not being afraid. My strongest feeling at the moment was slight embarrassment. I hated the fact that I was lying here totally naked; I have always rather modest. Also, I was not aroused like the previous times Matt had seen me without clothing. This was the first time I lay before him being completely flaccid. This condition, however, did not last long, for Matt then pulled the desk chair over and placed it in front of me, between my legs. "Spread em," he said, as he sat down in the chair. He had picked up his duffle bag from the dresser and it was now on the floor beside him. He reached into the bag and pulled something out. I could not tell what it was and did not want to ask. I closed my eyes for a few seconds, and then felt his hand against my privates. He was cupping my nut sac, rubbing it gently. I felt my penis spring to life rather quickly, as he ran his fingers back and forth. The sensation made me squirm a little bit; I had always been really ticklish. I opened my eyes to look at him, and he seemed to look pleased. He smiled at me as he gently rubbed me with just the tips of his fingers. "Ticklish, huh?"

"Yes sir," I managed, stifling a small eruption of laugher.

111

His face then again got serious and he held up the object that was in his hand, allowing me to see it for the first time. He was holding what appeared to be a cordless hair clippers device. "Decided my pup needs a trim," he told me. "Keep your legs spread apart wide, and don't squirm around, even if it tickles. You understand?"

"Yes sir," I said to him. He then flipped the switch and I heard the buzzing sound. He was going to shave off my pubes!

I lay there quietly then, keeping my arms at my side and my legs spread widely open for Matt, as he ran the edge of the clippers across my testicles. He used his free hand to push back my cock, gently pulling it up towards my navel. As I lay there totally exposed to him, I was surprised how incredibly good the sensation felt as he ran the clippers over my private parts. I felt the hair falling off against my inner thigh, and for the first time ever felt the air around my privates; it reminded me of a blowing breeze. It was sort of a tingly sensation. This, combined with the gentle way he held my cock in place against my body was causing me to become very erect. I lay there quietly and throbbed in his hand as he clipped off all of my pubic hair.

Matt was very gentle with me, being precise and cautious as he stripped me of my one single very masculine feature. I did not know why he was doing this to me; perhaps it was so that I would feel more exposed to him. Maybe it was so that with my smoothness I'd look and feel more boyish in his presence. He might have wanted merely to humble me. Or perhaps it was simply that he liked smoothness. Whatever the reason was, it wasn't for me to question. I just lay there, accepting the fact that he wanted this to be done. I already had admitted to myself that I would offer myself to him to do with as he chose, no matter what that might be. Now he was helping me to prove to myself just how true that statement had been.

When he had finished with the trimming, Matt then placed the clippers on the bed beside me and removed another object from his bag. This time he had an electric razor. He turned it on and pressed it against my body, rubbing it against the area he had just trimmed. He was removing the remaining stubble, making me totally smooth. The razor actually tickled me even more than the clippers had, and on a couple of occasions I laughed right out loud, in spite of myself. This did not dissuade him, and he continued with the procedure until he finally had achieved his desired result. Then he told me to roll over onto my stomach. I did as he said without question, and felt his fingers against my butt cheeks. I buried my head in my arms which I had pulled up in front of my face. He ran his fingers across my butt and pulled my cheeks apart gently. It was as if he was inspecting me, I think. He did nothing with the razor, for perhaps he saw that I already was totally smooth in that region. Instead he just rubbed me gently for a few moments. I lay there quietly, allowing myself to be touched, feeling as if I belonged to him now more than ever before.

After a few minutes he rolled me back over onto my back and told me to pick my legs up. As I did so, he pulled the towel out from under my butt and pushed my thighs apart again. He gently brushed off all of the loose hair, catching most in the towel. He then ran his fingers across my exposed private region, apparently reflecting upon his own handiwork. I then lay there and stared up at him. A part of me was so happy at that moment, for now I felt in some way marked by him. I felt that he'd altered my appearance for his viewing pleasure. I was not just his pup any longer. Now I was his shaved pup. I was so hard as I looked up into his eyes.

Matt then pushed back his chair and stood up in front of me. He was a towering presence to begin with, but in this position he appeared to be a giant to me. I lay there on the bed looking up at this heroic figure before me, feeling so tiny

113

myself. Not only was I now smaller than he in stature, but I felt even less a man that I had before. I was totally smooth, while he still had all his hair. I thought about the implications of this. I wanted to see myself next to him, to see the contrast of our bodies. I was glad he had done this. I was glad he had removed my hair. I totally felt like his boy. His *property*.

The large king-sized bed was raised much higher from the ground than was either of the two beds upon which we'd previously been intimate. Laying there before him, I realized that my body was at about waist level with him. I wondered if he planned to take me further tonight than he had the night before. I wondered if he was going to put his cock inside me as he had done with his finger the first time. My heart pounded with excitement as I thought about it. Suddenly I felt a wave of fear sweep over me. I did not know if I'd be able to do it. What if it hurt too badly? What if it did not feel as good as his finger, but instead hurt me? How was I supposed to respond to him when he did it? Would I be expected to just lie there and take it, or should I touch him, move my body in some way?

He gave me no indication, however, that his intentions were to fuck me. Instead he told me shift my position on the bed. He wanted my head over on the edge of the bed, where my butt currently was positioned. I obeyed him, and moved myself so that I was lying prostrate in front of him. My face was right in his crotch. Through his basketball shorts I then noticed that he was hard himself, at least partially. I wanted to touch it so badly right then. I wanted him so bad!

"On your back," he told me, as he pulled down the elastic waistband of his shorts. He was wearing boxers under the shorts, and he pulled the two down together. He stepped back a bit and I watched him upside-down, from my position on the bed, as he stepped out of them. He still was wearing his sneaks, tee shirt, and cap. "I've been waiting for this since early this afternoon," Matt told me. "Was even gonna have you blow me in the car. Thought it be hotter if I made you wait though...until I'd shaved ya." And then without further warning he stepped up to me and pressed his cock against my lips. He was nearly three-quarters hard at this stage, and I breathed in his scent as he towered there over me. All I could see was an inverted view of his thighs as I instinctively opened my mouth wide for him. He leaned over and grabbed me under the armpits, pulling me further over the edge of the mattress, so that my head was completely off the side. Then he cupped my head in his hands, holding it in place firmly with both of his hands. He slid into me!

It was far different than before, for in this position it allowed for a very smooth entry. He thrust into me in one clean movement, burying himself into my throat upon his initial entry. I craned my jaw open as wide as possible and concentrated upon controlling my gag reflex. I heard him moan in pleasure as he savored the tightness of my throat. An image of him flashed through my mind, as I lie there humbly in my servile position. I saw him standing there in his gym shoes, his legs spread apart and feet planted firmly on the ground. I saw him in this position which allowed him total control, enabling him to thrust his hips as he drove himself into me. I loved the mental visualization. I loved the idea that I was being used by him in this fashion. I felt like I was his pleasure hole. I was so rock hard as my smooth body lay stretched out in front of him.

He did indeed begin to thrust himself into me. He gripped my head with fierce intensity as he rammed himself into me. I thought of how he'd informed me that he'd been waiting for this moment since early afternoon. It made me so hot to think he had dwelled upon it. He had actually thought of our intimacy so much that he planned out this encounter in advance. He then had patiently shaved and cleaned my body, knowing all the while that when he was done, he was going to be fucking my throat. He did this all for his own pleasure. I loved every single second.

115

The only direct comment that Matt made to me during the ensuing moments was the reiteration of an instruction that I already knew so well, "Don't touch yourself, and don't cum!" I simply lay there, clinging tightly to the bedspread beneath me with my clenched fists, as he fired his cock in and out of my throat. I learned so quickly that I could not breathe while he did this. I concentrated on the brief moments when he was sliding partially out of my mouth, and at those instants I made quick intakes of breath through my nostrils. I heard his moans of pleasure as he deliberately ground his hips, apparently tightening the muscles in his buttocks when he was buried balls deep into me. He had found the place of tightness within my throat that gave him the best sensation, and he revisited it over and over. This place, however, was truly the least comfortable for me. It was at these moments when he was buried in my throat that I was unable to breathe, and I had to work very hard not to choke on him, keeping my mouth open as widely as possible. It made my jaw sore actually, but I did not pray for it to be over. I did not wish away these moments when I was being used for the pleasure of this man who owned me.

This man who *owned me!*

Within only a ten minute time frame of violent face fucking, I was starting to wonder if I would be able to continue. It was not like I really was being afforded much choice, however, but it was starting to become so uncomfortable to me. My throat was hurting, and my jaw ached as he continued to drive himself into me. He seemed not to even be thinking about any of this. He seemed to be relishing how good it felt to have his cock inside me. I willed myself to be submissive, to show virtually no signs of resistance. I wanted to learn to take all of him whenever and however he wanted, and for however long he wanted. I formed a mental picture again, this time of myself. I visualized myself kneeling at his feet. I thought about the first time I'd knelt before him on the sidewalk when I was petting Petey that day. I knew in my heart then that I would ultimately belong to him. I had to. It was as if this were the single thing I was born to do.

His thrusting became more and more rapid, and he began to verbalize his pleasure, as he generally seemed to do when he was approaching orgasm. "Oh yeah!!" he said, "Tight fag throat! Eat my cock boy. Take it!" He pumped hard then, pistoning himself in and out of me ferociously. I felt his cock swelling up against my tongue. He was rock hard, and I did my best to keep my lips as tightly around his shaft as possible, pressing my tongue firmly against him. I wanted it to feel so wonderful to him! He rammed deep into me finally and remained there. I felt the cum firing into his dick, and knew that eruption was only seconds away. And then it was there again finally...that incredible moment of ecstasy. The pump!

He drained himself into me, moaning loudly with sheer pleasure! I did choke on him then, on his load actually, but kept right on gulping, trying so desperately to take every drop of him inside of me. I was his. I belonged to him. I was *owned by him*! His pup.

6

That night, for the very first time in my life, I slept with another person. I curled up beside him, both of us being completely naked, and felt the warmth of his body. Matt pulled me into himself, allowing me to find a comfortable, restful position, where my head was cradled in the crook of his shoulder. His arm was around me as he lay on his back, and I moved my hand across his chest, touching him gently-almost reverently. This must be heaven, I thought. I felt so very secure, so protected and safe. Not only did my body feel warm, but also the very core of me burned with a glowing radiance, a relaxing and peaceful feeling of contentment. I had not felt this way since before my parents had died. Finally, I was not alone any more. Finally, I was where I belonged.

Tears came to my eyes as I lay there then, a moment of unexpected emotion having swept over me. I clung to him, allowing my teardrops to drip down onto Matt's shoulder. He made no comment, but instead slightly tightened his grip around me, allowing me to feel the strength and security of his embrace. "Sir, I don't know what I did...I don't know how..." My words were merely a whisper. "I don't know why I deserve you. I don't even think that I do."

Without looking at me, or even moving any part of himself, Matt finally responded to me. His voice also was quiet, though not really a whisper. He spoke as he generally did, with confidence, making a statement of fact to me, "You deserve what I say you deserve. I want you to always remember one thing, pup. Every single time that you feel freaked like this, every single time you are insecure, I want you to think about one thing: *I chose you.* It's not for you to wonder and to worry about why I chose, it's your job just to accept it. You're down on yourself too much. You let yourself think all of these bad thoughts about yourself. I told you already, you are chill. If you were not exactly what I wanted, I would not be here. Doesn't that say something to you? Can't you let that be enough?"

I was clinging to him then, my small arm wrapped around his chest. I pressed my body against his, as tightly as I possibly could, feeling that I could not ever get too close to him. "It's enough, Sir. It's all I ever wanted, that's all. It just seems too good to be true."

He shifted his body then, and within an instant I was lying on my back with him leaning over me. Without any further warning, he kissed me. His kiss was not foreplay; it was the main event. It conveyed to me everything he had just said to me with words. He was so right. It truly was enough to have been chosen by him. Why should anything else ever matter?

That night I did not have an orgasm. I did not even think about it, actually, or want it. All I had wanted was to please him. I'm not exactly sure if he sensed these feelings from me, or if it simply did not matter to him. Truly I did not want it to matter, for I wanted him to take what was rightfully his— me—and to fulfill his own desires in any manner he chose. This genuinely gave me far more pleasure than any physical sensation ever could have.

We fell asleep together, resting together like spoons. I had my back to him, feeling the entirety of his body surround me. My position was fetal, and I felt so small. I simply lay there feeling him around me, smelling him, hearing his breathing...even his heartbeat. I slipped into dreamless sleep and awoke in what felt like moments, still in his arms. It was already the next day.

* * *

119

My throat was sore. It was not the same kind of soreness that you experience when you are ill. It just sort of ached. I did not regret this feeling at all, though; in fact I sort of liked the fact that I had a reminder of how I'd served Matt just hours before. Every time I swallowed, I'd be thinking of him that day. It wasn't like it hurt or anything...just felt different than usual.

I did not move after I woke up. I wanted instead to simply lie there and continue to enjoy the warmth of Matt's embrace. It was a matter of less than ten minutes, though, before I felt Matt stirring. He pulled his arm off of me and rolled over onto his back. As far as he knew, I was still asleep. I smiled to myself, being so grateful be there in that bed, next to the only person on earth that I totally worshipped and idolized. It was such a euphoric feeling.

Although he had put me to sleep with his wonderful kisses and his tender embrace, I was soon to discover that his method for waking me was far less romantic. I heard him moan very quietly, I thought possibly he was rubbing himself...rubbing his dick. I lay there very still, not wanting him to know I was awake yet. Suddenly he slipped his arm under me, quickly pulling me over to him, twisting my body so that I faced him. I closed my eyes, pretending to be moving in my sleep. "Wake up!" I felt his hand move to the top of my head, as he pushed me down, swiftly moving my head into position, so that I was suddenly eyeballing his hard cock. He had thrown back the covers with his free hand, and was stretched out comfortably, his legs spread. His far-larger body took up most of the bed.

"Suck!" he said, as he shoved my head down further. I immediately opened my mouth as he rammed me all the way down on his cock. He had grabbed the base of his shaft so that it was sticking perfectly upright, and was pushing me down with his other hand, the one still holding tightly onto my head. Once he was deep in my throat, he let go of his cock and grabbed a hold of the other side of my head. "Get between my legs! Kneel." I crawled over his leg then, all the while having his cock still buried in my throat and assumed a crouched, kneeling position. He let go of my head and dug his elbows into the mattress, pushing himself up onto the bed further. I followed him, leaning forward so that I kept his cock in my mouth at all times, and glanced up at him, seeing him as he shoved my pillow behind his head. He was getting comfortable. When he finally was situated in exactly the position that he wanted, he then grabbed my head again.

This time he did not thrust into me, not at all. Instead he pumped me up and down on his cock. He did this so slowly, as if he were enjoying every sensation. I was grateful, for this allowed me plenty of time to focus, to concentrate upon forming a tight suction with my mouth, to press my lips tightly around his shaft, to commit myself to keeping my tongue against the underside of his cock every single second. I had never experienced the feeling of a mouth on my cock, yet somehow I knew from my own masturbation that it would feel best for my tongue to press against him. I bet it felt so smooth and wet, like when I put lotion on my hand to jack off.

He never took his hands off my head, continuing to control the depth and speed of each pump. I focused all my energy upon how I was using my mouth, and completely relaxed the muscles in my neck, offering virtually no resistance to his control. I kept thinking of his words to me, "I chose you," as I involuntarily bobbed on his shaft. He must have been very relaxed and very comfortable, for he just lay there pumping me on himself for an incredibly long time. He did not increase much in speed, but remained rock hard in my mouth at all times. My jaw was again getting so tired, yet I absolutely refused to let him see this. I forced myself to continue with the pressure on his cock, with the suction and the movement of my tongue. I had to have a distraction; I had to somehow think about something other than how tired and sore my jaw was, or else I wouldn't be

121

able to continue. I began to count the pumps. Every single time his cock went into my throat I added a number. I wanted to see how many strokes it was going to take before he came.

Seventy-eight. Seventy-nine. Eighty. His pumping was very methodical, and most definitely unapologetic. I sucked hard, drawing my own saliva into the back of my mouth. I was learning just the right time that I needed to swallow my spit. I wanted to keep his cock slick and shiny with my mouth, but not saturated and slimy. I loved the feeling of his hardness. Ninety-four. Ninety-five. Ninety-six. My ankles were sore from sitting on them. In the kneeling position it often is the case that the ankles become numb, but prior to arriving at that point, they get extremely sore. I could not think of it though. I had to keep sucking!

The numbers got higher and higher, as I willed myself to concentrate. I did not want to lose count. Gradually his speed was increasing. I loved the fact that he was setting the pace, controlling every single second of my servitude. I felt so extremely submissive; and it felt wonderful. It was so right. This was where I belonged. This was what I wanted to do. I was so hard myself, realizing that he had woken me up with no greeting other than "Suck!" Why should it ever be any other way?

Two-twenty-three. Two-twenty-four. His pumping suddenly got much faster. It was as if he had all of a sudden shifted into overdrive. He tripled the speed. Quadrupled it. He was pumping me fast now on his cock. There was no point in even trying to breathe. I simply yielded myself to his will. I was fully aware of when it was happening, for I'd already learned the signs. I felt his cock throb against my tongue, his grip tighten on my head. Then I felt the cum firing into his cock as it had done every time before. I pushed myself down on him all the way. It was not necessary though, for he was holding my head tightly in place. Then he shot. I sucked. I swallowed. It was over, and he rolled out of bed, leaving me there without so much as a thank you. I heard him relieving himself in the bathroom.

I lay there on the bed exhausted, and rock hard. Serving him was so hot; it was unbelievable! I closed my eyes and rubbed myself, almost ready to erupt myself. I knew I must not, though. I knew I could not cum without his permission. I heard him in the bathroom. He had turned on the shower. I started to stroke myself. Oh God! I was going to lose control. *Hedge! Don't let yourself cum!* I squeezed my eyes tightly closed as I gripped my cock, and suddenly heard his voice.

"You do realize that no form of disobedience is without consequences," he said calmly.

I froze.

Quickly I pulled the bed sheet over me, letting go of my quickly diminishing hard-on. I now knew what it felt like to be literally caught with my dick in my hand. "Sir!" I gasped. "I didn't cum. Honest I didn't"

"Don't play naïve with me, pup. You know the rules. When you are with me, you do not touch yourself without my permission. EVER!"

"I didn't know Sir! Honest. I thought I just only was not allowed to cum. I thought I could still jack myself, if..."

"Quit rationalizing." He was very calm, and perhaps it was this calmness that frightened me the most. "You knew you were not allowed to jack off. That's why you waited til you thought I was in the shower."

I looked away from him, staring down at the mattress. "I'm sorry sir. I don't want to disobey. I don't want to be bad." I was nearly crying, my voice cracking. "Please don't be mad at me."

"I'm not mad, not at all, but you do have to learn. You must obey. If you choose not to obey, you face the consequences. It is that simple. You will not cum *at all* for the next ten days. In fact, you will not even get hard. You'll take whatever steps are necessary to make sure that these

123

orders are followed. Other than to bathe yourself or to take a piss, you will not even touch your cock. In fact, when you do piss, you will do it sitting down, with your cock tucked between your legs so you do not even have to hold onto it. Do you understand?"

My face was red. I could feel it. I felt so ashamed, so embarrassed to be caught doing what I knew I should not be doing. And I was frightened by the consequences that I now faced. I did not even know if I'd be able to do comply with them. "Do you understand, pup?" he repeated.

"Yes sir," I said quietly.

"Now get in the shower. We need to get ready to go; it's almost seven-thirty."

Alone in the shower, I did cry. How could everything have changed so quickly. I had served him the night prior, just before we went to bed. Then we slept tucked together so romantically. I had thought I was in heaven. I awoke in the morning to serve him again, and I did so better than I had ever done before. Then all of a sudden I messed up. Why had I done it? Why had I started to play with myself like that? It was so stupid, for I really did not even care if I came. I only wanted to please him. I was just really horny at that moment. I didn't think! And now I have ended up disappointing him.

I did not even worry about the fact that I'd be going for ten days without orgasm. It was not a punishment to me, for I probably would have imposed the same sentence upon myself, if not one far more severe. I was a bit concerned about keeping myself from getting aroused though. What if I woke up hard? What if I got hard accidentally? I was going to have to do as I'd done before, using the string. The thing that upset me worse than anything was that I had failed him. This was the first time since I had begun serving him that I'd met with his disapproval, and it was crushing to me.

The sudden movement of the shower curtain startled me. Matt stepped in to join me. He wrapped his arms around my shoulders and reached down to my chest, rubbing his fingers across my smoothness. He shifted me so that he could step directly under the water, then reached over to grab a bar of soap. I wondered if he would see my tears, or would instead mistake them for droplets of water from the shower. "You've been crying," he said. "I told you I am not mad at you. I am not even punishing you, pup. I just want you to learn that every one of your actions has a reaction. You have to live up to the consequences of your choices." He sounded very paternal, as he stood there with a bar of soap, lathering my shoulders. "If I were going to punish you, I'd just bend you over and spank your butt. Do you see the difference between 'consequences' and 'punishment'?" I nodded. Then I grabbed a hold of him and buried my head in his chest.

"I wish I had not done it sir. I wish I had obeyed. I'm so very sorry. Honest I am. Please believe me! And I'm sorry not because of the consequences either. I'm sorry because I... because I ..."

"Because you want to please me. You want to please your owner."

"Yes sir. I want that more than anything."

"I know you do pup. But you are just like my other Petey. Sometimes you are just impulsive. That's all. But you know what happens to Petey my dog when he disobeys? He learns that he has to endure the consequences. It's all a part of his training. Doesn't mean I think any less of him or that I care for him any less. Just means I have to do my job as his owner. I have to teach him."

I looked up into his eyes. "So you really are not mad at me sir?"

"No," he shook his head, "I don't often get mad, and when I do, I get over it quickly. Believe me, you will know if I am ever mad." I prayed that I never would find out. I took the soap from him then and proceeded to clean him. I was not about to ever again allow myself to disobey him. Not ever!

* * *

On the ride back into the city, I was wearing an entire
new set of clothing that Matt had gotten for me. The clothes
were preppy— a polo shirt, cargo pants, and even a brand
new pair of boarder sneaks. I could not believe he had spent
this kind of money on me, but he also informed me that
from now on he would be in charge of my wardrobe. I was
not to buy any new clothing for myself unless he was with
me. I also was not allowed to get my hair cut, buy new
glasses, or make any changes to my appearance without his
consent. To every single one of these orders I responded
with a respectful, "Yes sir." It was unthinkable for me to
even consider questioning him at this point.

When Matt dropped me off at the bookstore, I once again
apologized for my misbehavior. He told me that he did not
want to hear another word about it. Case closed. "I wish I
had made you breakfast sir," I said before getting out of the
car.

"I don't usually eat breakfast anyways, pup, but thanks
for thinking of it anyways. I fed you your breakfast though,
remember?" He was referring to his load that I'd swallowed,
and I did in fact remember very well. Even after brushing my
teeth, I still could taste it somewhat.

"Yes sir, I remember. Thank you." I smiled at him.

"Get to class now, and keep your cell with you."

I got out of the car and watched him drive away. Instantly
I thought the same exact thing I did every time we parted
from one another. When was I going to see him again?

I did not see Matt again that day, or even the next. When
I got home from class that Wednesday, I checked my email
while woofing down a sandwich, my first bite of food for the
day. I emailed Matt a listing of my new work schedule which
I probably should have just given to him the night before,
but I was too busy concentrating on other things to think of
it. I then did some of my homework, which took up a couple

hours of my time, and finally began making dinner, knowing that Kathie worked until six that evening. Hopefully she would be home after work, and not on a date with Carter again. Just as I was pulling the garlic bread from the freezer, I noticed the answering machine flashing. I set the loaf on the counter and walked over to press the play button.

"Hey Kathie, are you there...its Tracy. Pick up if you're there!...Well, guess not... Anyways, I'm so glad I ran into you last night. I have missed you so much, and I hope we can put all this ... um...stuff behind us. We have been friends for too long to just throw it all away. I'm so happy for you and Carter, too. He seems like such a cool guy...cute too! Well, I wondered if you and Carter might want to double-date with Matt and me sometime. Friday night, maybe. We're going to a party over at Mark Beeson's house, on the corner of Giddings and Franklin. Give me a call, okay? I'm sure you still have my number."

"Fuck!" I said, right out loud. For a moment I toyed with the notion of erasing the message. That would not be a good idea, though, for Tracy was sure to call back. If she found out I'd erased it and then mentioned it to Matt, I'm sure he would not be happy with me. Why did he have to even see her anyways? She was so conceited and such a bitch. She seemed nice enough to Kathie on the phone, I had to admit, but I knew that she almost never was nice without some kind of ulterior motive. I was sure that she did not even love Matt. She certainly did not feel about him the way that I did. He was only a trophy to her— a big jock stud that she could show off to all her friends.

I tried not to think of Matt or of his upcoming date with Tracy as I continued to make my spaghetti dinner. When Kathie did get home a few minutes later, she looked beat. Apparently she had stayed out quite late with Carter the night before. I was glad that I had dinner waiting for her, as was she. She noticed the answering machine blinking and played her message without comment. Then we sat down together to eat.

"So are you gonna do it?" I asked.

"Do what, kiddo?" She rubbed her eyes briefly, then looked over at me.

"Go on a double date with Tracy and Matt," I said.

"Oh, I don't know. Carter and I were thinking of doing something together Friday night, just not sure yet what it will be. Tracy is right though, we have been friends too long to throw it away. Especially over some guy."

"Yeah," I said, trying to sound sincere, "and she is right about Carter too. He is very nice. I liked meeting him."

"So what did you and Matt do last night? You stayed out all night with him huh? I guess its true that you two have become really close."

"Well, yeah, we have. We went up to his cabin. He owns property out by Crystal Lake, or his parents do, I should say. You should see this place. They call it a 'cabin,' but it is this gorgeous three bedroom home. We just hung out together there and chilled for the night."

"You get your reading done?"

"Oh yeah. You know me, I always get my reading done. Kathie, I hope you don't let Tracy do anything to you again. I mean, I hope you don't trust her too much. I know she is your friend, but there is just something about her..."

"Don't worry, Petey. I've known Tracy a long, long time. I know what she is like. Plus, I already told you, I'm just as concerned about you and Matt. I don't want him to hurt you either."

"I don't even see why you say that, Kathie," I said defensively. "Matt is not going to hurt me. He is the one who saved me from getting killed probably. He is the best friend I've ever had."

"I know," she said, "You just are sensitive, that's all, and he is not. It's like Mom used to say, you wear your feelings on your shirtsleeves."

"I never really understood what the heck she even meant by that," I responded.

"She meant that you are a totally open person. You're emotional, and it's easy for people to see that. In some ways that makes you vulnerable. It also makes you the wonderful person that you are though. There isn't anything wrong with it. It's just that sometimes I feel protective of you. After all, you're the only family I've got left, remember?"

"Well, I feel protective of you too. But still, you can't deny me my friendship with Matt just because you think I might get hurt."

"True," she said, "and you can't deny me my friendship with Tracy either. We still can worry about one another, though, right?"

I nodded. "Deal," I said, and shoved a fork-full of spaghetti in my mouth.

7

I woke up Thursday morning in some serious pain. I had tied a string around my penis before going to bed, just as I had done previously. This time, however, it did not work! I had gotten a rock hard erection in my sleep and the string was cutting deeply into my flesh. I could not believe that I'd actually slept through it. I was totally throbbing as I threw on a robe and dashed to the bathroom. I flung back the shower curtain and turned on the cold water, full force. Quickly I stepped under the stream, gasping as I did so, for the iciness of the water was shocking, to say the least. I stood there shivering under the blast of frigid water as my erection subsided. I then stripped off the string and noticed it had literally cut into my flesh. I was sure to be sore from that, but what was even worse, I had failed Matt again!

I adjusted the water, allowing myself the luxury of at least a tepid shower, wanting all the while to just bash my head as hard as I could into the wall. How could it have not worked right this time? How could I have actually slept through an erection? I just wanted to cry. There was always the option of simply not mentioning any of this to Matt, but already I knew that this would not even be possible for me. I'd have to tell him the truth. Every time he looked me in the eyes, it was like being force-fed a huge dose of sodium Pentothal, the truth serum.

I did not know how Matt was going to react when I told him the truth. Maybe it would help if I stressed to him that I had become aroused accidentally, and in my sleep. I doubted that would matter, though, for he had said to me that I needed to take steps so that this would not happen, not even by accident. Damn it! Why did this have to happen?

I got out of the shower and wrapped a towel around me. I was absolutely freezing. I shivered my way back into my bedroom and locked the door. It was only six o'clock in the morning. I was going to have a long day ahead of me, for I had to go to class that morning and then work. After work I wanted to attend the meeting at the Student Services Center. I wondered what Matt would think of that. I had not bothered to mention it to him, and so he did not even have it on his copy of my schedule. I decided that what I would do is send him an email. I could tell him about my erection too, and beg for forgiveness. Might as well get it over with and just face my medicine. Then if for some reason he did not want me to attend the meeting tonight he could call me.

When I logged on I was startled to see his screen name in my buddy list. He was online, and at six in the morning!

Ptboy1982: hello SIR..I am surprised to see u online

MattJock82: ditto

Ptboy1982: I was going to send u an email, sir

MattJock82: bout what, pup?

Ptboy1982: please don't be mad at me

MattJock82: you get a boner?

I paused for a couple minutes, starting to actually shake. I stared at the screen and moved my fingers back into position on the keyboard.

MattJock82: answer me

Ptboy1982: yes sir...I did

MattJock82: didn't you do what I told you to do? Take precautions?

Ptboy1982: yes sir, honest I did. I got hard anyways. I'm sorry...it was an accident

MattJock82: then what did u do? Did u jack off?

Ptboy1982: NO SIR!!!!! I jumped into the shower...cold

MattJock82: good boy

I sat there staring at the screen. This was unbelievable. It seemed like he was not even upset with me, even though I had failed.

Ptboy1982: sir?

MattJock82: yeah...?

Ptboy1982: I'm sorry I failed u. again.

MattJock82: u didn't fail, pup...u did good...don't worry, I will help u to not get hard. I have a plan.

What was he talking about? A plan?

Ptboy1982: I don't understand sir.

MattJock82: don't worry bout it. You'll see.

Ptboy1982: yes sir...I have a question for u too sir...if I may...please

MattJock82: hit me

It cracked me up whenever he said that. I visualized myself actually taking a swing at him.

Ptboy1982: would it be ok for me to go to the meeting at the college tonite...about the vandalism

MattJock82: u wanna go?

Ptboy1982: yes sir

MattJock82: then go ahead

MattJock82: why u up so early pup?

Ptboy1982: when I woke up hard...I sorta freaked about it, I guess...so I was gonna send u an email

MattJock82: u were a good boy to tell me right away

Ptboy1982: thank you sir

MattJock82: go back to bed for a couple hours

Ptboy1982: I think I will...still tired...sir?

MattJock82: yeah

Ptboy1982: I luv u

MattJock82: KISS!

Then he was gone. I sat there for a few more minutes before logging off. I just stared at my screen, not checking email or playing any games...just staring at the place on my buddy list where his name had been. I had seen him less than twenty-four hours prior, and it seemed an eternity. I missed him so much already. I was so glad that he did not become upset with me for the erection that I'd had. I also was glad I'd told him everything. After finally logging off I curled up in my bed again and hugged my pillow. I fell asleep pretending it was he that I was clinging to.

* * *

I almost backed out of my plans to attend the meeting, but for some reason went ahead and rode my bike down to the Student Services Center after work. I was tired after a long day, and I did not really think that I wanted to risk being associated with a "fag organization." But still, there was a certain curiosity. I wondered who I'd see at that meeting, how many straight people would be there, and if I'd be able to even tell the difference between the gay ones and the straights.

I pushed the entry door open cautiously and heard the sounds of people talking. It was sort of a dull roar, people chatting together amongst themselves. Apparently the meeting had not started yet. I slipped into the main auditorium and found an empty seat near the back. The room probably had a seating capacity of about two hundred, and there could not have been more than thirty or forty people present. I looked at my watch; it was 7:55. I still was about five minutes early.

"Hi there. Excuse me, is this seat taken?"

I looked up to see a blonde guy who was probably in his mid twenties, staring down at me. I wondered why he'd bother to ask about the seat when there were 150 others that were obviously available. "No, not at all. Help yourself."

He held out his hand to me. "Andrew Tompkins," he said, "Most people call me Drew."

"Nice to meet you Drew," I smiled up at him as I shook his hand. "I'm Peter. Peter Drinkell."

"I haven't ever seen you around. You are a student here?"

I nodded. "I am a freshman. I kind of keep to myself, I guess."

"Well, glad you decided to break out of your shell. You gay?"

I looked at him, wide-eyed, shocked by his very candid question. "Um... I thought this meeting was for gay and straight people both," I said.

"It is. That's why I asked," he laughed. "Sorry, didn't mean to be nosy."

"Its okay." I looked down at my lap. "I guess I am not sure if I am or not."

"Well don't worry about it. Doesn't even matter one way or the other. I *am* gay, by the way. So is my boyfriend!" He laughed at his own joke and I just looked over and smiled at him. He seemed like such a sincere person, and he really was very cute. Drew was probably only a couple inches taller than me, a little bit stockier build, but still very slender.

"Is your boyfriend here?" I asked. It seemed weird to be referring to a guy as being another guy's "boyfriend."

"Yeah, he is the speaker. His name is Alex, and he is president of the Gay Student Union."

"Oh..." I said. "Is that him up front."

"Yeah. That's my man," Drew said proudly.

"Are you seeing someone?" I thought it strange of him to ask me this when I'd just told him I was not sure that I even was gay. Probably it was his genuineness that prompted me to be honest. I nodded.

"Well, I ...um..."

He looked at me sweetly, staring right into my eyes. "It's okay," he said. "You don't have to share if you aren't comfortable."

"No, it's not that. I just never have ... um...I never have been asked before. We just started to ...you know...um...see each other a couple weeks ago."

"What is this person's name?"

I wondered if I should tell him. Well a first name only probably wouldn't hurt. "His name is Matt," I said. "And he is a jock." *Why did I just say that?*

Drew laughed. "I like you already," he said. Before we could say any more to one another, Alex called the meeting to order. Alex appeared to be much taller than Drew and myself. He was nearly Matt's height, I'd say. He seemed to be a bit older than me, maybe mid twenties himself, just like Drew. I guess it made sense.

"Thank you everyone for coming tonight," Alex said. His voice was extremely masculine, far different than what I had anticipated. I suppose I had expected to have some effeminate, stereotypically gay person conducting tonight's meeting. "As I'm sure you all know by now, there have been several incidents of vandalism and blatant hatred on this campus within the past weeks, all targeting gay students. The Gay Student Union, representing the gay, lesbian, bisexual, and transgendered members of our student body, has been compelled to respond to these incidents. This is the reason we are here tonight. In addition, we are disturbed by the virtual non-response of the school administration."

As Alex continued to deliver his rehearsed speech, I was somewhat amazed by the way that he conducted himself. He clearly was very self-assured and confident, and he did not seem to exude any of the classic stereotypes associated with homosexual men. At some point in his message, he surprised me by referring to himself as a "bisexual man." This seemed rather revealing to me, and in stark contrast to Drew's earlier comment that his boyfriend was "also gay." After the opening remarks were finished, Alex outlined very clearly the facts relating to each incident that had occurred on campus. He then called for a resolution condemning the acts. This I thought was rather silly, for surely everyone in attendance would be in agreement on this issue. I did not see the point in having a vote. He then passed around a petition, asking us each to sign it, condemning the violence and demanding the administration take appropriate steps. Alex then invited another speaker to step forward and to brief the audience upon the "success" of Monday's protest rally. The speaker was a lesbian named Tina Bianchetti. She had flaming red hair, and seemed rather obnoxious and overly boisterous. For a few seconds I was concerned that she might be going to lead us in a cheer, "Hell no way won't go! We're here, we're queer, get used to it."

I glanced over at Drew and he seemed to be staring up at Tina with a disdainful expression upon his face. I must not have been the only one who had reservations about her. I did not at all disagree with the sentiments expressed at the meeting, although I had to admit that the methods of the Student Union seemed to me to be rather futile. Perhaps I was sort of expecting there to be some great plan of action laid out at this meeting. With all the posters and flyers up around campus, I expected this to be much bigger than it was. Honestly, the whole event was rather anti-climactic.

When the meeting concluded, those in attendance were invited to partake in refreshments which were being served in the front lobby. I got up from my seat, snatching up my backpack, and headed for the front door. Drew was right behind me. "You want a pop, or some punch or something?" he asked. I stopped in my tracks and turned to face him. What the hell?

"Sure, why not?" I smiled at him and followed him back in the other direction to the table where the refreshments were laid out. Just as Drew was handing me a Diet Pepsi, I heard a voice behind us.

"Drew, come here." We both turned, and I saw that it was Alex. Drew stepped away, and they both moved a few feet from me, to speak to one another privately. I did not want to appear to be eavesdropping, so I stepped over to an adjacent table to peruse the literature that was displayed. The two of them talked for a few moments, and all that I heard was Drew saying to Alex, "Yes sir." Then he returned to me.

I looked back over at Alex, who had already turned to walk away. I wondered why Drew had not even introduced me to his boyfriend, but gave it no more thought at the time, for Drew was then offering me a cookie. He resumed his place beside me, just as if we had never been interrupted.

"Your boyfriend is very attractive," I confessed to him.

"I know. I'm lucky," Drew laughed. "I bet yours is handsome too, though."

"Oh...well, he is not really my boyfriend. It's not like that. Like I said, we just started seeing each other a little while ago."

"So you are not all that serious about him then?"

"Oh...no, that's not what I meant. I'm serious about him...*very* serious. I just don't know if he'd like that label... 'boyfriend'."

"Oh, okay. Well...the reason that I asked is...um..." he was hesitating. "You wanna go outside with me for a bit? I think I could use some fresh air." I nodded, surprised by his sudden nervousness.

When we got outside, Drew reached into his pocket and pulled out a pack of cigarettes. He offered me one, but I declined. I thought it was funny that he had just said he needed fresh air, but was now sucking carcinogens and toxins into his lungs.

He took a big drag and then exhaled slowly. "Well, as I was about to say, there is a reason I asked about how serious you were with your ...friend."

I smiled at him, being somewhat confused by the things he was saying to me. "Okay...what is the reason?"

"Well, I was wondering...or actually...my boyfriend was wondering...we both were actually—"

I laughed right out loud at him then. He was cute when he fidgeted like that. "You were wondering what?" I asked.

"If you would like to come home with us."

"You mean for a visit?" I was totally lost upon the intent of his invitation.

"Well, yeah, sure. I mean a very *friendly* visit. How should I say this?...um...Well...Alex...he *likes* you."

"How can he like me? He doesn't even know me. In fact, you never bothered to introduce us." My remarks were not malicious, but rather lighthearted actually. "I already told you I think he's handsome, so sure, I'd like to meet him."

"Oh geesh," Drew sighed. "I don't even think you understand what I'm saying, do you? Are you sure you don't want a cigarette." I shook my head. "Alex sometimes picks out boys that he finds attractive. Then he gets me to bring them home. That is my job...I do it for him. And then...then he gets it on with them."

I was taken aback, astonished! "You mean, you find guys to have sex with your own boyfriend?" I asked, in sheer disbelief.

"Well, it's not like he is cheating or anything. I'm always present when they service him."

"*Service* him?" I asked. "What do you mean 'service' him?"

"You are totally new to this, aren't you?" he placed his hand on my shoulder. "Let's sit down." We both sat down on the steps upon which we'd been standing. "Okay, let me explain this...somehow. Alex is not just my boyfriend. He is...well...he is more than that. He is my 'sir'."

I wondered if he meant it the way I was starting to think he did. I wondered if that was why he had said "Yes sir" to Alex when he was talking to him. I wondered if his Alex was like my Matt. "You see, I am submissive, and Alex is Dominant. Do you know anything about what that means?"

"I think so," I said. I was smiling at him now. "My Matt is dominant too."

"Ohhhh...." Drew said. "Well then forget I ever said anything about coming over. I didn't realize it was like that for you."

"What do you mean? You didn't realize it was like what?"

"I did not realize that you already had a SIR."

I thought for a second, as I looked over at him. I guess he was right, I did have a Sir. I just never had really thought of it that way. "Okay, well let me ask you something, okay?" I said.

"Sure."

"If he is your Sir, and you belong to him, the way that I belong to Matt, then why is he getting you to get other guys for him? Doesn't he like you enough? I mean, aren't you enough for him?"

"It's not for me to say," responded Drew, matter-of-factly. "I just do what he tells me to do. If he wants me to ask someone home for him, I do it."

"Doesn't that bother you? I mean, that he wants someone other than you? Don't you get upset seeing him with other guys?"

"Oh sure, I mean, I'd be lying if I said it never bothered me. But I did come to realize finally that his pleasure is my pleasure. If he is turned on by being with someone else, it's not up to me to question. He never does it to hurt me or anything. In fact, he is very particular about making sure that I am included. Sometimes he even lets the other sub...um..." He lowered his voice, "he let's the other sub blow me sometimes."

"Really?" I asked. "I have never had that done to me before...I only have...um...sucked. I never have been blown by anyone else."

He laughed. "You really *are* new to this. Shame you are taken. Alex would have had a lot of fun with you."

"Can I ask you something about him...please?"

"Sure, hit me." I almost laughed, hearing Matt's phraseology coming from someone else.

"Has he ever ordered you not to cum?"

He laughed right out loud then, putting his arm completely around me. "Yeah, of course. That is pretty standard. Your Sir always decides when you get to cum and when you don't."

"Well, I will tell you a secret," I said, getting really quiet. He looked over at me, seeming to be feeding off from my innocence. "I am not allowed to cum for eight more days. It is sort of like a punishment, even though Matt says it is not a punishment exactly. I can't cum and am not even supposed to get hard."

"What'd you do? Jack off when you weren't allowed?"

"How'd you know?" I asked.

"Been there. Done that," he laughed again and took another drag from his smoke. "So does he have you in chastity?"

"What's that? You mean like a chastity belt? I thought those only were for girls."

"No, they make 'em for guys too. It's a bitch at first, but after a bit you get used to it. I take it he has not introduced that to you yet, since you don't even know what it is."

I shook my head. "Wow, this is so cool that we met each other. I mean, I did not think there was anyone else like me out there. I mean anyone else who was ...um...owned."

"Yeah, there are lots of us. It's called a Dominant/submissive relationship, or 'D/s'...I can introduce you to a few people like us. Do you have a computer?"

"Yup."

"Give me your email address. I'll sent you the url's for some cool websites. You'll see, you're not alone at all."

"Well, I think I should get permission from Matt before I start meeting other people like that."

"Of course," he said, "that goes without saying."

I leaned into Drew then as he continued to sit there with his arm around my shoulder. *I think this is going to be the beginning of a great friendship.*

8

The following morning I was in the kitchen waiting for a piece of toast to pop up when I heard a buzzing sound coming from my bedroom. It was my cell phone. I raced into the bedroom, and snatched up the phone off from my bedside stand. I knew that it had to be Matt, for nobody else had my number. "Hello, Sir," I gasped.

"Why you out of breath pup? You been running...or jackin off?"

I laughed. "You know I'm not jacking off Sir. I don't usually make the same mistakes twice. I was in the kitchen and had left the phone in the bedroom."

"Thought I told you to keep it with you at all times?"

"I'm sorry sir," I said, my heart suddenly sinking.

"Jus messin with ya, pup. You're chill. But listen, I'm headed over to your house, should be there in five. Kathie leave for work already?"

"Yes sir. Yes, she did. I'm alone."

"Good," he said. "See you in a few." Then he clicked off.

For a second I panicked, wondering why he was coming over so early in the morning. Seems that every time he was about to meet me, I'd get frightened. I guess it was just my insecurity. Maybe I should quickly make him some breakfast. No, that's right, he said he didn't eat breakfast. I went back out into the kitchen to get my toast, but then stopped in my tracks. I ran back to the bedroom, forgetting the toast and pulled back the closet door to look at myself in the mirror. I ran my fingers through my hair, doing little or nothing to alter my appearance, but somehow believing I was making a difference. God, I hated this shirt. It made me look so fucking fat!

I pulled off my shirt and flung the closet door back open. What should I wear? I grabbed a striped polo shirt. No, this makes me look like frickin sailor boy. I grabbed an A&F pullover. This one was all right. No, I hated that color. I'd grab a dress shirt. What about this burgundy Ralph Lauren? No, too dressy. Shit! I heard the pounding at the door. He couldn't be here already. I bent over and picked up my recently discarded shirt from the floor and pulled it back on over my head. I guess it would have to do. One last look in the mirror. *I look terrible.*

I slammed the closet door and raced to the living room. I stopped, tried briefly to calm myself when I heard the pounding again. He was getting impatient. I lurched towards the door and swung it open. "What took you so long to answer the door, pup." I was practically panting, gasping for breath. "You must be doing a lot of running around this morning," he laughed. "You're out of breath again."

"Oh..." I said, taking a big gulp of air, "I was not done getting dressed when you called. Sorry."

"No problem, little guy. Just chill out. You're gonna have to take your clothes off again for me anyways, I'm afraid."

I looked up at him, smiling, "Oh really?...um...Sir."

"Well, not what you think, but you always like to get naked for me no matter what the reason, don't ya?"

I was puzzled by the last question, especially being that I was so modest that I hated getting naked for anyone...even Matt. Yet still, I think I was starting to get used to it. "I like doing whatever makes you happy." I noticed that he was again carrying a package...another gift?

"Let's go in your bedroom," he said.

He led the way this time and I followed. "Sir, I met a new friend last night. His name is Drew. He is...well, sort of like me. He has a boyfriend named Alex. He calls him sir, just like I do you."

"Oh really?" Matt said, "Was this Alex there too?"

"Yes, and you wanna know something really funny?"

"What?"

"Well at least I hope you think it is funny. Anyways, this Alex, he made Drew ask me to go home with them. Alex wanted me to *service* him. Can you believe that?"

Matt's face became very serious. "What?" he said, quite incredulously. "I don't think you need to be hanging around those guys."

"No, sir, please. It's not like that. They did not know about you and me."

"Why is he getting his boy to pimp for him? Doesn't sound like a very chill dude to me."

"I don't know, sir. I mean, I didn't really even talk to Alex. Drew is cool, though. Plus he answered a lot of questions for me. He has been Alex's boy for like four years now."

"How old is he?"

"Well, when I first met him, I thought he was like maybe twenty three or something. Turns out he is twenty eight. He goes to college though. He must have decided to go back. He looks really young, and Alex is only twenty-four himself. Alex looks like a jock...like you, sir."

"Hmm, don't know, guess I'll have to meet him before I decide. Want you to just chill though til I do. I don't think I like the idea of them pimpin on my boy."

"You know I would never do anything with someone other than you sir, don't you?"

"You better not. Now take off your clothes and get up on the bed."

"All of them?" I asked, rather surprised.

"Yes," he said without emotion. I began to strip. "Remember I told you I had a plan, to help you keep from disobeying me?" I nodded. "Have you started to feel prickly yet?"

I nodded again. "Yes sir, and very itchy."

"Okay, I'll shave you again, keep you smooth. Long as you shave every couple days, you won't start to get that itchy stubble. I'm also gonna put this device on you. It's called a chastity device."

I felt my face getting red. "Will it hurt?" I asked.

"No, it won't hurt at all. In fact, if it does hurt, or even feels uncomfortable, you need to let me know. I should warn you though, there will be pain if you start to get hard. The whole purpose is to keep you soft. But from what I've read about these things, after you wear it a little while you learn to not get hard at all. It just is automatic."

"Can I see it, sir?" He pulled a box from the package he was holding. It did not look very big at all. "It's called a CB2000. Guess that stands for 'chastity belt' even though there is no belt to it. It just attaches right to your cock."

"I don't know how I will go to the bathroom sir." My voice was getting shaky. "How will I even be able to pee?"

"There's an opening at the end, so you will be able to piss. Your dick will always be pointed down though, so you are gonna have to keep sitting down when you do it, but you have been doing that already." I was naked, sitting on the edge of the bed. "Lay back," he said. "I'm only gonna be shaving you while you have the chastity on. After your ten days are up, and I take it off of you, then you will have to keep yourself shaved. It's not really my job." I nodded, as I lay there flat on my back next to him. He sat down beside me and pulled the razor from the same bag in which he'd had the CB2000. He ran his fingers across my chest affectionately. "Did my pup miss me?"

"Very much. I missed you more than anything sir." He leaned over and kissed me on the lips.

"You're a good boy, you know. I missed you too." I smiled up at him, hardly able to believe he had just said that. "You know that you are not being punished by me putting this on you, don't you? It is very important that you realize that."

"I know sir. It is to help me."

"That's right." Without further warning he flipped on the razor and started to shave me. It did not take long this time, but the sensation of his touch and the tingly feeling of the razor caused me to become somewhat aroused. He did not seem a bit bothered by it though. When he was done, he set the razor down on the bedside stand and started to open the box containing my chastity device. "Now it's gonna be challenging to get you into this thing if you are hard, so you better just relax. Close your eyes and think of something dull." He laughed. "Think of your least favorite subject in school or something."

I did as he said, smiling in spite of myself. I could not believe how gentle he was being with me now. After what I had done Wednesday morning, you'd have thought he'd pin me down and force me into this thing. You would have thought that he would make sure I knew that I was being punished, rather than insisting to me that it was not a punishment at all. I thought about how Drew had proudly told me how lucky he was to belong to Alex. He was not the lucky one, though. I was. I would not trade my Matt for his Alex for anything in the world. I lay there completely relaxed, when I felt him suddenly slide the ring around my penis. He did it quickly, I think to get it on without causing me much sensation. Then I felt another ring slide on after the first, and my penis slid into this tube-like thing. I did not look down at it though, for I was afraid if I saw him touching me I would get hard.

He worked on the device for about five minutes altogether. When he was done, he attached a very small padlock to the front of it. Then he told me to open my eyes and stand up. It felt so odd. I stepped in front of the mirror and looked at myself. The device, and my penis within it, looked so very small, but it felt incredibly bulky on me. It felt like it was huge.

"Don't worry, you will get used to it pup. After a bit you won't even realize you have it on. Put your clothes back on. I wanna make sure you can't tell that your are wearing it by looking at you." I pulled on my briefs and to my surprise, my package tucked nicely into the frontal pocket of my underwear. He examined me carefully and then told me to go ahead and put my pants on. I did so. "See, no one will ever know. How does it feel?"

"Different," I admitted, "But it doesn't hurt. It's not uncomfortable."

"Good. Now get over here and kneel down." He unzipped his jeans and pulled out his cock. I was surprised to see that he was rock hard already. He then pulled his jeans and boxers down below his buttocks and sat on the edge of the bed. "Take off my shoes...and my pants," he ordered. I obediently knelt there then and did as he had told me. I was still shirtless and wearing no socks. All I had on were my briefs and cargo pants.

When I had successfully removed his pants, he stood up and moved over to the desk chair. "Crawl over here, boy!" I obeyed. "Does this web cam work?" I nodded in response to the question.

"I hardly ever use it though, sir. It was free with the computer...package deal." He turned in his chair to face the computer and used the mouse to click onto a desktop icon for the camera software. I knelt there, watching him. He then pulled out the globe-shaped cam and placed it on the edge of the desk, positioning it at my face. In a couple seconds I saw my image on the screen. He swiveled around in the chair then, to display his rock hard cock to me. "What do you want, boy?"

My jaw dropped open as I stared at him, almost in disbelief. I'd seen him several times, had even tasted him, yet each time that I knelt before him I was just as excited as I was that very first time. "I want you Sir. I want to please you. I want to taste you!" My voice was again high-pitched and whiny.

"Beg!" he commanded. And as I had done with him before I knelt there and begged, but this time with much more intensity, and most definitely, much more sincerity.

He was absolutely all I wanted...ever. I wanted him with every fiber of my being. My heart pounded, my cock throbbed within the chastity device. It was as he said though, it did not get hard. Once I felt the pressure and then ultimately the pain, the fullness in my cock subsided. I stared up at him imploringly, almost to the point of tears.

Click! He right-clicked the mouse beside him, snapping my picture. Click! He did it again. Three times. Four. Then he finally turned to direct his full attention to me. "Suck it, pup! Suck my cock!" I knelt there obediently, and I hungrily devoured him. He just kicked back and enjoyed, until finally he drained himself into me. Then he allowed me to continue kneeling at his feet for a few moments, resting my head against his leg.

"Good pup. How did it feel to serve me, when you could not even get hard yourself?"

I looked up into his eyes. "It felt...right, Sir. It just felt so right." He affectionately ran his fingers through my hair.

"Am gonna have to get goin' here in a minute." He stood up, stepping back into his boxers and jeans. "Now your ten days started over again this morning, because you got hard yesterday," he said, in a tone that was matter-of-of fact. "So that means that you go until a week from next Tuesday without cumming or even touching yourself. Got it?"

"Yes sir."

"Save these pictures I just took of you and email them to me. Keep your phone with you at all times. Since you are off work on Sunday, we are going shopping together. Don't hang with Drew either until I meet him. If you have his email, though, you can see if he wants to meet us on Sunday. You got all that?"

"Yes sir," I nodded as he was zipping up his jeans. I was holding onto his shoes, prepared to put them back on him. He sat back down and allowed me this privilege. When I was done, he stood up. "Go get yourself some breakfast, pup, before you leave for class." Then he kissed my forehead and turned to leave. I did not even get up from my kneeling position until he was out the door.

I loved him so much.

Fortunately for me, I did not have a first hour class that morning. I followed all of his commands, saving the pictures, emailing them to him, and then sending an email out to Drew. I put Drew's screen name in my buddy list but then blocked him from seeing me online. I did not want to talk to him at all until I had Matt's full approval. I then went out to the kitchen and ate my cold, dry toast. Surprisingly, it went quite well with the cum taste that already coated my mouth.

* * *

I was very glad to have the evening off from work, for I was extremely tired when I got home from school that Friday. I was somewhat surprised to see that Kathie was already there when I arrived. "I thought that you had to work until three."

"Yeah, hon, but I got out early. It was kind of slow. I'm glad though, cause I think I'm gonna take a nap. Carter and I are going out later. In fact..." she said, "We decided to go on that double date with Tracy and your friend Matt."

I just stared at her then, not really sure how I was supposed to respond. I'd already known there was a possibility that this would happen, but it still did not make the confirmation any less a shock. "Oh, did you?" I said.

"I kind of thought you'd be glad, actually, seeing that you like Matt so much. What's the problem with us hangin' out with him and his girlfriend?"

"There's no problem," I said, "Why do you think that I have a problem with it?"

"Well...by your tone of voice, for one thing. You're not jealous or something, are you?"

"Of what? What's there to be jealous of?"

"I don't know; you tell me. Maybe because I'm hanging out with your friend, and you were not invited?"

I looked at her coldly. "That doesn't make sense, Kathie. Why would I be jealous because of some stupid double date? Matt and I spend way more time together than what he spends with Tracy anyways!"

She stared at me. "So you are jealous of Tracy... not me." It was like a light switch had been turned on, as she came to a stark realization. I shook my head violently.

"It's not like that. That is crazy. Of course I'm not jealous of Tracy. I just don't like her, that's all. You know I never have. And I think Matt deserves a whole lot better than her, to be honest!"

"Petey," she looked at me affectionately, "do you think that maybe you might be spending too much time with him? He's a good guy and all, but it seems almost like in some ways you are becoming obsessed with him. You even are getting cell phone calls from him in the middle of dinner. And by the way, where'd you get the money for that phone?"

"He bought me the phone, because he *is* my friend."

"Sit down," she said, motioning towards a kitchen chair.

"I thought you were gonna take a nap," I reminded her.

"I am, but I think we need to talk about this whole thing some more."

"Well I don't really think there is anything else to say. Matt is my friend. Tracy isn't. Period!"

"Petey, you do know that there is nothing you cannot tell me, don't you? You do know that I love you more than anything in the world? I will always love you, no matter what." She moved closer to me. "Please...what is going on between you and Matt?"

"Nothing! God, why do you keep asking me stuff like this? Is it so unbelievable to you that I could actually have a *friend* for once in my life? Matt is my best friend. I think that is a good thing, not something you should act all freaked out about."

"And you are telling me that it is not something more than just a friendship?" She stared into my eyes.

"What are you even suggesting?" I sneered. "Are you saying that Matt and I are a couple of faggots?"

"I'm not suggesting anything," she calmly responded, "I'm asking. And even if you were gay, it totally would not matter to me."

"Well, when you are out with Matt tonight, take a good look at him. Ask yourself if he looks like a fag or not. Better yet, why don't you just ask *him* what he is. Ask him in front of Tracy!" I whipped around, turning from her and bolted for my bedroom, slamming the door behind me. God, I wish I could rip this fuckin chastity thing off of me! Everything was annoying to me at that moment. I dove into the bed, burying my face in the pillow and cried.

Eventually I dozed off to sleep, and did not wake until after seven o'clock. I groggily stumbled out into the kitchen, and found a note on the table.

Petey

Carter and I are going out for a bite to eat, before we go to the party. Please don't be mad about our conversation earlier. I'm sorry if I said anything to offend you or to hurt your feelings. I honestly was not trying to accuse you of anything. Like I said, I love you...no matter what.

Love

K

I placed the note back down on the table and went to the refrigerator. I grabbed a bottled water and chugged it. I was so famished too. I pulled out some lunchmeat and some mayo, placing them on the countertop. Then I retrieved the bread from the upper cupboard and began assembling a sandwich. As I was spreading the mayo, a wave of emotion swept over me again, and I could not even see the bread through my tear-filled eyes. I just wished that he would stop seeing her altogether. I wished that he would just tell her the truth. But then, what was the truth? Maybe it was me that was blind to the truth at this point. Maybe he did not really love me the way that I thought. After all, he had never said it to me. He never once said "I love you." Even when I told him that I loved him, all he said was "KISS." What does *that* mean?

I pressed the pieces of bread together and moved the sandwich to my mouth, taking a small bite. Almost immediately, before I'd even finished chewing it up, I wretched. I dropped to my knees and grabbed the nearby trash can, spitting my mouthful into it. Then I continued to convulse, gagging up the juices from my empty stomach. I was not sick; I knew better than that. It was nerves, that's all. I often puked when I got really upset. I got up from my knees then and grabbed a paper towel, wiping my mouth. Then I tossed the sandwich into the trash, and changed the trash liner. After tying up the trash bag, I placed it on the linoleum by the front entry, knowing I'd have to take it out in a bit.

After pacing around the living room for a couple of minutes, I then headed into the bathroom and stripped off my shirt. I finished getting undressed after adjusting the water in the shower, and then stepped in. I looked down at myself, seeing the weird little plastic device that was securely attached to my privates. He probably was going to be out fucking Tracy tonight, and here I was, not even able to touch myself.

When I got out of the shower, I wrapped a towel around myself and went back into my bedroom, plopping myself in front of the computer. My hair was still dripping as I logged onto my internet account. When I pulled up my email, I immediately noticed I'd received a message from Drew. I opened the mail and read,

Hey Pete,

Thanks for the email! It was really cool to meet you last night. Alex said to make sure that I told you he did not realize you were already taken. No hard feelings. I'd love to meet your Sir on Sunday, like you said, but am afraid I only will be allowed to do so if accompanied by Alex. Please convey this to your Sir, and express to him our appreciation for the invitation. Hope to hear from you soon

Drew

After reading the email, I immediately forwarded it to Matt. Well, at least that was good news. And even if Matt was out tonight on a date with Tracy, at least I had Sunday to look forward to. I realized I was starting to feel a little bit better, and so I got up and threw on some sweats and a tee shirt. Then I slipped on my sandals and took the trash out to the dumpster. When I got back, I grabbed an apple from the fridge and headed back to the computer. It was still logged on, and I surfed through some web pages, checking out the latest on *Harry Potter and the Sorcerer's Stone*, the movie version of the first book which was going to soon be showing in theatres. Then I played Word Womp for about an hour and finally curled up with a novel.

As I lay there on the bed, I kept thinking about Matt being at that party with Tracy. I wondered what he was doing right then. I wondered if he said anything to Kathie about me, and I was worried that maybe she had said something to him about me also. Did Matt kiss Tracy the way that he kissed me? Did he enjoy making love to her as much as with me? I was certain that she did not service him as well as I did. She was too much of a selfish bitch to service anyone but herself. Maybe he forced her to do it, the way he sort of did with me. I hoped that if he did, he made her choke hard on it. Maybe she'd choke to death!

At ten o'clock I went out to the living room and flipped on the television. I wanted to see what was on 20/20. I could not believe how Barbara Walters hardly even opened her mouth when she talked. It must be a real pain for lip readers to understand her. I tried to concentrate on the program, but it was extremely boring, so I surfed through some channels for a while. I stopped on Comedy Central. There was a black comedian who was kind of funny, but I really wasn't in the mood for stand up. I caught the tail end of a rerun of South Park, but even that did not tear me up the way it usually did.

At eleven-thirty I finally decided to lie back down. I placed my cell phone on the bedside stand, as I did every night when I went to sleep, plugging it into its charger. Surprisingly, I dozed off rather peacefully, not even thinking about the chastity device between my legs. I willed myself to not dwell upon Matt either; instead, I thought about one of my upcoming exams. Before I knew it, I was sound asleep.

I woke up with a start, hearing some sort of loud buzzing sound. I reached over reflexively to turn off my alarm clock, but that was not even the source of the sound. I looked at the digital clock on my stand, seeing it was 2:32am, and suddenly realized the buzzing was my cell phone. I swung my legs over the side of the bed and grabbed for my phone, "Hello?"

"Wake up! Wake up! Wake up!" It was, of course, Matt. Was he drunk or something?

"What's wrong, sir?" I said, suddenly panicked.

"What's wrong?" he repeated back to me. "What's wrong is that my cock is rock hard and it needs some attention...NOW! I'm in the laundry room of your apartment building. Get your ass out of bed, and get in here on the double. You have sixty seconds.

"Oh...and be naked...just wrap a towel around yourself." Click.

I leapt out of bed, my heart pounding in my head. Oh my god! I wasn't even awake yet. I stumbled over to the closet, catching a glimpse of myself in the mirror. Man, my hair was all mussed up too. I spun myself around, being disoriented and not really knowing what to do. I took a deep breath. Shit! I then went to my bedroom door and cautiously opened it. The apartment was very dark and quiet. If Kathie was even home, she must be in bed. I tiptoed into the hallway, wearing only my underwear and then dashed into the bathroom. I pulled open the linen closet in the bathroom and removed a large towel, then stripped off my underwear and threw them on the floor, finally wrapping the towel around my waist. Then quickly I headed back into the hallway and towards the living room.

When I opened the front door, I thought I might faint, my pulse was racing so rapidly. I tried briefly to calm myself; it was no good. I was shaking again, but I was not particularly scared, just excited. He thought of me! Even though he was out on a date with that whore Tracy, he thought of *me* and then called me in the middle of the night! I smiled to myself as I stepped into the hall and pulled the door behind me carefully. Then I darted down the hallway towards the laundry room. It was at the end of the corridor. Everything was completely quiet. When I pushed open the door, I was briefly blinded by the bright lights in the laundry room. I squinted as I let the door close behind me. And then I felt his hand on my shoulder.

Matt was standing beside me, fully dressed, but his cargo pants were unzipped, and he was holding his cock in his hand. I stared at him, thinking to myself how right he was. That cock did in fact need attention...badly. He said not one word to me, but instead pressed down on my shoulders, indicating to me the position that I was expected to assume. I dropped to my knees, peeling my towel off in the process. I wanted to be naked for him, totally exposed. I wanted him to be able to look down and see me, his property, confined by his chastity device, kneeling before him to serve. I belonged to him, every single part of me. I wanted him to see. I felt my own cock stiffen within the constraints of my cage. The points of intrigue ring that was pressing against my dick, stabbed me mercilessly as I became erect. I did not even care! I was far too excited.

I looked up at him, prepared to beg for his cock as I had done earlier that day. He was too horny for that though, and he grabbed a hold of my head quickly and shoved his cock in my face. Instantly, I opened my mouth wide, and he rammed all the way into the back of my throat. I choked on him reflexively, trying desperately to suppress my gagging. He paid virtually no attention though, and stepped into me, his body shoving me backwards while his cock was still buried inside of me all the way. I felt my head slam against the wall. He was still holding my head, preventing it from hitting the wall too violently. It jarred me, nonetheless, and I clearly got the message that he was in absolute control.

He then began thrusting. He did so with no apparent thought of my comfort or lack thereof. He just rammed into me without mercy, using my mouth and throat for his sheer pleasure. I knew that I had become only one thing to him, as my nose was flattened repeatedly against his pubes. I knew I was only a hole. *His* hole! Being unable to focus clearly on anything, I closed my eyes tightly, cranking my jaw as wide as I could while still trying to keep some suction around his shaft. It did not matter though, for he really wasn't even using my mouth at this point. He was using my throat! I wondered how it felt to him, if he felt the walls of my throat around his cock. I certainly felt him inside of me. I felt the hardness of him jabbing the back of my throat over and over again. Every single time I had to gulp slightly, which I quickly learned helped to suppress my tendency to choke. This was not entirely effective, for I did still gag on him, but everything was going so fast. Within less than five minutes I knew he was right on the verge of dumping his load.

He apparently had no desire this time to allow for a long and exciting build-up to his orgasm. He merely wanted to get off. He continued to thrust into me until he achieved his goal, finally digging his fingers deep into my skull as he forced me down the entire length of his cock, and pumped every drop of his juice down my tight throat.

He moaned loudly, and I thought for a second, even with my mouth stuffed full with his prick, "What if someone hears?" Nobody would hear though, it was two-thirty in the morning. They were asleep and we were inside of a nearly soundproof room. He continued to pump into me, and it felt by far to be the biggest load he'd drained into me so far. I tasted him almost immediately as the semen backed up onto my tongue. I gulped and gulped, over and over, eagerly eating the gift he was feeding me.

As quickly as it had begun, it was then over. I lay on the floor, gasping. "Get up and get back to bed," he said as he zipped himself up. I'll call you Sunday morning. In the meantime, send me an email and tell me how much you loved serving me." And then he turned and walked out, leaving me there alone. I had been wrong about the drinking, I noticed. He did not smell even slightly of alcohol. In fact, he appeared to have been stone sober. He must have just been extremely horny. Maybe Tracy had not put out for him. Maybe she wanted to, but he chose me instead. I smiled to myself as I lay there, not wanting to move at all, not wanting to step back into the real world just yet. I wished for a brief moment that I could rip off this chastity device and jack myself. But then as I thought about it, I was glad that I could not. I was glad that I had served so well, and had not even thought of my own pleasure. This was as it should be. This is what being his pup was all about.

I made my way back to my apartment and grabbed my underwear from the bathroom. I then crawled back into bed, noticing it was just a little bit after three o'clock. I slept so peacefully the rest of the night, savoring the taste of my hero in my mouth, and willing myself to dream only of him.

9

All of the anxiety and depression that I had allowed myself to suffer when Matt was on his date with Tracy had instantly vanished when he called me, waking me in the middle of the night. I was so relieved and so elated that he had thought of me, even after having spent the evening with her. He came to me to fulfill his needs, which said to me that he valued me more than her. It told me that I provided something for him that she did not offer. It allowed me to feel as if I were special to him. He could have gone home with her, taken her somewhere and had sex with her. He could have stayed with her until the early hours of the morning as he had done with me earlier that week, but he did not. He instead chose to call me.

It did not matter to me what Kathie thought. Even if she were to have told me point-blank that she bitterly hated Matt, it would not have dissuaded me. I was at a place in my heart where nothing else mattered to me, only pleasing and serving him. I craved his attention, his affection, his approval. I wanted to spend every single waking minute in his presence. I wanted nothing less than to be entirely his property. Never before in my life had I felt such contentment and such validation as I was now feeling, living in Matt's shadow.

Definitely it had begun as hero worship. He was the one who saved me. He was my Rescuer, my Savior. But then it gradually had begun to change, to become more than just that. I no longer just idolized him and emulated him, I also felt utterly incomplete without him. To not have him with me, to not speak to him, to not hear from him, to not see him every single day , was sheer and utter torture to me. And even the times when we were apart, whether they were very brief periods or days on end, they seemed an eternity to me.

How could I have been so selfish earlier that night, when I sat alone in my apartment brooding over the fact that he was out with someone else? Surely he was allowed to go out with whomever he chose. He definitely was entitled to go out for an evening and have fun. And without question, he should be able to do so without offering any explanations or without seeking the approval of anyone else. I belonged to him, and I was his pup. Shouldn't that have been enough for me? Shouldn't I be content with the knowledge that he cared about me so very much that he said I was "chill"? Shouldn't his affection, approval, and guidance be all that I needed? Why did I have to continue to torture myself so much over Tracy?

Really, what was it that I expected of him, anyways? Did I honestly think that a jock like Matt would announce to the world that he loved a little fagboy like me? Did I think that he ever would be completely satisfied with what I had to offer him? I did not even know that there actually was anything of significance for me to offer. I was weak, and geeky, and shy. I was vulnerable, and fearful, and unattractive. Why did he see anything in me whatsoever? Even if he had ultimately chosen to spend his time with Tracy or with someone else other than me, I think that I knew deep in my heart that I'd have gladly taken whatever part of him that he was willing to share with me, and I'd have taken it upon his terms. He was in control; he always decided the whens and the wheres.

How could it be any other way?

I was up by eight that next morning, getting myself ready to go to work, when Kathie called to me from the kitchen. Someone wanted me on the phone. I walked out to the kitchen and took the phone from her, smiling at her as if to tell her everything was cool. "Hello," I said.

"Peter? This is Drew...remember? ... from the meeting Thursday night."

"Sure, I remember. Did you get my last email?"

"Yeah, that's what I'm calling about. Alex wondered if you guys wanted to come over to our apartment tomorrow evening...around six...for dinner."

"I don't know. Matt is taking me shopping, I think, and I'm not sure what time we will be done. I will have to ask him if he wants to. Can I find out and call you back tonight? Oh, and how did you get my phone number?"

"I got it from the phone book, silly. Don't you remember telling me you lived with your sister Kathie? But sure, you can let us know tonight if you're coming. You want my number?"

I looked down and saw his number displayed in my caller-ID. "I got it already. We have caller-ID."

"Okay, cool. What you doin' today?"

"Oh, I have to work this morning...just until three o'clock. Just chillin after that."

"Why don't you and I get together this afternoon then...just the two of us, I mean."

"Hmmm...well, how bout I call you later, when I get out of work? We can decide then...if it's all right, that is."

"Sure, sounds cool. So I'll hear from you after three. Peace out."

"Bye," I hung up the phone and jotted down his number on a pad that was sitting nearby. How was I going to get a hold of Matt before three o'clock, I wondered. I could not call his cell phone. I guess I'll shoot him a quick email, and ask him to call me later.

My short six hour shift at work seemed to drag on for days. I really was not in the mood to even work that day. For one thing, my penis was very sore. When I'd gotten hard the night before, it had been stabbed quite mercilessly by the little plastic spikes that were inside of the chastity ring. In addition to that, I was still feeling a bit of discomfort from where the string had cut into me two nights prior. I did not really regret anything, though. In fact, I sort of liked having the constant reminder that I was in service to Matt. I did try not to think of it too much, though, for I was afraid I'd get hard again, and then I'd be in some really serious pain, for sure.

When my shift was up and I still had not heard from Matt, I decided that I'd just go home and check my email. If he had not gotten back to me, I'd just have to blow off Drew and then make up some excuse later. But as I was hopping on my bike, about to head home, my phone finally rang. I grabbed it from my belt and answered quickly, "Hello, Sir."

"Hey pup! How ya feeling? Did you get enough sleep last night?"

"Oh, yes Sir. Thank you for asking, did you?"

"Yeah sure. I'm cool. So you wanna hook up with Drew tonight huh?"

"Well I told him I would have to wait until I'd talked to you. I never said I would do it."

"I know pup. Just chill; that's why I'm callin you. It's fine for you to hang with Drew. Just be a good pup, don't do any messin with him at all, you understand? You know what I'm sayin to you?"

"Yes Sir. No sex." I sort of giggled as I said it.

"Right. And then we can meet the two of them tomorrow together. Tell him we will be at their place at six, but make sure you get the directions."

"I will Sir. I'll do everything you say."

"I know you will, pup. You're always a good boy. I'm gonna tell you right now, though, you won't hear from me again until tomorrow morning when I pick you up. I have plans for tonight. So don't freak about it or anything. Just go hang with Drew for awhile and have fun. Then I'll see you in the morning. Got it?"

"Yes Sir, I've got it."

"Okay. KISS!" He then clicked off the phone before I could say any more. I reached into my pocket and pulled out the piece of paper bearing Drew's number. I dialed it on my cell.

"Hello," the voice was not Drew.

"Um...hello. Is Drew there...please?"

"Sure, hang on." A couple seconds later I heard Drew's voice.

"Hello?"

"Drew, this is Peter. You told me to call you."

"Yeah sure. I was expecting you. What's up?"

"I can hang out with you today...if you still want me to, I mean."

"Yeah, of course I want you to. You are so silly sometimes. You want me to meet you somewhere?"

"Do you want to eat? I mean we could meet at Vinnie's Pizza down at Washington Street. I'm right close to there now."

"Sure, that would be awesome. I'll be coming alone though. Alex is going out tonight."

"Oh, that's good... or I mean, that's fine. Matt is going out too. It will be fun. We can just hang out together."

"Great. Okay, then, are you headed over there now?"

"Yeah."

"All right, I'll get goin myself then. See you there in about a half hour, okay?"

"Okay."

"Peace out," he hung up the phone. I rode my bike around for a bit and decided to do some browsing in the nearby shops to kill some time, so I wouldn't have to sit there waiting alone in the restaurant. Finally, about twenty minutes later, I headed back to the bookstore and re-locked my bike. Then I walked down to Vinnie's. It was almost exactly a half hour since I'd talked to Drew. I just hung around outside, sort of pacing, for about four or five minutes

161

when he finally pulled up in his little truck. I smiled at him as he got out.

"Hi," I greeted him.

"Hey there, guy. Oh man, you look cute in that shirt."

"Thanks, Matt got it for me." I beamed at him as we walked into the restaurant together. Drew requested seating in the smoking section and I followed behind him as the hostess led us to a booth.

"Guess what I did today?" Drew asked me, after we were seated.

I shrugged my shoulders and smiled sheepishly at him. "Dunno," I said, "What?"

"I got tickets to the 98° concert."

"You did? I totally love those guys! When is the concert?"

"They're gonna be here on the 24th, which is three weeks from today. I almost could not even get the tickets either, cause they have been sold out for the past two weeks, but then I found some tickets for sale online."

"Wow, that is so lucky. Are you and Alex going?"

He shook his head as he lit a cigarette. "Nah, Alex doesn't like em. He is not into boy bands at all. He doesn't even really like much Top Forty music at all, actually. There is this one girl that he sees sometimes. Probably will go out with her that night."

"Alex sees a girl? You mean like a girlfriend?"

"Yeah, sort of, but then not really. He likes 'pussy' every once in awhile. Isn't that gross?"

I laughed at him and the ridiculous face he made at me. "I don't know, I guess so. Matt has a girlfriend too. Her name is Tracy. I absolutely hate her, too. She is such a bitch."

"Yeah, well that is the bummer that goes along with having a bisexual boyfriend. On the one hand, you wouldn't want them if they were all faggy and shit like we are, but then on the other it drives you crazy that they fuck chicks. It was so hard for me in the beginning, when Alex would choose to be with her instead of me. Her name is Kelly. I used to call her 'smelly Kelly' cause she always wore way too much perfume. I think Alex finally told her to quit takin a bath in the shit, cause she doesn't smell like a whore so much any more."

"So it doesn't bother you any more that he sees her sometimes?" I asked.

He rolled his eyes as he exhaled a stream of smoke into the air, "Fuck yeah, it bothers me. Drives me crazy, but what am I gonna do about it? It is not like I have any right to tell Alex not to see whoever he wants to. The one thing I always tell myself, though, is that she is just a diversion to him. I am the one he has actually chosen to be with... in a relationship. He lives with me, sleeps with me, shares his life with me. She is nothing but a hole for his dick when he wants pussy."

"How come she doesn't freak about it then? I mean, I'd think it would be obvious to her that you and Alex are together."

"Nah. She is not too bright. I really think that it just is not even imaginable to her that Alex could ever mess around with guys. He is so straight-acting, that it never even occurs to her. She thinks that the two of us are just roommates. Can you imagine?" he laughed and took another hit off his cigarette.

"Well it doesn't even seem to me that Alex hides the fact that he is bi. I mean he stood up in front of all those people at that meeting and told everyone. Plus he is president of the Gay Student Union. It doesn't seem like he hides it from anybody."

"Yeah, you are right, I guess. It's hard to explain though. It is like his life is sort of compartmentalized. He doesn't really let Kelly see any of that part of his life. She does not go to the same college, and so he's never told her about the Student Union. Plus, sometimes he will go for three or four weeks without even seeing her. I don't see why she even would still see him. Probably she is just in love with his huge cock." My face was getting red; I could feel it. I looked down at my water glass and giggled. "Oh, you think that's funny?" he said, "well let me tell you, it's fuckin huge!"

"You just crack me up sometimes, Drew," I admitted.

"Hmm, well I do that to a lot of people. I'm a freak, I guess. Seriously though, he does have a huge dick. What is Matt's like?" he asked me, much too casually.

My mouth dropped open, as I looked around us to see if anyone was close enough to eavesdrop on our conversation. "I don't think I can tell that," I whispered. "I mean... um... it's kind of personal."

He busted up laughing then. "Well, let me tell you something, kiddo. If you think it wouldn't turn Matt on to know that his boy was bragging about his awesome cock to some other fag, then you probably don't either don't know him real well yet, or else he is very unusual. Most Dom guys would be turned on knowin that fags talk about them like that."

"Oh, well to be honest, I am not sure it is big or not. I mean it's a lot bigger than...um...than I am. But Matt is the only guy I have ever ... um...been with."

"Really? And you are such a cutie too, but that's right, you already told me you're just new to this. Don't you look at porn though, like on the internet?"

I shrugged. "Well sometimes I do...now. I mean, I started to a little after we...well...after we were together the first time. I started to want to see how other people did it and stuff."

"Well, how many inches would you say it is?" he asked, rather too seriously.

I laughed at him again. "How would I know?! Do you think I measure it or something?"

"Yeah sure," he smiled. "I've measured Alex. He is eight and three quarters inches, base of shaft to the tip of head. And fat!"

"Wow," I said, "I think that is big. I bet Matt is at least that big too, though. I think so, but I'm not sure. I wonder if he will let me measure it?"

"Probably. He probably will get turned on by it, even. Has he fucked you yet?"

My mouth dropped open, "You sure do ask a lot of personal questions!" I looked up and the waitress was standing at our booth. Oh my god, I hoped she had not heard any of our conversation. I quickly grabbed a menu.

"You just wanna get a pizza?" Drew asked. I nodded quickly in response. "You like vegetarian?"

"Yeah. Perfect. No mushrooms though, okay?"

"Sure," Drew said, as he looked up to the waitress. "Medium, please...deep dish."

"Anything to drink, gentlemen?"

"Diet Coke for me," said Drew.

"Iced tea, please," I said.

"Okay, any breadsticks or appetizers?" We shook our heads. "Okay," she smiled, "be right back with your drinks."

"Do you think she heard what we were saying?" I asked, after she was gone.

He laughed, "Who cares? Like it isn't obvious we are a couple of queer boys. So has he fucked you yet?"

I crouched down in my seat a little, and then leaned forward, looking over at Drew as if to reveal my innermost secrets of the heart. "He did it to me with his finger." I actually laughed a little as I said it, sort of excited to be sharing this with someone else for the first time.

"Finger fucked ya, huh? Well, he must be getting you ready for the main event." He smiled affectionately at me. "Sounds like he is being very gentle with you... training you."

"Training me?" I asked, "What do you mean?"

He crushed his cigarette out in the ashtray. "I mean that you are so new. He is teaching you. He's taking things slow for ya. That's good. That's what a good Sir does. You're lucky."

I nodded. "Sometimes it seems too slow though. I want him to do more."

"Yeah," he said, "that's understandable, but it really is not for you to decide. You just have to relax and let him give ya stuff when he knows you're ready."

"You know what he did to me yesterday?" I asked. Drew smiled at me, as if he were talking to a small boy who had just come from the circus.

"What?"

"He put me in one of those...devices. Those...um..." I lowered my voice again, "those chastity devices."

"Oh dude, that is so hot. Then did he make you blow him?"

I was blushing again; I knew it. I nodded. "And plus he came back last night in the middle of the night. He called me on my cell phone and I had to meet him in the laundry room of my apartment. And I served him there. Then he just left, like it was no big deal."

"Yeah. Well you did your job. It *was* no big deal. So how does it feel to be wearing it? What kind is it?"

"Feels weird sort of. I was starting to get used to it, but then today it is hurting me so bad. It's called CB2000."

"Yeah, those are the kind they usually get for beginners, but it is not supposed to hurt you...ever. Did you tell him it's hurting you?"

I shook my head. "No, I'm not going to be a baby about it. I probably deserve it, really. Cause like I told you before, he caught me...you know...playing with myself."

"Dude, you'd better tell him. He is gonna be pissed if you go around with that thing hurting you and he doesn't even know. He might not have it on exactly right."

"Well, it did not hurt at all...but then I got sort of hard last night...when I was in the laundry room. And my dick got stabbed by those spike things."

"He has the spike things on it already?" he asked, astonished. "Those are called 'points of intrigue' and are generally only used for more advanced subs. They are specifically designed to cause pain. But usually beginners don't have them, cause they can't control their erections as much. You better tell him, Petey. He needs to get that thing off of there, before you get hurt. Are you bleeding at all?"

I nodded. "Only a little. Let's change the subject though. I don't want to talk about it."

"Okay...but dude...*tell him!* I'm serious."

My conversation with Drew was so natural, and so very relaxed, that it seemed we had been best buds for years. I loved every second that I was with him, and I was starting to think of him as being like the next-best-thing-to-Matt. After we finished our late lunch, we drove over to the mall. Drew took me in to this one hair salon so that I could meet one of his friends, Larry. He was a stylist there, and was this really lanky, forty-ish blonde guy who was balding yet still very attractive. He was extremely effeminate though, and very outspoken. "He is the best hair stylist I've ever had," Drew confided, "but then he knows it. He's pretty cocky sometimes about how good he is. He's expensive though, and usually you have to book an appointment way in advance." We had caught Larry between customers, and he took a couple of minutes to chat with us.

"So when you gonna let me get my hands on your hair, little guy?" he asked me. "I'd love to play with you for awhile." He smiled.

"Just simmer down, Larry," Drew warned, "Peter is taken already."

"Can't blame a guy for tryin, though, huh? Figured you were taken already; too cute not to be."

We then went over to this one adult shop in the mall. It was called "Erotic Expressions," and featured mostly lingerie and heterosexual novelty items. They did have a smaller gay section though, in the back, and so Drew and I went back and looked at some of the videos and toys. As we were browsing, Drew picked up a leather collar that was studded with metallic beads. "Has Matt mentioned collaring you yet?" he asked me.

I shook my head. "Why would he do that?" I asked sincerely.

"Oh, to mark you...to claim you as his own property. It's a great honor to be collared, actually. See?" He peeled back the neckline of his polo shirt and revealed a gold chain. It had a very small padlock attached to the front. "This is my collar from Alex. I wear it 24/7. Only he has the key to it."

"Wow," I said. I examined it more closely, realizing that it was about the same thickness as a dog's choke chain collar. "So you like wearing it?"

"I totally love wearing it, dude. Whenever we go out to a bar or something, or to a gay pride event or something like that, I have to display it in the open. It makes me feel so proud to be owned by him, and when I wear it, it's like telling the world that I belong to him."

"That's so cool. I wish Matt would get me one... but I doubt it. He is more private, I think. I don't think he would ever want me to display myself like that."

"Well, you never know. It's really not so much that you are displaying yourself. It is that you are simply making a statement that you belong to someone. Sort of like a wedding ring, I guess. If you had been wearing a collar Thursday, Alex would never have had me proposition you."

"Yeah, that makes sense. I think it is awesome that you have a collar from him. Do you ever just reach up and touch it, to remind yourself that you are his?"

He smiled... "Constantly."

We spent nearly four hours together that day, Drew and I. We hit up all the cool shops, and he even bought me a gift. It was a baseball cap that sort of matched my shirt. Finally Drew took me back to the bookstore where I showed him around. He bought a couple erotic novels, and I let him use my discount card. Then he threw my bike in the back of his truck and drove me home. I did not invite him up to the apartment, but assured him that we would see him the next day. He had written down the directions to his house for me, and before I left, he leaned into me and kissed my cheek. "See you tomorrow, guy. Was a lot of fun today."

"Thanks...I think so too.... Drew?"

"Yeah?"

"I like you a lot. Thanks for being my friend."

He laughed. "Well, thanks for being mine. I like you too. You know, you are one of the most sincere people I have ever met." I looked into his eyes, sort of surprised by the statement.

"See you tomorrow." I got out and closed the door. He waited while I removed my bike from his truck bed. Then as he pulled away I parked my bike in the carport and headed inside. Wow, how did I get so lucky...first Matt and now Drew. I realized how much things were getting better for me. I'd been so lonely and sad every since Mom and Dad had died. Maybe everything was going to be all right. Maybe there actually was a chance I would end up being happy.

Maybe.

10

Sunday morning was hectic at our apartment. It started off that we had run out of coffee creamer. "Shit!" I heard Kathie yell. I told her to just use milk, like any normal person would do. "I hate using milk. It makes the coffee taste curdled." So reluctantly I offered to run over to the market to pick up some coffee creamer for her. When I got back, Carter was there. He was picking Kathie up for brunch. As I walked through the door, creamer in hand, the phone was ringing. I lunged for it, hoping it was Matt, but was disappointed to hear Tracy's voice on the line.

"Is Kathie there?"

"I don't know," I said, "I'll check." I held my hand over the receiver, "Kathie, are you here? It's Tracy."

"Well, yes I'm here, Bozo." She grabbed the phone from me as I made a face at her, while shoving the coffee creamer into her hand. I then went into the bedroom to check my email. I had just sat down at the computer when I heard Kathie say to Carter, "Tracy is gonna meet us at the restaurant; is that all right, hon? She's gonna try to get a hold of Matt and invite him too."

I shot back up out of my chair instantly and headed back to the kitchen. "Matt is not going!" I yelled. "He's not going to brunch with you 'cause he already has plans with me."

"Oh," said Kathie, "Well that's okay. We aren't trying to ruin your plans. Just inviting him to brunch that's all. You know, you could come too."

"No thanks," I said. "He is gonna be here in a few minutes, I think. I doubt he'd want me to go to brunch with you guys if Tracy was gonna be there."

"Why would he feel like that?" asked Kathie. "What difference does it make if Tracy is there? She's his girlfriend for heaven's sake."

"Well...um...he knows we don't like each other so much. I don't think he would want there to be any bad feelings or anything. You know...tension."

"Whatever," she said sarcastically. "Anyways, Carter and I are going and if any one of you guys—you, Matt, or Tracy—want to join us, you are welcome. Just keep me out of this childish bullshit of you two being jealous of one another. If I were Matt, I'd just tell both of you to grow up. You're his friend and she's his girlfriend. You two ought to try getting along with each other."

"Whatever!" I repeated back to her mockingly. I turned and headed back to my bedroom. Now I was pissed. That bitch was gonna ruin Matt's plans today, plans he had with *me*. I closed the door behind me and sat down in my computer chair. I winced from the pain in my groin. Damn this chastity thing. It hurt like crazy! The night before I tried to clean myself in the shower. As soon as the water hit my privates it felt like I was pouring acid on myself. Now today, every time I moved a certain way it was almost unbearable.

After logging on, I opened my buddy list and changed the settings to remove Drew from block status. Instantly his name appeared on my screen. He was online.

Ptboy1982: hi Drew

Boydrew75: hey peteyboy

Ptboy1982: watcha doin?

Boydrew75: nothing just got up

Ptboy1982: I'm waiting for matt. He is coming over today so we can go shopping. Then we are coming to your place.

Boydrew75: yeah I know

Ptboy1982: his gf just called here. She wants him to go to brunch with her and my sister and my sister's bf. Hope that he doesn't go.

Boydrew75: oh, well just chill. So what if he does, you still have the rest of the day to be with him.

Ptboy1982: yeah, but this was supposed to be our day together. Why's she got to ruin it?

Boydrew75: well don't get all freaked. Not for you to decide. Even if he does go with them, doesn't mean he won't still go shopping with u afterwards.

Ptboy1982: I know. Sometimes I get so pissed at myself. Why do I have to be such a baby about everything?

Boydrew75: not being a baby. You just r jealous, that's all. It's natural. I'd be jealous too.

Ptboy1982: why's everyone think I'm jealous?

Boydrew75: lol...um cuz u are

Ptboy1982: whatever

Boydrew75: ur a good guy, just be calm. Matt's not gonna diss you so jus chill.

Ptboy1982: hope not

Boydrew75: how's ur chastity feel today? Any better?

Ptboy1982: not really...worse actually

Boydrew75: he's probably gonna see it today, ya know

Ptboy1982: well, maybe he won't notice anything

Boydrew75: I doubt that. You need to tell him about it anyways. Right away!

Ptboy1982: well I gotta go, okay? He is gonna be here any minute.

Boydrew75: k...see u at six Peace Out

Ptboy1982: bye

I logged off and pulled up a game of Scrabble. I was such a schmuck. Why'd I have to make such an ass of myself to my own sister, and in front of her boyfriend? Shit! I got back up out of my chair and went back to the kitchen. Kathie and Carter were standing together at the counter, both looking at the same Sunday paper together. "Kathie?" I said.

"Yeah, hon," she said as she looked up at me.

"I'm sorry."

"For what?" she asked sincerely.

"For being such a jerk. You're right about me and Tracy. If Matt wants to go to brunch with you guys, it doesn't matter to me. I'll even go too...if he wants me to, that is."

"Well you're not a jerk, silly, and if he's already made plans with you, I'm sure he'll just tell Tracy that anyways. Let's not argue about them any more though, okay? Let's just call a truce."

"Deal," I said as I smiled at her.

"Deal," she repeated. There was a knock at the door just then. I grabbed her hand quickly and squeezed it, and then headed for the front door. I opened it to face the man in question, Matt.

"Hey there," he said, "You up and ready to go, guy?"

"Yeah, come on in S—, um, Matt." I motioned for him to come inside. "Tracy just called here. She is going to breakfast with Kathie and Carter and wants you to go with them."

"I know," he said. "She got a hold of me. Told her I already had plans though." He smiled down at me.

"You did? Well, um...if you want to change your plans, it's okay, you know?"

"Course I know that. But I don't wanna change em. That's why I'm here." I wanted to grab him and hug him just then, but instead just looked up into his eyes adoringly. He grinned at me.

"See Petey, I told you he'd say that," said Kathie. "But you guys are both welcome to join us, if you want," she added, addressing both of us.

"Maybe next time," Matt replied. "Thanks anyways."

"Sure. Well we had better get going."

"How ya doin Carter?" Matt said, finally greeting him.

"Everything's cool, I guess," he said. "Very busy lately."

"Yeah, I bet. Work, school, girlfriend. Those things all can be very demanding."

"Hey!" said Kathie lightheartedly, "Watch your mouth!"

"Well dude, we better run," said Carter. "Nice seein you again."

After they had gone, Matt and I went into my bedroom. "You have fun yesterday?" he asked.

"Yes sir," I said. "Drew and I went to the mall. Wanna see what he bought me?"

"Sure." I grabbed the b-cap from my dresser.

"See? It goes with the shirt you got me."

"Cool. Come here." He sat down on the bed. I walked over and stood in front of him and he grabbed a hold of my butt, pulling me into him so that I was standing between his legs. He then kissed me. "You miss me?" he asked.

"Oh my god, more than anything!"

"Take off your pants, pup. Wanna check your chastity."

"Um, it's okay sir. I just checked it awhile ago."

He laughed at me. "I want to check it myself. Do as I say," he said reprovingly.

"Yes sir," I said. I unbuttoned my pants and stepped out of them, now standing in front of him in just my shirt and underwear.

"Now your briefs," he said, starting to sound a bit annoyed.

I looked down at the ground. "Sir?"

"Yes? What's wrong. Why aren't you obeying me, pup?"

"Can't we please do it later, Sir? Please?"

"Do it now. Now take off your briefs." He was very firm with me, and I knew I could not delay any longer. I reached down and grabbed the waistband, finally pulling them down onto my thighs, but not stepping out of them yet. He reached out and gently grabbed the base of the device, underneath my balls. Instantly I winced from the pain.

"Does that hurt?" he asked. I nodded, reluctantly. "Get em off and lie on the bed, pup." I obeyed, removing my underwear the rest of the way, and crawling up on the bed. He had stood up while I did so but then sat back down on the edge of the bed to examine me. He had a small key in his hand, the one for the padlock. As he unlocked my cage, I put my hands up behind my head, trying to lie perfectly still and not to show him I was in any pain. But as he removed the first ring, I reflexively jerked my body, pulling my legs slightly up off the bed.

"Oh my god, you have been bleeding," he said. "Your cock is all torn up. Why didn't you tell me about this?"

"It doesn't hurt too bad," I lied, "It only does hurts once in awhile."

"Didn't I tell you that if it hurt at all you were to let me know, right away?"

"Yes sir," I said, embarrassed. "But I did not ... um...I dint' wanna be a baby about it, Sir."

"Damn it Petey! It's not for you to decide. I gave you very specific instructions. I gave you an order to tell me if it hurt at all, didn't I? Do you have any cream or anything around here? A first aid kit?"

"Under the sink in the bathroom Sir." He got up off the bed.

"Don't move," he said as he went to retrieve the ointment. When he got back, he placed the first aid kit next to me on the bed. "It looks like these spike things poked into you pretty bad. Plus you have a nasty scab around the base of your cock. How'd you get that? Was it from when you had the string around yourself?" I nodded. "How come I did not notice that when I put this on you?" I shrugged.

"It wasn't scabbed yet Sir. You probably couldn't tell since I was soft at the time."

"Well you should have told me," he scolded. "You know this is a bunch of total bull shit! Is this how you take care of yourself, pup? You don't just neglect yourself like this, that's majorly wrong. I'm not happy right now! Not at all!"

"I'm sorry sir," I was on the verge of tears. "Please don't be mad."

"Well I *am* mad! And do you know what I'm maddest about of all?"

"That I didn't tell you?" I whimpered.

"That's right! Especially after I told you to tell me *right away*. I expect you to take care of yourself, pup." His voice was getting calmer. "That is as much your responsibility as it is mine." He squeezed some ointment onto his finger and rubbed it on me. It felt so good to have the chastity off, and to have him touching me, even though I was very tender. "You know if you weren't already in so much pain, I'd roll you over and spank your ass."

I did not know if this statement was entirely serious, but was not about to press my luck, so I just responded, "Yes Sir." I lay there quietly as he rubbed in more ointment.

"You still got those boxers I gave you?"

"Yes sir. They are in my drawer."

"Okay, well you are gonna wear boxers until this heals up. Nothing tight. No chastity either. But that still doesn't mean you are off restriction." He pulled out the bottom drawer of my bedside stand and threw the chastity device into it. "Get those boxers and put em on." I rolled off the bed immediately and did as he instructed. "How does it feel?" he asked as I pulled up the boxer shorts. "Better?"

"Yes sir, much."

"Come here," he patted his hand on the bed next to him, and I walked over and sat beside him. Then he put his arm around me, pulling me into him. "Pup, I don't want to do things to hurt you. Why would you ever think that I would want you to be in pain like that? And why would you try to hide it from me?"

I looked down at my lap. "I don't know, Sir. I just thought it was my own fault. I was not even supposed to get hard, but what happened is that I got so hard that one night...Friday...when you called me. I got so hard and I stayed that way for awhile. It ended up ... well...it ended up that those things got stuck in me, those spikes. It was my own fault. Not yours."

"Maybe we should think about not having the spikes just yet then. I think I can take those out of there. You should have told me about this yesterday when I called you. Or you should have sent me an email. You know I check my mail several times a day."

"I know Sir. I'm sorry. It was my fault. I was bad."

"Stop it. When you are bad, I'll let you know. You're not bad. You just did not make the right decision, that's all. Doesn't make you bad." I reached my hand over and placed it on his leg. I wanted to drop to my knees in front of him then. I wanted to show him I knew my place. I just sat there, though, and let him hold me.

Everything that Matt had said to me—the way that he scolded me and reprimanded me for not telling him about my situation—it was all true. I did know that he'd been very specific with me regarding the chastity device. His instructions to me had been very clear. It was not supposed to hurt me. If it did hurt me, I was to let him know right away. At this point I was not even entirely sure why I had failed to obey him; it made no sense even to me. I remembered that I had been concerned about having gotten so hard Friday night when I was serving him. I remembered that I had thought that the pain was a very small price to pay for belonging to him. I remembered that I had not wanted him to see me as being too weak or too much of a baby. My thinking was certainly rather convoluted, I now realized in retrospect. Perhaps I had over-thought the situation. Maybe I'd mistakenly assumed that I had options, when in fact there was really only one simple and very clear option to choose, and that was obedience.

Was I ever going to be worthy of him? Was I ever going to learn how to be the kind of pup that Matt truly deserved? Instead of focusing upon following his instructions and doing exactly the things that he said for me to do, I'd wasted so much of my energy fretting and worrying about extraneous issues. I'd worked myself into a frenzy over Tracy and what Matt was doing with her, rather than remaining focused upon what my own role was supposed to be. Why did he put up with me? Why did he tolerate the constant cycles of failure that I seemed incapable of escaping?

The summation of my feelings at that moment were a potent mixture of sadness and self hatred. I failed, just as I always had done. But now it was worse than ever before, for I was doing more than just failing myself. I was also failing the one single person in my life that I had loved unconditionally; the one person other than my family, that is. I knew why Matt had never told me that he loved me. How could he ever tell me something like that? How could that ever in a million years be true? I hated the weak and dependent person that I was. I hated the fact that I lacked everything necessary to be classified as a real man. He had seen these qualities in me, most definitely, right from the beginning. He had seen how very much less than him I was. And now the verbal chastisement that he had leveled at me cut me to the core. It was so true. I was indeed bad, regardless of his efforts to ultimately make me feel otherwise.

I held onto him, clinging to him as if I were terrified he'd simply vanish. I believe that a part of me actually did fear that. I felt he was going to be torn away from me the way my parents had been . I feared that one day I'd wake up and he would no longer be in my life. I could not bear to lose him. I squeezed my eyes tightly shut as I buried my head into his chest. *Don't leave me Matt. Please don't leave me Sir.*

"Hey, we should get ready to go pup. I made an appointment for you. Gotta be there in about a half hour." He gently pushed me away from him, holding me in a position where he could look into my face. He moved his hand so tenderly to my cheek and brushed away the tears. "Don't cry pup. I told you that you are not bad. Remember? You're a chill dude. Remember?" His voice was so calming to me, so very paternal and patient. I nodded as I looked up at him.

"I promise to obey you always, Sir. I promise. I promise with all my heart."

"I know you do, pup. I believe you." He kissed me then, not at all with passion, but with such gentleness. His strength overpowered me as I melted into his loving embrace.

"I love you so much, Sir."

"Love you too."

My world stopped for a few seconds. The tears came flooding back into my eyes as I was overcome with a wave of tremendous emotion. He loved me too. He loved me too! He loved me too!!!!

And so began the best day of my entire life. We then readied ourselves as I got re-dressed, and headed out for a day of being together, Owner and pup. This was heaven. There was no other word to describe it.

* * *

I did not question Matt about the appointment that he had said was scheduled for me. When we arrived at the shopping mall, I realized that he had made an appointment for a haircut. The appointment was at the same exact salon where Drew and I had visited the previous day. Ironically, my hair stylist was Larry. "See hon, I just knew I'd get to play with your hair sooner or later, but this is even sooner than I expected." Matt looked over at me, shaking his head. Apparently this Larry was a bit over the top, as far as Matt was concerned, but Matt also must have known that Larry was very good at his job. "Now what's it gonna be today, little guy?" Larry said to me, leaning over my chair and staring me right in the face. I smiled at him in spite of myself but then quickly turned to look at Matt. "Oh...." Larry said, "I see, well what's it gonna be today?" Larry repeated the question, but this time directing it to Matt.

Matt proceeded to lay out very specific instructions as to how he wanted my hair cut. He wanted it done in a style that was almost identical to his own, except a bit shorter. I was so excited when he said it that I could not wipe the smile off of my face. Matt wanted me to look like him, to be sort of a miniature version of himself. It was totally perfect. It would have been exactly what I'd have chosen were the decision to have been left to me. "You two are such a cute couple," Larry said, being as boisterous and extroverted as ever. I wondered if Matt was self conscious at all of the other patrons around us. Nobody seemed to raise an eyebrow , though, and I suddenly realized that pretty much everyone in the salon probably was gay, except for maybe a couple of the female customers. I guess a hair salon is not really a place that sexual orientation is much of an issue. Larry certainly made no effort to conceal his sexual identity.

"So have you two been together for very long?" Larry asked as he scrubbed shampoo into my scalp. I was tilted back in the chair with my head lying on the edge of the sink.

"No sir," I said, "Only for maybe a few weeks, I guess."

"Honey, you don't have to call me sir." Larry leaned down as if to whisper in my ear, "You can reserve that formality for your man here. I bet you call him that all the time, don't you?"

"Yeah," I grinned up at him, wondering if Matt was paying attention to our conversation.

"How old are you, if you don't mind me asking?"

"He's nineteen," Matt said, "and so am I."

"Oh man!" Larry sighed, " I feel like chicken tonight, like chicken tonight!" Matt and I looked at each other bewildered, not understanding what the hell Larry was talking about.

When Larry was done washing, cutting, and styling my hair, I looked at myself in the mirror. Only thing I really had to do was maybe get rid of these glasses, I thought. Then I would look a lot better for Matt. I bet he hated that I was such a four-eyed geek. "Do you like it, Sir?" I asked him.

"Looks cool," he said, "Perfect." He handed Larry a twenty dollar tip which Larry quickly pushed right back in his hand.

"The privilege of doing it was enough of a gratuity in and of itself. You need a trim yourself? On the house," he offered. Matt shook his head, declining graciously.

"I'm all set, thanks. Plus we got a lot to do today." Larry shook both our hands and led us to the register where Matt presented his credit card.

"Sir," I said, gently grabbing Matt's arm. "Will you please let me pay for it?" I reached into my pocket, pulling out my own bank card.

"Nope," he said without any further comment. I knew better than to argue, and was so incredibly proud as we walked out together. Now people would look at us and know we were together. I wondered if anyone would ever think I was his little brother. I sort of looked like it with this haircut. I kept glancing up as we walked down the mall, trying to catch glimpses of us in the reflection of the different windows and mirrors we passed. Matt seemed to not even notice, taking everything in stride and leading the way confidently to our next destination.

After we left the salon, Matt led me to the NuVision Eye Center where he bought me a pair of contacts. He informed me that he liked me just fine in my glasses but that now I'd have the option of being able to see even without them. The optician spent a good thirty minutes helping me practice putting them in and removing them before we were ready to move on.

Matt then took me into several different shops, beginning first with Foot Locker. There he bought me two really cool pairs of shoes and a pair of hiking boots. We then went A&F where he got me a couple of rugby shirts. We also hit County Seat, the Gap, Ralph Lauren, the Leather Barn, Target, and

Gliks. He bought so many different things for me that I was
losing track of what they all were and how much he was
spending. He had me try on many of the items and wear
them out of the fitting room, walking around a bit in front of
him so that he could evaluate me. He ended up buying cargo
pants and shorts, basketball and baggy shorts, wind pants
and matching jackets, fleece pullovers, a whole bunch of tee
shirts, sleeveless tees, and a couple baseball shirts. It was
almost four o'clock by the time that we got done with all of
the shopping, and finally Matt announced that he was
starving and that we were gonna go eat. He loaded me up
with all of these packages then in my arms so that I could
hardly see in front of me and shoved his car keys in my
hand. "Take this stuff out to the car and then meet me back
at the food court."

"Yes sir," I said, smiling over the bundles in my arms.
"Matt?"

"Yeah?" he looked down at me, perhaps about to laugh at
how ridiculous I must have looked.

"Thank you." My voice was starting to crack, as I was
again feeling emotional.

"You're welcome," he said, as if it were no big deal. "Now
do what I said, and hurry back."

When I stepped out into the huge parking lot, I realized
that I had a long walk ahead of me. Matt had parked like a
frickin mile from the damn entrance. Now which row was it?
Was it Row C or Row D? I started roaming around aimlessly,
looking for the car. My arms were starting to feel like lead,
carrying all of these packages. Finally about five minutes
later I eventually spotted the car. I thought I was gonna drop
everything as I fumbled for the keys. I leaned against the car,
dropping a couple of the bags I was carrying, and as I did so,
the damned car alarm went off. Shit! The lights were
flashing, the horn blowing, and I was starting to panic. Oh
Shit! I dropped the rest of the packages onto the ground,
freeing my hands as I started pressing buttons on the key

remote. Finally I managed, by sheer luck, to press the correct button, disabling the alarm. I then unlocked the driver's side door and dumped all the packages into the back seat. I crawled in and straightened them, not wanting Matt to get back to the car and think that I had been careless.

When I was finally done, I closed the car door and raced back to the mall entrance. I was completely out of breath when I made it to the food court. I scanned the room, looking for him. Finally I spotted him and headed to his table. "Took you long enough," he said casually.

I was gasping for air. "Sorry sir..." I heaved a big sigh, "I accidentally set off the alarm. And that was after I roamed around for five minutes. I couldn't remember where we parked."

He just laughed. "Sit down, I got you a sandwich."

"Oh, thank you, Sir." I sat down and took a big gulp of my beverage before diving into the sub.

"I got you something else, too, pup," he said. I stopped chewing my sandwich and looked into his eyes. His voice was so serious all of a sudden. I gulped down the bite of food and took another quick sip of my pop.

"Sir, you've bought me so much already," I said.

"This is special, though. This is something I picked out just for my pup, to remind him who he belongs to. That's why I sent you to the car. I had to go get it."

I looked at him wide-eyed, not really believing what I was hearing. Why would Matt do all of this for me? Why would he spend all of this money on me, get me a haircut like his, buy me contact lenses, give me shoes and clothes, and spend the day with me? Maybe it was true. Maybe he really did love me. I just felt so unworthy though, having done nothing to deserve this showering of attention and gifts. "Sir, I can't ever pay you back for all you have done. I don't even deserve it." I was so choked up as I spoke to him, wanting to grab a hold of him right there in the middle of the mall.

"Did I say that I wanted anything paid back? Did I tell you any of this was a loan?"

I shook my head, "No Sir."

"All right then. It's my decision whether or not to do things for my pup. Your job is to just accept it and quit worrying so much." He then reached into his pocket and pulled out a small square box. He opened it and placed it on the table in front of me. I looked down and saw a very simple beaded necklace- a choker. He was giving me jewelry, but it was not just any jewelry. It was like— like a collar?

"Is it ...um...is it a collar Sir?" I asked meekly.

He nodded. "Sort of. It's a necklace. But when you wear it, we will both know what it really means. It means you are mine. You belong to me."

"Oh Sir!" I was openly crying now, tears streaming right down my face. "Thank you. Thank you so much." He then reached down and removed the necklace from its box.

"Lean forward," he said. He then reached over with the necklace and wrapped it gently around my neck. "Turn around." I did so immediately, shifting in my chair. He then clasped the back of the necklace below my hairline. I felt the coldness of the beads against my skin and reached up to touch the front of it with my fingers. I wished I could kiss him then, or even kneel before him. I wanted to do it right there, right in the food court. Instead, though, I just turned to face him and looked into his eyes.

Unfazed, he took a bite of his own sandwich. "Looks good," he said casually, with his mouth full. I knew his assessment was not just of the necklace either. He was referencing the entire package, his pup, fashioned in his own image. I smiled at him affectionately and proudly, finishing my lunch in silence. There was no need for any further conversation.

11

On our way over to Alex and Drew's apartment, I sat in the front seat next to Matt and rifled through each one of the bags that contained our purchases from that day. I was so thrilled, literally overjoyed, to have an entirely new wardrobe selected by Matt himself. Part of me just wanted to skip our dinner date with the guys and head right home so I could try everything on...again.

"So what do you like best, pup...of all the stuff we got today?"

"The necklace, Sir," I said without any hesitation.

"Good answer."

"And the haircut too, Sir." I pulled down the visor in front of me and looked at myself in the mirror. "I'm glad you got me contact lenses too. I don't want to look like such a geek any more."

"Well, I'm glad you like the contacts; that's cool w'me, but you don't look like a geek either way. I like you just the way you are, isn't that enough?"

"Oh yes, Sir," I agreed, "but I just want to look my best for you, that's all."

He glanced over to me, smiling, "When we get done with dinner, I'm gonna take you back to my house. You can spend the night. Probably have to stop over to your apartment though, so you can grab your books for tomorrow, and tell your sister."

"Okay! I'm so happy, Sir, cause I just don't want today to end. I don't want to leave you, not ever."

"How does your dick feel?"

I laughed at the question. "You want to touch it and see for yourself, Sir?"

"You know what I mean."

"It doesn't feel bad, Sir," I said seriously. "Doesn't hurt like before, just kind of itches." He reached into his pocket then and pulled out the tube of ointment.

"After we get over to Drew's, ask to use their bathroom. Take this with you and re-apply some of this ointment on yourself. All right?"

"Yes sir, thank you."

When we finally arrived at their apartment complex, I noticed right off that this was a much more upscale development than the apartments in which Kathie and I lived. These seemed to be closer to condos than apartments actually. I wondered how they afforded it, though, being that both Drew and Alex were currently attending college.

"I should have made a dessert or something to bring with us, shouldn't I?" I said, suddenly feeling ashamed.

"Nah, I don't think this is supposed to be that formal, pup. Just a group of buds chillin. If anything, we could have brought some beer, but it's no big deal. Don't worry so much."

I laughed, realizing that I was over-doing it again. "I'm nervous though. I never have talked to Alex before."

"Don't be nervous. I haven't even met either one of them, don't see me pissin myself over it, do ya?"

"No sir, but you're not like me Sir. You don't worry bout stuff like this."

"How do you know what I worry about, pup? Maybe I'm just better at hiding things than you. I think you just are far more open with your emotions than I am."

"So you are nervous too?"

"Didn't say that either. Just sayin that ya don't always have to express everything that ya feel, or I don't anyways. But you are you and I am me. We're both chill. Right?"

"Yes Sir," I smiled. "I wish I could blow you right now!"

He laughed. "You want me to have you blow me right here in the car?"

"Can I, Sir...please."

He laughed again. "Nope. Maybe later." He then reached for the door handle to let himself out. "Come on, pup, let's go."

Drew was the one who greeted us at the door. Immediately he extended his hand to Matt, introducing himself. "A pleasure to meet you, please come in." Alex stepped up behind Drew, smiling as he shook our hands. "Can I get you something to drink?" Offered Drew.

We both opted for a soft drink, and as ordered, I politely asked to use their restroom. Drew pointed me down the hall, and I went in, locking the door behind me. Wow, this bathroom was about the size of my bedroom, I thought. I walked over to the commode, pulled down my pants, and sat down, having to relieve myself. I was actually getting used to taking a piss this way, and even though I no longer had the chastity on, I was unclear as to whether or not this restriction was still in place. I decided I would still obey the order not to piss standing up until Matt specifically told me otherwise. When I finished, I liberally applied the ointment as Matt had instructed. It did feel so much better already. After zipping back up and washing my hands, I then returned to the kitchen area of the apartment to join the others.

Matt was already engaged in conversation with Alex. "So Drew teaches at the college? I thought he was a student."

"I did too," I interjected.

Drew smiled. "No, I just told you that I attended the college. Never said I was a student."

I laughed. "Wow, I don't even see you as being a professor. I...um...well, you seem too young for it."

"Just a job," he said nonchalantly. "Alex is a student, though. He's in the university program and will have his bachelors this year."

"Do you have a Master's Degree?" I asked.

Drew shook his head. "No, don't really need that to teach at community college. I teach political science. Boring, huh?"

I was totally amazed. Drew seemed so very young. We had hung out together, talked about boy bands and gone shopping just yesterday. He seemed like he was my own age. Never once had he mentioned that he already had a degree and was a college professor. Even now, he was downplaying his own accomplishments. It sort of made sense though now- the nice apartment and the new truck. Maybe Drew was just one of these people who would always be young at heart. I wondered how this reality—the fact that Drew was the bigger financial provider— affected the dynamic of his relationship with Alex. How was it possible for Alex to be his superior and his owner when he was so much younger and had accomplished so much less than Drew already had?

It soon became obvious to me, though, that Alex simply had that personality that made him dominant. He had a confidence about himself, not unlike Matt, where it seemed so natural for guys like Drew and me to defer to him. In his conversations with us, he often made references to Drew that identified him as his owned property. He was not being condescending at all, simply stating things in a matter-of-fact manner.

We had moved into the living room, and Matt was seated on the sofa. I initially moved to sit beside him, but instead elected to sit on the floor, next to his legs. This did not seem to surprise either Alex or Drew, even though there were plenty of other seating choices available. Alex sat comfortably in a recliner and Drew sat beside him on the arm of the chair.

"Yeah, I am doing my internship at a computer software company," Alex was saying. "It is likely to turn into a permanent position when I graduate."

"Then he will be making the big bucks," Drew interjected. He looked over at Alex and smiled. "And we can vacation every year in Bermuda or Southern Europe." Alex put his arm around Drew, playfully digging his fingers into the little guy's ribs. Drew jerked spasmodically, erupting with a child-like giggle.

I sat there on the floor, looking up at them. I could not help but smile, they seemed so perfect together. Alex was so breathtakingly handsome. The frame of his body was incredibly muscular, and perfectly toned. I wondered how many times he worked out. He was slightly bulkier than Matt, and far more dark- complected. I bet if he were shirtless, he'd display a big furry patch of hair on his chest, unless of course he waxed or shaved. Drew looked so small beside him, and everything about the couple seemed just so perfect. Drew obviously idolized this man, his owner.

I could not believe how well Alex and Matt actually hit it off. As we continued to converse, Drew and I became more and more quiet, offering nothing really to the conversation. We just listened quietly as the two of them spoke. They had begun discussing sports, speculating on the prospects of the Marlins for the upcoming season, and Drew and I became lost after the first few sentences.

Drew looked at me and moved his head slightly, indicating that I should come with him. "Want to help me with dinner, Petey?" I looked up at my owner, who nodded his approval, and then immediately stood up. "Let's go out on the balcony first, okay? I wanna have a cigarette."

After stepping through the sliding-glass door and closing it behind us, Drew said to me, "Oh my god! Your Matt is unbelievable! You are one lucky fag, you know?" I smiled broadly, very proud of the compliment.

"Do you like my haircut, Drew? Matt had me get it just like his."

"I noticed." He said, as he lit his cigarette.

"Guess who did it? Your friend Larry down at the mall."

"Really? I didn't think he worked Sundays. He must have liked you a lot in order to do your hair this soon. Usually he has a waiting list a mile long."

"Oh, well Matt had scheduled the appointment."

"Oh, that explains it. No way Larry would refuse someone like Matt."

"And look at this!" I said excitedly, "Matt got me this necklace. He said it is like a collar for me."

Drew held his cigarette between his lips and stepped over to me, examining the necklace. "Nice," he said. "See he is training you. He's gonna get you used to the necklace probably before he gets you a real collar. You must be so happy, huh?"

"Yeah! This has been the best day of my life. Plus he bought me all kinds of clothes and stuff. I totally feel like I don't deserve it though."

"Long as he thinks so, that's all that matters. Did you tell him about the chastity?"

I nodded. "Well...um, not exactly, but he knows. He wanted to check me this morning and then he saw."

"Bet he was majorly pissed, huh?"

"Yes, I should have listened to you."

He laughed. "Yup...but you gotta learn yourself. Just the way it is."

"How come you never told me you were not a student at the college?" I asked.

"Does it matter? No matter what I do with my life or where I choose to work, it is never gonna change the fact that I am sub. Plus until Alex gets his degree and is making more money than me, I don't want to ever put myself in a position where it may appear that I'm superior to him. Actually, we both know that no matter what, I'm not superior. I just am older. Still I think it's an ego thing. Me a teacher. Him a student. It's sort of role reversal."

"Was he ever in any of your classes?"

"Nope. Thank god. If he had been, then I never would have started seeing him in the first place. We actually did not even meet at the school."

"If you are a teacher, then why do you attend the Student Union meetings?"

"I do it to support Alex, since he is the president, silly."

"I just can't believe that you are a professor and I never knew. I thought I pretty much knew all the teachers at the college."

"I keep a low profile," he laughed. "Sub boys like me are good at that, don't you agree?"

"Yeah."

When we went back in, Drew immediately went into the bathroom and brushed his teeth. "Alex hates that I smoke. I'm surprised he has not ordered me to quit." I stood next to him, watching as he brushed. Then we went into the kitchen where Drew pulled out a marinating container from the fridge. "I already put the baked potatoes in the oven," he said. "Perfect timing. They only have about ten more minutes." He then flipped on the knob of the broiler. "How do you guys like your steaks?"

"I like mine medium," I said, "but I don't eat much red meat. I'm practically a vegetarian."

"Me too. I like other kinds of fresh meat, if you know what I mean."

I laughed. "Let me go ask Matt how he likes his, okay?"

"Sure."

When I returned from the living room, I told Drew that Matt wanted his medium-rare. "Just like Alex," Drew said. "You want to toss the salad?"

"Sure," I said, and opened the refrigerator to pull out the ingredients.

"Everything is in the crisper," Drew told me. "Here's a bowl." He reached into a cupboard above his head and took down a big salad bowl set, complete with matching tongs. "Do you like to cook?"

"I love it," I said. "Last week I made Matt a huge dinner for the first time. We had chicken parmesan. That was the night he finger-fucked me." I giggled.

"Sounds like you must be a good cook," Drew laughed. "Wonder if I make Alex a big meal, if he will reward me like that."

We laughed together. Then I became more serious. "Drew, how did you know about yourself? I mean, how did you figure out that you were sub?"

"Well...I had known for a long time that I was gay, ever since I was a teenager. In high school I used to just totally worship the jock-types. Sometimes I would get lucky and get to blow them, ya know. After doing that enough times, it just started to seem so natural. I started to understand that I was not ever gonna be happy unless I was serving a guy like that. You see what I'm saying?"

"Yeah, but I think it was so different with me, though. I never did anything with anyone before Matt. I was too shy. The first time that I ...um...sucked him...well, that was when I actually figured it out, that I was gay, I mean. It was weird. Was like he knew it before I did."

"Well, I'm sure that he did. Dom guys seem to know who is sub and who is not. It's sort of like a high-tech version of gaydar." He laughed.

"What is that?"

"You've never heard of gaydar?" he asked, incredulously.

"No," I admitted.

"It is when a gay guy can pick out who else is gay, without them even saying so. It is sort of a sixth-sense. Haven't you ever spotted some guy that you just knew was gay, but you could not put your finger on why you thought that?"

"Um, well, I never really thought of it. I never really even thought that I was gay, so I wasn't really worried about anyone else. Up until a month ago I was still hoping I'd find a girlfriend."

He busted up laughing then. "Hate to burst your bubble, dude, but I wouldn't hold my breath if I were you. I don't see that happening anytime soon. You're as sub as I am, and then some."

"Thanks a lot!" I said sarcastically. We then both laughed and continued with our dinner preparations.

At the dinner table, I sat quietly and ate while Matt and Alex were discussing the movie *Matrix*. I'd seen the movie and actually liked it, but not for the reasons that they did. I liked it because Keauna Reeves was in it. I thought the conversation was sort of funny because when Drew mentioned the movie Sweet Home Alabama, both Matt and Alex said in unison, "chick flick." Drew rolled his eyes and leaned over to me, whispering in my ear, "Any movie with a plot to it apparently is a 'chick flick'." I laughed.

Alex said, "What's that Drew?"

"Oh nothing sir, I was asking Petey to pass the salt." I reached quickly in front of me to grab the salt shaker and hand it to him.

I could only eat about half of my steak. I was wishing we had not had such a late lunch at the food court. I offered to wrap the remainder for Matt to take home to Petey2. Matt then shared with our hosts the story of how he had found the dog at the humane society the day after nicknaming me 'pup' because of my striking resemblance to the Little Rascals dog.

Alex looked over at me and said, "Thought maybe you were a pup cause you like to be on all fours." I blushed.

"He's my pup because he belongs to me, right Petey?" Matt said. I nodded and pulled my necklace from under my shirt collar.

"That your collar?" asked Alex.

"Yes sir, well...um...sorta. I don't have a real collar yet, just a necklace. Matt bought it for me today." I looked over at Matt, broadly smiling at him. "But it's just as good as a real collar to me. It means the same thing."

Drew had gone to the kitchen for the dessert and returned with a blueberry pie and a stack of plates. "I'm not the cook that you are Petey; I bought dessert from the bakery this morning." He handed me a roll of aluminum foil that he was carrying under his arm. I thanked him and tore

193

off a piece with which to wrap my piece of steak. I then cleared Matt's and Alex's plates from the table and took them to the kitchen. I returned and did the same with Drew's and my own.

After dessert, Drew and I rinsed the dishes and loaded them in the dishwasher. We then joined Matt and Alex on the balcony. I was shocked to see Matt smoking a cigar. He and Alex each had one. I wanted to tell him that I did not know he smoked, but opted to say nothing. Drew lit up a cigarette himself. Not wanting to be left out, I reached over to Drew and held my hand out, trying to act casual as I asked for a smoke. No sooner did I have the cigarette to my lips than I was suddenly taken aback as Matt reached over quickly and ripped it from my hand.

He handed the cigarette back to Drew and said firmly, "He doesn't smoke."

"Sorry sir," I said as I looked down at my feet.

"Drew shouldn't be smoking either, actually," said Alex. "Pretty soon he's gonna be quitting."

Drew put his arm around me gently and said quietly in my ear, "It's okay, you'd have just choked on it anyways." I felt the redness in my face.

We stayed at their apartment for about an hour after dinner, and I was very pleased that Matt and Alex had decided to hook up with one another later in the week. They agreed to meet on Tuesday to go to the gym together. I knew that as long as Matt and Alex were friends, then I'd have no restriction regarding my friendship with Drew. Before we left, Drew put his arm around me affectionately and hugged me tightly. "Thanks for coming, Petey." He then shook Matt's hand and thanked him as well. "I hope you will let Petey and me be friends, sir."

Matt smiled, "Actually, I think you are good for him"

"Thank you sir," Drew said. "And I was wondering something. Would it be okay for Petey to come with me to the 98° Concert on the 24th? If he wants to, I mean."

"Prob'ly...we'll see," Matt said.

When we got out to the car I was excited about how well our evening had gone and was just as excited about the fact that I was going to be spending the night at Matt's house. I could not wait to see Petey2 either. "Sir, are your parents home tonight?"

"No, they stayed at the cabin this weekend. We have the house to ourselves."

"Cool," I said.

He then drove me back to my apartment where I gathered my school supplies and left a note for Kathie. This truly had been a wonderful day so far. I did not know it yet, though, but the best was yet to come.

* * *

"Where's Petey at?" I asked as we walked through Matt's front door.

"Out back, in his kennel," Matt said as he kicked his shoes off. "Why don't ya go get him, pup."

"Okay! Should I give him the steak out there?"

"Nah, he has a food dish in the utility room off the kitchen. Give it to him there. Just go right down that hallway past the kitchen and you'll see the back door."

After setting down my backpack and shopping bags, I immediately complied with Matt's instructions. When Matt had told me that Petey was in a kennel, I envisioned a small crate, but what it actually was, though, was a rather spacious fenced in area in the back yard. It was probably 20x25 feet at least. He began jumping up against the fence as soon as he saw me, wagging his tail furiously. "Aw, were you lonely, pup? Huh? Come here little Petey. Good boy! I have a treat for you." As soon as I opened the kennel gate Petey was all over me, jumping up excitedly. I knelt down to pet him, allowing him to lick all over my face. I hugged him and laughed, and then picked him right up to carry him inside.

I gave the pup his treat when we got inside, having left it beside his food dish on my way out to get him. Immediately he snatched it up in his mouth and bolted for the carpeted living room. Matt appeared out of nowhere in the hallway doorframe. He was pointing his finger, "NO! You eat your dinner out here, on the linoleum." The pup stopped in his tracks, immediately hanging his head. I laughed at him giddily, for he was so cute, though it was not without empathy. I understood what it meant to be reprimanded and instructed by my owner.

"He is so cute when he hangs his head like that," I said. "He knows you're the boss." Matt stepped over to me.

"Just like my other pup," he said, wrapping his arms around me. I stared up at him, suddenly aware of how he towered over me. I loved this feeling of smallness when I was next to him. I loved feeling so overpowered by him, so dwarfed by his mere presence. I clung to him then, wrapping my arms around his torso so tightly. I never wanted to let go, and I never wanted this perfect day to end. I realized then that this was the first real intimacy we had had that day other than when he held me on my bed that morning. I inhaled his scent as I buried my face into his chest. His body was so hard as I pressed against it. I cocked my head back and stared up at him. He leaned down, bringing his lips down to meet my own. We kissed so gently then, and I simply melted into his embrace.

"Sir, you taste like smoke," I laughed, "but I don't care. You taste good no matter what."

"Yeah whatever. Deal with it." He had so much tenderness in his eyes as he spoke to me. I knew that even in his directness, his manner exuded such sincerity. He made me feel so valued. The way that he showered me with presents today, the way that he spoke for me when others addressed me, the way that he took for granted that the instructions he gave to me would be followed— these things all were beacons to me. They demonstrated what I meant to him. I was without question his property, but more than that, I was his valued property. I did not know if he ever would consider me to be his boyfriend, but that did not really matter so much, for that was merely a label. What I was feeling for Matt right then was something that was far more special to me than a typical gay boyfriend relationship.

It was such a wonderful combination of seemingly paradoxical realities. On the one hand I felt so much less than Matt. I was without question his subordinate. I took orders from him, deferred to his judgment, and constantly sought his approval. On the other, I felt so valued. I felt he helped make me a better person, or perhaps simply helped me to realize that I already was better than what I'd previously believed. He never degraded me or made me feel that I was inherently an inferior person. On the contrary, he was teaching me that I was loveable. He was helping me to see that I had potential to do things I did not think I was capable of doing. He was soon to expand upon this, and to guide me into taking on challenges that I'd have previously been too timid to even attempt.

At this very moment, though, the only challenge I faced was to adequately express to him even an inkling of the gratitude that I so strongly felt. Even as I clung to him, right there in that utility room, I felt the urge to slide down his body and assume my respectful position, kneeling at his feet. As I began to do just this, though, he held me in place. "Let's go upstairs," he said, "We have the whole house to ourselves."

He then scooped me up in his arms, like he had done only once before, and carried me all the way through the kitchen and living room, up the two-tiered staircase, and into his spacious bedroom. Petey scurried behind us, wagging his tail excitedly. Matt then lay me on his bed. I was on my back, staring into his face as he sat down beside me. "You're my pup," he said, and his words were so filled with sincerity and emotion that it actually choked me up. He did not need to say more; those three words said everything to me. I belonged to him, he valued me as his own, and most importantly, he loved me. He had said it earlier that day, and I believed him. I felt it in my heart.

"I love you so much, Matt" I said, not even aware I was using his first name. "I really do, with all my heart." Then he leaned and kissed me, this time with passion unlike anything I'd ever known. I felt him around me, inside me, on top of me. He was consuming me, connecting with me in a way that made me feel as if I were merely an extension of himself. As I responded to his kisses, my eyes moistened with teardrops. This was paradise, far too good to be true.

When he pulled himself back from me, I felt how aroused I'd become. I was a little alarmed, but as his hand gently groped me, feeling my hardness, I knew he expected nothing less. "Pup, I want you to go draw us a bath. I'm going downstairs to get your bags. Take off your clothes and wait for me in the bathroom...in the tub. There should be some bath beads or something under the sink."

I nodded. "Yes sir." He then kissed me again, gently, and left me.

Matt's bathtub was not the typical rectangular-shaped, normal-sized tub that I was used to seeing. It was a big garden tub that reminded me of a Jacuzzi. As the basin began to fill with water, I added some bath oil beads that I found under the sink, just as Matt had indicated, and I stripped off my shirt. I walked over to the large, full-length mirror and looked at my shirtless reflection, seeing myself now clearly for the first time since I'd gotten my new haircut and my necklace. The beads of the necklace seemed to sparkle, or was it merely my imagination? I was so happy that he somewhat changed my appearance. It felt as if he had marked me, given me a branding of sorts, that would identify me as *his*. A chill ran through my body as I stood there half naked, and I then proceeded to remove the remainder of my clothing.

I crawled into the soothing water of the tub. It was just the perfect temperature, and I lay back and rested my head against the edge of the tub, completely submersing my body in the warm water. I closed my eyes and waited, enjoying the luxury, and feeling totally relaxed. I stirred slightly as I heard Matt walk through the door. Opening my eyes, I looked up to take in his image. He was shirtless himself, and had on only his boxers. He peeled them off as I watched with pure awe. No matter how many times I saw him this way, I'd never be over that incredible feeling of astonishment. He was far too good to even be true.

I leaned forward and scooted up towards the center of the tub as he stepped in behind me. He lowered himself, snaking his legs around my much smaller body. He embraced me, pulling my back against his chest. I sank in, feeling cradled by him, and he hugged me tightly. Turning my head while leaning back into him, I was able to press my lips again against his. It was like snuggling; in fact it *was* snuggling. I did not think at that moment it was even possible to get too close to him. I wanted him so badly.

He grabbed a bar of soap and gently ran it across my chest, working it into a lather. He moved down further, slowly forming circular movements with hand, touching me so tenderly. I squirmed in his embrace as he made his way down to my abdomen, feeling extremely sensitive and ticklish. He playfully dug his fingers into my sides as I burst into a tiny fit of laughter. "Sir, it's tickling me!" I protested.

"Oh, really?" he said innocently, and then immediately repeated the same exact action, achieving identical results. I laughed right out loud and squirmed uncontrollably, though I made no real effort to free myself from him. The laughter subsided when he silenced me with his kisses once again. I felt his tongue sliding into my mouth as I parted my lips slightly. I had shifted to face him, and wrapped my arms around his shoulders, clinging to him. I felt his hands on my body, they moved so smoothly up and down my sides, across my buttocks.

He pulled his lips away from my own and buried his mouth into my neck, kissing me passionately. Again I reacted by wriggling my body and laughing. He'd found another ticklish spot. I relaxed myself though as he continued to kiss my neck and ran my fingers through his short hair. He leaned into me further then, moving his lips down onto my chest. He found my nipple and darted his tongue across it. It was very hard and extremely sensitive to his touch, and I held onto his head tightly, again trying to control my laughter.

It felt so wonderful, though, as he continued to hold onto my torso with both hands all the while using his tongue to stimulate my nipple. He then moved quickly to the other nipple, producing all of the same glorious sensations all over again.

His hands moved across my body then, gently caressing my chest, my abdomen, finally finding my groin. He slid his hand under my privates, cupping me so tenderly. I was so very hard then, aroused in a way I had not been in almost a week. "I'm glad I took it off you, pup," he whispered. "I like feeling my boy so hard. I like that *I* make you hard."

"You do Sir; it is only because of you."

"Just relax. Lean back and close your eyes." I obeyed. "I want to be inside of you pup. I want to make love to you."

My body trembled then, not of fear or nervousness though. I'm not even exactly sure what caused it, for I had no misgivings about submitting to Matt's desires. Truly at this point, his desires were my own. I too wanted him within me. I wanted all of him, and nothing less. As I lay there against him, my smaller body on top of his far more masculine frame, I felt his hardness against me. I felt his arousal, as his rock hard erection pressed against me. He was resting right against the hole that he'd previously only entered with his fingers. It both excited and intimidated me, but stirred within me a desire unlike any I'd ever experienced. "I want it sir. I want it so bad!" My voice was so shallow, so high-pitched at that point that it almost sounded whiney to me. This however did not seem to bother him, as he seemed to understand my excitement.

"Just relax," he said, as I lay there in his arms. He shifted me in his embrace so that I was cradled against his shoulder, lying beside him. His other hand was free, and he moved it up and down my hard cock so slowly, tracing it with just his fingertips. He pulled me up slightly with the arm that was around my shoulders, gently sliding one leg under my buttocks. It was such a smooth movement, so graceful and tender. He did this all the while continuing to touch me in my private region. I lay there, continuing to keep my eyes closed as I felt his finger move down below my penis, below my testicles, and into the region just between my rectum and ball sac. He pressed against me with a little more firmness. I'd never felt this sensation before, never been touched in this place. It made me throb. It was such an incredible feeling, as he continued to massage this area of myself that I had never even known existed.

His finger moved down further, and was pressing against the hole that he had entered only once before. He found it again and carefully pushed into me. It was so tight this time, and even though I was lying in a pool of warm water, it felt so dry as he tried to poke himself into me. He removed his hand slowly and apparently applied some sort of lubricant. It was the body wash that was on the ledge of the tub. He then submersed his hand back into the water and quickly found my hole, entering it smoothly before the lube could wash off his finger. I moaned as he plunged himself into me. There was nothing about the experience that was painful, and I remained rock hard. He instructed me look at him then, and I opened my eyes. He was staring down at me, both of his hands on my body. His left arm was around my shoulders and his right hand was inside me. He leaned in and kissed me.

I felt his tongue enter my mouth as his finger entered my other hole. I squirmed in his embrace, responding to his kisses. I pressed my hands against his hard smooth chest, as he buried his long finger inside of me. "Do you want more of me pup? Do you want more of me inside you?"

"Yes sir...oh god."

"Say it!" he prodded, "Say what you want."

"I want you , Sir. I want you inside of me. I want to make ... I want to...ughhh... I want to make love to you!"

He pulled me forward then and smoothly removed his leg from under me. He released me from his embrace, pulling his arm around the back of my shoulder, as I lay back again to lean against the ledge. Then I felt his finger slide out of me. He stood up very quickly, stepping out of the tub, and almost immediately resumed a crouching position beside me. His was crouched down next to the tub, all wet and dripping, as he scooped both of his strong arms under me, one under my knees and the other under my neck. He stood up, picking me up easily, and I grabbed a hold of him, wrapping my arms around his shoulders. He then carried me back into the bedroom and again placed me on the bed. We were both soaking wet, but it did not seem to be a concern of his at the moment.

He grabbed a towel that he had laid out on the bed. It was an enormous bath towel, almost the size of a blanket. He pulled me up against him and wrapped the towel around my body. Then he kissed me once more. I felt so warm against him, not shivering as I normally would have been right after exiting the bathwater. He placed me back down against the bed again, this time moving my body so that I was lying comfortably against the pillows. He then grabbed another smaller pillow and slid it under my behind. I thrust my hips upwards slightly as he positioned the pillow. Then he picked up a tube of some sort of gel that he'd already placed on the bed. It was apparently waiting there with the towel. He removed the cap and squeezed some onto his finger. He slid back into me, almost the same way as he had done in the tub. He was a bit more forceful though, driving himself into me all the way. I moaned once more, and felt myself throb uncontrollably.

I rolled my head to the side then and saw Petey, Matt's pup. He was lying on his doggie pillow, his very own little bed beside his Master's. He lay there staring at me, his head resting on his paws. I smiled down at him, wondering if he somehow understood that I too was his master's pup. I turned to meet Matt's gaze, then, staring directly into his eyes. "Sir, let me suck you...please. Let me taste you like I did before...oh please."

"You want that huh? You want my hard cock in your mouth? You wanna taste it, pup?"

"Oh god! Oh please!!"

He made no movement to remove his finger from inside of me, but instead shifted his body, pulling his legs up onto the bed. He stretched out beside me so that his groin was lying next to my head. I rolled over slightly as I reached for him, grabbing a hold of his hips. I opened my mouth to take him into myself. I was hungry for him. I wanted it so badly. He slid in so smoothly as I took the entirety of his cock into me, cranking my jaw open wide to accommodate him. He was in my throat. I sucked passionately, wanting to return to him all of the pleasure that he was giving me, while my nostrils pressed against his ball sac.

I continued to suck him as he kept his finger inside of me, pumping in and out with increasing speed. The pace was still not fast though, merely rhythmic. He then gently pulled out of me, once again squeezing the gel into his hand. I heard him as he lubed up both his fingers again. "Stay relaxed," he instructed, and then slid his finger back into me. He pulled out and then immediately drove himself back in. He did this about four or five times, twisting his finger slightly as he did so, making a circular motion of sorts. After repeating this movement several times, he then entered me with two of his fingers. I felt very little difference, he did it so smoothly.

He continued to very gently twist his fingers inside of me, telling me several times to stay relaxed. He instructed me to close my eyes then and to just enjoy the sensation. I did so, disbelieving how wonderful this actually felt. Then he pulled his cock out of my mouth and moved himself back between my legs. He kept his fingers inside of me, but was now pressing his body against mine. His lips were again pressed against my own. I kissed him back, wrapping my arms around his shoulders. I felt him pull his finger out of me.

I then opened my eyes and looked into his as he continued to lean over me. He backed off slightly and stared down at me. "Say it again, pup. Say what you want."

"I want you inside me Sir," I said it this time far more confidently. "I want all of you inside of me...please!"

He picked up the lubricant then for the third time and once more squeezed some into his hand. This time he squirted it into his palm and dropped the tube back onto the mattress. He then moved himself into a position where he was kneeling more upright, so that I could see the entirety of him. I could see his rock hard erection clearly as he wrapped his palm around it. He slid it slowly back and forth on his cock, which was already shiny from my spit. He began spreading the lube out evenly on his cock. I watched how it shined, slick with both his lube and my spit. His cock was huge, throbbing there in his hand as he seductively jacked himself.

Then he inched himself even closer to me, to where his knees were pressing right against my thighs. He removed his hand from his cock then, and slid each of his palms under my thighs. I planted my feet flat on the mattress as I bent my knees, pushing myself even closer to him. I thrust my hips slightly into the air to raise myself from the pillow, and he moved himself against me so that the tip of his cockhead was pressing against the hole which he had just lubed so liberally. He released my left leg, the one he was holding onto with his right hand, but I retained the position using my feet to balance myself. He then used his free hand to grab his cock once more, guiding himself into me. He held onto it firmly as he thrust his hips forward.

He was very slow and cautious as he poked just the head of his cock into me. I stared at him wide-eyed as he looked back at me. He did not remove his gaze from my face as he slowly pressed himself into me. But now, suddenly for the very first time, I felt a tremendous wave of pain in my rectum. It felt as if he were shoving a baseball bat inside of me. I grimaced from the pain and my body jerked reflexively. Immediately he backed out. "Ride out the pain, pup," he said soothingly. "Just ride it out and relax. It will pass in a few seconds." I closed my eyes tightly and did as he said, forcing myself to relax. He was right, the pain did subside. When it had, I opened my eyes again to see his smiling face. "You all right?"

"Yes sir."

He then re-entered me. This time there was far less pain. In fact, I don't think it felt like pain at all, much more like slight discomfort. He slid into me further than the first time. I pulled my legs back, bringing my knees up towards my body. He moved his hands so that they were both against the bed just behind my legs. He then used his arms to press against my thighs, forcing my hips up further off the mattress. This enabled him to slide into me a little deeper. I stared at his face. A look of pleasure swept over him as he experienced the tightness of my hole for the very first time. He was all the way in!

He closed his eyes briefly, enjoying the sensation, and then opened them again to look down at me. He moved his hands off the mattress and up my thighs. He followed my legs up until his palms were holding my ankles. He pushed against them, raising them into the air. He was holding them tightly when he pulled himself back out of me slightly. Then he plunged back into me again. He repeated this, three or four times, each time pulling out a little further than he had previously. He leaned into me, still pressing against my ankles. I felt the weight of his body on top of me and the heat of groin against my ass.

He ground himself into me then, over and over. He was not forceful to begin with, but as he progressed he did so with much greater intensity. He was thrusting his hips now. It was a sensation that was unlike anything I'd ever felt. There was no longer pain, as there had been upon entry; instead, there was a sort of stabbing sensation deep inside of me. It was similar to what I'd felt when he'd finger fucked me that first time, but it was so much more intense.

When he had first entered me and I'd felt that seemingly unbearable wave of pain, I'd gone quite soft. But now, as he leaned on top of me and thrust his cock deep inside me, I again throbbed. I throbbed so hard I thought I was going to lose control and shoot. I moaned so loudly. "Shoot it pup! Shoot your fuckin load for me! Show me how much you love having me inside you! Fuckin shoot it!"

"AAHHHH!" I cried, grabbing onto the bed sheets with both of my hands. "AAHHH!" then I blasted away. I fired my load so violently it was like a volcano, shooting up into the air, some of it splashing against my face and against the wall above my head.

I was trembling from the most intense orgasm of my life as Matt continued to thrust in and out of me. He held firmly to my ankles, pounding himself hard into me with his throbbing cock. And then as I looked into his eyes, I saw for the very first time that look of sheer ecstasy! I knew he was going to pump. Then he did, as he loudly moaned himself. He stopped thrusting, instead forcing and holding himself all the way inside of me. His body sort of convulsed as he drained himself. He was moaning as he did so.

"Fuck yeah!" he screamed. "Take it boy! Take my load."

As he released my ankles I wrapped my legs tightly around him. I did not want him to pull out of me. I did not want it to be over, not ever. He then leaned down and kissed me, as he was still buried deep inside.

12

I felt cold after it was over, my body shivering visibly. I just wanted to be close to him, to have him hold me, embrace me, wrap himself around me. He did exactly this, after having first used the big towel to wipe up my mess. Never in my lifetime had I experienced such serenity as I did just then at that moment while I was cradled within the protectiveness of his embrace. I felt small and vulnerable. I basked within the overpowering awareness of his strength. Nothing in the world existed just then, only he and I. This feeling consumed me, and it actually came to mind that I was more than just his property. I felt one with him; I felt like an extension of him.

Our voices were quiet as if we were somehow reverent of the beauty of this precious time together. "Thank you, Sir. Thank you so very much." My expression of gratitude was a very feeble attempt of conveying the magnitude of my emotion. "I truly do love you...I love you with my whole heart."

We lay there silently for such a long time until I became aware of the fact that my thoughts were drifting. I was thinking how I did not want this euphoria ever to end. I did not want this blissfulness to ever go away. How could I bear it if that happened?

"What are you thinking, pup?" he said without looking at me. He was lying on his back staring up towards the ceiling and I was cradled against his shoulder, my hand flat against his smooth chest.

"I'm thinking how scared I am, Sir."

"Scared? Of what, pup?" he asked.

"Of this ever going away...this feeling. I'm afraid eventually you will no longer want me, not the way that you do now."

"Pup," he said somewhat reprovingly, "why do you worry so much? Why can't you allow yourself to enjoy what you have right now at this minute, instead of freaking about what you might not have later?"

"Don't know, Sir," I said honestly, "Maybe it is just the way I am. My mom always said I was too much of a worrier."

"Your mom was right. Now I want to tell you something, something honest from my heart, and I want you to listen to me. You know that I do not say things to you that are not one thousand percent true, don't you pup?"

"Yes Sir," I said, awaiting the statement he was about to make.

"Never before have I wanted another person the way I wanted you today. Never, *ever* before. And never before have I made love to someone the way we just did together. Don't get me wrong, I'm not saying that I have not had hot sex before. I've had lots. In fact, probably I could honestly say I've had *hotter* sex. But what I mean is that this was the most special. This was...different. Do you understand, pup?"

"Yes, Sir, I do understand. I understand it with my heart, honest I do."

He squeezed me, pulling me tightly into himself. "So stop worrying. Enjoy it. Enjoy *us*. You better believe that I'm going to, so you need to do the same. Got it?"

"Yes, Sir, I've got it."

"Good."

After a few more moments of silence, I began speaking again. "Sir, what are you planning to do with your life? What about after school? Do you even have your major selected yet?"

"Oh yeah, sure," he responded. "Do you know what 'Fitness Unlimited' is?" he asked.

"Yeah, that gym down on Coolidge Avenue, right?"

"Yup, that's one of 'em. There are actually four stores here, plus another thirty-one stores statewide. My dad owns them."

"He does?" I asked. That explained the money that they had, I thought.

"Yeah, and I probably will eventually take over the business."

"Do you ever work there now, Sir?"

"Not officially," he said, "I mean I'm not on the payroll or anything. I do spend a lot of time there though, especially the one over on Spruce and Jennings Streets. That's where I work out."

"So do you go in there and boss the employees around?" I asked. I looked up at him and smiled as I said this.

"Who me?" he laughed. "No, seriously, I'm not like that. If I notice something wrong, I'll tell 'em, and they end up fixin it, but I'm not bossy with them. Not yet." He again laughed in spite of himself.

"So why are you even going to college then, Sir? Why don't you just work at one of the gyms?"

"Well, 'cause I want an education, for one thing. And plus, my dad is not ready to sign everything over to me. That probably won't happen until he retires. He is sixty-one right now, though. I'm the baby of the family."

I laughed at him. "You are the baby, just like me. I'm the youngest too. How many brothers and sisters do you have?"

"Two sisters," he said. "One lives in L.A. and the other in Phoenix. The one in Phoenix is married to a bigshot lawyer. She has no interest in the business whatsoever. Her name is Karen. The other one—the one in L.A.— she's a dyke."

"Your sister is gay?" I was surprised.

"Yup. Don't really know her that well. She's the oldest, and we really didn't grow up together. Her name's Amanda."

"Did your parents freak when they found out she was like that...gay, I mean?"

I felt him shrug his shoulders, as I continued to lie against him. "I don't know, so what if they did? It's her life. I don't think they freaked, though. What's there to freak about?"

"Well...um...some people just do. I mean, it's like parents get this idea in their heads about who their kids are, and when they find out differently, it's like they don't really even know them any more. It makes me wonder what my own mom and dad would say...if they knew about me."

"And you don't think that they might have had an idea of it? I mean, I think parents usually know their kids pretty well. They just don't like it when things are different than what they want them to be... so they pretend that they're not."

"I think my mom would have known, or I mean I think that she did know. She knew I was different from other boys. I just hope it did not make her..."

"What?"

"I hope she was not sad about it, that's all. I don't want to think that she might have been disappointed in me."

"Pup, you are one of the best kids any parent could ever want. There's nothing about you that would have ever made either your mom or your dad sad. Trust me. If you only knew the shit that my parents put up with raising me." He laughed.

"What do you mean? You seem like the perfect son to me. Jock. Smart. Handsome. Polite...most of the time." This time I laughed.

"Yeah, but guess I have always been kinda spoiled. It's all right though. I deserve it."

"Yes you do!" I said, leaning over to kiss his chest. "You deserve everything you have, everything you want. You deserve everything."

"Just so we have that straight." He gently ran his hand down my back, squeezing my butt playfully.

"Sir?" I asked.

"Yeah?"

"Remember how you said to me that sometime you'd let me come and watch you work out? When you gonna do that?"

"You mean here, or at the gym?" he responded. "Sometimes I just work out here in my room."

"Wherever you want, sir. I'd like to see you in the gym though, really. Pumping your big biceps in front of the mirror." I giggled as I visualized it. "I'll just sit there, watching you. My hero."

"Your hero, huh? Why do you say that?"

"Cause it's what you are, sir. I can't believe you don't know that."

"Maybe I just wanted to hear you say it."

"Well, I'm saying it, Sir. You are totally my hero. You saved me from getting beat up...even worse than I did, I mean. And you keep saving me every single day. I don't ever want to disappoint you. Not ever."

"Then don't let yourself get hurt, like you did this week, and not even bother to tell me. I still have a notion to spank your ass for that one."

"I'm sorry, Sir. I didn't mean it. I'm so sorry."

He hugged me tightly. "Just remember who you belong to. You're my property, and I don't want the things that I own to be neglected or abused. You got it?"

"Yes Sir, I've got it." I then lay my head restfully against his chest and just listened to the beating of his heart. The feeling was remarkably surreal. How could this possibly be real? How could I be here in the arms of this man? I concentrated on the words he'd said to me. *Enjoy the things that you have now instead of worrying about what you might not have later.*

* * *

When I woke up the following morning, that surreal, euphoric feeling had vanished. Instead all that I felt was an intense desire to pull the pillow over my head and sleep a couple more hours. In addition to that grogginess I also had an acute awareness that my butt would never be the same as it had been just a few hours previously. Oh my god, it hurt! How could it feel like this, after Matt had been so careful with me, using all of that lube and being so slow and gentle with me?

Then as I lay there in the bed, with my eyes still closed, I smiled to myself. It wasn't so bad. It would be like a reminder to me of how we'd made love. Every time I became aware of the soreness, I'd think of him. Plus, I probably would not have hurt like this if he were not so damn huge! I wouldn't trade that for anything though. It was a small price to pay.

I rolled over and discovered that Matt was still beside me. It had not been merely a wonderful dream. He actually *had* made love to me, and I actually had slept beside him in his bed. And now here we were together still. *Don't let the day start just yet. Oh please...let us just be together for a little while longer.*

I craned my neck over the side of the bed and squinted to see the clock on the stand next to me. It was after seven, and I knew the alarm would be ringing in a few minutes. As I lie there I thought about how Matt had told me that he hardly ever ate breakfast. It was a shame, for I'd have loved to get up and serve him breakfast in bed. Finally I pushed back the linens on the bed and rolled out. My clothes from the night before were still in the bathroom on the floor, and I was somewhat self conscious as I darted across the room naked. It was strange that I'd be that way, for the only person who was even in the room to see me was Matt, and he was sound asleep. Plus he'd already seen me naked several times.

As I stood there in the bathroom relieving myself, I suddenly realized that this was the very first time in a week

213

that I'd done so standing rather than sitting on the commode. I then became a little bit concerned, thinking that maybe I was disobeying him. He'd said I had all of the same restrictions. Then on the other hand, he had lifted the restriction of getting hard. He told me he liked that his pup got hard. He had even allowed me to cum. I also thought about how he'd allowed me to kneel at his feet when he had relieved himself that day, the day that I started to freak. I was terrified that he was going to force me to drink his piss. It seemed silly to me now. If he were to want me to do it now, I don't think I'd be so scared. I don't think I'd be really that scared of anything he did at this point. There was no one on earth I trusted more than him.

I wondered what it would be like actually, what it would taste like. What if it made me sick? What if it were so incredibly repulsive to me that I vomited? But how could that be the case? I already had tasted his cum many times. I already had had his cock in my mouth and my throat, and nothing about it was repulsive. In fact, it really tasted rather good to me. How could his piss be worse? It came from him after all. But then again, it was waste, wasn't it? It was not meant to be consumed, but instead to be gotten rid of. In spite of these worries, I still allowed myself to think about that feeling I'd had kneeling at his feet. I'd knelt there right in this very spot I was now standing and watched him. What could be more subservient? What could show him any more how much I worshipped him than to kneel before him while he relieved himself?

Were I to actually have tasted it that day, what would have happened? I doubt I'd have gotten sick. I don't think that his piss would have made me feel that way at all. In fact, as I stood there relieving myself I felt my own flaccid cock start to swell a little. The thought of it was slightly arousing me. I watched the stream of my own piss as it splashed against the water in the toilet. Holding myself with my right hand, very carefully I moved my index finger towards the stream. I then quickly shoved it into the line of fire, just for a brief second, soaking it with my piss. I held it out in front of me, looking at the droplet of piss as I finished draining myself. Then I moved it towards my face, opening my mouth. I slid my finger in past my lips and onto my tongue, tasting my own piss for the first time. There really was no taste to it at all. I reached back down and ran my finger across the underside of my dick, catching another droplet and pulling it back to my mouth.

"What are you doing?" Matt said, standing in the bathroom doorway. Quickly I bent over, reaching for my boxers that were on the bathroom floor.

"Nothing sir...um...I'm sorry. I forgot to sit down this time. I'm so sorry!"

"I didn't mean that. What were you doing with your finger in your mouth?" I felt my face getting red, as I stepped into my shorts. I did not want to look up for fear of making eye contact. "Tasting your piss, huh? Why were you doing that?"

"I dunno, sir," I lied.

"Yes you do. Tell me. Why were you tasting your piss, boy?"

I was starting to shake a little bit, trembling in spite of the fact that only seconds before I'd told myself how much I trusted this man. "I was...um..."

"You were what?"

"I was thinking of you, Sir, of that one time...when you were p—"

"You were thinking of me standing here pissing when you knelt beside me, weren't you?"

I nodded. "Yes, Sir," I confessed.

"And...?" he prodded.

"And...um...I was thinking...wondering what it was like, I mean to taste it. Remember? I was afraid. I was scared you were going to make me do it...to taste it, I mean."

"Yeah, I remember. Get on your knees." Immediately I obeyed him. He stepped over to me, standing in front of the commode. "Some day you will beg for it. Some day you'll be on your knees begging to take my piss." He then grabbed his cock, aimed it, and began pissing into the toilet. As I knelt there staring at the stream I moved my hand closer, finally bringing my fingers into contact with his piss, allowing it to drench them, and then pulling my hand away slightly. I continued to stare at him until he was finished.

"Look at me," he ordered, and I stared up at him. He seemed to tower over me as he looked down into my eyes. "Taste it. Taste my piss." I then stuck each of my fingers into my mouth, one at a time, licking them off, all the while staring up at the man who owned me. "Lick my cock...clean it off, boy!" Obediently I wrapped my lips around his flaccid cock, tasting the droplet of piss that was dripping from his slit. I sucked on it a little, looking up at him, and then I felt him squirt into my mouth. It was just two quick little squirts, the remainder of piss that was in his shaft. Without even thinking, I gulped it down. He was so right: I too knew I'd soon be begging for this.

I did not pull away from him when he had finished draining himself. Instead I kept the entirety of his cock in my mouth, sucking it passionately. I felt it start to swell in my mouth, and then his hands were on my head. As he got harder, I stretched my jaw to accommodate him. His cock grew to full size in my mouth and then eventually my throat. Keeping himself buried, he then shifted his position for his own comfort so that he was standing with his legs apart and feet flat on the ground. I knelt there between them. Then he started to thrust. He had done this before, yes, but never with such fierceness. Never before had he rammed me the way he did this morning. At a certain point I did not feel as if I even existed to him. I was simply a hole for him to fuck. I knew that he must be staring at himself in the mirror as he fucked my throat mercilessly. A few times I had to struggle, suppressing a violent gag, but I truly was at this point starting to control this reflex. He must have been aware of this, for from that day on he never again was gentle with me when it came to oral servicing. I wondered then, with his cock shoved down my throat, if he was proud of me for submitting to his training. I wondered if he was pleased by the fact that he had taken me from the stage of being virgin to cock sucking and had turned me into a pro. The way he drilled me then, gave me little doubt that this indeed was true.

Finally I sensed that the moment of anticipation had arrived, as he gripped my head tightly and thrust deep into my throat, holding me firmly in place. Then he drained himself, this time of his cumload. I gulped madly, eagerly swallowing his seed, and savoring the taste as some backed up onto my tongue. Then it was over.

"Go make me breakfast," he ordered. "I'm hungry this morning for some reason."

"Yes, Sir!" I gasped, still out of breath, and headed down to the kitchen.

13

"Drew, guess what happened?!" I was speaking to him on my cell phone, standing outside of the bookstore.

"What, Petey?" he asked, laughing at my excitement.

"He did it last night! I mean, Matt did. He um...he made love to me." I lowered my voice, looking around me to make sure no one was within ear shot.

"He did? So you're not a virgin any more," he laughed into the phone. "How was it?"

"Oh my god! It was the most incredible thing I've ever experienced. He was so...so absolutely wonderful. We took a bath together and then he literally carried me into the bedroom. Can you believe it?"

"He sounds sort of like Alex. Did he put a pillow under your ass?"

"Yeah, how did you know?"

"Oh, it makes it a little easier, especially for the first time. Did you bleed?"

"No, I don't think so. But oh my god, my butt hurts today."

He busted up laughing then. "You'll get used to it, don't worry. After awhile you'll actually look forward to that feeling."

"Oh don't get me wrong," I responded, "I'm not complaining. It was so beautiful, the way he kissed me so much. Then afterwards we cuddled together."

"Awww! That's sweet. He sounds like such a romantic."

"Well not this morning though."

"Oh? Did he fuck you again?"

"No...but...well, I will tell you about it later." I felt myself blushing.

"Tell me now, dammit!" he demanded.

This time I laughed. "Well, um, have you ever...um..."

"What?"

"Have you ever tasted Alex's...um...urine?"

"He made you drink his piss?!"

I began pacing back and forth in front of the store. "Just a little, and then he face fucked me. It was so hot."

"Wow, that *is* hot! So when are you gonna do it again?"

"I don't even know when I'll see him again. He didn't say, but I can't wait. I just wanna be with him all the time. I never want to be away from him. Not ever."

"You're so in love. Isn't it cool?"

"Yeah. Hey, I am gonna be late for work. What are you doing later?" I asked.

"Nothing. Wanna come over?"

"Yeah, if you want. Or maybe we can go to a movie or something."

"Sure, but I have to check with Alex though. Should be all right though, 'cause he has a class tonight."

"Cool. I'll call you after work."

"Kay...peace out." He then hung up.

That entire day I was totally on cloud nine. During the first part of the day, when I was in class, I'd find myself drifting off into daydreams, thinking of Matt and of our incredible night together. Then later at work, I thought of him even more. I wanted to run into the bathroom a couple of times to beat off, but then I realized that it would not be a good idea. How embarrassing would that be to have someone find out, and plus I was still on a no-cum restriction. Even that, though, was not upsetting to me. It actually made me feel so good to know that he controlled me that much. He even decided if and when I had an orgasm; that was total ownership!

Matt made no further mention of the chastity device, and so I did not bring it up. My penis was still quite sore and even scabbed. When he had stroked me the night before it felt wonderful, but afterwards it sort of burned. So had I not been so overjoyed by the memories of what Matt and I had done together, I may have been quite miserable. My ass hurt like never before, and my dick was sore as hell. It was a small price to pay, though, for he was the whole world to me. Nothing but Matt Porter mattered to me at that moment.

When I got out of work, I called Drew, and we decided that we would meet at my apartment. He had never been there, and I wanted to show him all of the clothes that Matt had bought me. I gave Drew the directions and told him to meet me there in an hour. I then headed out on my bike, stopping first at the grocery store on the way home. I would get some stuff to cook for us, and we could have dinner together and then just chill. Drew had said he'd bring over a video with him and we would just hang out at home instead of going out to the theatre. I thought that was a great idea, 'cause I was a little bit tired and wanted to just relax. When I did get back to my apartment I found a note from Kathie on the kitchen table. She was going to be staying overnight at Carter's.

I was in the kitchen slicing potatoes when I heard Drew at the door. "Come on in Drew!" I called to him. "Door's open."

He peeked his head inside the door, "Hello?"

"I'm in the kitchen," I said, suddenly realizing he'd never been here. I put down my knife and ran out into the living room. He smiled at me and walked over, placing a bag on the table along the way. I returned his smile with one of my own, and he reached out and hugged me.

"Oh my god," he said, "you just are absolutely glowing." I busted up laughing.

"That sounds so stupid, you know," I countered. "Come out in the kitchen with me. I'm making cheese fries. I think we should just load up tonight on incredibly fattening junk food. Wanna?"

"Uh, here," he said, holding out his wrist to me. "Twist my arm." I laughed.

"So what did Alex think of Matt and me?" I asked.

"Oh he likes you guys. Well, you already know he thinks you're cute." I blushed. "But he likes Matt too. I'm so glad, 'cause if they had not liked each other, then maybe we couldn't be friends."

"Me too! That would have sucked."

"Have you ever tried this one caramel dip? It is so good, and fat free. We can have apple slices and caramel...yum."

"Cool. I should have brought over some junk food with me."

"Nah, I have plenty. Did you bring a movie?"

"Yeah, I brought *Matrix* and *Steel Magnolias*," he answered.

"Oh god, I love *Steel Magnolias*. That's one of my favorite movies. We should put on pajamas and sit in front of the T.V. with our junk food." I laughed as I said it.

Drew laughed himself. "Well, I don't usually wear pajamas."

I shrugged. "Have you tried these 'Wow' potato chips? They are really good, and totally fat free too. Cept some people get the runs from it," I giggled. "It's so cool. You can eat all these really good foods now and not worry about the fat grams."

"Why do you even worry about fat grams anyways?" questioned Drew. He was leaning against the counter, resting his chin in the palm of his hands. "You're so damned skinny to begin with. Plus, you said we were gonna be loading up on fattening food."

"I am definitely not skinny! But besides, everyone knows people who were slim when they were young, but then like ten years out of high school they suddenly get a big ole pot belly and go bald. I don't want that to be me! And plus I don't wanna be a fat slob for Matt...I want to be little and cute."

"Well you have a ways to go before you have to start worrying about that stuff. You just graduated high school last year. I'm the one who should be worried. I'm almost thirty!"

"Whoopty-doo," I said flippantly. "You don't even look older than me. You don't act it either. Um, I mean you're mature and everything. I don't mean it as a put-down. I just mean you are so young looking. I can't even believe you're a college professor."

He smiled at me. "Thanks, but actually the only reason I'm a college 'professor' is because I'm teaching at a community college. After Alex gets his computer science degree, though, I'm going back for my Masters. Then I will be able to teach in a real university."

"What's it like?" I asked, "being the one in charge all day long at work, and then coming home to where it is just the opposite?"

"That's weird that you'd ask that," he said, "'cause I was thinking about that just today. It's kind of strange, actually. It's like I'm two different people. Once I walk through the doors of that school each morning, I take on all of this confidence and I'm not really intimidated by anyone. But then when I walk out at three in the afternoon, I am back to my normal self, totally sub. Isn't that wild?"

"Yeah," I admitted. "Do you like your job?"

"I love it," he said as he dipped an apple slice into the caramel. "Teaching is what I have always wanted to do. I used to tutor kids in high school, mostly dumb jocks." We both laughed.

"Did you get lucky with any of em?" I asked.

"A few times, yeah. There was this one guy named Chris. He was a football player. Dumber than a rock. I tutored him in algebra for an entire semester. After about the third session he let me start blowing him. After that, I sucked him off at every single session. He was so hot."

I busted up laughing. "How'd you get him to let you do it? I mean, that first time."

"Hmm, I don't really know, I guess. It just happened sorta. I think that those kinds of guys can sense when another guy is sub, most of the times anyways. I think the way I acted all nervous around him at first, it made him aware that he was superior to me."

"But he wasn't really superior, though. Was he? I mean, you were the one who was the brain. You were tutoring him."

"Yeah, but you have to admit, from the perspective of a high schooler, knowing how to solve algebraic equations is far less desirable a talent than being a star quarterback. He was so popular. Good looking too. Man, he just made me almost piss myself whenever I was around him."

I laughed at his description. I was pouring grease into the deep fryer, almost ready to start making the fries. "Can you believe I'm so worried about fat free food and I'm *frying* potatoes? I'm such a moron sometimes."

"Well that is the only fattening thing you have here. I can't believe you call this stuff junk food!" He shoved a chip into his mouth.

"I'm glad that Matt isn't like that. Dumb, I mean. He is so super smart, and he's a jock too. It is like he is the perfect guy."

"Yeah, I can't argue with that. He seems pretty awesome. So what do you think of Alex?"

I looked down at the counter and then looked up at him quickly. "He's hot...but don't tell him I said so."

This time Drew busted up laughing really hard. "Why would you care if I said so? He already knows he's hot looking."

"'Cause I don't want him to know, that's all. Well, besides, what if he tells Matt? I don't want Matt to think that I'm checking out some other guy."

"Well, I'm sure Matt is aware that Alex is hot. He has eyes. I don't think that Alex is a threat at all to Matt though, or vice versa. They both are pretty confident in themselves."

"Yeah, that's true. I just get so paranoid though sometimes. I'm so scared that I will disappoint him. I'm afraid it is going to all end some day, without any warning. I told Matt that last night and he said I should stop worrying about what I might eventually lose and start enjoying what I have right now."

"Good advice," Drew said, "Damn these cheese thingies are good."

"I know. I love those things. So when did you first know that you were gay? Was it when you started messin with these jocks in high school?"

"Well, it's kind of odd, really. I sucked off four different guys while I was still in school. Never did anything else with em, just blowjobs. All the while I did not have a clue that I was gay, though. I guess I just thought it was a phase or something. Finally when I got into college, it sort of dawned on me."

"Did you date girls?"

"Nope. I was just one of those types who did not date. Maybe I was shy or something. But actually, I wasn't all that shy. You seem a lot more reserved than I ever was. I had plenty of friends, male and female. Not the class president or anything, but I did all right." As I looked over at him, he had this pensive look on his face, as if he were ruminating over his high school memories.

"Did I tell you how Matt and I met? I mean, how we officially met. I had known of him for a long time before, but we never were friends or anything. One day towards the beginning of this semester I got off the bus at the college and these two guys jumped me. They started teasing me and stuff. Bullying me, you know. And then they started to beat me up."

"Oh my god! Did you report it?"

"Not to the school. We reported it to the police, though. They got into a lot of trouble. Matt was the one who saved me. He stepped in and kicked their asses."

"Wow! He took them both on?"

I grinned at him. "Yeah. Well, he didn't even have to do anything to the one. Soon as he punched the first guy, the other one took off."

"I wish you had reported it to the school. That is a hate crime. Did they call you a fag and stuff?"

"Yeah, all kinds of stuff like that. They actually started to pick on me when we were on the bus. Both of them are in high school still, but they go to a vocational tech class or some shit. I don't think they are in the program anymore, 'cause I never see them. I have a restraining order against them."

"That's good. What an amazing story. So was it like love at first sight... you fell head over heels for your hero?"

I laughed. "Not exactly. I was really crazy about him, for sure. I did not really understand what I even was feeling, 'cause I knew Matt had a girlfriend and stuff. I did not even really think of myself as being gay then. Sometimes I don't really think of it that way even now. I am just me, I guess. It wasn't until there was that one rally at the school— after the vandalism— that I really thought about it.

"It was like two months that went by before I even saw Matt again. I ran into him about a month after Christmas. He was walking his new puppy over here, near my apartment. When I first saw him I was so excited, 'cause his dog was so adorable. Guess what he named it?"

"Petey... you told me last night at dinner," Drew smiled at me. "Now I understand why he thought you looked like the dog from Little Rascals. You must've had a black eye. That's cool he named his puppy after you."

"And you know what else is cool? Now I'm his other pup. Now he has two Petey pups."

We both laughed. I flipped the button on the deep fryer to release the basket. The potato slices were turning a nice golden brown. "Do you like your fries crispy or soft?" I asked.

"Soft," he said.

"Cool, me too. These are done then. Do you want to take some of this food into the living room and I will finish getting these fries ready. You do like cheese fries, don't you?"

"Is the Pope Catholic?" he answered.

"You're a bonehead sometimes, Drew. A cute bonehead, though."

"Aw...I'm not sure if that was a compliment or not."

"I should show you the chastity device that I had to wear. Matt left it here in my bedroom. Do you wanna see it?"

"Sure."

"Okay, pour this cheese sauce over these fries. I will get it. Then we can move everything to the living room together." I darted into the bedroom and pulled out the drawer beside my bed, snatching up the chastity. I could not believe how small it was. It sure felt bigger when it was on me. "Here it is," I said when I'd returned to the kitchen.

"Oh yeah. The CB2000. Never saw one before, only pictures. Alex had me in a different kind for awhile. Mine was a lot less friendly than this little thing."

"Really? How long did you have to wear it?"

"Few weeks at a time. He makes me wear it still sometimes, when he is training me for stuff. He doesn't like it when I get to the point where I'm starting to focus on my own pleasure. I totally understand, though. It is so easy to do that, ya know. He is so hot that it turns me on, and then I get all excited and aroused. Next thing I know I'm thinking about getting off myself instead of concentrating on only his pleasure. Not my job, though, to worry about my pleasure. Only he decides if and when I get any at all. My only true pleasure should be to please him."

"I know what you mean. I only want to please Matt. I want that more than anything. But then you know what he told me yesterday? He said he likes seeing me hard. Can you believe that?"

"Sure. A pup should be hard when he serves his owner. Shows you are turned on by him. Still that doesn't mean you are there to satisfy yourself. You always have to remember that you are there to serve him. He is the one who decides if you get any pleasure of your own."

"I know. Still it made me feel so good. I kind of like the fact that I don't always get to cum. Then when he does let me, it is even better."

"You do understand that when he lets you cum, he does it mainly for himself, right? He does it cause he likes seeing you get off. You still are serving him when that happens, not vice-versa."

"Yeah, I know that. I can tell he likes it. I can tell by what he says to me. He tells me to shoot for him. He tells me exactly when to do it."

"Can you? I mean, can you do it exactly when says to, or does it take you awhile?"

"I am right on the edge of shooting when he says it, so all I have to do is let go," I said, no longer embarrassed at all by sharing these intimacies with my new best friend.

"Eventually you'll be able to do it even when you are not on the edge. You will be able to cum on demand."

"How will I learn that?" I asked, astonished by the mere possibility.

"He will teach you, don't worry. And with him being friends with Alex, he will probably come up with some stuff that's gonna blow your mind. Just remember to trust him."

"I do, Drew. I do trust him, with my whole heart."

He smiled at me. "I know you do. I can see it in your eyes, all the time."

We carried the food in the living room and placed it on the coffee table, then sat down Indian style on the floor. As we pigged out that evening watching our movies and then later sorted through my whole new wardrobe , I grew more and more comfortable with Drew. It was like he was my best friend on earth. Never before had I had such a confidant, someone with whom I could confide so many things. I hoped that Matt would understand how important this friendship with Drew was becoming to me. I hoped that he would not ever feel that what I had with Drew ever infringed upon my devotion to him. On the contrary, Drew seemed to help me serve Matt better. He was the one single person who understood everything.

* * *

Later that evening, after Drew had left, I sat down at my computer to check email. Of course, the very first thing that I looked for was a message from Matt. There was none. I sighed, somewhat disappointed, and then got up and walked over to my bed. I sat down and picked up my cell phone, checking it carefully to make sure there were no unanswered calls displayed. There was not. I was not going to worry, though; I'd just spent the absolute best day of my life with Matt the day before, and we had even made love. He would call me when he was ready.

Maybe he would call tonight! Maybe he'd call and wake me in the middle of the night like he did that one time. That would be so awesome. I went back to my computer, debating whether or not I should email him. I sat down and pulled up a blank email, typing in his address in the recipient box.

"Dear Matt," I typed. Then I looked at it and backspaced immediately, deleting the salutation.

Sir,

I have missed you so badly today. I know it was just this morning that I saw you, but it seems an eternity ago. All that I can even think of is you and what you did to me last night. It was the most beautiful experience of my life, and no matter what ever happens to me, I will always remember and cherish it above everything else.

How did I find you, Sir? How did I get so incredibly lucky? You are so absolutely perfect to me. I mean, I know that you are not actually perfect, but to me you are. To me you are the whole world.

Sometimes I feel things for you that are so very intense that it actually scares me. I never thought it was possible for me to love anyone the way that I love you. I never thought that anyone would love me, either. But you told me that you did. You told me yesterday that you loved me. I just wanted to pinch myself right then, to make sure that I was actually awake and not dreaming this awesome dream. I was awake though, and I even have the sore butt to prove it...lol.

Tonight Drew came over and we ate so much junk food. In fact, I'm still stuffed from it. I showed him all the things that you bought me, and he was totally amazed. Know what he said to me, though? He said that now whenever you see me in these clothes it will remind me how totally you own me. It will show everyone else too...it will show that I'm your property. He said that was especially true of the necklace.

I'm sitting here waiting, hoping you will either sign online or else call me. I know I have no right to ask it of you. I know that everything is on your time table and it is up to me to be a good pup and wait for you. Sometimes it's so hard though, Sir. Sometimes I just think I cannot wait one more second to see you.

Well, I think I will sign off now...I have a little bit of homework to do. I will continue to wait for you, and plus I'll keep my phone on beside the bed. Even if you call me in the middle of the night again, I won't even care. In fact, I will get on my knees and thank you for it. I promise I will Sir. Then I will beg to serve you, just like I did this morning, and I will take whatever you decide to give me, no matter what. I'll never be afraid of what you want from me...not ever again...I promise. I will always obey you. Always.

I love you with my entire heart.

Your puppy

Petey

I read over the letter after I'd finished, checking to see how it sounded. I was a little trepidatious, debating for a few seconds on whether or not I should delete it and start over, or perhaps to simply send him no email at all. Then finally, out of pure impulse, I clicked "send" and immediately logged off.

I then crawled into bed and pulled my backpack over beside me. I should read over my English Comp worksheet, because I was pretty sure there'd be a quiz the next morning. I tried to focus my attention as I pulled out the workbook. It was no good though, for I kept thinking about Matt. I wondered where he was right then. What was he doing? Who was he with? I wondered if he would call me. I hoped so badly that he would. Maybe if I concentrated on it hard enough I could will him to call. It would be like a telepathic message.

I lay there for a few moments, closing my eyes tightly and concentrating. *Please call, Matt. Please! Please!* This strategy did not seem to work, though, and after a couple of minutes I gave up, realizing it was stupid. I also realized how aroused I was. I was totally rock hard. I thought about how he had made love to me. I thought about how he had made me cum when he was still inside of me. I thought about that next morning, when I knelt before him in the bathroom, taking his entire cock down my throat. I closed my eyes, envisioning him, remembering how he had looked as he towered over me. I thought of how small I was compared to him, how much stronger he was, and how his mere presence dominated me.

Oh God! I want to be with him so bad! I was nearly in tears as I lay there, fantasizing about my hero. I couldn't take it any more! I have to talk to him! I have to!!

I reached over to my bedside stand and snatched up my phone, not even thinking. I did not even give it any consideration that it was almost midnight, nor did I think about the fact that Matt had specifically told me to never ever call him unless it was an emergency. I quickly pulled up my phone book on the digital display and selected his number, initiating the call. My heart was pounding so fast by the second ring that I thought I would stroke out right there.

"Sup? Where are you?" It was Matt's voice on the line.

"I'm at home, Sir...in my bed."

"What's wrong?" he repeated. "Why are you calling me?"

I heard another voice behind him, a female voice, "Who is it?" the voice said. It had to be Tracy. I could recognize that bitch's whiny tone anywhere.

"Is that Tracy , Sir? Are you with *her*?"

"Why are your calling me?!" Matt demanded, obviously getting pissed. "Is this an emergency?"

"No," my voice was nearly a whisper.

I was getting nervous now, but also a little angry myself. Why was he with Tracy? Didn't last night mean anything to him? Didn't he really love me like he said? If so, why would he then immediately go over and be with her?

"Matt, hang up!" I heard Tracy saying. "You promised to be with me tonight. Just fucking hang up!"

He was ignoring her. "You listen to me, and listen good. You are not gonna say one more word to me. When I'm done talkin, I'm hanging up. Then I will deal with you tomorrow. Don't *ever* call me on this phone unless it is an absolute emergency. Never!" Then he clicked off.

I lay there on the bed, staring up at the ceiling with the phone still up by my ear. Oh my god! What had I just done? I'd called him on his cell phone even after he'd specifically told me not to ever do it. Just minutes ago I'd sworn to myself I'd always trust him and always obey him in every way. And now here I was totally fucking up. My face was beat red; I could feel it. I'd failed him again, and what was worse, I'd made him really angry this time!

Then I thought about what he was doing right then. Tracy was right beside him obviously. Were they somewhere in bed together? Was it his house, in his bed— the same bed upon which he'd made love to me the night previously? How could he do it? How could he have told me just yesterday that he loved me, and then be sleeping with a woman today? I felt my eyes welling with tears. How could I have believed it? How could I have actually believed someone like Matt was capable of loving me? I was so fucking stupid!

I pulled the phone away from my ear, moving it in front of my face, focusing on it through my tear-filled eyes. Then I reached up with my other hand and did something I'd never done before. I pressed the "off" button, and the display when blank. Then I placed it beside me on the bedside table and flipped off the light. I buried my head in the pillow and cried then. I cried so hard and so long that I lost track of the time. Eventually I must have fallen asleep because it was daylight when I opened my eyes. It was the next day.

14

I did not go to class that Tuesday morning. It was only the second time since I'd started college that I'd missed a day, the first time being when I was bashed. None of what had happened that previous evening seemed real to me. It did not seem possible that I could have gone from being so ecstatically happy one minute to the point of being devastatingly crushed the next. I hated myself for having disobeyed Matt by calling him on his cell phone in a non-emergency situation. For a few moments I tried to rationalize with myself, saying that it had felt like an emergency at the moment. I had wanted him so desperately that I had felt as if I could not wait another single minute to talk to him, but then I remembered his very specific instructions. He had told me when he programmed his number into my phone that I was not to call him if I were simply horny or missing him. Why hadn't I remembered those instructions last night before I'd called?

I also could not get the images of him being with Tracy from my head. Even though I had known and even thought I'd accepted the fact that he was going to be seeing her when he chose, it still was like a knife in my heart. I did not understand how he could love me as he said that he did and still choose to be with her. Then as I thought about these things, it occurred to me that if I had not called him in the first place I would not have even known about Tracy. Most likely he'd been with her several times before when I was not aware of it. How could I even expect otherwise?

But was it even possible for him to love me, as he said that he did, and for him to still choose to be with her? Maybe when he'd told me that he loved me, he had not meant it in the same way that I had. Perhaps he loved me the same way that he loved Petey, his dog. Maybe he loved me as a friend. Or possibly he drew a distinction between loving someone and being "in love" with them.

During these hours of reflection, I was able to recall some things that I had not even been capable of thinking about the night before. I remembered the loving way that Matt had rescued me. I thought about how he demonstrated constant support and patience towards me. He had made love to me so tenderly and beautifully. I recalled all of the gifts he had showered upon me. As I looked around my room I could see so many reminders of him. I also thought about how he had shown some trust in me. All of this time I'd focused upon the fact that I was trusting him, but I never thought about how he was trusting me as well. He trusted me enough to give me his cell phone number, believing that I'd never use it unless absolutely necessary. Now I had shattered that trust. Not only had I disobeyed him, but I'd demonstrated to him that I was immature and untrustworthy.

It was so frightening to me; I was terrified I'd lost him. He told me that he was going to deal with me today, but I had no idea what that even meant. Was he saying that he would punish me for my misdeeds? Was he going to show up to my house? Maybe he was going to call or email me and tell me that it was over between us. Maybe he was going to completely deny me access to him for awhile. That would be sheer torture. I wouldn't be able to go on if he did that! I could not bear such a punishment.

Why was I such a loser? Why did I always fail? I should box up all of these gifts that Matt had given me and have them ready for him when he showed up. Surely he would not allow me to keep all of the clothes when he dumped me. And the necklace too, oh god, I was going to have to give that back as well. I touched it with my fingers, running them across the smooth beads. I did not even deserve to wear it. I sat there on the edge of my bed, unable to do anything but cry. I didn't even want to face the day. I wanted for this to all go away. How could it possibly be happening?

I never should have allowed myself to believe that I was loveable. I never should have felt even for a second that I was capable of pleasing and satisfying someone like Matt. The words I'd said to him the previous night in my email were true, he was perfect to me. Oh my god! The email!! I had completely forgotten that I had sent it. I had gone on and on about how much I loved him. I told him I would obey him always. What would he think when he read those words? He probably would print it out and bring it here, then shove it down my throat. He'd think I was a liar, to have made such proclamations only to then turn around and immediately refute them with my actions.

I got up from the bed and walked over to my computer. I had to check to see if he had read the letter. If he hadn't then maybe I could unsend it. I rubbed the back of my hand across my eyes, clearing them of tears enough to see the screen. I was sniffling as I typed in my login information and waited for the homepage to open. As soon as the screen finished loading, I clicked on my mailbox, waiting anxiously for the messages to display. There it was...Matt's response. My hands were shaking as I simply sat there, staring at the computer screen. I did not think I even had the courage to open it. What was he going to say to me? I had to do it though. I had to.

When I clicked on his message to display the words, my heart sank as I read the response

I told you that you'd know it if ever I were pissed. I AM! What a joke, when u say u will obey me always. Be at home today at five. I'll be there.

Matt

Oh no! He truly was angry, and now I had over eight hours to wait to find out what was going to happen. How was I going to handle it? What would I say to him when he told me that he was breaking it off with me? I wondered if I should have all of the clothes and gifts ready for him, to show him that I knew I did not even deserve him. I wondered if I should get on my knees before him and beg for his forgiveness. I wondered if I should just not be here at all. I was not even worthy of seeing him. But then I also knew that I absolutely had to be here. I had to obey him this time, even if it were the very last opportunity for me. I would not hide from him or run away; I'd face him and accept whatever he doled out to me.

I wished so badly that I could talk to Drew right now. He would know the best thing for me to do. I could not call him though, for he was at work. I decided to send him an email. I would just tell him I had an emergency and needed to talk to him ASAP. Maybe he'd check his mail sometime during the day. If not, maybe he'd be home in time to call me before Matt got here. I pulled up a blank email and typed in my message, sending it to him quickly.

Matt and Alex were going to be meeting today to work out, I also remembered. I wondered what time that would happen. Would Matt tell Alex about our situation? Would he tell him what I had done? If so, I wondered what Alex was going to then think of me. Would he give Matt advice? He probably was gonna tell Matt to just dump me. Maybe he'd advise Matt to do that so that I would be free, and so that he could then proposition me like he wanted to before. No, he'd never do that. He really wouldn't even want me at all once he found out how disobedient I was.

Truly that day was the longest of my life. I paced the apartment, unable to eat, watch television, or even take a nap. All that I could do is worry. I showered, did some cleaning, and paced some more. I ran into the bathroom three different times to throw up. There was no food in my stomach, so I just puked up bile. Many times I went back to the computer to check my email. Nothing. Nobody was online for me to talk to, and nobody had sent me any mail. All I kept getting was spam.

I knew that Kathy would be working late tonight. She'd slept at Carter's house the night before and must have gone to work right from there. So I did not even have her to talk to about the situation. Really, I would not have told her anyways. She never would understand how I could be in love with Matt, especially not with her best friend being his girlfriend. I wondered if she thought of this entire scene as being twisted. She seemed to have an inkling that I was had feelings for Matt. She had prodded me to confide in her, but I just couldn't. I think I was sort of scared. What if she advised me not to see him? What if she could not understand a relationship like Matt and I had? She probably would want me to find some boyfriend who was equal to me or something. She'd expect it to be like it was with her and

Carter. I could never be in that kind of relationship though. It just was not me.

Around two o'clock the phone finally rang. I ran over to it and looked at my caller ID. I did not recognize the number. "Hello?" I said.

"Peter, it's Drew. What's up?"

Immediately I started crying, sobbing into the phone. I was gasping, trying to formulate intelligible words, but failing miserably. "Oh my God, calm down," he said. "I can't understand you. Do you want me to come over?"

"You can't...you're working," I cried, attempting to pull myself together.

"No, I am off this afternoon. I'm going to come over, all right? Are you going to be okay until I get there?"

"Um...no...I mean, yes...I don't know! It's Matt. I think he is gonna dump me today."

"What?! What are you talking about?— No wait, just calm down. You can explain it to me when I get there. Okay?"

"Okay."

"Okay, ten minutes. See you then."

"Thank you," I sniffled into the phone.

By the time Drew arrived it was about twenty past two. I had stopped crying and resumed my incessant pacing. I bolted towards the door when I heard the knock. He stepped in and grabbed me immediately. I cried in his arms, not able to yet tell him what I was even crying over.

"Come on, let's go sit down, and you can tell me about it." He grabbed a hold of my hand and led me to the sofa where we sat down beside one another. "Now what is this crazy stuff about Matt dumping you? He was at our house this morning to meet Alex. They went to the gym together. He did not say anything like that to either of us."

"He didn't?" I asked as I suddenly looked up at him. "Really? What did he say...did he say anything about me?"

"Um, yeah. He asked me if we had a good time last night, thanked me for coming over and being with you. He was

237

very polite. I don't know why you'd think he wants to break up with you."

"I disobeyed him last night," I confided, looking down at my hands as I told him. "I called him on his cell phone. I'm never supposed to do it unless it's an emergency. I couldn't help it though. I missed him so bad."

"Well, that is no reason for him to dump you, silly. You fucked up, is all. It is no big deal. Every boy disobeys sometimes. You just have to take your punishment and get on with it."

"You don't understand, though, Drew. He was—" my voice was trembling as I started to cry again, "He was with her!"

"Who? His girlfriend?"

I nodded. "Oh," he said. Then he sat there quietly for a minute. Finally he said, "Listen, what did you really expect, Petey? You knew that he still was going to be seeing her, right? It's not like that should have been a surprise to you. And he didn't do it right in front of you to flaunt it or anything. You probably would not have even known, had you not called him...like you weren't supposed to do anyways."

"I know! But he sent me an email. It said he was pissed. He sounded really angry. He said for me to be here at five tonight and he was coming over."

"What time was that email sent?"

"One o'clock this morning," I answered.

"And what time was it when you called him last night? Let me guess, 12:30?"

"Midnight," I corrected him.

"Well, duh! No wonder he was pissed. If he shot out that email at one in the morning he must have been still steaming from the phone call. I can tell you, though, by eight o'clock this morning he was very calm. I'm positive he is not coming over here to dump you. If he were gonna dump you, he wouldn't waste his time."

"What will I say to him?" I looked into Drew's eyes, pleading with him for some advice.

"Well, to be honest," he said rather thoughtfully, "I think you should say as little as possible. Tell him you were wrong and that you're sorry. Don't make *any* excuses for yourself. None! I mean, don't say, 'I'm sorry but....' That will be like rationalizing. It will not impress him, believe me. And don't question him about the chick either. If you start telling him shit like that he hurt your feelings, it is gonna piss him off all over again. He probably will say you deserved to have your feelings hurt 'cause you were disobedient to begin with."

I nodded. "Should I get on my knees?"

He smiled at me. "Well, not to begin with, but hopefully before he is through, he will have you in that position. Right?" He was grinning at me.

"Do you think he is gonna punish me?"

Drew laughed. His laughter was not malicious though, just an expression of his awe of my innocence. "Yes, honey, he is gonna punish you. I can guarantee it. If he didn't, he wouldn't be much of a Master."

"A Master?"

"A Master, Owner, Dom...whatever you choose to call it. He is responsible for you now, you know. It is all very paternal. He has to discipline you when you do wrong. It's his job. You really wouldn't want him to just ignore it when you fucked up, would you?"

I nodded furiously. "Yes!" I said through laughter and tears.

He laughed again. "No you wouldn't. You just feel that way at the moment. After this is over, you will be thankful. He is gonna be fair to you. I just know he is. I can tell what a good person he is. You both are good people, and I bet you anything he talked to Alex about this whole thing this morning. Alex would never advise him to do anything to hurt you, not in any way."

239

"Thank you, Drew," I said, squeezing his hand. "I'm sorry that I called you away. I'm such a baby."

"Don't be silly. You're my friend, plus you didn't call me away. I already told you, I get out a little earlier on Tuesdays, no afternoon classes. Generally I stay and grade papers and shit at the school. I was just going to head home today though 'cause I'm all caught up. Did you eat anything today? You look terrible."

I shook my head. "Well, come on, let's go get you some lunch, my treat. I promise to have you back here in plenty of time before Matt gets here."

"You are taking me in public after just telling me I look like shit?" I asked.

"Yeah, for once I can be the pretty one! Now go wash your face, little guy." I reached out and hugged him, wondering how he had done it. In the matter of ten minutes he'd managed to take away every bit of anxiety I had. He set my world back to where it was before. Drew was amazing.

"Drew, thank you. I love you...I mean, as my friend."

"I know. I love you too. Now go get ready." He then gave me a quick kiss.

* * *

When five o'clock came and went, and I still had not seen Matt, I was extremely worried. Drew had brought me home by 4:30. Although I'd have wanted desperately for him to stick around, we both knew that it would not have been a good plan. Matt was going to need time alone with me, and truly this was a very private matter between only the two of us. Finally at about a quarter past five, I heard Matt's knock at the door. I was terrified, but did not waste any time in getting to the door to invite him in. The very last thing on earth that I wanted to do was to make him wait.

When I opened the door, there he stood. Frozen, I stood there staring at him. I knew I must have had that wide-eyed, deer-in-headlights glaze in my eyes, for he just looked down at me, as if puzzled. "You gonna let me in?" he asked.

"Yes sir," I said, stepping aside and then closing the door behind him. Matt was carrying a duffle bag. Of course, I did not dare to inquire as to its contents. After he was inside he turned to look at me, and I opened my mouth to speak.

"Sir—"

"I'll tell you when you're allowed to talk. Sit down." He pointed to the sofa. I nodded and immediately did as he said. "That little stunt you pulled last night was totally a bunch of bullshit. You know it, and so do I. Funny thing is that I read your email right afterwards and had to laugh. You promised to always obey me. What a crock!"

I wanted to tell him how sorry I was. I wanted to tell him that he was right and that I was nothing but a complete loser. I did not dare speak though. Instead I looked down at the ground in front of me, tears welling up in my eyes.

"Look at me," he ordered. "Don't ever take your eyes off of me when I'm addressing you." I looked up and met his gaze. His face was very serious, but did not convey any malice towards me. I did not sense that he hated me. "All right, there are two issues here that we need to discuss...that *I* need to discuss. All you need to do is sit here and listen til I'm done. Number one is the issue of your cell phone. I bought that phone for you for two reasons, first to be able to reach you whenever I wanted and second to give you a way of contacting me in an emergency. You have abused the privilege of your phone, however. I've given it some thought, and my immediate impulse was to yank phone privileges from you altogether. I'm not gonna do it though, cuz I still wanna be able to call you when I feel like it. So instead, I bought a new phone for myself today, with a new number. You will not get this number until you have proven yourself trustworthy. Do you understand?"

I nodded, "Yes sir." My voice was so quiet compared to his. I had an incredible urge to look away from him, to hang my head and stare at the floor. Instead I continued to look into his eyes, willing myself to obey.

"Second issue," he said, "is who I spend my time with. You were all pissy about the fact that I was with someone else, someone other than you. This sort of attitude will never be tolerated...NEVER! Who I choose to be with is my business, and mine alone. If you don't like it, tough shit. Deal with it. And also, if you had not disobeyed me in the first place, you never would have gotten yourself all worked up over me being with Tracy. You never would have even known. I could go on and on about what you mean to me versus what I feel for h—which, by the way, is nothing— but I don't have to justify myself to you. It should be obvious to you after this weekend how I feel. That's just a side issue though. Your call was such bullshit! Then I had her goin' off on me.

"I'm not gonna put up with you questioning me and asking who I'm with. If you cannot deal with the fact that I am the one who decides when and where I spend my time, and with whom I spend it, then you need to fuckin walk. Period. You got that?"

"Yes sir," I answered.

"Good. Now, let's talk about your punishment. First of all, no Drew for one week. You are not to call him, talk to him online, email him, go to his apartment—nothing. Alex has already informed him of this restriction, and assures me he will comply. I am the one who decides who you spend your time with, not vice-versa. Do you understand?"

My heart sank. A whole week without Drew, oh my god! "Yes sir," I responded.

"Second, you will write a letter of apology to Tracy for calling me so late last night. It was extremely annoying, and she was pissed. Justifiably so, I might add. The letter will be very polite, with virtually no underlying messages or rudeness of any kind. You will complete this assignment tonight and give it to me tomorrow morning. Do you understand?"

"Yes, sir," I said, wondering how I ever was going to compose such lies. There was nothing that I felt sorry for, relating to her. I could care less if she dropped dead.

"Third, get up and go to your bedroom. Strip down to your underwear and wait for me. Now!"

I shot up out off the sofa automatically and did precisely as he said, walking briskly to my bedroom, not even looking back. My hands were shaking as I unbuttoned my jeans and stepped out of them. Then I took off my shirt and socks. I stood there shivering, standing in the middle of the room looking down at the floor. I was afraid to even move. What was he going to do? I waited there for him then for almost ten minutes. It seemed more like ten hours, and I wondered what he could be doing alone out in the living room. I did not dare try to find out though. I just stood there.

When he stepped through the door, I looked up to see him standing there. He seemed ominous, towering over me. In his right hand he held a wooden paddle. It was big, about eighteen inches long and about an inch-and-a-half in thickness. I stared at it, wide-eyed, disbelieving for a moment what I knew was about to happen. Tears were in my eyes again as I stared at the paddle.

"Quit crying, and prepare to take your punishment like a man," he said. "Move over to the chair and put your hands on the back. Now." I obeyed him, feeling my face redden as I did so. I stood there, right next to the chair, unable to see him behind me. I looked straight forward, staring at my computer monitor. "Now step back two paces and spread your legs apart." Again I obeyed, and the results were that I was in a position where I was bent over uncomfortably, my butt totally exposed to him. "Put your head down," he said as he stepped over to me. He placed his left hand on the back of my head and gently pushed it forward so that I was staring straight down into the chair in front of me. "What do you have to say for yourself, boy?" he said, still pressing against my head.

"I'm sorry, Sir," my voice squeaked out a pathetically timid reply.

"What?! I can't hear you!"

"I'm sorry, Sir," I repeated, this time a little louder.

"You're sorry for what, boy?"

"For disobeying you, Sir," I began to cry again, tears streaming down my cheeks. He did not scold me for it though, but remained in his position of dominance beside me. "And embarrassing you in front of your— in front of Tracy, Sir. I'm so sorry. Please forgive me."

Almost instantly I felt the jolt of the first whack. I steadied myself, gripping the chair firmly as I felt the sting of the paddle through the underwear fabric. "Do you remember what I said to you about consequences, boy?"

"Yes Sir," I cried. "Every action has consequences."

"That's right, boy. You disobeyed. Now you pay the consequences." I heard the rush of air as he swung the paddle the second time, again connecting with my tender ass. I winced as I felt the second blow, a little bit more severe than the first. I remained immobile though, firmly keeping my feet planted in position and holding onto the chair tightly. He released my head, then and stepped away from me slightly.

"Ten whacks," he said. "Count them out!" He swung the paddle again, connecting for the third time.

"One," I cried, wincing from the pain. It was like fire on my butt, stinging me terribly. "Two ... Three...Four." I was crying openly now, whimpering from the humiliation more than the pain itself. When he got up to the seventh blow, which was actually the ninth, he paused. "Take off your underwear," he ordered. I stood upright, almost unable to bear the blistering pain in my ass. I grabbed the waistband of my briefs and pulled them down, stepping out of them. I then resumed my position.

Whack! The crack of the paddle against my bare skin sounded as if I had been slapped , and the stinging sensation was wickedly painful. "Unghhh! Eight," I cried. He paused, allowing me to compose myself. As I stood there crying in my servile position, I wondered what he was thinking. I wondered how it made him feel to discipline me this way. Whack! "Oh Sir!!! Unghhh! Nine!" His last blow was delivered quickly, right on top of the previous. "Ten!" I gripped the chair so tightly then that my knuckles were white. I stared down at them, trying to focus on anything but the pain, allowing it to pass. It did so very gradually, and I did not think I was going to be able to even move afterwards.

"Stand up and turn around, boy. Face me," Matt instructed me. I did as he said, without any hesitation. My ass was burning unlike anything I'd felt before. "Kneel!" he commanded, and I dropped to my knees instantly, enduring the pain as my ass connected with my bare legs. I was staring directly at his crotch now. He was rock hard too, for I could clearly see the outline of his cock in his wind pants. "I own you boy, I own every part of you! Do you understand?"

"Yes Sir," I said as I craned my neck to look up at him. He towered over me, and I simply knelt there in awe.

"And you will obey. You will always obey! Do you understand?"

"Yes Sir," I said, now no longer crying, although the pain and humiliation had subsided only slightly.

"Give me your necklace." I stared up at him, disbelieving what he was saying. He was going to break it off with me after all! Oh no! I immediately felt myself starting to lose control of my emotions. I was weeping there in front of him, not like a series of violent sobs, merely horrible tears of grief. I reached up, running my fingers across the beads. I wanted to beg him then, to plead with him not to take it away from me. But I could do nothing but obey him. I reached behind my neck and unfastened the clasp, removing it.

245

He held his hand out, and very gently I reached over and placed the necklace in his palm. I was so terrified, I did not want it to now be over. "I'm not taking this away from you, cause you are still my pup, but you are not going to be wearing it either, not until you earn the right to be seen as mine. You will keep it here on your stand and will not remove it or put it back on until I feel you deserve to do so. Do you understand?"

"Yes sir," I said, instantly relieved that he said I was still his. He then stared down at me, and I looked directly at the outline of his rock hard cock.

"Serve me," he said. "Suck my cock." He pulled down the waistband of his wind pants and boxers, exposing himself to me. He tucked the front of the waistband snugly under his balls and stepped up to me, his rock hard cock right in my face. I opened my mouth instinctively and took his throbbing hardon into me. I sucked as never before then, trying so desperately to redeem myself. It was only a matter of minutes before he was ready to shoot. He held my head firmly in place, ramming into my throat forcefully. I struggled to breathe, choking on his cock several times. He simply ignored my discomfort and continued to use me to get himself off. Finally, he jerked my head away from his cock and pulled out of me, grasping his shaft at the base as he leaned backwards slightly. He shot his load high into the air over my head. Some landed in my hair and on my face, though most of it went right on the floor. "You haven't earned my cumload," he informed me. He then stepped back up to my face, still holding his cock, he smeared the cockhead against my cheek, wiping it clean of the last drops of his load, and finally pulled his wind pants back up to their proper position.

"Complete your assignment. I'll pick you up tomorrow morning at 8:30 for school. Be ready. You also will not be going to that concert with Drew." Then he walked out, leaving me kneeling there on the floor.

15

I was fully dressed and waiting for Matt at 8:30 the next morning, when my cell phone rang. It was him. "I'm just pulling into your parking lot," he said.

"Yes, sir. I'll be right down." I picked up my backpack and was already headed out the door when he clicked off the call. I did not want him to have to wait for me at all.

The previous evening had been absolutely excruciating for me. I kept reliving my punishment, which was really not surprising, since my butt was on fire the entire evening. I'd never been paddled like that before, and would have had no idea how long the stinging and soreness persisted even after the punishment was over. I actually had slept on my stomach that night, which is something I never ever did. Generally, I slept curled up on my side, in sort of a fetal position.

Worse than the physical pain, though, was the reality that I'd disappointed Matt. Every time I looked over at my dresser and saw the beaded necklace lying there, I felt a wave of guilt. Sometimes this affected me in a very emotional way, causing me to cry. Other times I was embarrassed or just sad about the whole situation. I wanted so much to call Drew and tell him about my punishment and to see what he had to say. I wanted to confide my feelings to him, to lean on his shoulder for support. Now I could not even do that, but it was really my own fault. I refused at this point to be angry at all with Matt. He only was doing his job. He was training me. If I had been a better person, he would not have had to punish me in the first place.

I ran down the stairs and out into the parking lot, catching up to Matt's car even before he came to a complete stop. I swung the door open and climbed in, easing myself carefully into the seat.

He looked over at me, "Little tender, huh?"

"Oh, it's all right sir, I'm fine."

"Guess that's why corporal punishment is such effective discipline. It sticks with you for awhile, reminding you of what you did wrong."

"I know, Sir," I said, hanging my head shamefully and staring into my lap.

"Look at me," he said. I turned my head and looked up into his face. "You do know that everyone does things that are bad sometimes, right? Doesn't mean they are bad people. Even I have had to be disciplined before."

"I know, Sir, but…"

"But what?"

"But I just keep failing you. Why can't I just do the right thing, ever?"

"Hold out your arm," he said. I looked into his eyes, puzzled by his instruction, but I obeyed. He reached up to the visor above his head and pulled it down, grabbing a black Sharpie pen that was tucked away there. He moved it to his mouth, grasping it between his teeth. Then he grabbed a hold of my outstretched wrist with his left hand, and pushed up the sleeve of my rugby shirt, exposing my upper arm. "Hold this," he said, and I reached over with my right hand and held the shirt sleeve up for him. He then took the marker from his mouth and removed the cap. He brought the tip down to my arm and wrote in big bold letters "OWNED." I was watching intently as he traced the letters onto my skin, and when he was done I looked into his eyes. He smiled at me. "Unzip your pants," he said.

I wanted to question him as to whether or not it was wise to do that here in my apartment parking lot, but I knew I must obey without question, so I did exactly that. I reached down and unbuttoned my cargo pants and then proceeded to unzip them. "Pull your shirt up," he instructed me. I did so, exposing the smooth flat area between my naval and the waistband of my briefs. He pulled down the elastic waistband of my briefs. He moved the marker into position

and wrote the word "PROPERTY." Then he pulled back the
waistband so that he could look inside. "Looks good," he
said, "When did you shave?"

"Last night, Sir," I said. "I tried real hard to remember
every order you gave me and to obey them all."

"Good boy," he praised me. Then he re-buttoned my
pants for me and zipped me up. "Now turn to face the door,"
he said. I shifted my body in the seat immediately, and
stared out the window. He pulled down the back of my shirt
slightly, and I felt the marker make contact with my skin.
"I'm writing the word 'Puppyboy' on your back," he told me.

I smiled immediately. "You are?" I asked.

"Yup. That's what you are, aren't you?"

"Yes Sir, I'm *your* puppy boy."

"Yeah, and my owned property too. Now you are
marked...by me. But I have an assignment for you. Turn
around and look at me."

I slid around smoothly in my seat so that I was looking
directly at him. "Okay, are you ready to hear it?"

I nodded quickly. "Yes Sir, I'm ready."

"Okay. Sometime today, either at school or work, or
sometime in-between...doesn't matter when...you are to
show your marks to three different people. I mean you have
to show each one of these three people one of your markings.
You don't have to show all three markings to each of the
people— just one per person. You understand?" I nodded.
"And then you will be showing them that you belong to me,
that you are my property."

I was still smiling at him, but then suddenly I became
more serious, as a wave of concern overcame me. "But how
Sir? How will I show my marking that is down in my
underwear to anyone?"

"Think about it, pup. When do you always have to pull
down your pants?"

"When I pee?" I asked.

"Right."

"But I have to pee sitting down, like you told me, so I go into the stall."

"Well I'm rescinding that order. I want you to pee standing up again. You just are gonna have to make sure that you do it while standing next to someone, and you're gonna have to get him to look over at you so he can see the marking."

"What about the one on my back, Sir?"

"Hmm, guess maybe you will have to take your shirt off at some point, don't you think? You could do two at once if you did that."

"Thought it had to be two different people," I said.

"Yeah, but if two people who are together see you walking around with your shirt off and they notice your markings, that would count."

"Okay, I said. I will try to do it, Sir. I will obey you."

"You can do it pup, I have confidence in you. When you do, I'm gonna be so proud of you. But then what you gotta do tonight is send me an email just as soon as you get home from work. You will report to me exactly how you obeyed. You got it?"

"Yes, Sir," I said.

"Then after you do all this just like I've ordered, I will reward you. You'll be allowed to jack off tonight. You gotta think of me when you do it, though." He smiled at me as he added the last part.

"Well at least that part won't be hard," I said. I was starting to get excited.

"Okay, now listen carefully, 'cause I'm gonna give you a chance for an extra special reward, okay?"

"Okay!" I said excitedly, leaning forward slightly in anticipation.

"If you show your 'property' marking to more than one person, I will let you spend part of the day tomorrow with Drew."

"You will, Sir? You'll let me see him even though I am being punished?"

"That's right. I make the rules about your punishment. I have a right to change them whenever I want. If I say you can see Drew, then you can. Period."

"Oh Sir, thank you so much!" I said.

"Well, no need to thank me yet. You gotta do your part. I'm not giving you anything until you earn it. Did you get your assignment done from last night?" he asked.

"Yes, Sir," I answered and reached down into the side pocket of my backpack. I removed a folded piece of paper and handed it to him. It was my letter of apology to Tracy.

He took the letter from me, unfolding it, and read it. I looked down into my lap as he did so, and then he looked back over at me. "Good job. Did you mean what you said in the letter?" he asked.

I was about to say "Yes Sir," but instead I just sat there, looking down, unable to answer.

"Pup, I asked you a question," he said after a few seconds.

"Sir, it is true, I am so very sorry that I disobeyed you. I'm also sorry that I interrupted you and called you so late at night, and I know it was inconsiderate. But I would be lying if I told you that I am sorry towards Tracy, 'cause I'm not."

"Don't you at least think that she deserves a little respect? If she is someone who is in my life and is someone that I choose to be with, isn't that enough reason alone to be polite to her? Not to mention, you should be polite to people anyways, friends or not."

"Yes, Sir...I agree. But— I um— I think that I should be polite to her and respect her, and I'm sorry that I was not, but I'm not sorry really for her sake. I'm sorry because it disappointed you, and because it made me feel bad about myself too, 'cause I don't want to be a selfish person." I was speaking very quietly, still not looking up at my owner.

"Pup, that is all I am asking of you. I don't want you to necessarily like everyone that I do, but I want you to treat people respectfully, that's all."

"She does not respect me, Sir. She treats me awful. She always has."

"So? Does that mean you have to be the same way? You are a better person than that, I think. You are *my* pup! And I expect more from you. Plus, I can guarantee you, she won't treat you disrespectfully around me. No one will. You understand?"

"Yes, Sir," I said. I smiled and looked over to him.

"So I think you did mean the words you wrote. You are sorry for your behavior and sorry that it was inconsiderate, in spite of the fact that you don't really like Tracy. Would you say that is accurate?"

I nodded. "Yes, Sir, that's right."

"Good boy," he said. And then he folded the letter back up and ripped it right in half, right in front of me, then handed it back to me. I smiled at him broadly. "You look really cute today, pup, but you should be wearin a b-cap with those clothes."

"Want me to run back upstairs and get one, Sir?" I offered.

"Nah, we are gonna be late if we don't get goin." He then reached up and removed his own cap, placing it on my head instead. It was too big and the visor slid way down in front of my eyes. He laughed. "Better adjust that," he said.

I laughed back at him, almost giggling. I was so happy to be marked by him, and now to be wearing his cap. He made me feel so good about myself. "I love you, Sir," I said.

"Love you too."

Then we fastened our seat belts, and he drove us to school.

* * *

When I got into my first hour class that morning, my heart was racing as I thought about how I was going to carry out my orders from Matt. I already had a plan, though, at least for showing off my first marking. I was gonna show my "Owned" mark, the one on my arm, for that would be the easiest. I'd work my way up to the more difficult ones after I got this first one out of the way. I looked around the room and saw there was an open seat in the back row right next to this girl named Kim. She was always very quiet in class and seemed rather shy to me. She would be a good one to expose myself to the first time, I thought, because it was unlikely to cause much reaction. I was not sure what she would think when she saw that word written on me, but I did not really care. All I was concerned about was my obedience to my owner.

We sat through nearly forty-five minutes of the hour before I finally had the courage to even consider following through with it. I was determined, though, and was so focused upon this determination that I was paying little attention to the class instructor. I was watching the clock, realizing that I only had about five minutes before the end of the period. I glanced over at Kim, watching her as she took notes on the lecture. How was I going to get her attention? Damn! I looked around the room. Everyone was facing away from us, looking either at their desks or up towards the professor at the front of the class. I reached up with my right hand and pushed up my left shirtsleeve, sort of rolling the cuff under, as if to create a sleeveless shirt. The word "OWNED" was now clearly visible. Then I picked up my pencil and tapped it lightly on my desk. I glanced over to her, and she did not respond, giving me no indication that she was even aware of my presence. I stared over at her while I continued to tap the pencil, a little bit louder. I had to get her to look at me, but I did not want to get any unwanted attention from anyone else! I paused, and then finally for a third time tapped my pencil repeatedly on the desk top and

this time also cleared my throat. I glanced over at her, and as
I did, caught her eye. She turned her head slightly and stared
directly at me. She got a puzzled look on her face and then
shook her head very slightly, quickly looking back down at
her notebook. She saw it! She definitely saw it! I pushed my
sleeve back down into its rightful position then and smiled
to myself. I did it! I obeyed him!

* * *

In my next class, I stared out the window, checking to see
the weather conditions. I was praying for a really hot day,
otherwise how could I ever walk around for even a second
with my shirt off? It was only the end of February, and
although we had some pretty warm days, it was not really
the time of year that you saw people walking around
shirtless. I just couldn't think about it yet, though. I'd get too
worried. I had to instead focus upon my other marking first.
I would have to do that one inside...in the bathroom, of
course.

After my second hour class, it was lunch time, and I
headed for the cafeteria. Instead of going in, though, I went
into the men's restroom. There were a couple of guys at the
urinals, and I walked up to the sink. I removed my backpack
from my arm and placed it beside me on the ground, leaning
it against the wall. My heart was racing again, just like the
first time. I turned on the water and began to wash my
hands. I just stood there, trying to act natural as each of the
two other students zipped up and stepped away from their
urinals. Both walked out without even bother to wash first.
The bathroom was now empty. I dried my hands and picked
up my backpack, stepping over in front of the urinal closest
to me. I just stood there then like a statue, waiting for
someone else to enter the restroom. It seemed like an
incredibly long time, and I really did have to pee. I did not
want to relieve myself yet though. I wanted to wait until

someone was beside me. I moved over then to the middle urinal. If I did not do that, then when someone did come in, they would not likely use the urinal closest to my own. By being in the middle, I ensured that I'd end up right next to someone.

The sound of the bathroom door opening literally startled me. I was so nervous, but tried to act natural. It was a single person who had entered. God, I hope he uses the urinal and not the stall, I thought. I stepped closer to my urinal then, reaching down to unzip my pants. The guy who had just entered the bathroom walked over to the station to my left. Thank god! He was a student, although he was not familiar to me. I thought he looked kind of cute actually, and he was also wearing a baseball cap, just like me, although he was a good five or six inches taller than me. I looked straight ahead, staring at the wall in front of me. As he positioned himself in front of his urinal, assuming the masculine position of legs apart, feet planted firmly in place, he reached down and unbuttoned himself. He seemed to be unaware of my presence, ignoring me and simply taking care of his own business.

I was unsure what to do. How was I going to get him to look over at me? Even more than that, how was I going to get him to look down at my groin. I thought for a few seconds. I could glance over at his dick first and see if he checked me out in return, but what if he got pissed, thinking I was making a pass at him? I did not want to relive the Devin Baker experience. I pulled my fly open then, still standing there with my underwear yet untouched. The other guy already had his dick out and was pissing. I wondered if he was aware of the fact that I was taking so long to even get my dick out. I glanced over to him, and then quickly looked away, returning my gaze to the wall in front of me. I did this again, three times. I wondered if he noticed. I could hear him pissing, a steady stream striking against the porcelain surface of the urinal. He would be done before I even got started. *Oh my god! I cannot do this!*

My heart skipped a beat when suddenly this cute guy turned his head and looked over at me. He was staring directly at me, trying to make eye contact, it seemed. Suddenly I was embarrassed. Here I was hoping he'd look at me, and now that he was, I did not know what to do. I did not even want him to look any more. I had temporarily forgotten my mission to carry out Matt's orders and was instead self conscious of this cute guy who seemed to be checking me out in the men's room. As quickly as that fear had overtaken me, my determination to be obedient kicked back in. I forced myself to turn my own head again, this time to meet his gaze. I grinned at him, trying to convey shyness and passivity, yet also to encourage him to continue pursuing me. Then I leaned backwards slightly and looked down, shifting my eyes in a very obvious way to check out his groin area. As I did this, I pulled down the waistband of my underwear while using my elbows to slightly slide up the tail of my rugby shirt. I wanted to make sure the entire word "PROPERTY" was visible. I looked intently at his cock, which he was holding proudly in his hand as he pissed. I stared at it for a good five seconds and then very quickly shifted my eyes to look up at his face.

He was checking me out at the same time! I caught him doing it. Yes!! I had obeyed. Immediately I looked back to the wall and stepped up as closely to the urinal as possible, grabbing my own dick. I then relieved myself and refused to even think of glancing back at the cute guy beside me. When I finally got done he still had not moved, even though I could hear that he had finished pissing several moments previously.

I zipped myself up quickly and flushed the toilet. Then I grabbed my backpack and bolted for the door, not looking back.

* * *

After my third and final class of the day was dismissed, I already had a plan of action for exposing my third marking. I immediately headed for the college bookstore. When I got there I walked around a bit until I found the display of tee shirts and sweatshirt that bore the school's logo. I picked out the least expensive, a gray sleeveless tee and headed for the cashier. I pulled my wallet from my backpack and paid the cashier quickly, thinking of nothing but my plan of action. I then headed outdoors to the courtyard area. It was here that many of the students hung out, a lot of them being smokers who were getting their hourly nicotine fix. I looked around until I spotted a single person, a guy, standing alone over against the wall of one of the buildings. Directly to the left of him there was a large flower garden which was surrounded by a cement, waist-high ledge. I walked over to the structure and sat on the ledge, positioning myself in clear view of the guy who was resting against the wall.

I placed my backpack beside me and pulled out my new tee shirt. Thank god the weather was nice today, I thought. It was mid-seventies, and so a lot of the students had stripped off their sweatshirts and were walking around outside in short sleeves. I knew that I could pull this one off rather inconspicuously. I sat there, realizing that everything was going well. I was in a position that was directly in the line of view of this bystander. The only concern I had was that when I stripped off my rugby shirt, he might look away. I'd just have to take my chances. I stood up, turning my back to him. He was less than ten feet from me.

I then reached down and grasped the shirttail of the rugby. I breathed deeply and then quickly went for it. I pulled the shirt over my head in one swift movement, and was then standing there naked from the waist up. I knew that if the guy was still looking in my direction, he would surely see the word "Puppyboy" etched across my shoulders.

I did not immediately move to pick up the tee shirt. Instead I just waited a few seconds, somewhat embarrassed by my half nudity. I'd always been overly modest, but my will to serve Matt completely outweighed my self-consciousness at this point. After a few seconds, I made a fist with my right hand and moved it in front of my mouth. I then started to cough. It was a fake cough, but I tried to sound convincing. I coughed several times, over and over, trying hard to imitate an uncontrollable spasm. After about ten seconds of this, I immediately whipped around and caught the direct gaze of my target. He was looking right at me! Yes!! I did it again.

Quickly I turned away from him and pulled on my new tee shirt. I then stuffed my rugby shirt into my backpack and headed for the bus stop.

* * *

On the bus ride to work, all I could think of was how proud Matt was going to be of me. I had completed all of my assignments already, even though I had not even been certain that I'd be able to do it. Now all I had left to do was the one extra exposure. I knew that it was optional, but I wanted to do it so badly because then Matt would know how much I desired to please him, and also I'd be able to see Drew. How would I ever do it at work though? I certainly could not expose my groin area to a coworker. I'd probably get fired, or at the very least they'd think I was a major pervert. Plus even if I didn't lose my job, I'd then have to work with them afterwards. It had to be a stranger, but then as I thought of it, that could be even a worse scenario. If it were some customer, I could end up in big trouble, especially if they complained to my boss.

Matt had said "at school, at work, or any time between...sometime during the course of the day." Okay, so I had to think of something other than work then. But what? I had lucked out in the men's room at the cafeteria. I could not be so fortunate a second time, I was sure. Wait! I just thought of something. There was that one park downtown. I'd read about it in the paper. Several people had been arrested for soliciting sex. They were men who were busted by undercover male cops. That must be a park where guys hung out looking for someone to hook up with. That would be so risky though! Oh my god, I could end up in jail if I got caught.

But just a minute, I thought. I am not going to be soliciting sex. I'm only gonna be exposing myself, and really I could do it in a way that I didn't even have to show my dick. I could just pull the waistband of my briefs down far enough to expose the marking and then get the hell out of there as fast as possible. My heart pounded excitedly as I worked out the details of my plan. I still had almost a full hour before my shift started at work. I could make this happen; I knew I could!

I got off the bus two stops earlier than normal, about three blocks from the park. As I walked down the sidewalk towards my destination, I stopped to check myself out in the refection of a storefront. Maybe Matt was right. I did look sort of cute with my cargo pants and b-cap. Now with the sleeveless shirt, I definitely looked like what you might call a "twink." That was good, though. It was exactly what I wanted for my plan.

I resumed walking, picking up the pace, as I headed directly into the park. I was nervous for I'd never done anything even remotely like this before. I wasn't even sure how I would be able to tell who was going to be interested in anything more than conversation. What if I hooked up with some psycho or some basher who wanted to hurt me? What if I could not get away from them after I'd exposed myself? Well, I told myself, it is broad daylight. It won't hurt to walk around a bit and check things out. If I see someone who is a good target for my plan, then I can go for it, but if I feel scared too much or unsafe, I will just abandon it. I already had completed my main assignment anyhow. This was just sort of like an "extra credit" project.

I started to stroll around, observing a few people who were actually utilizing the park for its intended purpose, picnickers and the like. I walked over towards the restroom facilities. I wondered if this was where all the "hookups" took place. So far, I had not witnessed anything that indicated there was any sort of action at all going on in this place. I walked up to the building, turning to look around me as I paused at the door. If there was someone watching the building, I wanted him to see me, to get a good look. I wanted to use my "cuteness" as bait. After all, Drew had told me that Alex thought I was attractive. Maybe someone else would too.

I went inside, and it was eerily quiet. I walked over to the sink, checking my reflection in the mirror. Then I went to the very back stall, furthest from the door, and stepped inside, pulling the door shut behind me. The walls of that bathroom stall were covered with various types of graffiti. Specific sexual messages were written all over these walls, which looked as if they had been repainted several times. It was a futile attempt to mask the graffiti. The messages stated dates and times when guys would be available to either suck or be sucked. Some of the messages bragged of big and hard cocks, and others were advertising expert cock-sucking ability. I was intrigued as I read them, laughing to myself. I never realized how entertaining it could be to read bathroom graffiti.

Suddenly I heard the bathroom door open. I started to get excited, as I had three times previously that day. I quietly placed my backpack on the back of the toilet seat, and stepped over close to the door of the stall. There was a small slit through which I could peer, the space between the door and frame of the stall. I put my eye up to the slit and looked out into the main section of the restroom. I could see the big mirrors above the sinks on the opposite wall. The guy who had entered was probably in his late twenties. Whew! That was a relief. I was afraid I'd end up encountering some old person, like forty or fifty. This guy, though, was not old. He actually was quite attractive. He had a stockier build than the other guy from the cafeteria, but he was very masculine. I sort of thought that maybe he was legitimately here to take a piss, because he looked so straight.

He stood in front of the mirror though, as if he were admiring himself. I watched him intently as he casually ran his fingers through his short black hair. Then he clasped his hands together behind his head, as if he were stretching. He had a really nice body. I could see the definition of his muscular chest through his somewhat tight fitting tee shirt. He was wearing faded Levi jeans, and I could clearly see the roundness of his tight, toned butt. I wondered briefly what it would be like to watch him getting fucked by someone like Matt. I bet he wouldn't seem so straight to me then. I was smiling to myself as I stared at him through my peep hole.

Then he moved his arms away from his head and suddenly brought his left palm down to rest it on his thigh. He slid it over, edging it closer to his groin. He then rather quickly moved it the remaining distance, sort of seductively groping himself. Oh my god! He was staring right at me. He spotted me in the reflection! By reflex I immediately stepped back away from the door. He had to know I was there. He surely must have seen my feet from below the stall. My heart pounded in my chest, and I breathed deeply, trying to calm myself. Okay, this is; I can do this, I told myself. I picked my backpack up from the toilet and flung it back over my shoulder and stepped over to the door, unlatching it and walking out.

Now we were staring directly at one another's reflection in the mirror. I tried to act casual, and I walked up to the sink. There was one other sink in between his and mine. We both continued to look at the others' reflection in the mirror. I straightened my shoulders and stood there, staring at his reflection, and then glancing back at my own. I moved my hand down to my own thigh, trying to imitate what he had just done. I slid it across my cargo pants and placed my fingers against the flap that housed my zipper. I moved my other hand in place, keeping my backpack on my shoulder. I moved my fingers to the button of my pants, doing so in a way that was slow and rather seductive. I wanted to make sure he was getting into this. Before I continued, though, I stepped back a bit away from the sink. I then pulled my hands away from my waist altogether. I glanced up at him, seeing the intent look on his face. I knew he wanted me to continue. I turned then and walked behind him, moving over to the sink on his opposite side. This was the sink closest to the exit door, but it was also right next to him.

His gaze had followed my reflection the entire time. I repositioned myself so that I was in front of the mirror just as I was before, only this time next to a different sink. I moved my fingers back to my fly and this time did unbutton the pants. I slowly unzipped myself, feeling my pulse pound in my head. I then turned towards him, looking away from the mirror and directly at him. He did the same so that we were facing one another. Without saying a word, I pushed up the tail of my shirt with the sides of my arms while at the same time pulling apart my fly to expose my underwear. Then I gripped the edge of my waistband slowly. He was staring now, realizing he was about to get a show of some hot twink cock. I then pushed down the waistband...slowly, teasingly. I pushed it down as far as it would go before it got to the point of exposing my dick. I knew the word was visible. I knew he had to see it: "PROPERTY." I stood there frozen for just a few seconds, staring at him. Then finally I backed up a couple paces.

Quickly I turned, bolting for the door. I flung it open and then immediately grabbed my pants, re-buttoning them as I ran. I ran as fast as I could without even looking back. I kept running until I was well out of the park and almost to the

bookstore. I did it! I did just what he told me. I obeyed him!!
Matt was gonna be so very proud of me, I could not wait to
tell him.

I could not help smiling throughout the rest of my day.
Kathie picked me up from work at the end of my shift. She'd
called the store to see if I needed a ride. When I got home,
the first thing that I did was type that email to Matt, telling
him all that had happened. I told him about the girl in first
hour, the capped guy in the restroom at the cafeteria, the
smoker in the courtyard, and finally the muscle hunk at the
park. I had shown all of these strangers who I was. I was
Matt's pup, his owned property.

16

I spent a great deal of that evening refocusing upon my
studies. I had neglected homework and even had an
upcoming due date on a term paper that was heavily
weighing on me. I spent a good three hours pouring myself
into these tasks, and it felt rather refreshing, actually. I did
not want to spend the entire evening obsessing over the fact
that I was under restriction and being punished. I also was
thankful that instead of the terrible feelings of guilt and
regret that were constantly plaguing me, I now had
something else to dwell upon. I hoped that my obedience
today would be enough to redeem myself with Matt. I prayed
that he would see that I could be a good boy too. It just was
so awful that the one incident where I had impulsively
chosen to disobey totally outweighed all of my efforts to
please him.

As I sat at my desk researching for my term paper,
occasionally I'd glance over to my bedside stand to look at
the beaded necklace. It was still there, waiting for me to be

worthy of again wearing it. Maybe after Matt received my email he would grant this privilege. I would not ask though — never. It was not up to me to ever ask something like that. It was solely his decision, and I knew that I had to trust him with the timing.

I was shirtless and wearing only a pair of sleep pants when my cell phone rang at 11:52 p.m. It was initially a shock to me, for I had not even been thinking about the possibility that Matt may call me. Instead I'd been buried in my homework. "Hello?" I said.

"Hey pup! Whatcha doin?"

"Hello, Sir," I said, swiveling in my desk chair. "I'm at the computer, just doing some home work."

"You were a good boy today. Got your email."

I smiled to myself, finally hearing the praise I'd craved all afternoon. "Thank you Sir. I did not even check my mail yet though to see if you wrote back. I was sorta swamped with school stuff."

"It's cool. School's gotta come first. Don't want my pup to flunk out." He then laughed. "You jack off yet?"

"Um, no Sir. Honest I didn't. I know I can't without permission." Instantly I was concerned, thinking he had some reason to believe I may have disobeyed again.

"Well I told ya you could, pup. I said if you showed your markings to three people you could jack tonight, remember?"

"Yes Sir, I remember, but still I thought I had to wait until you decided if I did everything...um...right."

"Ohhh, well I'm glad ya waited. You did great though; made me proud. Not sure I want ya hangin in that park though, not unless I'm with ya. Don't want you getting yourself arrested or beat up."

"I'm sorry, Sir," I said, immediately feeling deflated.

"Nothin to be sorry for, guy. I said ya did good, didn't I? An owner's gotta look out for his pup's safety is all. Was smart the way you did it today though, moving towards the door and not letting the guy corner ya. Plus you did it in broad daylight— lot safer like that."

"Thank you, Sir." I was relieved by his clarification.

"What ya wearin?"

"Batman sleep pants," I giggled. "I'm in my jammies."

He busted up laughing. "Cool. Anything under 'em?"

"Just me, Sir."

"Ohhh... get on your bed."

"Yes, Sir," I said, immediately standing up and moving to the bed. I sat down on the edge. "Okay, I'm sitting on the bed now."

"Good boy. Now lie down on your back." I did so. "How'd it feel today to show some strangers that you were owned property?"

I smiled. "Wonderful, Sir. It...well, it just felt cool, like I was proud of it, ya know."

"Yeah? You think those dudes knew what it meant when they saw the word PROPERTY written over your dick?"

I laughed. "Probably not, Sir, but I knew. Made me feel good to obey, and made me feel like...um...like you'd see I could be good too, not just bad all the time." I could feel myself getting aroused as I spoke to him.

"Pup you dwell on shit too long. You did bad and we dealt with it. Move on."

"Yes, Sir...it's just that I'm afraid I won't ever be able to make up for it."

"Don't gotta make anything up, pup. Ya just gotta try to learn from your mistakes, that's all. Everyone does wrong sometimes. Can't always think about the bad, though. Gotta try to think about the good things about yourself. You know, I do. I think about how good my pup is, not how he sometimes messes up. It's like my other Petey. You think I'm gonna disown him or something when he messes? Wouldn't be a very good owner if I did that, would I?"

"No, Sir. I did not mean it like that. I never meant you were not a good owner!"

"I know, but just chill, okay?"

"Yes, Sir."

"You hard?"

"Yes, Sir, very much," I smiled as I offered this admission. "Makes me hard to talk to you."

"It should. Take your pants off." I obeyed him, pushing my hips upwards as I slid my pants down over my thighs. I cradled the phone between my chin and shoulder to free my hands. I pulled my knees up towards my chest so that I could slide the sleep pants down past my ankles. I then tossed the pants on the floor and lay there totally naked.

"I took them off Sir," I said.

"Totally naked now?"

"Yes Sir."

"Good boy. How's your butt feel?"

"It's a lot better Sir, doesn't hurt any more, just maybe a little...um...tender. You know what's weird, Sir?" I asked.

"What?"

"I felt so bad yesterday, when you...um...when—"

"When I paddled your ass?"

"Yes, Sir. I felt so bad about everything. I was so embarrassed and stuff. I felt so awful. Then today I was thinking about it. I thought about it when I was on break at work, and it made me so hard. Isn't it strange I'd get hard thinking of that?"

"What about it made you hard?"

"I don't really know...I mean, not exactly. Maybe cuz you made me serve you afterwards."

"Yeah, but you have served me lots of times before. I think it's more than that," he said.

"I think I got so hard cuz it turned me on that you were so much in charge. You were so superior."

"You like that, huh?"

"Yes, Sir, I liked it a lot. It was sort of like you— well— like you put me in my place or something."

"What's your place?" he prodded me.

"Under you, Sir. Below you. My place is at your feet, on my knees, like you made me see that very first time, when I came over to your house."

"Feels good to know your place, doesn't it?"

"Yes, Sir. It feels right."

"What else did you think of when you got hard, pup?"

"I thought of the details, Sir. I thought about how you made me stand there in my underwear while you still had on all your clothes. It was ... humiliating, I guess. You made me feel so humble. And I thought of how you put your hand on my head, pushing it down. It felt shameful, reminded me of how I'd done bad. I thought about how I kept wishing it was over, but I just had to stand there and take it until you decided that you were done. I thought how I had no choice about it, cuz it was punishment."

"What else?" He was urging me to go on.

"I thought about how you spanked me two times first, and then made me start counting again at one. I thought about how you made me take down...unghh...take down my underwear." I was getting excited, groping myself.

"You touchin yourself, boy?"

"I'm sorry, Sir. Yes." Quickly I removed my hand from my throbbing dick.

"It's okay, stroke it, just don't cum."

"Yes Sir. I thought about...um...well...I thought about the last few whacks. You were slower at first, ya know, showing me some mercy, I think. Then the last few you did quicker, didn't give me a chance to recover, I guess."

"Bet it smarted, huh?"

"Yes Sir, hurt like crazy, but I couldn't even move. I had to stand there and take it. Then you know what made me hardest of all Sir?"

"What's that, pup?" he asked, "What made you rock?"

"The fact that when I turned around and dropped on my knees, you were so rock hard yourself. I was humiliated and in pain, but you were rock! And so then you forced me to...to suck you. You—"

"I fucked your face!"

"Ohh God! Yes Sir!"

"Don't cum, boy, you better not cum til I tell you."

"Yes Sir...I won't."

"You wanna cum?"

"Yes Sir, I want to. I wanna do it so bad!"

"How long's it been, boy? How long ago was it you came?"

"Sunday, Sir. It was when we made love."

"Almost four days. Bet you wanna cum real bad then, huh?"

"Yes Sir."

"How bad you wanna shoot your load boy? How bad do you wanna do it for me?"

"Real bad, Sir. I wanna shoot my load for you, Sir. I want to so bad!" I was stroking myself fast, feeling my cock throb in my hand. It was as if I'd never been so turned on. "Please sir. I beg you!"

"Beg boy! Beg me to shoot!"

"Oh god!! Oh please, I'm begging you!" My voice was high-pitched and whiney, almost to the point of crying. "Please let me shoot it Sir. Oh please!"

"Bet you wanted my load yesterday too, didn't you? Bet you wanted your owner's cum."

"I wanted it so bad. I wanted to feel...I ...unghh...I ... I wanted to feel you...unghh... pump it into me, Sir!"

"Yeah, you wanted it so bad, you'd have begged for it, wouldn't you boy?"

"Yes Sir!! I would have begged — on my knees."

"You're close now, aren't you boy? You wanna shoot so fuckin bad right now!"

"I do Sir! I want to shoot it. Oh please, please let me do it Sir! Please let me shoot my load for you!! Oh...Oh...Oh!!!"

"Stroke it pup! Stroke that fag cock of yours and tell me who owns you!"

"You own me SIR!! Oh God, you own all of me. I belong to you. I'm your owned property. I'm your pup!"

"That's right! I own your ass, boy!"

"Oh please SIR! Please let me shoot it, please let me cum. Oh please, I beg you Sir!"

"Do it! Shoot that fuckin load. NOW!!"

I erupted like a volcano. My cum spurted from my cock in huge jets, globs flying up on my chest, hitting my face, the pillows, filling my navel. I literally screamed with ecstasy, "AAAAHHHH!!!"

"Good boy, drain that load," he was saying to me as I continued to moan, pumping out every drop of cum from myself.

"Lick it up boy, lick up that cum load for your owner. Do it boy, NOW!" I scooped up some of the cum from my chest, sticking my finger into my mouth. I sucked on it, so he could hear me obeying him. I continued to do so as he spoke to me, "Eat that cum, boy. You know your place, don't you?"

"Yes, Sir."

We both got quiet, as I continued to lick, finally allowing myself to breathe more normally. I lay there, waiting to hear what more he had to say. "You shoot a big load for me?" he asked, his voice now much calmer.

"Huge, Sir. It went all over."

"Good boy. You deserved it; you were very good today, very obedient. You get to see Drew tomorrow too, just like I promised."

"Thank you, Sir."

"You working tomorrow?" he asked, "Can't remember your schedule."

"Yes Sir. I work tomorrow and Friday both, cuz it's my turn to have the weekend off."

"That's right. Well, I got plans for us this weekend. It's a surprise though." I was excited by this revelation. "You done with your homework?"

"Yes Sir, was about to crash when you called."

"Okay, well get yourself cleaned up and then get some zee's. I'll take you to school tomorrow and then pick you up from work. We can go over to Drew's afterwards. Sweet dreams."

"Good night Sir. Thank you. I love you!"

He then clicked off. After wiping up my mess, I did exactly as he had instructed, drifting off to sleep and having wonderfully sweet dreams.

* * *

I got out of work that following evening at 6:30, and as he had indicated, Matt was there to pick me up. It had been a really long day for me as I'd been so anxious to see Drew. I hoped that I'd be allowed to spend some time alone with him. There was a part of me that was actually even concerned that he'd be angry with me. If I had not screwed up, then I would not have been denied the privilege of his friendship. What if he held that against me? Still another part of me, though, knew that Drew was the sort of friend who was not like that. He would not be angry at either Matt or me. He'd understand that Matt had the right to discipline me as he saw fit, and he'd also know that I was human and made mistakes sometimes. He pretty much had told me that the night of my paddling.

When I opened the passenger-side door to get into Matt's car, I looked in and saw what he was wearing. Instantly all thoughts of Drew left my head, as I wanted nothing other than to get Matt alone and worship every inch of him. He was wearing a backwards b-cap, sleeveless muscle tee, Umbros, and a pair of basketball sneakers. As I stood there in the doorway staring in at him, he finally said, "Get in pup. What's wrong?"

"Oh nothing, Sir...I ... um, oh nothing." I climbed inside, tossing my backpack over the seat into the back.

"Don't say 'nothing' to me. What is it?" he prodded.

My face must have reddened, for it felt about fifty degrees warmer. "Oh, it's just you, Sir. You look so—um—so hot."

He smiled at me. "Yeah, I know, but why is that any different than any other time?" He busted up laughing then. "Actually, Alex and I are goin to the gym while you visit with Drew."

"Oh, okay."

"How was your day?" he asked.

"It was so long, Sir, and I had this one really difficult customer. I just wanted to strangle her."

"Why's that?" he glanced over at me as he pulled out of the parking lot.

"Oh, she just ran my butt off. Then she had me look up all this stuff for her on the computer. Finally when her credit card was declined, she got all mad and screamed at me, and then didn't even end up buying anything."

"Probably she was embarrassed."

"Yeah, well she should have been embarrassed by her own self. She was acting like a moron."

He laughed. "People can be jerks sometimes. You eat anything?"

"No Sir, but it's okay. I'm not really hungry."

"When did you eat last?" he asked.

"I had an orange at lunch, oh, and some pretzels."

"What a weird combination. Why didn't you eat a normal lunch?"

"I had the orange for lunch, Sir. I ate the pretzels on my break at work," I explained.

"Well, I'm gonna stop and get you something. Actually, I'll just have you order a pizza or something from Alex's house. You and Drew can share it."

271

"Maybe Drew will have eaten already, Sir."

"Maybe, but I doubt it. Alex won't have eaten, not before goin to work out."

"Oh , I would think it would be a good time to eat. Then you go and burn off all the calories."

He laughed. "Don't think Alex is too worried about calories pup."

When we got to their house, I could clearly see that Matt was right. Alex definitely didn't need to worry about being fat. He was standing in the kitchen wearing only his wind pants and sneaks, getting a bottled water from the fridge. His upper body was rock hard and smooth, and I thought he looked like someone who should be posing in an underwear commercial. "I'll be ready in a sec," he said to Matt. "Drew, is this our last bottle of water?"

"Yes, Sir," he said. "Sorry, I forgot to stop at the store after work."

"Shit," he said. "Well, run over there while we're at the gym."

"Yes, Sir," he said, and then he turned to me. "Come here." He held out his arms and I stepped over to him and hugged him. "How ya doin?"

I smiled as I grabbed a hold of him. "Good. How are you?"

"All right." He then whispered in my ear, "Alex is in a really pissy mood. He'll be better after he works out, gets rid of some of his tension."

I laughed. "I can go to the store with you if you want."

"Duh!" he said teasingly, "Like I'd leave you here by yourself."

"Do you want to get a pizza? Matt said for me to order us one." I looked over to Matt.

"Why don't you call and order one? You can pick it up when you go out to the store."

"Okay, sure," said Drew. "I'm starving too. All I ate today was a bag of yogurt pretzels."

"You fags are ridiculous," said Matt. "Pup, run down to the car and get my wallet out of the glove compartment. He tossed me his keys.

"I can get the pizza, Sir," said Drew.

"No, I'll get it," Matt responded. "Hurry up pup." I dashed behind him and headed out the door. I loved the fact that he was willing to give me orders like that even in front of Drew. When I got to the car, this time I knew the correct button to press so as not to set off the alarm. I got in through the passenger-side door and opened the glove box. As I reached for the wallet a thought entered my mind. I should look inside his wallet and see his driver's license. Then I could find out his birthday. I had been thinking about that earlier in the day, actually. I was meaning to ask him. I picked up the wallet and looked around me. I leaned into the car and held the wallet under the illumination of the dome light, opening it quickly. His driver's license was in a plastic sheath and sported a remarkably good picture of him. March 5th, that was the birth date. Oh my god, that was only four days before mine! And it was this Sunday! I wondered if that had anything to do with the plans that Matt had said he'd made for us.

Quickly I closed his wallet and shut the car door. Then I ran as fast as I could back to the apartment. After Alex and Matt had left I was bursting to tell Drew what I had just found out. "Sunday is Matt's birthday! I looked at his driver's license. Plus he told me that he has plans for us this weekend, and I have both days off work."

"You getting him a gift?"

"Yeah, but I don't know what. Oh my god! What am I gonna do? You know what else is cool though? His birthday is only four days before mine. His is the fifth and mine's the ninth."

"Wow, and you are even the same age. See you two were made for each other. So how did it go Tuesday night? I know that Matt borrowed Alex's paddle. Sorry."

"Oh, that was Alex's? Does he use it on you?"

"He has before. Hasn't had to in a long time, though. Hurts like a motherfucker, doesn't it?"

"Yes! I didn't think I would ever be able to sit down again, and he only spanked me twelve times."

"Why twelve?" Drew asked.

"Supposed to be ten, but he had two warm-ups, I guess."

Drew laughed. "But who's counting, right?"

"Me! Me and my ass." We then both laughed. "I can't even believe I'm laughing about this. I was so sad about it. Worse than the spanks though, was that I had to take off my necklace."

"He take it from you then?" Drew looked at me sympathetically.

"No, I still have it, but I'm not allowed to wear it."

"Well it's good he didn't take it from you. Bet that means you will get to wear it again pretty soon. He told Alex that I could not see you for a whole week, but then he must've changed his mind, huh?"

"You aren't gonna believe how that happened." I turned around then and pulled up my shirt. "Look at what he wrote on me. Plus he wrote this," I turned back around and pulled up my shirtsleeve. "And there is another one down underneath my underpants. I had to show these markings to four different people—strangers! That was how I earned the privilege of seeing you today."

He laughed. "That's cool. You see what he's doin, don't you?"

"What?" I asked, naively.

"Well he knows you feel bad cuz you fucked up, so now he's giving you a chance to succeed. He made it something he knew you'd be able to do, but also it was not something that was too easy. Then it makes you feel good about yourself."

"I never thought of it that way. Why do you think he's doing that when I'm supposed to be getting punished right now? Why would he be rewarding me instead?"

Drew put his arm around me. "You are a smart guy, ya know, but sometimes you can be so ...well...so innocent," he laughed at me in such a gentle, loving manner. "Matt has already moved on. You fucked up, he gave you your punishment, the situation's been dealt with, so now he has put it behind him. You need to do that too, silly."

"Then how come I still have the restrictions? No necklace. No you, other than tonight, I mean."

"Well cause that was part of the punishment. You did the crime, and now you gotta do the time. But as far as he is concerned, it's been dealt with. Period. So quit your fuckin worrying, okay?"

I smiled at him, putting my own arm around him now. "Thanks, Drew. I just knew that you'd know the right thing to say."

"It's cuz I'm so OLD and experienced," he laughed at himself. "I'm not young and cute like you any more."

"Shut up! Let's go get our pizza, and then you can help me decide what to get Matt for his birthday present."

"Cool."

* * *

We were on the balcony when Alex and Matt got back from the gym. Drew had just lit up a cigarette. "Shit, I hope he lets me finish this," he said. "It's only my third one today; I'm working on quitting."

"Why don't you just quit altogether if you only smoke three a day anyhow?" I asked.

"Psychological, I guess. It's sorta like my crutch maybe. I just love smoking, even though I know all the bad stuff about it. The one single reason why Alex hasn't made me quit though is that he used to smoke himself, not for very long though. After he quit, though, he hates it now, but he also knows how hard it is to quit, so he goes easier on me."

"Alex is so quiet to me, Drew. It seems like he never talks to me," I confided.

"Oh don't worry about that. It isn't that he doesn't like you or anything. He does, really. I know he does. He just knows you belong to someone else. He respects boundaries, that's all. He probably is gonna take his cues from Matt. When Matt starts to show that he is comfortable with you being around Alex, then he will warm up to you more."

"Matt's not really like that with you though, Drew. I mean he talks to you and stuff, at least more than Alex does to me."

"Yeah, but Matt is kind of the novice here. Alex has been my Master for a lot longer. In some ways Matt is learning stuff from Alex. I bet he advised him about your punishment. After all, he did loan Matt the paddle."

"I'm embarrassed that Alex knows I got spanked," I said. "That's so humiliating."

Drew shrugged. "Hmm, well I don't know of any boys who have never gotten spanked before. Not unless their Masters are real wusses or something. It's just part of their job to discipline us, not anything for anyone to be embarrassed by."

"I know, but I just can't help it. Sometimes I just feel a certain way, and it doesn't really matter if it's logical or not."

"Well, you are very emotional. It's cool though; that's just who you are." He exhaled a big stream of smoke, deliberately blowing it away from me. "But if you are talkin humiliation, that can actually be quite hot."

"What do you mean?" I asked.

"Well, I mean like the piss thing, when you tasted some of Matt's piss. Imagine if he made you do that in public. Wouldn't that be sort of humiliating?"

"We'd get arrested!" I retorted.

"Well, this is just hypothetical. Plus I didn't necessarily mean 'public' public. I meant private public, like in front of his friends or something. Or say he made you kiss his feet, or piss yourself in front of people—anything like that, where other people could see him controlling you. It would show how far you were willing to go in order to serve him and obey him. No limits, even though it was embarrassing."

"Yeah, that is sort of hot." I smiled as I thought about what he was saying. "But that's different than getting punished. He could make me do that stuff just cuz he liked it, not because I'd been bad."

"True. But still, don't you think it was hot the way he spanked you? Afterwards, didn't it turn you on, make you feel controlled?"

"Yeah, but not really til yesterday. I was thinking about it in the afternoon and I got a big boner." I laughed. "Then Matt let me jack off last night while he was on the phone with me, and that's what we talked about. We talked about him spanking me."

"See, it still was humiliating to you, but because of the humiliation it actually was also hotter than fucking hell. Right?"

I nodded. "Yeah, weird, isn't it? Do you think that makes me a pervert or something? Some kind of a masochist?"

"Yeah, right. Just like me." He took another drag off his cigarette.

Suddenly the sliding glass door opened. It was Alex. "Put out that cigarette and get in here. Both of you," he said. Of course we wasted no time, obeying immediately.

As we stepped into the living room, Matt was sitting comfortably in the same recliner that he'd sat the first day we visited. He had his feet propped up on a footstool. Both he and Alex had obviously showered. Matt was now wearing wind pants and white crew socks. He had on a different beater shirt but the same b-cap. Alex had on his same wind suit, having obviously worked out in the clothes he'd had on underneath it.

"Drew, go get Matt and me a beer," Alex said. I walked over to Matt, not really sure why I'd been called in. I stood there in front of him, waiting to see if he was going to give me any instructions. He did not speak, but instead pointed to the ground. I knew immediately that I was to kneel and did so.

I then knelt there at his feet, looking up at him. He did not return my gaze, though, or even acknowledge my presence. Alex had sat down on the sofa, and he was holding the television remote. He clicked through the channels until he got to the sports channels. He and Matt started talking to one another about what was on TV, and when Drew came in with the beer, neither of them even acknowledged him with so much as a thank you. Drew did not wait as I had for instructions to kneel, he just seemed to know it was expected and did so, right at Alex's feet. This was the first time I'd ever seen Drew in the subservient position to his Master.

Alex shifted his position on the sofa and propped his bare feet up on the edge of the coffee table. He was somewhat sprawled out, and Drew was on the floor next to the coffee table, right beside his owner. I probably should have been watching Matt, being that I was his property, but I wanted to see what was going to happen with Drew. Matt did not reprimand me, though. He allowed me to continue to observe, perhaps knowing that it was a good way for me to learn. Alex seemed to pay no notice to his boy whatsoever and still focused all of his attention on the game he and Matt were watching. They continued to talk to one another as if Drew and I were not even in the room.

Carefully Drew then reached up to Alex's left foot and took it in his hands, beginning to rub it. Finally Alex spoke to Drew for the first time, "No hands." That was all he said. Immediately Drew pulled his hands away and clasped them together behind his back. He held onto his right wrist with his left hand. Then he slid himself on his knees over to where he was as close to the coffee table as possible and leaned in to bring his mouth down to Alex's toes. Alex was acting as if nothing was even happening, and then I turned to look over at Matt. His composure was the same as Alex's, and as I looked up at him he casually took a swig of his beer.

I then moved over to the footstool, imitating the position that Drew was in, and clasped my own hands behind my back. Unlike Alex, Matt was wearing socks. I wondered if I should remove them. I did not know what to do, though., so I just bent down and kissed his socked feet. Apparently this was acceptable, for Matt did not tell me otherwise or make any effort to pull his feet away from me. I glanced over to look at Drew, while continuing to kiss my owner's feet and saw that he was doing the same. His kisses were worshipful, almost passionate. It was as if he revered them. I glanced up to Alex, and from my position on the floor saw him as being almost godlike, the way he reclined there, towering over his boy, while his feet were being served.

I then looked back up at Matt, staring up at him wide-eyed. I was almost pleading with him for instruction. Should I take his socks off? If so, did that mean I could use my hands? When he did look down at me, it seemed to be with no interest whatsoever, as if everything that was happening right then was perfectly normal and acceptable. I continued to stare up at him while I again kissed the sole of his foot. I unclasped my hands from behind my back then and reached up to grip the edge of his left sock. I was going to begin removing it. Finally he spoke to me. "No! Use your mouth." Startled, I resumed my former position, pulling my arms back behind myself. I then glanced over to Drew. He had not even seemed to look up from his position. He now was licking Alex's feet in between his kisses.

I moved my mouth down then to where I had just had my hands, and gripped the edge of Matt's sock with my teeth. I did it so carefully so as to only touch his sock, and not his skin. Matt pulled his heel just slightly off the footstool as I tugged on his sock, bringing it down below the heel. I then released my grip and moved my mouth up to his big toe. There was a tiny excess of fabric at the edge of the toe, where I could safely grip with my teeth without scraping him at all in the process. I carefully bit down into the fabric and pulled my head back, pulling the sock off in one smooth movement. His naked foot was then in front of me, resting comfortably on the footstool. I then slid over and duplicated my actions with his right foot. I managed to do it much quicker the second time, even though when he lifted up his heel it was hardly noticeable. It was more like he just took his weight off of it, but did not actually pick it up.

Now I knelt there, hands clasped behind my back, staring at my owner's feet. I took a brief moment to again glance up at him. I wanted to see him the way that I had just seen Alex. I wanted to see him sitting there in his towering position of comfort and dominance. He looked like a king on a throne, even more so than he had that very first time I served him in his bedroom. He did not have to instruct me to kiss his feet. I did so very passionately then, out of genuine awe and worship. I kissed them over and over again, first the left, then the right, never removing my lips from them other than to switch back and forth to the opposite foot. I began using my tongue, licking them, tasting them for the very first time. I licked and kissed his toes, sliding my tongue in between each of them. I kissed his soles, every inch of them, and bathed them with my tongue. I worshipped his heels, his ankles, every single square inch of his feet, including his toenails. His feet were very clean, as he had just showered, but did smell slightly of the inside of his sneakers. They had a slightly musky, perhaps sweaty smell. They did not taste unlike the other parts of his skin which I'd had in my mouth though, and to be honest, even if they had not been clean, I would have worshipped them just the same.

280

I loved him so much at that moment, and felt so small kneeling there in front of him. I felt so very much less than him, and it was a feeling that was so satisfying to me. It was right— very right. I thought of how Alex had a clear view of me kneeling here serving my own Master. I loved that Matt was being worshipped in front of his friend. I loved that I was the one doing it.

As I knelt in that servile position, I felt myself become so aroused. My thoughts remained focused upon showing Matt how much I worshiped and adored him, so much so that I was able to mentally block my own discomfort. My own feet were becoming numb as I knelt on them, my neck was getting sore, and even my mouth was tired. I continued in my efforts to serve him, though, all through the rest of the game. At one point Alex ordered Drew to get up and get them each another beer, but when he returned, he resumed his position.

Finally without warning, the time was up, for the game had apparently ended. Matt removed his feet from the stool without even telling me he was going to do so, and then he did say to me, "Put my socks back on. You can use your hands." I obeyed him immediately, and held his feet in my hands, one at a time, as I re-socked each of them. Then I crawled around to the other side of his chair to find his shoes and brought them back to him. I put them on for him and tied them, and continued to kneel there. When he was finally ready to go he stood up. I waited for his permission before I stood myself. When I did get up, I noticed that Drew had already done the same. I looked at Matt imploringly, seeking his permission to say goodbye to my friend. I knew it would be almost a full week before I saw him again. Matt simply nodded.

I walked over to Drew and hugged him. "Thanks Drew. Thanks for being my friend."

"You're welcome, silly. Thank *you* for being mine." I thought it interesting that neither of us made any comment about what we had just done for the previous hour-and-a-half. I guess we both just knew it was our place to serve and that what we'd done was right.

17

Although it made perfect sense that Matt would get horny after having worked out and then having been worshipped non-stop for ninety minutes, I was not really prepared for what that was actually going to mean to me. When we exited the apartment and descended the stairs, Matt grabbed my arm before I could head for the car. "Over there," he said, nodding to a dark corner of the parking lot. There was some sort of outbuilding, a wooden structure. I believe it housed the dumpsters for the apartments, as my own complex had a similar structure itself.

When we got behind the building, there was very little light. A street lamp from the parking lot illuminated one corner of the area where we were, thus allowing us the ability to see somewhat, but we ourselves were completely in shadows. The space we were in was an ally of sorts, for there was a section of about five feet between the back of the building and the big wooden fence which surrounded the property. There was literally no possibility of any passersby spotting us unless they were to make a very deliberate attempt to walk back behind the building to join us.

Before my eyes could adjust to the dimness, I tripped on something, almost completely losing my balance. As I lunged forward I thrust out my palms and caught myself against the back fence. Matt was immediately behind me, pressing his body against mine. He slid his hands up my sides, sending shivers throughout my body, and instantly I giggled. I was very ticklish in that spot. He quickly moved his hands further up my sides, and before I knew it he had bent his elbows and clasped his hands together behind my head. My arms were then pinned helplessly within his own; I was in a full-nelson headlock.

"Watch your step, fag," he said, "or you could end up getting hurt." This statement surprised me somewhat for only three times before had he ever referred to me as a "fag," and the one time was in a lighthearted, joking manner. His voice was very serious now though. The other two times were when he was fucking my face and just about to achieve orgasm. "You fuckin little pussyboy, I know your type. I know exactly what you fuckin want." He leaned into me, pushing the side of my face against the fence. His mouth was right next to my ear, as he leaned down. Due to the difference in our height, it felt as if he were pulling me right off the ground. I kicked my feet slightly, scraping my tiptoes against the pavement.

I struggled a bit within his grasp, for a few seconds forgetting that this even was Matt who had me pinned. My arms were twisted unnaturally, and I winced from the pain. "Please sir...it's hurting me!" He then took a step back and then suddenly thrust me forward, releasing the grip of his hands around my neck. I hurled into the wall with a smack, hitting my head as I did so, for I was not able to bring my arms down quickly enough to break the impact.

"Unghhh!" I cried in response to the searing pain that shot through my face. Suddenly I thought of what had happened the first day Matt and I had officially met. I thought of what Devin and Kyle had done to me. "Please don't hurt me!!" My scream was out of pure reflex, as I pulled my hands up to cover my head. I was crouching down, tucking my head down towards the ground, trying to protect myself. Matt was no longer there with me, but instead these other people—these strangers-had taken his place. I lay there, terrified, trembling as thoughts of Devin and Kyle taunting me flashed into my memory. *You look like a fuckin dog, you faggot!! If you want it, crawl over here and get it! Here faggot!* I saw them towering over me, both of them. *You heard him, faggot...he said beg...like the dog you are!* I fell over on the pavement, pulling my knees up towards my chest, waiting for the blow. I remembered the way he kicked me right in the side. "No!! Please don't hurt me...Please!" *You want it back, fag? Here!* I buried my hands in my face, sobbing, as I relived the forceful blow of the hardcover book connecting with my nose. "Aaahhh! No! No!" My sobs turned into weeping as I lay there trembling, not even fully conscious of where I was.

What was happening to me? "Please, I beg you! Please give it back!" I repeated this cry over and over as I lay there, burying my hands in my face. I lay there shaking, reliving the terrifying fear, waiting to again be kicked and then hit. It was like the day that Devin had come into the bookstore, I'd been somehow transported back to the very moment when he'd pummeled me.

Suddenly Matt's arms were around me, "Petey, it's me Matt, calm down, I'm sorry. I'm so sorry." He pulled me into him, but I was still scared, pressing my fists against his chest, trying to get free. "Petey, wait! Please calm down. I won't hurt you, I promise. Remember? I promised you, I will never hurt you!" I was crying uncontrollably at this point, barely hearing anything he was saying.

"I never meant to scare you. Please believe me. I didn't think you would hit your head. Oh god!" As I knelt there on the ground shaking and crying he gradually tightened his grip around me and pulled me closer to him. "Pup, listen to me, please... please, it was just a scene, that's all. Just a stupid scene. I thought it would be hot to do you behind the garage, fuck you real rough. I didn't mean to hurt you, honest I didn't."

I wrapped my arms around his neck then, grabbing a hold of him fiercely and hugging him with all my might. I could not come up with words to say, but just instead held onto him, wanting to again feel the security of his loving tenderness, the way he'd saved me that day at the school, carrying me across campus and taking me to the hospital. I wanted him to be that gentle and heroic savior and to feel his protective strength the way I had the first day he'd made love to me that at his house. He knelt there with me, holding me without saying any more, allowing me to feel that it was really him and not some stranger who was trying to hurt me.

"I'm sorry Sir," I sobbed, "I'm so sorry." I was still crying as I held onto him.

"No, pup, don't be sorry. It's okay. Don't be sorry at all. I was stupid—so fuckin stupid. After..."

He did not finish the statement, but I felt that he had somehow suddenly remembered how we met. He remembered how he'd rescued me when I was truly getting beaten. He had not realized that I'd interpret his aggressiveness in the same light. He'd only wanted a hot scene, and I understood that now. "I should have trusted you, Sir. I'm sorry . I did not mean to freak. Please forgive me, I'm sorry."

"Stop it," he said calmly, "Stop saying you're sorry. Are you hurt? Did I hurt your head?"

I shook it violently. "No Sir, see? It is not hurt at all. You didn't hurt me, really you didn't."

He then scooped me up in his arms as he stood. "Let's get over to the light. He carried me out from behind the building and walked towards the lamp post. "Let me see," He said. I turned my head to show him, to prove to him I was fine. "It's just a little red, that's all," he said, and then moved his lips over and kissed the side of my head, just below the spot in question. "You know I'd never hurt you, don't you pup? I never, ever would."

"I know Sir. I'm sorry, I ruined it for you. We can go back! Please! We can go back and you can do it to me, just like you wanted. I will not cry this time, I promise. Please let's go back, okay?"

He cupped the back of my head in his big hand then, still carrying me in his arms, and moved his lips down to meet my own. He kissed me then so beautifully and passionately. I at first thought his kisses were to silence me, but they truly were so much more. When he pulled his mouth away finally, he said to me, "No, let's go to my house. I can make love to you there." Then he carried me back to the car and placed me carefully in the passenger seat.

When we got over to his house, even then he took responsibility for my safety, not even allowing me to walk to the door. He carried me up the steps and inside, not putting me down until he was all the way upstairs in his bedroom. How is it that I could have thought under any circumstances that he would ever do me any harm? How could I have confused him with my tormentors? "Matt, please forgive me. I wish I had trusted you."

"It's not your fault," he said. "It's my fault; I should have known better—"

"No! How is it your fault, Sir? I'm the one who was the baby. I'm the one who freaked out!"

"My job's to protect you, even when you freak." He had placed me on the bed and was sitting beside me. "I'm going to undress you now," he said, not at all asking permission of me, but telling me specifically what he was doing. "I loved the way you worshipped me tonight, pup. That's what got me so hot."

I smiled up at him. "Sometime we will do what you wanted Sir. Sometime I will serve you that way...I mean the scene like you wanted."

"Don't worry bout that now, pup," he said as he ran his fingers across my smooth, bare chest, sliding his hand underneath my shirt. Then he proceeded to strip me.

"I want so bad to feel you inside me again, Sir." I stared up into his eyes. "Please be inside me again like you were before. Please make love to me."

He did in fact make the most passionate love to me imaginable that night. I awoke in his arms the next morning, my fear just a memory. I was where it was safe, in the arms of my owner.

* * *

When Matt and I arrived at my apartment the following morning Kathie was already up and in the kitchen. She was leaning against the counter drinking a cup of coffee when I walked in. "Hey," I said, "Long time no see."

"Yeah, where were you last night?" she asked.

"With Matt. I stayed at his house."

"Would've been nice of you to leave me a note," she retorted. "I was kinda worried."

"Oh, I'm sorry. I actually didn't plan on spending the night. It just got late and so he asked me to stay. I'll leave you a note or call next time, I promise. I'm sorry."

"All right. It just seems like we never see each other any more. I was actually planning on spending the evening with you for a change. It's okay though, did you guys have fun?"

"Yeah, we went over to our friends' house, Alex and Drew. I hung out with Drew while Matt and Alex went to the gym, and then we watched TV when they got back. We had pizza too."

"Did Matt drop you off just now?" she asked.

"No, he's waiting for me in the living room." She stepped over to the archway where she could see into the living room.

"Hey Matt, how ya doin?"

"Not too bad. You?"

"Been very busy. What's Tracy up to?" she asked. I felt my blood pressure rise slightly from her question.

"Don't know," he answered, "I haven't really seen her lately, not since Monday."

"Oh wow, I got the impression that you two were pretty serious about each other." I detected a note of sarcasm in her voice and wondered if Matt knew her well enough to pick up on it.

He laughed. "Oh really?"

"Never assume anything," I interjected, then quickly turned to go towards my bedroom. The first thing I saw when I walked in was my beaded necklace on the stand. I wondered if Matt even thought about it and if he was gonna make me go without it for much longer. I gathered up my books and stuffed them into my back pack. I'd already showered at Matt's house, but I was wearing my same shirt and pants as the day before. I stripped out of them and stood in front of the opened closet door, unsure of what to put on.

Matt walked through the bedroom doorway. "Boy, she's one who needs her coffee in the morning, huh?"

"Yeah," I said, "I don't know what's up her ass."

"She's just protective of you, that's all. She just lectured me about not letting you get hurt. Was like it came from out of nowhere."

"She did?" I asked, instantly getting angry. "I'm sorry Sir; I'll talk to her about it."

"Nah, don't. Just let it go. Like I said, she just is concerned about you."

"Does she have a short memory or something? Doesn't she remember how you saved me before and how you bought me all this stuff?"

"Hmm, well maybe she thinks I'm not trustworthy, that I've got an ulterior motive or something."

"That's bullshit. What if I said that about Carter?" Matt closed the door behind him as I was beginning to raise my voice.

"Shhh" he said. "Just chill. So what ya gonna wear?"

"You pick it out, Sir. Please."

"Wear these," he said, pulling out a shirt and pair of pants very similar to what he was wearing himself. "We can match today." I smiled up at him. Then he stepped over to the stand and picked up the necklace. "And this too."

"You mean it Sir?" I asked excitedly. "Oh thank you! It's only been two days; seemed like forever though." I walked over to him, looking up into his face, feeling so excited and proud. "Sir, I have never wanted anything more than to belong to you, and to wear your collar, as a symbol that I am your property."

He looked down at me, not smiling, but conveying such warmth with his eyes. As I stared up at him, I sensed that he too was proud to own me, although I did not exactly understand why. I did not feel as if I were much to be proud of. Then out of pure instinct I did what came natural. I knelt down in front of him. There was no more appropriate way to receive a collar, I realized. As I knelt there I bowed my head, feeling so humbled and subservient. I felt him reach down and place the necklace around my neck, and I lifted my chin slightly to allow him access. He attached the clasp in the back and continued to stand there, towering over me, assuming his stance of domination.

I had to lower myself even further. Never before had I felt such an overpowering need to demonstrate my humility. I bent myself forward, placing my hands flat on the ground, now in a position where I was on all fours. I did not look up at him. I couldn't, but could only stare at his feet. He was wearing his basketball sneakers, and I lowered my face to the ground, right next to them. Closing my eyes briefly, I kissed them. I kissed first the left, so slowly and reverently, and then moved over to the right. I opened my eyes while doing so, worshipping my owner's feet, trying desperately to convey to him how very much he meant to me. I wanted for him to see how well I knew my place. I wanted him to feel the power that he held over me. I wanted for him to take for granted that I belonged to him, that I was less and he was more. I kissed and licked his feet over and over, and did not even think of stopping until he told me to do so.

He stepped back from me finally, while I remained bowed respectfully before him. "Look at me, pup," he said, and I

289

moved myself into an upright kneeling position, staring up
into his face. "You can see Drew again too, but it has to be
when I'm with you, or when I give you permission. Still no
concert though."

"Yes, Sir," I said, beaming up at him, tears rolling down
my cheeks. "Thank you, Sir. Thank you so much!"

Throughout the day, I continued to touch my necklace,
running my fingers across the smooth beads, as I now had
an even far greater appreciation for it and for what it
represented. Matt had told me when he handed down my
punishments on Wednesday that I would not be allowed to
wear it until I had proven I was again worthy of being seen
as his pup. He apparently now felt that I had proven myself.
I could not wait to tell Drew about it. My only
disappointment was that I had to find a gift for Matt today at
some point. It would have been so cool if I could have
included Drew in this quest, yet Matt had been specific that I
could see him but only with his express permission. It was
not like I could ask Matt to let me go shopping with Drew for
a birthday present, for it would then totally spoil the
surprise. After Matt and I had parted company at school, I
thought that I should have asked for permission anyways,
and simply told him I wanted to go shopping with Drew but
just not mention the item for which we'd be shopping.

Since I had not thought to ask this in time, though, I
resigned myself to the fact that unless I ran into Matt at
some point on campus that day, I'd have to shop by myself.
It totally sucked that I was scheduled to work that afternoon,
too, for that meant I'd either have to squeeze in some time
between school and work or else wait until the end of the day
to find the gift. What I ultimately decided to do was to cut
my last class of the day. It was a boring class that I was acing
anyways, and I knew that nothing major was forthcoming in
terms of tests or quizzes, so it would be fine.

At lunch I got out my bus schedule and checked to see the
route I'd need to take to get to the mall. I mapped it out

mentally and then grabbed a chicken sandwich from the cafeteria. I wrapped up the sandwich and tucked it carefully in the top of my backpack and then headed for the bus station. As I sat in my seat on the bus, nibbling on my sandwich I kept worrying about where I should go to find the perfect gift for Matt. What exactly did you buy someone who already had everything he could ever want or need? He certainly had the money to go out and get any new item that he desired. My choice would have to be something that was not so much practical, but instead an expression from the heart. It would have to be something that conveyed to him how much he meant to me. I was not sure that such an item actually even existed, because the depths of my feelings for him seemed to transcend any tangible, material possession I could think of.

Initially I began to focus upon getting him something that had to do with puppies, but then quickly dismissed that idea, remembering that I'd already bought him the stuffed dog from the grocery store. Jewelry items also did not seem appropriate for it seemed that he was the one who would be more apt to buy that sort of thing for me. He was really into sports, but I did not have a clue what to get him along that line. He liked to dress nicely, but I could not think of any articles of clothing that I could pick out for him that he would not already have.

I had had to change busses once in order to get on the correct route to the mall, and when I finally stepped off the bus at the mall entrance, I checked my watch. I had a little less than two hours before I had to catch the bus back. That would be cutting it close, in fact, leaving me only a small window of time to make it to work. As I began strolling through the mall, I quickly came to a realization that I would not be able to settle on just one gift. To my surprise, I found several "perfect" items that I just had to get for him. The first was in a cigar shop. I bought him a humidor storage case for cigars which came with a sample set of "the world's finest cigars." That item alone was almost seventy dollars. I handed over my debit card eagerly, though, knowing he was worth the money.

The second two items I found were in the jewelry store. The first was a monogrammed cigar lighter that came complete with a cutter. I would have to arrange to pick up the lighter later that day or the next morning somehow in order to allow for completion time of the monogramming. I also found my favorite item of all— a silver plated key chain which was itself shaped like an older skeleton key. It had an inscription on it that said "Key to my heart," and the upper part of the design bore an inscription of a heart. It did not look feminine at all and was small enough to where it could be placed on a key chain without anyone particularly noticing.

The fourth item that I picked up was a pair of 2(x)ist silk boxers. I could not resist them, thinking of how sexy he would look.

Then I stopped into the A&F store and picked him up a cool b-cap. I knew he had tons of them already, but this one would be the only one from me.

The final item was a puppy gift after all. I found him an adorable mouse pad that had a picture of the cutest puppy I'd ever seen. That one was the least expensive of all the gifts, yet I was very excited about it for it was so absolutely adorable.

I sat down at the café then, not far from where Matt had first collared me with his necklace, and had a diet cola. I added up my receipts and realized I'd spent a little over two hundred dollars. My savings account still would have over six hundred left in it, though, and I remembered all the money he's spent on me less than a week prior. He was worth every single penny.

The bus was due to arrive in about ten minutes so I picked up my purchases and stuffed them into my back pack, being very careful not to damage the baseball cap.

Then I headed out to catch the bus. I was so excited as I waited, anticipation bubbling from inside me. He would be so happy.

"Hey Petey," I heard a familiar voice behind me. I turned around to see it was Carter. "What are you doing here?"

"Oh, I just had to do some shopping. How ya doin?" I asked.

"Good. Hey you want a ride somewhere?" he offered.

"Oh, well thanks, but I can catch the bus. I'm going to work now."

"Well let me give you a lift. I'm going that way myself already."

"You sure?" I asked.

"Yeah, of course I am. C'mon." He then led me to his car and pressed a button to release the door lock for me. "How's everything going for you? Any one else hassling you?"

"Oh no, not at all. Everything is going cool. You and Kathie sure spend a lot of time together; you must really like her."

He nodded, "Yeah, I definitely do that. I've never been so happy before. It's like we were made for each other. What about you? How come you don't have yourself a girlfriend?"

I shrugged. "Don't want one, I guess. I have enough other stuff to worry about anyhow. Girls seem like they just are a big headache."

He laughed. "Yeah, they can be, for sure, especially when they are as headstrong as your sister."

"Tell me about it," I agreed. "This morning she bitched out my friend Matt for no reason at all. She told him that she was afraid he was gonna hurt me."

"She's just being protective of you, that's all, but I don't see what she has to worry about with Matt. He seems like a great guy. Seems like she'd be glad you two are such close buds. I mean, look how he saved you from those dudes beating you up."

"Exactly!" I said. "But she thinks we spend too much time together or some shit."

"Have you ever thought that maybe she is just a little bit jealous? After all, she always had been so close to you, but now all of a sudden you don't see one another much any more."

"Yeah, maybe," I said, "but does she expect for me to sit at home alone all the time while she is out with you? No offense to you, Carter, but if she can have a boyfriend then so— or I mean then I can have friends too."

He paused before responding, perhaps noticing my near slip of the tongue. "Like I said, just give it time. She is gonna eventually see that everything is cool with Matt. Trust me. If you think it'd help, I can talk to her about it."

"I don't know, Carter—maybe, but it could make things worse. I think I will just try to find a way to spend some more time with her, like we used to do. Maybe then she will chill out about everything."

"Good plan, I think," he smiled over at me. "You two are lucky to have each other. You're both great people."

"Thanks," I said.

When I got to work I still had a few minutes to spare and so I went to the outdoor café adjacent our building and got myself an iced tea. I sat down at one of the tables and pulled out my cell phone. I dialed Drew's number, even though I knew Drew would not be home from school yet. It was not my intention to talk to him anyways, but instead to Alex.

"Hello?" It was Alex.

"Hi Alex...um...Sir, this is Peter Drinkell, Drew's friend."

"Hi Petey," he said. "Drew's still at work."

"I know Sir, but I wanted to talk to you anyways. Um, is that okay?"

"Sure," he laughed, "Wassup?"

"Well I have a favor to ask, sorta. You know I can't see Drew right away, least not without Matt's permission, right?"

"Yeah, I'm aware of that."

"Well I need to get a message to him, Sir."

"You should give the message to your Master, boy, and let him decide if he wants it to be delivered."

"Oh, I know sir, but you don't understand. It is about a surprise for him, for Matt. Sunday is his birthday. I bought him a gift at the mall and I need to figure out how to pick it up. It's already paid for and everything, and I just wondered if he could pick it up for me, if it's not too much of an inconvenience Sir."

"Well, I can do that. Where in the mall is it?"

"It's at Crestwood Jewelers. It's a cigar lighter. I can't believe you'd do that for me, Sir."

"It's no big deal. Don't gotta call me sir either, not unless Matt tells you to."

"Um, okay...Alex. Well it won't be ready til about five o'clock tonight. It could even be picked up tomorrow. If you know when you plan to be there, I can call them and tell them you'll be picking it up for me."

"I'll go there tonight, then drop it off to you. If you want, though, I could pick you up and just take you there to get it yourself."

"I'm at work, Sir—er, I mean Alex."

"Oh okay. You at that bookstore down by Vinnie's Pizza?"

"Yes, yes I am."

"Okay, I can drop it off to you there. Don't worry, I won't tell Matt either. I'm meeting him later tonight. We're goin to a club together."

"Cool," I said. "Well, have fun! Thank you so much Alex for doing this. Otherwise I'd have had to find a way out there tomorrow morning, and I know Matt had made plans for us, so I'm not sure how I'd get away with it."

"Everything's cool. I'll see you in a few hours, okay?"

"Okay, thanks! Bye!"

"Bye," he said and then clicked off.

It was a little past seven when Alex arrived at the bookstore. I still had another hour of my shift left to complete. Right as I was about to go greet him, Mr. Bartlett stepped up to me. "Peter, you wanna knock off early tonight? It's kinda slow in here."

"Sure, that would be great Sir, thank you."

"Okay, finish up your cleaning stuff and you can go."

"Yes Sir," I said.

I then turned from him and greeted Alex. "Hi!" I said excitedly. "Thanks again for bringing that over to me."

"Sure," he said, handing me a small white bag. "The lady at the store showed it to me, for my approval," he laughed. "Cool gift. I bet he'll like it."

"You think so?" I asked honestly.

"Yeah sure. When you get out of work?"

"Right now, actually. I just have to put this stuff away and then I'm done."

"You walkin home?" he asked. "I'll give you a lift if you want."

"Um, well, I don't know. Do you think you should, sir?"

He looked at me somewhat puzzled. "Of course I should. Why not?"

"Cuz I don't want Matt to find out and be mad at us."

"I don't think Matt would be mad at us for that. He doesn't care if I give his boy a ride home, I'm sure. Plus it's not like we're gonna tell him, or it'd ruin the surprise of his gift."

"Yeah, you're right. Well thanks ... again. Let me put this stuff back, and then I'll be right out. Okay?"

"Okay," he said, and turned to browse the store while he waited.

When I returned, carrying my backpack over my shoulder, Alex met me by the front door. "I'm ready," I said, and he opened the door for me as we stepped outside.

"My car is that Lexus over there," he pointed. Just as we began to move towards it, a familiar car pulled in front of us, right into the parking lot. It was Matt. He cut us off, stopping right in our path, rolling down his window.

"Hey, wassup?" Alex said to Matt.

"Was gonna ask you the same thing," he responded, staring at Alex. Then he turned to me, "Petey, get in the car."

Without arguing, I did so immediately. Oh shit, how was I gonna explain this? "I was just gonna give Peter a ride home," Alex said.

"Don't bother, that's what I'm here for. Remember me? Petey's owner, your friend — or so I thought."

"Dude, chill out. It's not like that, not at all. I just was givin the kid a ride home, no big deal. I don't want your property."

"Why would you be spending time with him in the first place without telling me?"

"Dude, take a pill. I'm not interested in your boy. We're buds, and I don't do shit like that."

Matt looked directly into his eyes, as if trying to read him. "All right, it's cool," he said. "Still wanna meet up later? Eleven o'clock?"

"Was countin on it," Alex responded.

"Okay, see ya then."

I sensed that Matt was not really cool with the situation though. He seemed to still be angry, saying nothing to me at all as he drove me home. "Sir..." I said to him when he pulled into my parking lot, "I'm sorry, please don't be mad. I only was getting a ride from him, that's all."

"Why was he there to begin with? I didn't see him carrying any books."

"I think he was there to browse, Sir. Maybe he didn't find what he wanted."

"Petey, don't fuck with me. I'm not an idiot."

"I know sir, I didn't—"

"It's not your problem anyways. It's between Alex and me, so don't worry about it."

I hung my head shamefully. "Sir, don't be mad at Alex, please."

"Drop it!" he ordered.

I continued to stare down at my lap. Softly I said, "Sir, can I please just say one thing? Please?"

He sighed, "What?"

"I called Alex and asked him to come over, that was why he was there, but it's not like what you are thinking. It was not ...um...it wasn't like I was..."

"All right, spill. What the fuck are you talkin about ? Why did you ask him to come over to where you work without telling me first?"

I was starting to feel very intimidated, as I sensed Matt getting angrier. "It was for a surprise Sir...for ...um...for your birthday."

"What?" he asked. "I don't want any surprise for my birthday."

"He was bringing me over my gift for you." I unzipped my backpack then and pulled out the white paper bag. "I was going to give it to you Sunday, but you can have it now Sir, please." I held it out to him. "I didn't have a way to get down to pick it up since I had to work, so I asked Alex to have Drew do it for me. He did it himself though."

"You should have just got Kathie to take you," he said, "or just not gotten me a gift at all! I don't expect my pup to buy me presents."

"I wanted to buy it Sir. It's your birthday!" I was starting to get emotional. "Plus I could not tell Kathie about it, not with her being how she is lately."

"All right," he said, holding out his hand to take the gift from me. "Let me see."

He reached above his head and flipped on the dome light, then pulled the small box out of the bag in his hand. He opened it and removed the lighter. He pulled it out of the box, examining it closely. He saw the monogram, MCP. "Pup, this is a very cool gift. Thank you." He then bent over and kissed me. "I don't want you spending money you don't have to spare, buying me presents though.

"I didn't Sir," I said. "It was money I had saved, honest. So are you still mad?"

"No, not mad. I never was really mad at you anyways, more so at Alex. With you, pup, I was a little disappointed though."

"You were?" I asked, suddenly feeling as if I were on the verge of tears. "I'm sorry, Sir. I told Alex I could not take the ride from him, not without your permission, but he said he was sure you would not mind."

"Well, pup, I probably would not have minded him giving you a ride, but it is not up to Alex to speak for me. You take your orders from only one person, pup, and that is me. Do you understand?"

"Yes Sir," I said, hanging my head shamefully.

"There may be some times when I tell you it is okay to obey another master, but that is for me to decide, not you and definitely not Alex. You should, of course, always be respectful to other people, especially other superiors, but I am your owner. Got it?"

"Yes, Sir," I said again. "Sir," I looked up at him, "I would never betray you. Honest I wouldn't. I belong to you, not Alex."

He then pushed a button on his armrest and his seat went back. He flipped off the dome light above his head. "Blow me!" he said. And obediently I lowered myself in the seat, scrunching my small body on the floor between my seat and the dashboard, and leaned over to serve him. He leaned back comfortably in his own seat, spreading his legs apart slightly as I undid his pants. He was only semi-hard when I carefully exposed his cock, pulling down the waistband of his boxers and holding them out of the way. I was using both hands to do so, leaving only my mouth with which to touch him. As I took him inside me he moaned quietly, and relaxed in his comfortable position. He was growing harder.

"Suck it boy, make me rock," he ordered. "Show me who you take your orders from!" I pressed my tongue firmly against the underside of his shaft, forming a tight suction with my mouth, and sucked him like a baby sucking a pacifier. He did in fact grow rock hard, within just a matter of seconds. "Yeah!" he said, finally bringing his hands down to grab my head. "Slide on it, boy! Suck my fuckin cock!" He gripped my head tightly and began to pump. He did not move his hips, not even slightly, but moved me instead. He jacked me on his cock, as if he were holding some sort of jack off toy. His grip only got tighter as he continued, forcing me down on him to the point where my nose was all the way in his pubic region. His cock head was choking me as it forced its way into my throat. As I struggled to breathe and to focus upon not gagging, it was as if he were totally unconcerned with my discomfort. He just kept slamming me down hard on his prick.

Finally, almost without warning, I felt the cum fire into his shaft. I felt it with my tongue which was pressed against him firmly. He held me in place, offering me no choice whatsoever, and drained himself into me, moaning loudly now. "Eat it, faggot! Take my fuckin load!" I did exactly that, once again tasting that incredibly bitter, unique flavor of his cum.

He held me there for a few seconds until he was completely drained and once again relaxed. Finally he released me. "Get to bed early tonight pup. Will be here at seven tomorrow morning to pick you up."

I then got out of the car, and he peeled out of the parking lot without so much as a thank you. I smiled and walked up to the apartment.

18

My phone was ringing when I got out of the shower at 6:10a.m. "Hey, what took you so long?" It was Matt's voice, of course.

"Sorry, Sir, I was in the shower," I explained.

"Fuck, am I tired. I got about four hours sleep. Not gonna be there for another hour or so cuz I just got up."

"Okay, Sir," I said. "What should I pack?"

"Gonna be hot this weekend. Bring shorts, a swimsuit, sleeveless tees. Pack your chastity too, and bring a couple big towels. We are meeting Alex and Drew at the water park later on this morning, then you and I are goin up to the cabin for the weekend. There's a club I'm takin ya to tonight, too."

"Really, Sir?" I asked. "I don't think I will be able to get into a club."

"If you're with me you'll be able to, don't worry. You alone this morning?"

"Not right now, Sir, but Kathie is gonna leave for work in about ten minutes."

"Okay, cool. When I get there, I'm comin inside, so just wait for me in there. Got a few surprises for you this weekend, pup."

"You do?" I asked.

"Yup."

"Guess what, Sir?" I said to him, "I have some surprises for you too!"

"Not your job to surprise me, pup," he warned.

"Well they are good surprises Sir. I promise."

"Oh, okay. Nothin I'm gonna need to spank you for, I hope."

"No — definitely not Sir. Never again. Did you guys have fun last night?"

"Sure did, but listen I'm gonna get in the shower and I'll be there by 7:30 or so. Don't eat anything cuz we're going out for breakfast."

"Thought you didn't eat breakfast?" I asked.

"Not usually, but I'm hungry today. Okay, be ready, and make sure you're shaved!"

"Yes, Sir. Was just about to do that."

"All right. Later." He clicked off.

I was so excited when I hung up that I was actually giddy, running around my bedroom wearing only a towel, pulling clothes out of my closet and throwing them on the bed.

"Hey Petey, I'm leaving for work now." Kathie was standing in my doorway. I turned to look at her, holding a pair of Umbros in my hand. "What are you doing?" she asked.

"Matt and I are going to his cabin for the weekend. I don't have to work until Tuesday, and tomorrow is his birthday. Can you believe his birthday is only four days before mine?"

"Really?" she asked. "Well, I was thinking about your birthday, actually. I wondered if you wanted to have some of your friends over Wednesday night. I'll make you a cake."

I smiled at her. "Thanks, sis, but are you sure you shouldn't just buy one? Remember the last time you tried baking a cake?"

She laughed. "Don't be mean. It's the thought that counts, right? Well so maybe I will *buy* you a cake, or else I'll let you make your own and just take the credit for it. Whatever you want, Petey."

"Kathie?" I asked, "Have you been mad at me?"

"No, of course not — not at all. Why do you think that?"

I looked down at the pair of shorts in my hand. "Um... I don't know. Just seems like it. It seems like you are pissed about me being friends with Matt."

302

"Honey, I'm not pissed about your friendship with him, honest I'm not. I just want to make sure he doesn't do anything...well, how can I say this without hurting your feelings?"

"Just say it," I said, "I want you to be honest."

"All right. Well, I don't think Matt is exactly the kind of person that you might think he is. I mean, it was wonderful how he saved you from getting beaten up, or at least worse than you did anyway. But from the things Tracy has told me about him, he just...well... he just seems sort of selfish to me. I don't think he treats her right."

I was trying not to get mad, because I had asked her for her honest opinion. "I don't really see it that way, Kathie. Really, I don't. He has never been selfish to me. Look at all this stuff." I waved my hand over the bed. "He bought this all for me, and he gave me this necklace too. He is always doing nice things for me, and never once has he asked for anything in return." *Other than my obedience*, I thought.

"Don't you think it's weird, though, that he doesn't do those things for Tracy? I mean after all, she is his girlfriend."

"Maybe she just thinks she's his girlfriend. Have you ever heard him say that?"

"Well, he allows her to think it. If he isn't serious about her, then it is up to him to make sure she understands. She is totally nuts over him."

"Why's she gotta be so snotty all the time then? You should have heard her the one night I called Matt when she was there. She was such a bitch in the background."

"Well, did you stop to think that maybe it's because she doesn't get to spend very much time with him, and then the one time she does, someone else calls?"

"That is such bull. People get calls all the time, and Matt's my friend. Why should it surprise her if I called him."

"I'm gonna be late for work, Petey," she said. "All I know is that Matt seems to spend a lot more time with you than his own girlfriend."

"Like I said, I don't think he considers her his girlfriend!"

"Okay, well can we talk about this later, hon? I gotta get going."

"Yeah, I don't want us to argue. You know I love you, right?" I offered.

"And I love you too. Let's not let this whole thing with Matt affect our relationship, okay? I don't want to be telling you who you can be friends with. I just want you to be happy, that's all."

"I know. Have a good day at work." I reached out and hugged her then. "Thank you for worrying about me — even though you don't have to."

She smiled down at me and kissed me gently on the forehead. "Don't do anything I wouldn't do this weekend. And tell Matt I said happy birthday."

"Okay."

When she left, I resumed my task of packing, making sure I remembered everything he'd said to me. Then I went into the bathroom and dropped my towel. I splashed some warm water on my privates and lubed up my groin area with shaving cream. I stood there then, over the towel, and shaved myself in front of the full length mirror. I wanted to look perfectly smooth for Matt. The wounds on my dick were now completely healed, and I looked a lot better. He deserved for me to look good for him. It was like he'd said to me before, I was his property, and so he expected me to take care of myself.

When Matt arrived at about ten minutes to eight, I had been ready and waiting for thirty minutes. I, of course, did not say one word about him being later than he'd indicated, but instead remained very quiet. I was trying to gauge his mood, for I knew that on such little sleep he may be grumpy. He seemed his normal self though, and he greeted me with a gentle kiss. "Let me see that chastity thing," he said.

Obediently I retrieved it from one of my two bags, remembering precisely where I'd packed it. I handed it to him, without saying anything. "Alex told me that this thing can be used without those spikes, so there's no way for it to hurt you." He examined it closely. "We are gonna try it again this weekend to see. If it doesn't work right, I'll get a different one."

"Yes, Sir," I said. It was strange, because you'd think that I would be sad about him making me wear a chastity device. I was not though. In fact, it didn't bother me at all. I liked the idea of him having control over every part of me. I liked it a lot. "Did you want to put it on me now, Sir?" I asked.

"Nope. Not til tonight, before we go out. Remember, we're goin to the water park today. Not sure it would be practical to wear under your swimsuit."

"Okay, Sir," I said, "but I would if you wanted."

"Of course you would," he said, as if it were ridiculous of me to even suggest there was any other option. "All right, you got the towels?"

"Yes, Sir."

"Let's get goin', then." He tucked the chastity back into my bag and zipped it up. Then he picked up both bags and headed for the door. I locked up behind him, and hurriedly followed him down the steps to the car.

When we got to the restaurant, Matt ordered a bottled water. He did not ever drink the tap water that was freely offered, he explained, because it tasted like shit. He looked over the table at me and laughed. "I can't believe you actually drink coffee," he said. "It seems like an old person's beverage."

I shrugged. "I like it," I said, holding the cup with both hands as I sipped from it.

"Sometimes you're just so fuckin' cute," he said, and then reached over and playfully pushed down the visor of my b-cap. "I need you to do something for me," he said, sounding more serious. "Get up and go to the bathroom. Check it out and come back. Just look inside, wash your hands or

something if someone is in there so it doesn't look too weird.
All right?"

"Yes, Sir," I said, though uncertain of what it actually was
that I was supposed to be scoping out in the men's room. I
slid out of the booth seat then and casually headed to the
bathroom. I returned to the table about two minutes later.

"Well, what is it like?" he asked.

I laughed. "I dunno, Sir," I said, "like any other bathroom,
I guess."

"But is it several stalls or single-occupancy?" he asked.

"Oh, it's single," I said.

"Has a lock on the door?"

I nodded. "Yes, Sir."

"Okay good." he said, and took another big swig of his
water. "You're not eating much, pup."

"Not hungry really, Sir," I said. "Maybe too excited."

"Whatcha excited about?"

"Just this weekend, being with you, going to the park with
Drew. Just everything really. I talked to Kathie this morning
about you again, Sir."

"What did she say this time?" he asked. "She think I'm
the devil still?"

I laughed. "No, but she thinks you don't spend enough
time with Tracy. She says that you spend more time with me
than your own girlfriend."

"Well you already know she is *not* my girlfriend."

"I know, Sir. I told Kathie I wasn't sure you considered
her your girlfriend either. She said that you should then tell
her that."

"Well no offense to your sis, pup, but she needs to mind
her own business. Way I see it is that Tracy sometimes wants
to have it both ways. She wants a guy to be her 'boyfriend'
but she doesn't wanna act like a girlfriend. I think she knows
she's just my bitch. If she didn't like it, she'd have been
history a long time ago."

"Why do you call her that, sir? That sounds kind of mean."

"It's not mean." He sighed. "Look, Tracy is nothing to me. She just is a chick that I fuck sometimes, whenever I want pussy. She knows that as well as I do. If that isn't being my 'bitch' then I don't know what else you'd call it."

"What am I to you, Sir?"

"You're my pup. Don't be silly, you already know that."

"And that's not the same as being your bitch? Like you call Tracy."

"Of course it's not. It's a lot more than that. I totally own you. You belong to me. You're a lot more than just a fuck," he smiled at me. "You're definitely my favorite fuck, though."

"You're mine too," I laughed.

"I'd better be your *only* fuck!" he informed me.

"I know Sir; I was just teasin."

He grinned at me. "Okay, so then are you done eating? You're not gonna even finish your toast."

I shook my head.

"Finish one piece," he instructed me. "That's an order."

I made a face, but obeyed him anyways, taking small bites off the bread.

"Oh for chrissakes! Bite it, don't nibble." I took a bigger bite then, feeling sort of self conscious, but obeying just the same. I took a swig of my coffee washing down the toast.

"Okay, now get up and go to the bathroom again. Lock the door when you get in there and wait for me. I will knock once, then wait three seconds and knock two more times. Got it?"

"Yes, Sir," I said, and once again slid out of my seat and headed for the john.

As I stood there in the bathroom, waiting beside the door, I wondered what he was going to do to me. Certainly he was going to have sex with me, make me serve him some how. Maybe he'd bend me over and fuck me. He'd never done it that way before. I bet that would hurt a lot worse, though, more so than lying on my back with my butt on a pillow. Maybe he was going to let me blow him, like he'd done the night before in his car. I was becoming excited, actually rubbing myself as I stepped over in front of the mirror. Maybe I should kneel down beside the door and wait for him, then I could just open it up when he knocked and I'd be in position for him as he stepped inside.

As I was thinking on these things, he did finally knock. It startled me at first, the one single knock. Then he paused and knocked two more times, just as he'd said. I stepped over hurriedly and unbolted the lock on the door, my fingers fumbling a bit in the process. He entered casually, stepping immediately over in front of the toilet. "Lock the door," he said. I did so automatically and then turned to face him. The bathroom was small to begin with and had suddenly gotten smaller with both of us inside. I was only about four feet from him as he stood there, assuming the stance that men take when they are about to piss. His legs were spread apart with his feet flat on the floor on either side of the toilet.

He then turned his head to look at me, while he unzipped his pants. "Come here, pup," he said, "and get on your knees." Not knowing where exactly he wanted me, I stepped over behind him, slightly to his left. I was actually more in front of the small vanity sink as I slid down into my servile position. I knelt there next to him, humbly staring up at him while I awaited further instruction. "I gotta piss," he said, matter-of-factly. I knelt there watching as he pulled his fly apart and un-tucked his cock, then holding it in his hand, gripping his shaft with his first two fingers on its underside and his thumb pressing down against the top, positioned up by the base next to his groin. "Gonna drain myself into this piss hole, boy," he said. "Then it's gonna all be flushed, gone forever." I continued to stare at him, wide-eyed, as my heart pounded excitedly, my own cock becoming erect in my briefs. "You wanna see my piss get flushed down the drain boy? You wanna see it wasted like that?"

I opened my mouth, trying to answer, but I was too excited. Instead I just shook my head, as he stared over at me. "Huh?" he said, "Don't shake your head. Answer me!"

"No Sir," I squeaked. "No Sir, I don't want...um...I don't want you to waste it."

"What else am I gonna do with it then? If I don't piss it into this piss hole, then where?"

I gulped, being very nervous and trying again to find my voice. "Me, Sir. You could piss it into me."

He then laughed. He leaned his head back and laughed hard, in fact. "You want me to let you be my piss hole, boy?" he asked. "You didn't want that before. Why now?"

"I was scared Sir. I'm sorry." I looked down at the dirty floor upon which I was kneeling.

"But you're not now?" he asked. I shook my head, not looking up at him. "Why not now?"

"I tasted it Sir. Remember? "And...um...and I'm not scared any more. I trust you Sir."

"Good boy," he said, "but do you deserve it? Do you deserve both my cum and my piss? Do you deserve to be my piss hole?"

"Please, Sir, please let me do it for you. Please let me."

"You're asking me to give you my piss, and you say you're doing something for me?!"

"I'm sorry Sir!" I corrected myself, "I didn't mean it, not like that. Please, please let me have...um...have the privilege of being your piss hole. Sir...please." I stared up at him, pleading, hungry to serve him in every way, begging to be used in any capacity. I pled using my eyes, imploring him to feed me his piss. "Please sir. I beg you."

He then turned to face me, planting his feet now on either side of me, instead of the toilet. He literally towered over me now, in a way that he seemed far more superior than he ever had before. He was grinning slightly, enjoying the view perhaps as he looked down. Maybe it was the hungry look in my eyes, or perhaps the submissive position that I had automatically assumed— whatever it was, I was thankful it pleased him. He continued to hold his cock in his hand and said to me, "Open. Open real wide, boy."

I craned my neck back and opened, thrusting my upper body forward slightly to align myself under his cock. "Yeah," he said, "you're my little piss hole. My urinal." Then without further warning he shot a stream of piss directly into my mouth. He must have aimed it for my throat, for it hit the target dead on. I gulped immediately, but did so with my mouth remaining fully open. He stopped after this one initial blast of piss, and smiled down at me. "You like that, boy?" he asked.

"Yes sir," I responded quickly as I finished swallowing, but then immediately assumed my open-mouthed position. He then moved even a little closer to me, placing the end of his cock right on my lower lip.

"Take it boy, wrap your lips around it." I did as commanded, taking in just the head and then sliding further onto his shaft, so that it was in about one full inch. Then he released more of himself into me, a more forceful stream of piss this time. I tasted it now, for it was spraying right onto my tongue. It was not a bad taste, no worse than cum. In fact, the cum was often bitter. His piss was fairly bland, but it was so warm, sort of the temperature of heated apple cider. I gulped hungrily, afraid I might not get it all, afraid I could not respond quickly enough and might actually even gag.

He was very controlled in his delivery though, and he did not allow me to choke. He pissed for a steady four or five seconds and then stopped again. It was like I had just taken a big drink from a fountain, and I gasped slightly as I gulped to get it all down. I smiled up at him then as he pulled out of me. "Good boy," he said, "You like your owner's piss?"

"Yes sir! Yes sir, I do!" I excitedly confessed to him. I opened my mouth again, and this time he was much less careful. He stood in front of me now, and I felt that he had

310

arrived at a place mentally where he actually did consider me his urinal, for he released his bladder this time, just as he would have into the toilet. His piss came streaming out forcefully, and fired directly into my throat. I did choke somewhat, but continued to swallow as rapidly as I could. Some splashed against my teeth and onto my lips. I was thinking it was not ever going to end, for I had to concentrate very hard. I knew now how those college frat boys felt when someone poured beer into their throats using a funnel. I squinted my eyes to avoid any splatter. He actually sighed as he relieved himself into me and then finally the stream began to trickle.

He remained towering over me, and flicked the droplets of piss from his cock onto my tongue. "Lick it clean, boy." He said, and I obeyed. Then he stepped back and tucked his cock away, zipping up, exactly the way he'd have done in a bathroom full of guys while standing at the urinal. He pulled a sheet of towel off the dispenser and handed it to me. "Wipe your face," he said, "and then meet me out at the car." Then he walked out, leaving me kneeling on the ground.

I quickly stood up, lest anyone walk in and catch me. I turned to look in the mirror. His piss had splashed my face good, some running down my neck even. I turned on the water and washed myself, wiping with the paper towel. Then I went to the car as instructed.

* * *

After we left the restaurant, without explanation, Matt drove us over to the mall. Obediently and unquestioningly I followed him inside. It became apparent to me that we were headed for the hair salon again. I wondered if he felt I needed another haircut already. It had not been that long since the first one. When we got there I discovered that it was not I who was scheduled for a cut, but him. I sat patiently watching as Larry cut Matt's hair. Larry apparently

311

already had figured out that it was not necessary to speak directly to me, for Matt generally spoke for me in situations like this, so I remained the quiet observer, very content to watch my owner being serviced professionally.

When he was done, he tipped the stylist and then we walked to the cashier. "We need to also get an ear piercing," he stated, "for him," and he looked over to me. I did not say anything, but simply looked up at him. I could not help grinning.

"I'm getting my ear pierced, Sir?" I asked quietly.

"Yup," he said.

"Maybe you could get yours done too, Sir," I suggested. "That way we can look alike — like we do with our hair."

"Nope," he said, without any thought. "Not getting my ear pierced now, or ever."

"I wonder if it is going to hurt," I said, a little louder.

"Just for a second or two," the receptionist said. I soon discovered that it was she who did the piercing, being apparently more than just a receptionist. The first order of business was to select an earring. I did not really participate in this process, although the stylist didn't seem to actually understand this. She continued to ask my opinion on which ones I liked and Matt would answer her. She shot him a couple of glances that I was rather concerned about, and I almost told her it was okay to do whatever he said. I thought better of it, though, and kept my mouth shut.

Finally Matt decided on a single diamond stud. Then the stylist wiped my ear with alcohol and held this funny looking gun-shaped device to my ear. She was rather chatty and was talking about how she thought we must be such good friends to have even selected matching haircuts. She was trying to talk Matt into getting his ear pierced when she suddenly pulled the trigger. I assumed that this distraction was deliberate, for although it was an instantaneous event, it was rather painful. But as she said, it lasted only a couple of seconds. "Ouch!" I sad, in spite of myself. "I wasn't even ready."

"It's better when you're not expecting it, honey," she said. "Then it's over with before you have time to worry about it. She then proceeded to give us detailed instructions on the care of the ear over the course of the next six weeks. You would have thought I'd just undergone brain surgery.

"Do you like it, Sir?" I asked as we walked out together. I was checking it out in my reflection from a mirror in the storefront.

"Sure pup, looks cool," he said. "Gotta meet Alex at the park in a half hour. We'll be lucky to get there on time."

"Thank you for the earring, Sir," I said, "and for everything." He put his arm around my shoulder as we walked out together. Had anyone seen us together, walking like that, they probably would have suspected nothing—two buds hanging together at the mall. Perhaps with our identical haircuts they may have thought us to be brothers, Matt being the older and I the younger. Were they to look more closely, though, I think they probably would see something in the way I smiled when I looked over at him. They may have seen some sort of glint in my eyes when I turned to look at him worshipfully, or perhaps have noticed that in every step we took, he would lead and I follow. They may even have found it cute, or at the very least amusing, to notice that I had to take two steps to each of his one. They'd have definitely seen his confidence, the upright way he walked, his body language exuding openness and self-assurance, and they'd have known that his arm around my shoulder was a display not so much of affection, but of ownership and protectiveness. Even if nobody noticed any of these things, though, I did, and my heart swelled with pride as I walked out beside him.

In the car Matt informed me that he and Alex had arranged a meeting place. Whichever pair of us arrived first was to wait for the others under the big tree that was directly in front of the main entrance to the park. This time of year, the park was actually not too crowded. Within a few weeks they would get much busier, with massive numbers of college students descending upon them over their spring breaks. During the previous weeks, however, the temperatures had not been much above seventy during the day, and most people did not really get the urge to visit a water park unless it was undeniably hot.

"Sir?" I said as we were pulling into the parking lot, "I almost forgot, I have to ask you something."

"What's that?" he said as he powered down his window to take the parking ticket from the mechanical gatekeeper.

"Well, when Kathie and I were talking this morning, she said that I could have some friends over on Wednesday, for my birthday. Do you wanna come over? And can I ask Drew?"

"Sure, don't see why not. That's cool," he said, "My pup's birthday is almost the same day as mine."

"Yeah," I smiled, "It's four days apart. My birthday is actually on Thursday, the ninth."

"How'd you know when my birthday was, anyways?" he asked me. "I don't remember telling you."

"I saw it on your driver's license Sir. Remember the other night when you had me get your wallet from the car?"

"Oh, so you were snooping around in my wallet, huh?"

"No, Sir, honest it wasn't like that," I quickly defended myself. "I didn't snoop, only looked at the license, really. Please don't be mad."

He laughed. "Do I seem mad to you? Might have to spank you again though. This time I'll do it in your wet bathing suit though."

"Ouch!" I said, "With that paddle?"

"Or maybe a belt, over the knee."

I giggled. "It would be like you were my dad or something, spanking me like that, Sir."

"Yeah, well sorta. My job is to discipline and train you just like a dad does with his son. In some ways it's the same."

"You're not my dad, though," I scowled. "I don't think I like that comparison at all."

"Then we won't use it. Sides, you are my pup, not my son. I'm too young to be anyone's dad." I wondered if Matt ever realized just how often I did miss my own father— both my parents, actually. "Okay, after we get a parking place, your job is gonna be to take one of your bags and empty it out. Put our suits in it and the towels too. Get my wallet from the glove box and put that in there. We will rent a locker once we're inside to keep our stuff in. Okay?"

"Yes, Sir," I said, "and I won't even look in your wallet this time."

Drew and Alex were already waiting for us by the tree when we approached the entrance. I was carrying the small duffle bag containing our things. Matt was walking beside me, drinking a bottle of Mountain Dew he'd bought from a vending machine in the mall. "Dude, you get enough sleep?" he said to Alex, who was sitting on the ground leaning his back against the big tree.

"Fuck no," he said. They both laughed. "Almost felt like canceling today; I'm a little hung over."

"Geesh! What a lightweight. You only had, like, three beers last night."

"Yeah, right," he said, while pushing himself up off the ground. Drew was standing beside him, carrying a bag of his own.

"Hi Petey!" he grinned at me. "Ready to get soaked?"

"No!" I confessed. "It's too cold to be doing this already."

"You're the lightweight," he teased me. "It's not even cold. Supposed to be eighty-five today."

"I should have brought some sun block," I said. "I'm gonna get so fried."

"I've got some," Drew said. "Waterproof too."

"Gimme my wallet, pup," Matt said to me. "Shit, I should have brought that wrist band that I have. It's got a pocket for my money, and it is waterproof. Not like I can carry my wallet around in my pocket."

"You can buy those inside, sir," said Drew. He glanced up at Alex right after saying it. Alex nodded to him, and I wondered what it was all about. "Would you like for me to go get you one, sir?"

"Sure, that'd be cool. He pulled out a ten from his wallet and handed it to Drew. "You guys thirsty?" he asked, referring to all three of us I assumed. Drew and I both shook our heads.

"Nope," said Alex.

"Okay, was gonna get us something to drink. I'll get you something special later, pup," he said to me. When I looked up at him I sensed that he was not referring to soda pop.

After we got through the main gate and had paid for our entry, Drew grabbed me by the arm. "Come with me, Petey. Let's go get that wrist band." I followed him unquestioningly, running along behind. Apparently, Drew had come here often for he knew right where to go. Although I'd lived in this city my entire life, I'd only been to the park a couple of times, and that was several years prior.

"I got a big lecture this morning," he said to me.

"From Alex?" I asked.

He laughed. "Of course from Alex. Who did you think, from my fairy godmother?"

I shrugged, laughing myself. "What'd he lecture you about?"

"Showing respect. I thought he was gonna punish me, actually, but he didn't. He told me that he'd talked to Matt last night, and Matt wondered why I didn't show him more respect. I don't call him 'sir' or anything. So that's why I have to do that now."

"Oh, well Alex told me not to call him 'Sir,' not unless Matt told me to."

"Yeah, that is pretty standard. That's kind of why I never did it with Matt, but now Alex *has* told me so, so I've gotta obey."

"I wonder why Matt wants you to call him 'sir' but Alex doesn't want me to do the same."

"Well it might change now. You'll have to just see if Matt says anything to you the next time you talk to Alex. If he wants you to call him 'sir' then he will correct you."

"Okay. I usually do it anyways cuz it's sort of a habit. Are these the wrist bands you were talkin about?" I asked, picking one up from the table.

"Yup," he said. "Let's hurry. Don't want em to get mad." We went to the counter and paid, and Drew put Alex's change in the pocket of the wristband.

"Wait, I should get one too, for myself," I said.

"No, just give your money to Matt. He should decide what you spend it on anyways."

"Okay," I said, and we headed back to the front gate. When we got there, Alex was just returning himself. He had gone to the locker rental to get locker keys. He handed one to Matt and the other to Drew. He also reached in his back pocket and removed his wallet.

"You got my wrist band in your bag, Drew?" he asked.

"Yes, Sir," Drew said, and unzipped the duffle bag to find it. "Here you go Sir." Alex removed some money from his wallet and then handed the wallet to Drew. I thought it was rather interesting that Drew was the one who made most of the money for them, yet Alex was the one who handled the cash. In the case of Matt and me, he handled the money, but it all came from him in the first place. I wondered if maybe I should offer to give him the money that I did have from now on. I'd have to ask him about it later.

"Let's go get our suits on," said Matt. We then all four headed into the showers and changing room area. It reminded me of the shower at a gym, having wooden benches lining the cement walls. The shower spigots were in

317

the open and not divided by any type of stall. I dug our suits out of the duffle bag and handed Matt his. He stripped off his shirt immediately and pulled down his shorts and boxers, suddenly standing there in front of us all naked. He acted very casual as he then slipped on his suit. I thought it was strange that he did this all without removing his shoes or socks.

When I turned to look at Alex, I saw that he was already changed himself. I had been so mesmerized by watching Matt get naked, that I hadn't even looked in his direction. "Hurry up Petey," he said, "What are you waiting for?" My face reddened. I had always hated stripping down in front of other people. Even in gym class at school, I'd slink off to a corner where no one was watching when I got changed, then when it was time to shower I'd wait til it was nearly empty and dash in real fast, wrapping a towel around myself as soon as I was done.

I sat down on the bench and started to untie my shoe, pulling my knee up to my chest so that my sole was resting on the bench in front of my butt cheek. I pulled off my shoe and then changed legs, doing the same to my other foot. Then I removed my socks. Finally I stood up and immediately turned around so I was facing the wall and pulled down my shorts and underwear together. I then picked up my suit and stepped into it, leaving my tee shirt on, untouched.

"Take your shirt off, pup," Matt instructed. I looked up at him without saying anything, hoping he'd see the pleading in my eyes. "Just take it off and quit being so fuckin modest," he said. "Then take my shoes off." I pulled the shirt over my head immediately and then dropped to my knees and began untying his shoe. I did not give any thought to the fact that there could be other people coming in and out of the building. After I'd gotten the shoes untied and removed and had also removed his socks, I looked up at him. "Good boy," he said. Then I got back up and stood in front of him.

"Isn't it silly for him to be so modest?" Matt said to Alex.

"Yeah, it is," said Alex. "He has a cute little body." I blushed and then looked over to Drew. I was initially concerned that his master had complimented me like that in front of him, but Drew was smiling.

"Put our shit in the lockers, Drew," Alex said to him. Matt then handed me the locker key and his wallet, as if to indicate that I should do the same. We then both picked up our duffle bags and headed out of the building to find our lockers, locating the corresponding numbers to match our keys.

"You notice anything different about me?" I said to Drew. He stepped back from me a bit and looked me over.

"What?" he said.

"You tell me," I said, turning my head slightly.

"You got your ear pierced!" he said. "Do you like it?" he asked.

"Sure, Matt's the one who wanted it."

"That's cool. I had my ear pierced once, but then I let it grow back. When I started teaching, I wasn't sure it was a good idea."

"I thought that lady who did it to me was gonna piss Matt off really bad. She kept on ignoring him."

"I had that happen once," said Drew. "Alex and I were at this restaurant and Alex ordered for me, of course. Well, anyways, this waitress looks over at me as if to get confirmation — my permission or something. I didn't say anything, though, cuz I did not want Alex to think that I actually felt I had to give my approval. She just kept asking me questions, you know...soup or salad?...shit like that."

"What did Alex do?" I asked.

"He just answered her every time, and I sat quietly. She was persistent though, continuing to direct all her attention to me. Finally I said to her, 'No offense, hon, but if you really want a tip you should be getting the order from him, not me'."

I laughed. "What'd she do then?"

"She just like sorta shrugged her shoulders and then turned to Alex. People don't understand what it means to be submissive. They think it's a bad thing—a weakness."

"It is though, in a way, isn't it Drew?" I asked. "I mean Matt is the strong one and I am weak. That's why I know he is superior."

"Petey, you are anything but weak, and a good sub definitely can't be weak. All these people who are so proud of themselves for being so independent, they couldn't do the things that you and I do. They could not follow orders the way we do and devote themselves to one person like we do. That takes strength, not weakness."

"But that's just it, Drew. I'm not strong. I have a lot of problems following the orders Matt gives me. Seems I'm always screwing up."

"You're just learning! Give yourself a break. Everybody screws up sometimes. Part of Matt's job is gonna be to make sure you see the successes, not just always the failures. And you know what, I bet there have been a lot more times when you have obeyed him perfectly than there have been fuck-ups."

"I wish I could be like you, Drew. You seem to be so much better at it."

"You are perfect just the way you are. The fact that you are so young and innocent is probably what attracted Matt to you the most. He probably likes the fact that he can train you and make you into the perfect sub for him. I think he's doing a pretty good job too, for what my opinion is worth."

"Your opinion is worth a lot to me, really. I thought I'd die when he banned me from seeing you."

"I doubt he ever intended for that to last long. From what Alex tells me, he likes that you and I are friends. He thinks I can teach you stuff."

"He's right," I said. "You have taught me so much already. You know what happened this morning, right before we went to get my ear pierced?"

"What?" he asked.

"Matt made me go into the bathroom of the restaurant and wait for him. Then he came and peed in my mouth."

"You take it all?" he asked.

I nodded. "I begged him for it, then I took every bit of it. Can you believe it?"

"That's pretty hot, taking his piss in the public john like that. Did you get sick at all?"

"No, why? Does it make people sick when they do that? I mean, when they swallow urine?"

"Not like give you a disease or something, but some people throw up their first time. I never did. I was like you. I wanted it, but remember when you told me about that first time, when you freaked cuz you thought he wanted you to take his piss?"

"Yeah."

"Well if he'd have forced you to take it then, I bet you'd have just puked. It's sort of psychological.—"

"Drew! What the fuck you doin'?" It was Alex's voice behind us.

We slammed the lockers shut and removed the keys, running over to him. "Sorry Sir. We were talking."

"I see that. I don't like to be kept waiting, neither does Matt, I'm sure," he said, looking at me. I hung my head but did not say anything. "You put your sun block on?" he asked.

"No Sir. I almost forgot."

"Drew, get your sun block for Petey. Help him put it on while Matt's in the bathroom." Drew did as instructed, reopening the locker he'd just closed and retrieving the lotion.

"How you like your earring?" Alex asked me. "Matt told me he was gonna get it for you."

"I like it, Sir. He surprised me with it," I said as I sat down on the bench in front of the lockers. Drew stood

321

behind me and spread some lotion onto my back. I shivered a little as it felt cold when it made contact with my skin.

"Ticklish, huh?" said Alex, grinning at me.

"Yes, Sir, but it's cold too." I picked up the lotion bottle that Drew had placed on the bench next to me and squeezed some in my palm. "You're supposed to rub it in your hands a little bit first to get it warmer before you smear it on," I instructed Drew. Then I proceeded to demonstrate, rubbing some into my chest.

Just then Matt rounded the corner, carrying his bottle of Mountain Dew. He stepped over beside Drew. "You boys still aren't ready?" he chided us. "Here," he said, handing me the bottle he was carrying. I thought it odd, for I didn't even like Mountain Dew, and I actually wasn't even thirsty. I obediently took it from him anyways and instantly noticed it was not cold. It was, in fact, very warm.

"This is warm, Sir," I said.

"I know. Told you I was gonna get you something special to drink." Suddenly it dawned on me what was in the bottle. "Take a swig," he said. I looked up and saw Alex staring down at me. Matt wanted me to drink his warm piss right in front of Alex. I stared back at Alex, never removing my eyes from him and unscrewed the cap on the bottle. Then I raised it to my lips, tilted my head back slightly and took a big gulp of the warm liquid. I swallowed in a very deliberate manner, allowing my audience of one to see the constriction of my throat as it went down.

"Good boy," said Matt. I wondered what Drew thought of this little scene. I could not see him because he was behind me. After what had happened last night with the situation at the bookstore, I was thankful for the opportunity to demonstrate my unwavering devotion to Matt in front of Alex. I wanted him to see there were no limits to what I'd do to serve my owner, and I wanted him to see that I knew exactly who my owner was. I was his property, and off limits

to everyone else. It sort of surprised me—my own bravado—
as I stared into Alex's eyes.

"You guys ready to go on that huge water rafting ride?"
asked Alex, acting as if what he'd just witnessed was totally
unremarkable.

I grinned, turning to look at Matt, licking the corners of
my lips with my tongue. "Can we Sir? I love that ride!"

"Sure, pup," he said, and then tapped the visor of my b-
cap affectionately as he often did.

I carried the Mountain Dew bottle with me the entire
morning, drinking from it whenever Matt instructed. After a
bit, the warm liquid was unsettling to me, and I lagged
behind the others hoping to get Matt alone. He seemed to be
aware of my hesitation and fell behind himself, "What's
wrong?" he said to me.

"Oh nothing, Sir. I'm having fun. Are you?"

"Sure," he said, water dripping from his lean body. We
had just gone on a gigantic water slide.

"May I please get something else to drink, Sir?" I asked. "I
mean like a pop or ice tea or something? Please?"

"You getting sick?" he asked.

"Um...maybe a little," I confessed.

"Okay," he said. "We'll get something in a minute. Let me
see that bottle." He took it from me and held it up. It only
had about a half an inch of liquid left in the bottom, not even
a big swallow. "Can you finish this without puking?" he
asked. I nodded. "Do it," he said, handing it back to me. I
unscrewed the lid and downed the remainder. I was thankful
it was such a small amount, for I felt the queasiness
revisiting me.

"You've been a good boy today," Matt said. "Proud of ya
for being so obedient."

"Thank you Sir," I said, as I beamed up at him. We then
hurried to catch up with our friends.

Drew turned to me, "Petey, you wanna go on the tubes
with me?"

"The tubes?" I asked.

"Yeah, the inner-tubes. See the river that runs through the whole park? They throw tons of inner-tubes into it. Then all ya gotta do is just wait for an empty one to come by, and you wade in and claim it. Then you jus kick back and ride around on 'em; takes you in a big circle."

"Yeah, I'll do it!" I said.

"Good, cuz Alex doesn't like it. Says it's boring. Don't you Sir?" he said to Alex.

"All right then," said Matt. "We'll split up and meet back here in about an hour. Petey, here's some money to go get you a pop. When we meet again, we'll go get a bite to eat."

"Thank you, Sir," I said.

"You got a place to put the change?" he asked.

"No, Sir," I said.

"Then here, take this five instead." I then looked up at him as I exchanged the money with him and for the first time that day I noticed something. He was absolutely unbelievable to look at. He was just incredible, standing there shirtless, his hair damp and uncombed. The short haircut suited him so well; he was so amazingly masculine. He must have seen the worship in my eyes, or perhaps just sensed it. He looked at me in such a loving way then. It was just sort of like the world had come to a stop for a few seconds as we looked at one another.

I wondered what thoughts entered his mind when he saw me—when he looked at me as he was doing just then. He must have seen someone small, and weak — vulnerable. He definitely must have been aware of the hunger I felt when I stared up at him. He was more than a boyfriend to me, more even than an owner. He was my entire world, my waking thought each morning, my daydreams, my hopes, my future. Matt Porter was my best friend and also my Savior. He was a hero to me, and nothing I'd ever felt for anyone before even held a candle to the depths of these feelings. Did he see this?

324

Did he even have an inkling of how much power he held over me?

Surely an observer may have concluded that Matt had power because I was submissive and because he was superior, or dominant. But these aspects of our personalities were not the true source of Matt's power over me. His superiority was merely a part of his character. It was what he was, just as my submissiveness was a natural part of me. The power he held over me actually stemmed from me, though, not from him. My willingness to serve was what made him powerful. I loved him so very much, with every fiber of my being, with every single component of my soul. This love was unconditional and incomparable. It transcended any reality I'd ever known. This devotion to him, for lack of a better word, was what fueled the power he held over me. It was so totally voluntary and yet at the same time automatic. It was a paradox, for I could not have ceased to submit to him any more than I could have ceased to breathe, yet I also knew that my submission was my one single gift to him. It was all I had to offer.

At any given moment I could have pulled away, at least theoretically, and denied him any further control over me; though I knew in my heart that this was not an option for me, for never before had I felt so complete, so satisfied, so content, as when I was bathing in the security of his control and guidance. It was a place where I felt safe, protected, and sheltered from any harm. It was a place where I knew I belonged. To walk away from that place would be suicide for me. How could I ever go on alone without him?

I stared up at him for those few brief seconds, all of these thoughts flashing into my mind, though condensed in a manner that was not really even understandable. I looked at him then, overcome with unbefitting emotion. Surely the others would not have understood where this display had come from, thinking it to have appeared from nowhere. "I

325

love you, Sir," I said to him, so very quietly that I don't think that anyone but he could have heard.

He leaned into me then, presenting himself in a way that was so casual and relaxed. So masculine and natural. So unnoticeable. He leaned in and said to me in the same quiet voice, "I love you too, pup. I really do."

I took the money from him without any further communication and turned to Drew. The tears in my eyes surely must have been masked by the dripping water that was all over the rest of my face and body, for he did not seem to even notice. "Ready?"

"Ready," he said, and we headed off to the concession.

* * *

Drew and I were both kicked back, relaxing on our inner-tubes as the current from the river carried us lazily through the park. There were points along the route where the water became more rough or cascaded into a mini-waterfalls, but for the most part it was just relaxing and refreshing. We chatted with one another, mostly about the previous rides we had gone on. I confided in Drew that I'd missed him so much over the past few days, and I invited him and Alex over on Wednesday for my birthday.

Drew mentioned to me that he was aware of what I'd been drinking from the Mountain Dew bottle. He said he thought it was really hot that Matt made me do it in public like that, and he told me not to worry about getting queasy like I had. He said that at first he'd been like that, but that eventually I'd get used to it.

We had nearly made a complete loop around the park and were approaching the spot where we had first claimed our inner-tubes when suddenly out of nowhere a blast of freezing water nailed me right in the face. Startled, I flailed my arms and inadvertently tipped my inner-tube, my head sinking immediately underwater and the tube flipping over on top of me. Sputtering I thrust myself up and gasped for air only to hear gales of laughter coming from the bank. Matt and Alex were standing there, each with huge water guns pointed right directly at me. I hardly had a chance to breathe when all of a sudden I got beamed again right in the face. I didn't have time to look around for Drew to see whether he had been assaulted as well but started to beat my arms furiously on the water, creating a spray which I intended to use as protection against the attack. This proved useless as the high powered jets of water from their weapons cut right through the splashing water and continued to drench me. Quickly, I turned away to face the opposite bank and ducked my head, tucking it under my arms. They showed no mercy to me, however, and I started screaming, "I give up! Stop!!" My pleas were combination of giddy laughter and delight along with a genuine dose of frustration at my own helplessness.

After several seconds their onslaught finally subsided, probably because they were running out of ammo. They both were laughing, and as I spun around I spotted Drew. He was still reclined lazily on his inner-tube laughing hysterically at me. I suspected that he was merely lucky, though, that I had been the first to approach Matt and Alex's well-planned ambush. They must have realized a full scale attack with two lethal weapons such as those water machine guns would be most effective if aimed at a single target. Had Drew approached first, he probably would have been the unfortunate victim. "You guys!" I screamed, "That was not very nice!" They busted up laughing again, probably because it was so amusing that my protests were so civil. Had I been any other victim I'd probably be cussing them out openly.

Suddenly, though, I became a little braver and realized it was not fair for Drew to be still sitting there so casually, mocking my misfortune. Without warning I reached under his inner tube and thrust upwards with all my might, immediately tipping him right upside down in the water.

327

Alex and Matt busted up laughing again, high fiving one another for their ability even to get the two sub allies to turn on one another. As Drew bolted up out of the water the first thing out of his mouth was, "You little fuckin shit!" He then dove for me, and I started splashing in the water again, trying to fend him off. My attempts were futile, however as he caught up to me and pushed my head forcefully under water. He released me and then began splashing my face furiously with what felt like a tidal wave.

I was again stunned and hysterical, flailing to get away from him as I headed towards the river bank upon which Matt and Alex were standing. As I approached them, Matt stepped over to the edge. He was laughing real hard as Drew continued behind me in hot pursuit. I lunged forward, grabbing for Matt's outstretched hand. As he reached down to grip my wrist I quickly swung my other arm around and grabbed his, pulling as hard as I possibly could. In any other situation I would not have been able to get the upper hand on someone as big as Matt, but due to the fact that he was leaning over and not really expecting anything, I was able to catch him off guard. He lost his footing then and I continued to pull furiously. Alex was behind Matt, and offered a tiny bit of assistance, bumping into him "accidentally" and Matt tumbled forward face-first into the water. His body slammed into mine, pushing me again under water. I did not care though, for I was already soaked.

When Matt came up sputtering I knew my ass was grass. "Ewww, you're gonna fuckin pay for this, you little twerp!" he threatened me. He leaned forward to grab me, but just as he did so, Alex landed beside us, having cannon-balled into the water. All four of us were laughing and screaming then, threatening one another as we began a no-holds-barred water fight. It was every man for himself at this point. Sadly, I was the most vulnerable of the four due to my size and paid dearly for it. Twenty minutes later, exhausted, we hauled ourselves out of the water, each flopping onto the grass on our backs. "Let's go get the towels," said Drew. Without argument, Matt and Alex handed over the keys, and Drew and I left them to return to the lockers.

We were still laughing and each bragging to one another about how we had at certain points nailed our owners during the fight, when we finally got to the lockers. "Damn, I gotta have a cigarette," said Drew.

"I hope Matt remembers that we are supposed to get lunch. I'm starving!"

"Me too. You having fun?"

I laughed. "I don't think I have ever had so much fun," I said.

"You looked so fuckin funny when they nailed you the first time, Petey. You should have seen your face." He laughed heartily, "I wish I'd have had a video camera."

"Shut up!" I said, "You got yours too, you know. I saw Alex dunking you, more than once too."

"I know! He can be viscous when he wants to be. Probably why I love him so much, though, come to think of it."

"Yer bad!" I said. He lit up a cigarette and then threw the pack and lighter back into the locker. I wrapped a towel around myself and picked up the remaining towels from the bench. We stepped over away from the lockers to an area where there was a disposal can for cigarette butts and stood there together while Drew got his nicotine fix.

"What are you guys doing tonight?" asked Drew.

"Matt is taking me to some club. He says he can get me in."

"Must be the Den," he told me. "It's sort of an ess and em bar."

"What's that?" I asked innocently.

"S and M...sado-masochism. It's a term they use for people who are into bondage and pain and shit like that. Lot of Dom-sub couples go there too. It is part of what's called the 'leather community'."

"Why they call it that? Does everyone have a fetish for leather or something?"

He laughed. "No, but some do. It's just the name for it. It's like a sub-culture of gay people who are not into just the vanilla stuff. If you do go there, don't be surprise if you see some weird shit."

"Like what?" I asked, staring at him wide-eyed.

"Oh all kinds of stuff. You might see guys wearing collars and leashes. Might see biker dudes, boys dressed like dogs, people with strange piercings or tattoos. Pretty much every fetish is represented."

"Wonder why Matt would wanna go to a bar like that."

"To show you off, silly."

"But we aren't into all that weird shit like that. Least I don't think we are."

"Don't have to be. It's just that he can take you out tonight and be totally open about the fact that he owns you. It is the perfect environment to do it in. Nobody is gonna think anything of it, and plus he knows all eyes are gonna be on you: the innocent little, smooth slave boy. And you totally belong to him. It will be a turn on for him, I'm sure."

I laughed at his description. "Why do you call me a slave boy?"

"Well that's what you are. Actually, I'd say you are more of a pup. That's even what he calls you, but it's all just a variation of the same thing. Fact is, you are submissive and he owns you. You are his property to show off. He must be proud of you to do it, too, you know."

"Really? You think so?"

He smiled at me as he exhaled a stream of smoke. "Yeah. Positive. You should have seen the look on his face when you took a drink of his piss in front of us in the shower room. He could not have been any more proud."

I grinned in spite of myself. "That makes me so happy, Drew," I said, hearing my own voice choke up with emotion. "Thank you for telling me that."

* * *

After we ate, Alex suggested that we go on a ride in the cable cars. This was the only non-water ride in the park. It was a pretty boring ride, actually, but it provided an awesome view of the entire park. All four of us were pretty relaxed at this point and just wanted to kick back. When we stepped up to get into the line, Drew commented on how short the line was. Because of the low park attendance this time of year, we did not have to wait at all to get a car. In fact, the attendant was only using every other car, which was nice as it allowed for more privacy, creating the impression that we were being given our own personal tour of the park.

Alex got in the car first and slid all the way to the back, stretching his feet out in front of him. Each car was rather spacious, with a big round turnstile directly in the center. Each could easily seat eight people, but it was just the four of us, giving us plenty of room. Drew slid in beside Alex while Matt and I got in on the opposite side facing them. We were required to fasten our seat belts, but once the ride started, I unhooked mine and slid over next to Matt, wanting to cuddle beside him. He put his arm around me affectionately, and then leaned over and kissed me gently. "There any security cameras in these cars?" he asked.

"Nope," said Alex. "There are cameras at two points on the ride but none in the cars." As we ascended, I looked over the edge of the seat and out the window to see the ground below. It was a magnificent view, not just of the park itself but of the entire outlying area of the city. We were extremely high in the air, and the people below looked like tiny army men moving around.

I lay my head against Matt's shoulders and looked over to Drew and Alex. Alex had clasped his hands behind his head and slid down very slightly in the seat, spreading his legs apart. He looked very relaxed and also very masculine in this position. Truly, he was a handsome guy with his dark

331

features and broad shoulders. Drew was lucky to be owned by him, I thought, even though I wouldn't have ever dreamed of trading my own Master for him. Drew was sitting beside him, though not touching him the way I was with Matt. He looked over at his owner then, taking in the sight of him. I watched as Drew stared at him and could see the same hunger that I so often felt for Matt.

Alex did not look at Drew though; he did not even acknowledge that he was there. Instead, he looked over at Matt and me, staring at us, perhaps taking in the way we looked as a couple, cuddled together romantically. Finally he pointed to the ground, and at first I thought he was motioning for us to look at something, but soon realized he pointed as an instruction for his boy. Drew slid out of his seat then and knelt on the ground in front of him. There was just enough room for Drew to slide between Alex's legs, and he did so, positioning himself so that he was face-level with his owner's crotch.

Then without instruction Drew reached up and grabbed the sides of Alex's waistband, pulling gently on his swimsuit as Alex thrust his hips forward to allow the suit to be pulled down over his thighs. Alex brought his feet together on the floor in front of Drew which allowed him pull the shorts completely down to Alex's ankles. Alex then spread his legs again, completely exposing his naked cock. I stared over at him, wide-eyed, never having seen him this way before. He sat there in front of us then, on display with his fully erect cock right in Drew's face.

I looked up at Matt, wondering if I was expected to mimic Drew and kneel to serve my owner. Matt just tightened his grip around my shoulder slightly, though, as if to indicate I was to remain in my current position. I was surprised by the size of Alex's cock, even though it was not bigger than the one I served regularly. My estimation would have been that Alex was endowed with a good seven-and-a-half inches, whereas Matt was a full nine. Alex's cock was really fat though, maybe a little thicker than Matt's, and it was so hard as I stared at it that it seemed to shine.

He then closed his eyes and relaxed as Drew opened his mouth to serve. He slid down on his owner's cock in a beautiful, smooth movement, immediately swallowing the entirely of it. He remained there for a few seconds and then slid back up about half way. He obviously knew what to do to please Alex, for he moaned lowly, appreciating the sensation of his boy's expert mouth. Drew never took his mouth off of Alex's cock, not even seeming to have to worry about breathing. He just sucked it hungrily and obediently, delivering nonreciprocal pleasure to this man he loved.

After about two minutes, Drew began to bob on the cock, sliding up and down smoothly, allowing his throat to be impaled. He kept his hands placed flat against Alex's calves as he sucked hungrily. Alex finally unclasped his hands and brought them down to Drew's head. He gripped it firmly as he opened his eyes to stare over at us. Then he pumped. He got this very intense look on his face, seeming very determined, and he seemed to be staring directly at me. I could not take my eyes off of him, but I held tightly onto my owner. Alex started pumping Drew hard, forcing him all the way down on his rock hard cock. As I stared back at him I thought of Matt, and what it was like for him when I served. I thought of the expressions on his face which I never was privileged to see. Now, for the first time, I was seeing a man being served from an observer's perspective, and it was so unbelievably hot.

I watched Drew's mouth, saw how his cheeks were indented, proving that he was providing constant suction. I saw how Alex's fingers were digging into Drew's skull; his grip was tightening. The pumping was getting faster and faster, and Drew submitted totally, allowing himself to be completely controlled. Finally it stopped, as Alex forced Drew down all the way on his shaft. He held him there tightly and looked directly into my eyes. He was draining himself into his boy and doing so while staring at me. Immediately I looked away, and looked up into the eyes of my owner. I pulled myself out of Matt's grip and slid to the ground, kneeling there at his feet.

Then I bowed humbly, bringing my face all the way to the floor, pressing my lips against the tops of Matt's bare feet. I kissed them over and over, reverently, demonstrating my absolute devotion to the one and only person in my life that I worshipped. I wanted Alex to see it, to understand that I was owned property, and not available to be had, not even in his fantasies! "I love you Sir," I said quietly between my kisses. "I love you with my whole heart. Only you. Only you, Sir."

19

On the ride back to Matt's cabin, I sat quietly in the car next to him, occasionally looking over at him as he drove. After the cable car ride, we had showered and changed, and I said my goodbyes to Drew. I was so looking forward to the evening ahead of me, being at Matt's side—on display—as Drew had stated. At the moment, though, I was content to merely be with him, relaxing in his presence. I felt this almost indescribable warmth inside me, a very happy and serene feeling. Words were not even necessary, for I sensed that Matt felt similar feelings himself. At one point, he reached over and placed his hand on my thigh, resting it there, perhaps to remind me that he was glad I belonged to him, or maybe to say something even more to me. Maybe it was an expression of his love. If he felt only a tiny fraction of the love for me that I felt towards him, it would be enough. It would be way beyond enough.

As we made the forty-five minute journey north of town, I began to realize how drowsy I was becoming, and I started to nod off. Matt did nothing to disturb me, allowing me to sleep quietly as he drove. I finally awoke as he was pulling up the forest-encased driveway. I reached behind me into the back seat and grabbed one of the duffle bags, digging into the side pocket to retrieve my watch. It was almost four o'clock. "Have a nice nap?" Matt asked me.

"I'm sorry, sir. I didn't mean to doze off."

"It's okay, all the sun must've tired you out. We have time if you wanna lie down when we get inside."

"Only if you do, Sir," I said. He just laughed as he pulled the car up to the edge of the drive. I stretched when I stepped out of the car, yawning as I tried to regain a sense of full alertness. It was so beautiful out here. The last time I was here it was dark, and then we had left early in the morning before I really got to take in any of the scenery. "This is so peaceful out here. It's just beautiful," I said.

"Yup. No one to bother us," he said. "One of these weekends we'll have to invite Alex and Drew up here. Not this time though, I want it to be just you and me."

I smiled at him. "I do too, Sir," I agreed, and picked up the duffle bag that I'd just moved to the front seat. Matt grabbed the other bag along with one he had packed for himself, and we headed inside.

"This is a very special weekend for us, pup. You know why?" he asked as he pushed the front door open.

"Because of it being your birthday tomorrow?" I said.

He laughed. "Not exactly, although I guess that makes it even more special. This weekend is special because it is important. I have a surprise for you."

"Really?" I said excitedly, "but you already have surprised me so much already. You got me this earring today, and then you took me to the park. You even let me...um...you know...um...take your urine."

"My piss," he corrected. "Sounds stupid when you say urine.

"But yeah, you're right, guess those all were nice surprises, but I have another one for you. This one is better—much bigger than the water park, the earring, or even the piss. You gotta go take your nap though first. Then when you get up, we can get some dinner and I'll give you the surprise."

"Oh Sir!" I whined, "I won't be able to sleep now. I'm not even tired anymore. Plus, all I will think about is the surprise."

"Are you questioning me?"

"No Sir," I said. "Are you gonna take a nap too?"

"Maybe, haven't decided yet, but I want you to cuz we're gonna be out really late tonight."

"Okay," I said, putting my bag down on a bench in the entryway corridor. "Do you want me to sleep in the same bed we used before?"

"Your choice," he said. "There are beds everywhere in here."

"I'll sleep in the same one, sir, cuz it is the one we were in together." He looked down at me, smiling, and again flicked the visor of my cap. I then turned and bolted up the stairs, eager to demonstrate my desire to obey him. Matt must have been right about me needing a nap, for in spite of the anticipation of the upcoming surprise, I dozed right off to sleep. When I woke up, it was already starting to get dark outside.

Slightly confused, I looked around a bit, until I was fully aware of where I was. I swung my legs over the edge of the big bed and yawned. I looked around for my shirt, not sure where I'd put it when I took it off to lie down. Quietly I stood up and padded out into the hallway. I had no idea where Matt was, and I did not want to make any noise in case he was sleeping. I heard sounds coming from the living room area, and as I headed down the stairs realized it was the television. I found Matt sitting in a recliner in front of the TV, his head tilted back and eyes closed. He'd fallen asleep. Quietly I tiptoed up to him and leaned in, looking directly at his face. He was so handsome that it almost overwhelmed me. I wished right then that I'd had a camera to take his picture. He looked beautiful, even when he was sleeping.

Suddenly he moved his arm very quickly, and grabbed my wrist. It startled me and I screamed, purely out of reflex. He opened his eyes and looked right into my own. "Tryin to sneak up on me, huh?" I shook my head, my heart pounding rapidly in my chest. "You know, I still gotta pay you back for what you did to me today, pulling me into the lake."

I wriggled my wrist within his grip, starting to realize that I was in a very vulnerable position at the moment. I knew he was being playful, but I had a feeling I was gonna be in store for something that I might not really want to endure. I wondered for a second if this ambush of his was the surprise to which he had earlier referred. "I'm sorry Sir!" I said, "it was only a joke."

"Ohh...only a joke huh?" He reached around and grabbed my other wrist with his opposite hand, now leaning sideways in the chair. He pulled me in front of the chair and straightened himself so I was now standing before him, between his legs. He then brought my two wrists together effortlessly, and gripped them both with his left hand. Even with both of my hands fighting against the grip of his one, I was still helpless, unable to pull either of them free. Using his free hand, he then reached up to my shoulder and pressed down; he was forcing me to my knees. I resisted him, though, and he removed his hand from my shoulder, but only to move it down to grab my groin. He easily found my nut sac and gripped it firmly, pulling downward as he squeezed. I immediately succumbed to his guidance, falling at once to my knees.

Matt's left hand still was holding my wrists and I was staring up at him. He kept eye contact with me, grinning all the while. "A joke, huh? Must have seemed pretty funny to you, seeing me fall over into the water like that, I bet. You think that was funny, boy?" I stared up at him wide-eyed, now starting to wonder just how serious he was being. Was he genuinely angry for my playfulness earlier, and was he now about to punish me for it? Afraid of avoiding his questioning, hesitantly I nodded. It *was* funny, after all. It was funny to all of us. "Oh really?" he said in a tone that was almost mocking. "Know what I usually do when I think something's funny?"

I knelt there, not knowing if his question sought an answer or was rhetorical. "I don't know sir," I said, my voice conveying the nervousness that I was now feeling.

He then reached over without warning, using his free hand, and gripped my bare side, digging his fingers into my sensitive flesh. I jerked spasmodically, and tried pulling away from him out of pure reflex. I instantly burst into laugher. "I laugh!" he said simultaneous with my outburst. As I twisted my body, trying to pull away from him, tugging my arms with all my might, he simply held them there while seeming to exert no effort whatsoever. He stared at me calmly as he dug his fingers into my side, tickling me unceasingly.

"Keep laughin, boy..." he said, "get a good laugh outta what you did." His thumb was pressing into my abdomen as his fingers worked the area just above my obliques. Unable to control myself as I was overtaken with a fit of hysterical laughter, I pushed my legs out from under me, landing on my butt. All the while he held firmly to my wrists and continued to tickle me. I was laughing harder and harder, getting to the point where I was needing to breathe, but I could not inhale.

He finally stopped tickling me after several seconds but continued to hold me in place. I immediately stopped the hysterical laughter but was very winded, gasping for my breath. "I'm...sor-sor-sor-sorry...sir!"

Calmly he looked at me as he slid himself to the edge of his seat. "Don't be sorry pup," he said, "it was funny. Let's just have a good laugh about it...together." He reached over and grabbed my left wrist with his right hand, pulling my arms apart. He was still holding both of my wrists firmly, but now using both of his hands to do so. He suddenly slid completely off the recliner, lunging towards me, as he dropped to the ground. He pushed my upper body backwards onto the floor and leaned over me and then assumed a kneeling position with each of his legs on opposites sides of my body. He had me pinned on my back and was staring down at me. He'd effectively pinned me this way so smoothly and quickly that I had not really even realized it was happening. Again he pulled my wrists together, this time over my head and grabbed them both with only his left hand. Holding me firmly in place on the ground, he turned himself slightly to reach behind his back and grab something from the chair. Apparently he had been hiding this item between the cushion and the inside of the chair.

As I looked up at him, the panic-stricken look on my face must have amused him, for he grinned at me in a way that almost seemed sadistic. He dangled the set of handcuffs over my head, allowing me to see them clearly and to speculate as to what he was going to do with them. "Sir, I'm sorry! Honest I only meant it as a joke! Please—." My voice was cracking as the panic swept over me. I felt myself tensing up, squirming underneath him as I desperately wanted to free myself. "Please— You're scaring me!"

Still dangling the handcuffs above my face, he stared down at me, looking me directly in the eyes. His expression, though, had softened. "Remember what I said, pup — what I promised you." A wave of guilt swept over me. How could I have feared him? How could I have mistaken his playful dominance as cruelty or sadism? He did not seem cruel or sadistic to me, not now or ever. He'd never hurt me. I just had to trust him. I relaxed myself then, ceasing to offer any resistance whatsoever. He let go of my wrists, and almost immediately I pulled my arms up, stretching them straight out in front of me into the air. I held my wrists together then, waiting for him to cuff me.

"I trust you Sir," I then said calmly. "I trust you completely." He slid one handcuff loop over my left wrist then and clicked it shut. As I heard the sound of the metal against metal, the cogs of the locking device making that unique zinging sound when he secured the loop around my small wrist, I felt myself becoming instantly aroused. Wide-eyed, I stared up at him, waiting for him to attach the second loop to my opposite wrist. Instead, though, he hesitated and let go of the handcuffs, allowing the set to hang down from my wrist. Using his knees, he pushed himself up into a more upright position then.

"Roll over, hands behind your back," he said. I did as he said, and then he attached the other loop, connecting my wrists together securely behind my back. I now lie face down with him sitting comfortably on my butt. He obviously was not allowing his entire weight to press into me, for I would have been crushed. He leaned forward then, sliding off of me and assuming a position beside me on the floor, lying down with his arm around my shoulder. I could not see him, for I was staring directly ahead, seeing only the carpeting in front of me. His fingers slid down my arm gently and then carefully back up, caressing me and causing goose pimples to rise the entire length of my arm. I lie there immobile, continuing to relax myself as he touched my smooth skin so lovingly. "Who owns you, pup?" he whispered into my ear.

"You do, Sir. You own every part of me."

"Good boy," he said quietly. And then he moved his fingers to the back of my neck, to the clasp of my beaded necklace. "It's time for me to take this off of you, pup, for good."

"Please Sir! Oh no, please—" Had I done something so wrong that he was punishing me again? Was he truly that displeased by my behavior at the water park that he again considered me unworthy to wear his necklace?

"Shhh," he said, calming me. "I'm not taking it from you, pup. I'm replacing it." Suddenly it dawned on me what he was doing! He was taking off the necklace so he could replace it with a real collar! I instantly was overcome with emotion, tears filling my eyes as I lie there next to him. He removed the necklace from its position and placed it in front of my face on the floor so I was staring right at it. "Kiss it," he said. "It's a symbol of your training, of all you and I have been through together so far." Reverently I pressed my lips against it, kissing it as he had instructed. "Good boy."

He then placed his hand on my shoulder once again and rolled me over so that I was on my side facing him. He pushed himself upright, into a kneeling position and then reached down to pull me to my own knees. Then finally he stood up. He turned and stepped over to the end table which was beside his chair and pulled open a drawer. From it he removed a smooth, black leather collar. It had a shiny silver buckle but was otherwise unadorned. He also picked up a small bone-shaped gold plate—a dog tag— and he turned to face me, stepping into position in front of me. As he towered over me, he held the tag in front of my face, allowing me to see it clearly. It was embossed on one side with a single word: PETEY. He turned it in his palm, showing me the backside of the tag. It had his contact information on the back—name, address, and phone number. It meant I was his. I belonged to him. His property.

I looked up at him as tears streamed down my cheeks. "I love you, Sir," I said quietly as he carefully fitted the collar around my neck. I felt the smoothness of the leather against my skin. When he slid the end of the collar through the buckle and tightened it, I knew I was smiling through my tears. I stared up at him the entire time, patiently allowing him to fit it around my neck perfectly. Then he crouched down into a squatting position in front of me and attached the gold name tag to the front of the collar, using the small silver ring that was there for that very purpose. He stood back up, now resuming his position of dominance. He was my owner now, officially. I was his collared pup.

I bowed down then, feeling overwhelmed with a sense of humility. It was paradoxical, the combination of my feelings. I was both humble and proud at the same time— proud to belong to him, yet so humbled by this very reality. I brought my mouth down to his feet, sensing how perfectly right is was for me to now worship him. My wrists were still secured behind my back as I bowed to kiss my owner's feet. I kissed them over and over, not ever wanting to stop, as the teardrops fell from my eyes. I worshipped first the right foot and then moved to the left. He just stood there accepting my worship, as I knew it should be.

Matt reached down, pushing me gently into a more upright position on my knees. I stared up at him through my tear-filled eyes, wondering for just a second whether I possibly was still in the big bed dreaming. It was real, though, and I was actually here kneeling before him, wearing his collar. He bent down and firmly grabbed each of my elbows, one in each of his hands. He picked my entire body up off the floor then, bringing me eye-level to him. Then he kissed me, at first softly. Our lips were pressed together tenderly as he leaned into me, applying more pressure. My mouth opened slightly in response to his, and he slid his tongue into me. The kiss grew passionate, and I hung there effortlessly suspended, as he displayed to me both his strength and passion in unison.

When he pulled me away finally, still holding me in front of him, I stared into his eyes. I'd never felt so much love, not even towards my own family. Without saying a word, he then quickly hoisted me, tossing me over his shoulder. I giggled as he did so, being totally at his mercy, but trusting him completely and loving every second of it. He carried me into the downstairs bedrooms then and placed me carefully on the bed. I was lying on my back, my cuffed hands underneath me. He pushed me up on the bed so that my head was lying on the single pillow that was already there in place. Then he moved away from me and stood at the foot of the bed, looking down at me. He reached down and grabbed my shorts and briefs together, swiftly pulling them off, exposing my shaved erection. He tossed the clothes carelessly behind him.

Then he reached down and grabbed my right ankle. I was relaxed, trusting him, as he pulled it over to the far side of the bed so that it was almost touching the baseboard. He reached down towards the ground and pulled something up, setting it on the bed. It was some sort of restraint which had apparently already been attached and waiting for me. He wrapped the leather strap around my ankle and secured it with the provided clasp. Then he moved to the other side of the bed, grabbing my left ankle. He pulled it in place and secured it with another restraint that also was already attached to the bed. As I stared up at him then, seeing him standing there at the foot of the bed towering over me, I was rock hard. My cock was throbbing against my belly, aroused to the point of leaking pre-cum. I was excited, my heart pounding, anticipating what he could possibly have in store for me, but not at all fearing him. I belonged to him now. I would trust him to do anything to me. Anything.

He stepped over to the side of the bed then, and reaching down, he ran his fingertips across my smooth ball sac. I jerked uncontrollably, having been recently shaved, I was extremely sensitive. "It tickles, Sir," I said as I smiled up at him. He then slid his index finger and his thumb each around opposite sides of my balls, caressing the area between my testicles and my inner thing. As he did this, his other fingers stroked the balls themselves. At this point I started to do more than jerk reflexively. I now was actually squirming. It was not that I was trying to resist him or even to express discomfort. It's just I was being tickled, and I could not control myself because I was so sensitive.

"Sir!" I protested, "It's so ticklish!! I can't stand it!"

He ignored my pleas and continued to gently and mercilessly run his fingers across my smooth balls. My cock stood totally erect, throbbing against my belly, as he continued his teasing. Finally I could hold back no longer and burst into laugher. I was twisting my upper body on the bed, flailing back and forth. He did not stop though, but continued as if totally unaware of my spasms. "Please stop!" I screamed. "Oh PLEASE!! PLEASE STOP!! I...hahahahahaha ....I can't take it!!" I was flopping my upper body around, twisting myself from side to side, while futilely pulling against the ankle restraints with my legs. The more I begged him to stop, though, the more determined he seemed to continue. Gales of laughter erupted from me, causing me to experience difficulty breathing. I was laughing so hard that I couldn't even inhale, and so somehow I'd have to find an opportunity to suck in a quick, deep breath, only to then immediately convulse into an even more hysterical fit of laughter.

"Yeah," he said calmly, finally pulling his hand away from my privates, "I think you're right, pup. I don't think you CAN take any more of this. The way you're flopping around, I'm afraid you might hurt yourself." He then reached down and slid his fingers gently between my collar and my neck. He gripped it firmly and pulled me smoothly into a sitting position. He sat down on the bed behind me, pressing his knee against my butt to hold me in place. Then he reached into his pocket to retrieve the handcuff key. He unlocked the handcuffs then, and I pulled my arms free, suddenly realizing how sore they were from having been underneath me while I was flailing around. I was still winded, trying to catch my breath as he grabbed my left wrist, the one from which the handcuffs were still dangling. He then put his other arm around my opposite shoulder and gripped it firmly, pulling me backwards. As I leaned back into him he slid himself out of the way and gently eased me back onto the bed. He then pulled my left arm up quickly and before I knew it, clicked the handcuff loop to the side of the headboard.

Now three of my appendages were securely locked to the bed in a spread-eagle position. Only my right arm was free. He got up and walked around the bed slowly, making eye contact with me the whole time. I felt my heart pounding in my chest, now fully aware of how very vulnerable I was to whatever he may have in store for me. "Sir," I said, "are you going to tickle me more?" My voice was high-pitched, betraying the fear that I had at the moment. It was not that I was afraid Matt would hurt me—I was just fearful of being tickled.

When I was much younger, I had suffered several encounters of tickle torture with my older cousin Allen. He and his family had vacationed in Florida one year and had stayed at our home, back when my parents had the house. Once he discovered how ticklish I was, he'd find ways to get me alone and then pin me down and mercilessly tickle me. I'd always go crazy when he did it, and sometimes I even lost control of my bladder from laughing so hard. This always cracked him up, knowing he was able to make me piss my pants. Every since those incidents, I'd always been very guarded about being tickled. Had it not been Matt who was just now touching me, I probably would have gone completely ape-shit, maybe even have thrown up.

Matt reached down and grabbed my last free appendage, grasping my wrist firmly. "Maybe," he said in answer to my question. "How could I possibly resist running my fingers through your pits when they're so — exposed — like this?" He then wrapped the restraint around my wrist, quickly securing it.

"Sir, Please!" I begged. "I'm too ticklish, I won't be able to take it!" He had climbed up onto the bed, kneeling over me. Each of his knees were on either side of me and he sat himself down gently on my waist. I felt the weight of his body on me as we sank into the bed.

"But you just got this nice new collar, pup. Don't you think you gotta somehow pay for it?"

I stared up at him, wide-eyed. "What do you mean, Sir?" I said. Surely he could hear the panic in my voice.

"Well nothing is free, ya know," he said. "It's up to me to set the price for your collar. I wonder…" he hesitated as he looked away, seeming to be reflecting upon the situation. "I wonder just how much this collar would be worth? What should I charge you for it?" I looked up at him as he turned back to me, staring into my eyes. "Hmm, say maybe five minutes of no-mercy tickling? Sound good to you?"

"No!!" I screamed. "No, please Sir!! Five minutes is too long! I can't take it!"

"Six minutes?" he said. "Ten?"

"No! No! Five!! Just only five, Sir!"

"Oh, okay, if you insist." He then reached both hands down instantly into my armpits and dug his fingers in, very softly at first. I bit down hard on my lip, trying to suppress the laughter as long as possible. Within five seconds I was wailing as never before, shaking my head from side to side, pulling furiously against the restraints, and laughing hysterically. After about fifteen seconds, when I was already to the point of breathlessness, Matt suddenly stopped. He got up from his position and moved to the head of the bed, to where my left hand was cuffed. He pulled out the key and unlocked it, taking my wrist into his hand, rubbing it gently. Then he held my arm up, examining it, and placed it back down on the mattress. "I'll be right back," he said.

I lay there, gasping for breath, my wrist aching—the one he had just rubbed. He re-entered the room, carrying something. It was apparently some sort of different restraint, neither leather nor a metal cuff. It was weaved material, sort of similar to what my duffle bag was made from, and it had a Velcro strap on it. He wrapped it around my wrist. "You were gonna hurt yourself with those metal handcuffs," he explained. "Is your wrist sore?"

346

"Only a little, Sir," I said. Had I not loved him so very much I might have strategized by exaggerating somewhat, possibly ending my session of tickle torture right then, but I simply could not lie to him. To be dishonest about any single thing would have been far worse than ten hours of tickle torture.

Once the strap was around my wrist and I was securely returned to my helpless, spread-eagled position, Matt resumed his position on top of me. "Okay...five minutes!" he said.

"No wait, Sir, shouldn't it be only four now?"

"Five minutes," he repeated, "Starting...NOW!" He then leaned in and began all over with the tickling. This time he did not pause at all, even when I got to the point where there was no laughter left in me. After I'd laughed for so long, I could not suck in breath right away, and so no sound would come out, just the convulsing of my body and the almost inaudible fits of silent laughter. Then after I was able to suck in a breath, an eruption of torrential laughter would explode from me, at which Matt would smile calmly, as he continued his torture.

"That's three minutes" he said calmly, as tears streamed down my face. The intense laughing made me shed tears, though they were not really from crying, just from intensity of the laugher perhaps. How could it only be three minutes? Oh god!!

"Please!!! Oh...Oh...Oh...Oh God...HAHAHAHAH!!!! Oh Please...s-s-s-s-s-s-SIR!!!"

"Gonna offer you a deal, pup," Matt said, having to raise his voice over my laugher. "Listen close." I was trying to listen, but since he continued to tickle me I could not stop the laugher. Finally he stopped, keeping his fingers pressed against me, though not moving them. "Okay, you have about one and a half minutes left, but I will stop right now, if you want to make a deal with me."

"Anything SIR!" I screamed. "I'll do anything!"

"Better wait and see first, pup. Okay, here's the deal. We take off your collar and I keep it until your birthday. Then you get it back."

"No!" I screamed. "No please Sir, don't do it!" Now my eyes were filling up with genuine tears.

"Calm down, pup," he said. "It's just an option. So you want the tickling to continue, or to give back your collar for a few days?"

"Tickling!" I yelled, without any hesitation. He then continued. He was very casual in the delivery of his torture, expertly finding exactly the way to touch me to send me screaming in a fit of hysterical laughter. He'd then revisit that spot, over and over, as I lay there stretched out underneath him, totally helpless. Never before in my life, not even when under the sadistic control of my cousin Allen, had I laughed so hard and so long. I laughed way beyond the point of even being able to make sound, for once I was out of breath, the only sound that would come out of me was what you might call silent laughter. My body was convulsing, and I was frantically pulling against the restraints. My resistance was not so much an attempt to free myself, but pure reflex. When being tickled in the bare underarms, the natural response was to immediately pull my arm down to protect myself. Being tied spread-eagled, this of course was not possible. Matt would pause briefly when I got to where I could not breathe for a few seconds, allowing me to catch my breath quickly, then he'd dive back in, beginning the torment all over. Each time he started over I'd go into another fit of laughter, very loud and hysterical.

After what seemed like hours, I began to again protest, "S-s-s-sir...Puh—leeez...oh god...oh puh.....puh...leeez, s-s-stop!!"

He smiled down at me, sitting comfortably on my waist, "Well, the five minutes were up a long time ago, pup. I just can't stop myself though." He then traced his fingers down my sides, introducing other parts of my body to his delightful torment. He found my abs, the smooth area just below my navel, and discovered this was a major hot spot. He dug in mercilessly as I went into another spasm. He pushed himself up onto his knees and reached behind himself, tracing the very sensitive area of my inner thighs. He revisited my nut sac. He continued downward, leaning backwards slightly, though still staring directly at my face. I was panicking as he moved closer to my feet, not wanting him to discover my most sensitive spot of all.

He slowly pulled his hands away from my legs and then stared down at me. I was gasping and thankful for the respite. "Please, Sir..." I heaved a huge sigh as I exhaled, "Please no more! I beg you."

"Yeah, you did your time, and a deal's a deal. Wanted to get to those feet though. Maybe save em for later, huh?" Then he slid himself up closer to my face, until his knees were resting against my underarms. He was wearing only a pair of shorts and his white crew socks. I saw the outline of his rock hard erection through the fabric of the shorts. "Kiss it," he said, as he thrust his groin towards my face. Craning my neck forward as far as I could, I was barely able to connect with his bulge, and he thrust his groin a little closer to me, finally reaching down and grabbing the back of my head with one hand. He pressed himself into me, grinding his hard-on against my mouth. I felt the wetness of the fabric which had been getting drenched with his pre-cum.

Matt then placed his hands on the wall in front of him and swung his leg over my body, pushing himself smoothly away from the wall, allowing himself to step down onto the ground. He stood there beside me, my eyes having followed his crotch the entire time. He pulled down his shorts in one smooth movement and stepped out of them. He then walked to the far end of the bed, down to where my feet were securely locked in place. He grabbed a hold of his cock with his right hand as he looked down at me, taking in the entirety of me, perhaps seeing how helpless and vulnerable I

349

was as I lay there collared and bound at his mercy. With his free hand he reached down to my right foot, and ran his finger up the length of my sole, beginning at the heel and then working up. He grinned as he watched my response. I immediately curled my toes downward and pulled my leg frantically against the restraint, finally bursting into laughter. He let go of his hard-on and reached down to my toes to push them backwards with his right hand. Then with his left, he dug his fingers into my soft sole. I went bonkers then, like never before.

He stopped after just a few seconds, again reaching to stroke his cock. "Ohh yeah...that's what I wanted to hear pup. I definitely think this is your hot spot. It is, isn't it?"

I stared down at him, wide-eyed with fearful anticipation. "Please sir," I said, "You said just five minutes."

"Yeah, you're right, pup," he said as he dug his fingers into the center of my sole, moving them rapidly back and forth. "But then, since I'm the one who makes the rules, I also can change them if I want." He grinned down at me. "Five more minutes on each foot!"

"No!" I screamed as he began all over again. He was very methodical as he worked my soles with his expert fingers, finding the absolutely most sensitive spot on my foot—the smooth area just below the instep—and working it relentlessly. During this part of the torture, my cock had gone soft, for it was no longer erotic pleasure, but at this point genuine torture. Of course, it was anything but torture to him, for he was rock hard himself, periodically releasing my foot long enough to stroke himself. After tickling each foot mercilessly for what seemed an eternity, he finally knelt down at the foot of the bed and stretched his arms out, easily reaching each of my feet at the same time. He then tickled them together, as I squirmed and laughed helplessly.

"Oh God!!! Oh God!...Pleeeez...oh pleeze...hahahahah...oh god...hahahahaha....please st—st-stop! I'm gonna pee ...oh sir...I'm...uh...ahhh...hahahahaha....if you...if you...hahahahaaa...if you don't stop!" Apparently this was what he was waiting to hear, for he then intensified his efforts so much the more. I burst into a solid fit of long, hysterical laugher then, and felt suddenly that I'd reached the point of no return, where my bladder was letting go. I laughed like crazy as the warm piss sprayed onto my belly. "Oh no!!" I cried, still laughing, but mortified at the same time.

Suddenly he stopped. He stood up as I lay there, tears streaming down my face, gasping for air. "You pissed yourself!" he exclaimed. "You fuckin pissed yourself. You baby!" It was almost exactly the same words that Allen used to say to me after I'd done the same with him.

"I'm sorry sir!" I cried. "I couldn't help it."

He then picked up my shorts and underwear from the floor and dropped them on my belly, rubbing them around in the puddle of piss. "How fuckin pathetic, you pissed yourself just like a baby," he repeated as he sopped up the mess. "I ought to make you wear these tonight. That way everyone can see what a baby you are. How do you feel about that, boy?"

"I'm so sorry sir! I couldn't help it," I said again. He clenched the soaked shorts in his hand then and moved it to my face, shoving it towards my mouth.

"Open up!" I opened my mouth obediently, as he roughly stuffed the urine-soaked bundle into my mouth, using his fingers to shove it in as deep as he could.

"Suck on it!" he ordered. And then he moved back to the end of the bed, quickly unfastening the buckle of each of my leg restraints. When free, I moved them around, feeling instant relief and freedom. This didn't last long though, for he then grabbed a hold of each ankle and brought them together. He pulled my legs up so they were directly in the air, and he held onto them together, using only his left hand. Then he pulled his right arm back, into a swinging position, and I knew I was going to get spanked. He held his arm back with his hand extended, perhaps allowing me to experience some anticipation. I bit down hard into the fabric in my mouth as he quickly brought his arm down and smacked my ass hard with his palm.

"Ungh!" I moaned, as he slapped my ass. He repeated this five or six more times.

"Bad boys who piss themselves get spanked!" he said, reddening my ass a little more with each blow.

Finally he stopped, having delivered about ten slaps to my bare ass. He dropped my legs onto the mattress. Then he resumed his position on the bed, once again kneeling over me. He jerked the wad of fabric from my mouth and threw it on the floor, sliding himself right up close to me. He edged even closer, pressing his hard cock against my lips. I felt his knees press over my tiny biceps as he unnecessary pinned me with them. I think he did this more for the purpose of positioning himself than for restraint. "Open!" he commanded, and instantly slid his hard, throbbing cock all the way into me. His thrust was so violent that I uncontrollably gagged. He pulled back less than two inches and then rammed in again, grinding this time. I struggled not to repeat the gagging, and pressed my lips down around his shaft, very carefully avoiding any contact with my teeth.

He grabbed a hold of my head firmly with one hand while pressing his other flat against the wall, using it to steady himself. Then he began thrusting into my throat. He pumped hard, ramming deep into me and staying there. In less than a minute, I knew it was coming. He brought his other hand down quickly from the wall, grabbing my head now with both hands as he buried himself balls deep into my mouth. Then he released his load.

"Fuck YEAH!!" he screamed, as he drained himself. The eruption was enormous and very forceful. I instantly gulped, trying to swallow it all as I felt his cock pulsing against my tongue. He held me there in place for a good twenty seconds after he was done emptying his load into me. Then he let go, and dropped down onto the mattress beside me, gasping for breath himself. "Oh god, pup! That was fuckin hot!" He reached over and unlatched the strap to my right wrist, then did the same to my left. Before I could even move and enjoy my freedom, though, he had his arms around me, pulling me into him. His embrace was so strong and so overpowering, that I just sort of melted into him, pressing my back against his body. We were lying there in the position of two spoons resting together.

"You were a good boy!" he said. "You were such a good boy."

"I'm sorry I peed sir," I said softly, feeling so ashamed.

He laughed. "It's a scene pup. I made you piss, so that I could discipline you. You did nothing wrong."

I then smiled to myself and leaned back into him. "Just a scene, sir," I repeated, "and I didn't freak this time."

"Nope. You trusted me. Good boy." He kissed the side of my forehead as he held me there. "See how hard it got me? See how hard my pup got me?" he asked.

"Yes sir. It was so hot," I admitted.

"And I'm still hard," he laughed. "Let's go get in the shower, okay?" He then reached down and patted my butt, this time very gently. "Hurry up!" I jumped up and dashed down the hall into the bathroom, as he calmly walked behind me.

* * *

I reached into the shower, turning on the water, and held out my hand to assess the water temperature. Matt was behind me merely observing. This weekend was turning out to be absolutely wonderful, much more than I could ever have hoped for or dreamt of. Gently Matt reached over and unfastened the buckle of my collar, removing it carefully and placing it on the sink behind him. I turned my head to look up at him, not speaking, but simply smiling, conveying to him the contentment I felt within myself at that moment.

How is it that I had gone my entire life up to this point without realizing how very incomplete I had been? He then leaned in and kissed me softly on the lips as I reached for his waist, sliding my hands around him as our mouths locked together. He used both hands to hold my head while he kissed me, demonstrating an expression of both love and ownership. I felt the powerful passion of his kiss while at the same time was aware of his control over me as he held my head in place. "I love you, Sir," I said quietly when he finally pulled away from me. His hands slid off from the sides of my face then and onto my shoulders. Slowly I dropped to my knees and removed each of his socks—the only articles of clothing he was currently wearing. Very delicately, I bent over and kissed the top of each foot before I righted myself and finally stood back up. Matt stepped into the shower first, and I stepped in after him. He had his back to the cascade of water, as it poured from the spigot onto his shoulders.

Once in the shower, I cuddled next to Matt, pressing my body against his. He lathered up his hands and ran his palms up and down my torso, reaching around me from behind. I leaned into him, enjoying the feel of him as his strength seemed to surround me. He picked up the bar of soap and held it in front of me, gesturing for me to take it from him. I reached up and grabbed the soap and then turned to face him. The water spilled down over his back, running down his smooth and chiseled chest. Worshipfully I stared up at him and guardedly moved my hand closer to him, doing so with absolute reverence. I was aware not only of his dominance over me mentally, but his physical supremacy as well. I felt so small next to him, a diminutive version of himself in many ways. He was my hero, my role-model, my idol. I touched his chest with my tiny hand, pressing the bar of soap against it, forming a small circle as I began to lather him.

Working my way down, I continued to clean his body, moving unhurriedly down his frame. I brought my free hand up to touch him as well, gently rubbing the soap against his skin. It was as if I were both cleaning and caressing him concurrently. I lowered my body as I moved down his torso, finally dropping to my knees. Then I moved to his feet. He picked each foot up slightly from the tile flooring, allowing me to clean every inch of him, scrub between the toes, wash his soles. I moved back up, past his ankles, then his calves, finally his thighs. I slid my hands between his legs, around behind him to his buttocks, and then rubbed the lather into his inner thighs. Then while kneeling there I faced his cock finally. I stared at it in awe, glancing to look up at him. I leaned forward, respectfully kissing it as I rubbed the soapy lather onto his nut sac. He repositioned himself slightly, moving his legs apart. I kissed him again, opening my mouth slightly as I pressed it against the tip of his cock head.

I opened wider, moving my mouth around his semi-hard cock. He did not protest, allowing me to take him into myself, this time not by force but of my own volition. Every reverential movement of my body was an expression of worship; I was crying out to him with my actions, demonstrating to him how deeply I loved him. If the movements of my hands and mouth were to be translated somehow into words, they would clearly have been these very three: *I love you.* I took more of him into my mouth, forming a suction around him, pressing my tongue against his shaft, feeling it grow in my mouth. I pulled away then after a few seconds and examined him. I saw how hard he was and looked up into his face. He was staring down, seeming un-angered and patient. I placed the soap bar between my two palms and moved them back and forth, lathering my hands thoroughly. Then I dropped the soap, unconcerned, and moved my hands back up to him, wrapping them around his now erect penis. I slid both hands around his fat shaft, soaping it up completely as I stared up at him.

Finally, he reached down, holding his palms upward as he did so. I placed my small soapy hands into his, and he pulled me up off my knees. Then he smoothly spun me in his arms, pulling me into him again, my back now against his chest once more. "Say what you want, pup...say it."

Almost tearfully I then responded, ever so quietly, "Sir, I want you inside me." He slid his hands down my body, resting them eventually on my hips. He pushed me forward, and instinctively I bent over, pressing my hands against the wall in front of me. I felt his hardness against my hole, the heat from it seemed to reach me before he even began to penetrate. He held onto me firmly, gripping my hips with intensity, as he poked his hard cock against my smooth and tight hole. Then he thrust forward, easing in slowly. He slid his soapy cock into my ass and I moaned, feeling it from this position now for the very first time. "Oh god," I said quietly, responding to the pleasure-pain mixture. It was indescribable.

Once inside me, he held himself there, possibly enjoying the feeling of my tightness, perhaps feeling the heat of my body around him. I loved the feeling of submission as I bowed there obediently, taking him inside myself. He continued to hold onto my waist, as he pulled out slightly. Then he thrust back in, and I felt the burning sensation all over again, as if he were entering me for the first time. I moaned, pressing my hands steadfastly against the wall. He repeated this action again, now for the third time, followed immediately by a fourth, a fifth, a sixth. He rocked his hips as he drilled his cock into me, picking up the pace with each thrust, ultimately forming a rhythm. I simply bowed there humbly, taking him into myself, allowing him to experience the pleasure of my tautness around his cock.

As he continued, his thrusts increased with intensity. He was rocking into me, riding me confidently. The physical feelings I was experiencing were very much mixed. The pressure of his cock against my prostate as he pounded into me was powerfully erotic, yet there was also some pain as his thick cock stretched me mercilessly. I allowed myself to mentally drift, visualizing myself kneeling at his feet, kissing them. I willed myself to think thoughts of servitude and humility as I stood there in this most humble position, assuming a stance of deferment before my owner. He continued his thrusts, unaware and unconcerned by any discomfort I may be experiencing. He rammed himself deep into me, burying his cock all the way each time. As he quickened the pace, he pulled out less farther with each pump. I sensed he was nearing orgasm, and I brought my mental realization back to focus upon the present.

"Oh god!" I screamed, "Fill me with your...ungh...your load! Oh please...just like...be-...fore...when you shot...ungh...ahhh... in...my...mouth, Sir!"

"You want it boy? You wanna take me in both holes? You want me to fill you up completely? Huh?"

"Yes Sir!" I screamed, "Oh PLEASE SIR!!! Ahhhh!"

He thrust into me then violently, gripping my hips tightly with both hands, holding me in place. I felt his cock throb against my hole as he drained himself, moaning openly. "Yeahhh! Fuck Yeah!" he exclaimed.

I remained in my position patiently, awaiting his signal to do otherwise, and then he finally leaned over, pulling me into an upright position. He was still inside me, and we both were panting heavily. He reached around me and grabbed my hard cock. "Shoot for me pup. Shoot your load." He slid his hand down my shaft, pumping me erotically. "Shoot it," he whispered in my ear, as he jacked me. Within seconds I moaned, spilling my seed all over the bathroom tile. "Good boy!" he said as he kissed the side of my face.

20

That evening I wanted desperately to give Matt the other
birthday presents I had gotten for him, but I held back,
forcing myself to wait until the actual day of his birthday.
We had dinner together before we started to get ready to go
to the club. After the shower, Matt allowed me to towel him
dry, occasionally kissing his various body parts as I did so.
He allowed me to put on a pair of shorts afterwards but
nothing else. He slipped on his boxers himself, and we
headed out to the kitchen together. "Sir, do you want me to
cook for us?"

He laughed, "Unless you plan to run into town to get take
out. Won't expect to see you til morning though; would be a
long haul on foot."

I opened the refrigerator door and to my surprise
discovered it stocked full of all kinds of food. "Wow," I said,
"Someone's been shopping. How hungry are you sir?" I
asked.

"Just do something easy, pup. After we eat, we gotta get
ready to go anyway. So easy and fast."

"Yes sir," I said, "Easy and fast." I pulled out a package of
ground sirloin. "Want a burger?"

"Sure," he said. "Make one for both of us."

"Hmm, okay. I don't know though, I don't usually eat a
lot of red meat."

"I said, 'Make one for both of us'," he repeated.

"Yes sir," I said. An occasional burger wasn't gonna hurt
me, and plus it sounded good. "Want me to do these on the
grill, sir?" I asked as I began unwrapping the white paper
from the meat package.

"Nah...fry em," he said.

I made a face. "That's the worst way to cook them sir, all that fat!"

"Fry em!" he repeated, obviously enjoying the fact that he could order me to do things I did not particularly want to do. I looked over to him and smiled.

"Yes sir," I responded.

We sat down at the table across from one another after I'd placed our plates down in front of us respectively. I'd prepared him much larger portions than my own, his plate heaping over with an enormous quantity of fries, macaroni salad, and a humongous burger served up on a toasted onion bun. My own plate had no fries, a small scoop of salad and a burger a third the size of his. He picked up the sandwich and stuffed a big bite into his mouth. "Mmm," he said, "Aren't you hungry pup?" He motioned to my plate.

"Sure," I said, laughing. "I'm hungry for you, sir."

"Good answer," he mumbled, his mouth stuffed with food. "You need to start eating more. No wonder you're so scrawny."

"You think I'm scrawny, sir?" I asked disappointedly.

"Don't get all defensive. You *are* scrawny — skinny, I mean. Not a bad thing; I like you just the way you are, but I think you need to take care of yourself. Don't want my pup malnourished."

I busted up laughing. "Yeah, right, as if I'd ever be accused of that!"

"Come here," he said, pointing his finger down to the ground beside him. I immediately pushed my chair back and slid out of my seated position, walking over to him. I stood next to him obediently in the spot where he'd pointed. "Down," he said. I knelt.

He then broke off a piece of his burger and held it between his thumb and forefinger. "Sit pretty, pup!" he said. I smiled up to him, but then instantly wiped the smile from my face, willing myself to be serious. I pulled my arms up against my chest in almost the same position as I'd done to amuse Devin and Kyle that day Matt had saved me. I knelt there, in only my shorts and collar and displayed myself before my Owner.

"Good boy!" he said, and held the portion of meat and bun above my head. I tilted my head back and opened my mouth as he dropped it in. I chewed it slowly, all the while looking up at him. He reached across the table and pulled my plate in front of him. "Ya know, I got my two pups matching collars," he told me. "Yours and my other Petey's are exactly the same. You like that pup?"

I nodded to him vigorously. I sort of did not think it appropriate to speak at the moment, having slipped into this doggy role. He picked up his sandwich again, taking another big bite. Leaning back in his chair casually, he tilted slightly backwards, rocking on the rear legs so that the front two raised off the ground. When he placed the burger back onto his plate, he picked up a french fry, tossing it to me indifferently. I tried catching it with my mouth but missed. I looked up at him then, wide-eyed. Did he expect me to dive for it, eat it off the floor? "Go on, pup," he said, "get it." Obediently I bent over, placing my hands flat on the floor on either side of the french fry. Hesitantly I bowed my head down, moving it close to the fry. I quickly grabbed it with my lips, pulling my head back instantly. I sat back up in my begging position, holding the fry between my teeth. As I looked up at Matt I sucked the fried potato into my mouth, chewing it rapidly. Before I'd even gotten it swallowed, he tossed me another. This time I caught it in the air. "Good boy!" he praised. I beamed up at him.

I knelt there then quietly, waiting patiently for him to feed me, one bite at a time. He began taking portions of my own sandwich from my plate to give to me while eating the rest of his own by himself. When the burgers were all gone, he picked up my plate and slid it onto the floor in front of me. All that was left was the macaroni salad. "Clean your plate, pup," he ordered. I resumed my canine position on the floor, getting back on all fours, and ate the few bites of salad without the use of my hands or a fork. When it was gone, I used my tongue to lick the plate clean. "Good boy," he repeated, "You were a hungry pup." I then lay down on the floor beside him, curling myself into a fetal-like position and pressed my face against his foot. He did not move it, but allowed me to rest my head there against him. It felt so good to be near him, to be touching him—even just his foot.

After our meal, Matt rose from the table. "Okay, get up and clean the table, pup. Then we'll go get ready." I shot up immediately, slipping back into my role as his boy. I did the dishes hurriedly, the excitement within me growing as I anticipated our evening out together. This would be my very first time in public at my Owner's side, clearly marked as his property. I'd be wearing my new collar for all to see. I'd be on display, as Drew had stated. I could not wait.

* * *

After finishing my clean-up in the kitchen, I found Matt in the bedroom. He had laid out on the bed my clothing for the evening. I was to wear a white beater shirt, cargo khakis, colored boxers, and white crew socks. "Grab my keys off the dresser, pup," he told me, "then run out to the car and get those two bags from the trunk."

"Yes sir," I said, obeying him without question. I was still only wearing my shorts, but we were far out in the country, and at this stage I was very much unconcerned about modesty. I shot down the hallway and then outside to the car. As he'd stated, I found two plastic bags in the back seat, both labeled clearly with a Footlocker logo on the side. It was obvious that each bag contained a large shoe box, and I was instantly aware that he'd bought us both a new pair of shoes. I was so excited as I ran back up the porch steps. I wondered if they were going to be identical to one another? Owner and pup in matching shoes was a thought that thrilled me.

I stood next to Matt when I returned. He was in front of the mirror, having gotten dressed already. His clothing was similar to what he'd laid out for me except he was also wearing a shirt over the beater. "No shirt for you, pup," he explained. "Want everyone to see your collar very clearly. You're MINE." He grabbed me affectionately by the shoulders and pulled me into himself. Carefully I placed the packages on the floor and snuggled up to his chest.

"You're all I want Sir," I said quietly. "You are all I ever, ever want." He kissed my forehead and then pushed me back from himself, holding me at arms length.

"Okay, gotta get you dressed." He picked up the boxers and handed them to me. "Put these on." Quickly I slid off the shorts I was wearing and changed into the boxers. He watched me the whole time, and although I was used to being naked in front of him, I could not help to feel a bit modest. It was one thing to serve him sexually, and yet another to be on display as he watched me strip. Certainly it was not that I minded him seeing me, just rather that I was a bit self conscious. When I thought of my body compared to his, I especially was freaked. He was so much more muscular than I. I was scrawny and geeky, I thought. At least I had replaced my glasses with contacts a while back, and plus he was dressing me a lot cooler than I ever had been before.

He picked up the cargos next and held them out in front of me by the waistband. He leaned forward, holding them for me to step into. He was actually dressing me, I thought, just like my mom used to do when I was a small child. I stepped into the cargos, one leg at a time and he pulled them up into place. He positioned the waistband in a manner that showed a bit of a sag, revealing the tops of the colored boxers. Then he reached over to the dresser and picked up a wide leather belt. "Here," he said, and then fed the belt through each of the loops on the pants. Then he cinched it up, fastening the buckle. He stepped back to observe his handiwork. "Cool," he said. Then he handed me the beater.

"Put this on," he said, this time allowing me to do it myself. After pulling the shirt over my head, he stepped up to me again, tucking the shirttail under the boxer's waistband. He examined it, apparently wondering whether to undo what he'd just done, leaving it untucked. Finally he decided it looked good the way he had it. "Put your socks on, pup," he told me. I obeyed, squatting down on the floor as I dressed each foot.

I then crawled over to the bed, now on my knees, and eagerly watched him as he picked up the packages from the floor and placed them on the bed in front of me. He removed both boxes from their bags and set them down on the bed. Then he pulled off the lids, revealing identical pairs of chalk-white Nikes. His were a size 13, and mine were a seven. As he pulled them from the box and set them on the bed, I thought mine looked so cute next to his. It was like they were a miniature version of the bigger pair. Mine were the baby shoes, and his were the grown-ups. I laughed right out loud.

"What's so funny, pup?" he asked.

"They look cute," I said. "I mean, mine do compared to yours."

He gave me somewhat puzzled look, rolling his eyes. "Oh brother!" Then he laughed. "Get over here and put mine on me," he said. Quickly I reached up and removed the larger pair from the bed, and then moved to position myself in front of him on my knees. He placed one hand on the dresser beside him and held onto the bedpost with his other, as he picked his socked foot up from the floor. He raised it to my face briefly, allowing me to kiss it respectfully. He was not seeking full blown foot worship at the moment, I knew, but merely allowing me the privilege to show my respect before dressing his foot. He brought his foot down closer to the ground then and held it there while I pulled the sneaker on. When I had it on his foot properly, he then pulled it away from me, planting it on the floor under him so that he could lift his other foot. He repeated the very same routine with his left foot then, allowing me to kiss it first and then put on the shoe. When I was done, I then leaned forward and tied each shoe. I bowed my head and kissed the tops of his shoes then, before sitting upright, still in a kneeling position.

Matt then reached over and picked up my pair of shoes, handing them to me together. "Okay, put yours on now," he said. I leaned backwards, pulling my legs out in front of me. I was now sitting on my butt on the floor. I put each of my own shoes on quickly, tying them exactly as I'd done Matt's. "Stand up," he instructed me.

We then stood together in front of the mirror, Owner and pup. I loved how we looked together, clearly a couple. We were not dressed as twins at all, our clothing being different, but our shoes were identical. We also each had on beater shirts and khakis. "Think I should wear a necklace, pup?" he asked.

I was a bit taken aback by the question, surprised he'd ask my opinion. "I think you would look awesome no matter what you wore, Sir."

"Didn't ask that, pup," he said, "I asked if you thought I should wear a necklace."

I smiled up at him. "Thank you for asking me, Sir," I said. "I don't know. Maybe not, cuz what if someone thinks it's a collar?"

"No one will think that," he laughed. "If they did, I'd have to punch 'em. Not that kinda necklace I mean, anyways. Something like a chain, maybe. A thick gold chain. What do you think?"

"You have one like that, Sir?"

"Well I wouldn't be thinking of wearin one if I didn't have it to begin with," he said. "I have that one," he reached inside of the duffle bag that was beside the dresser, pulling out a thick gold chain, "and I have this one." He pulled out a smaller silver chain.

"Hmm," I said. "Definitely I think it should be the gold one, Sir. Looks more masculine."

"Yeah, I agree," he said. He then reached up and put it next to his neck, reaching up to fasten the clasp.

"Want me to fasten it for you, Sir?" I asked.

"No," he said dismissively. "Pups don't collar their owners." I looked to the ground immediately.

"Sorry Sir," I said quietly.

When we finally were ready to leave, it was after 10pm. I knew it would be at least an hour's drive into the city, and if the club were where I suspected, we would probably get there a little bit past eleven. I wondered how it was the Matt was so certain he could get us inside. I mean, he wasn't even old enough himself to gain entry legally, and I looked even younger than him. When we did get there, I was not even aware of the location of the bar. There were no visible signs, as was the case with most clubs I'd seen. He parked the car, though, offering no explanation, and we got out.

"Where is it?" I asked.

He pointed up the street. "It's that gray building," he said. As I looked over, I realized that had I not been with him, I'd have never even seen it. There were no signs on the exterior, and the two small windows on the front were completely black, either covered or painted, I could not tell.

"Guy that works the door's named Ben," Matt said. "He has a membership at one of our gyms. He told me about this place." That explained suddenly how we were going to gain entry. "Want you to be real respectful of him, pup. He's my friend."

"Yes, Sir," I said, pulling the latch on my door handle in unison with Matt who was doing the same. We stepped out of the car. "I'll be respectful, Sir. I won't say anything."

"Didn't say that," he laughed. "You can talk, just remember your place. You are with me, my property. It's not like we are going to a restaurant or something. The whole reason we're here is to be together as owner and pup. Got it?"

"Yes, Sir," I said, smiling up at him as I walked briskly beside him. His steps were longer than mine and I had to practically run at times to keep up with him. When we got to the door, I did finally notice a sign. It was a small logo that was embossed above the door: THE DEN. Matt pulled the heavy door open and stepped inside. I followed quickly behind him, realizing instantly that it was a rather subdued atmosphere. The lights were rather dim and the room was very smoke-filled and surprisingly quiet. I did hear dance music, but it seemed to be coming from a distance. Perhaps the dance floor was in the back, away from the main bar area. As I looked around, I realized that the club itself was far larger than I'd expected from the view outside. It seemed rather expansive, stretching far beyond where I even would have thought the building ended. The décor was also much nicer inside than I might have guessed. It did not appear run-down as was suggested from the exterior.

The first person we encountered was the doorman. Obviously this was Ben. "Hey man," Matt said to him, reaching his hand out to shake with him. They did so non-traditionally, in a manner that indicated they were buds rather than business associates. I simply stood there quietly waiting to see if an introduction was forthcoming. Matt and Ben chatted casually for a couple of minutes, talking about how their weekends had been so far and about some new piece of weight equipment that was just installed at the gym. Finally Matt did turn to me, "This is my pup," he said. I looked up at Ben quickly, smiling but not saying anything. Ben extended his hand to me to greet me and I reached up and shook it respectfully.

"Nice to meet you Sir," I said meekly. That was all the attention he paid me, then returning his gaze to Matt. They talked a few more minutes before Matt decided to head on further into the club. Ben did not assess us a cover charge as was required, and made no mention of a need to see identification, although I did overhear him as we were walking away. He was asking the patrons behind us to show their I.D.'s, and requested a six dollar cover from each.

As we got further into the club, I became aware of why the music was so subdued. There was a huge circular bar in the center of the building and on each side of it a set of big double doors. Apparently on the other side of the doors was the dance area of the club. The bar was accessible from both sides and this allowed the sounds from the other room to spill out into our side, but you had to pass through one of the sets of doors to get to the dance floor. The side of the building that we currently were in was much more for socializing, I presumed. Most of the clientele also appeared to be more mature—the older set. I looked around myself, taking in many of the other customers, realizing that some were dressed rather unusually.

In the corner was a punk couple, each sporting heavy leather jackets and displaying brightly colored Mohawk hairdos. One of them had his nipples pierced with large silver hoops, and a chain was attached to each of them, connecting them together. His friend had an eyebrow piercing and was wearing a pair of jack boots which did not seem at all complimentary with the rest of his get-up. I shrugged to myself, being a bit puzzled by this oddity.

At the bar was a heavy set gentleman, probably in his late forties or early fifties. He was wearing a leather vest and a pair of saggy jeans. The jeans reminded me of what you might see a plumber wearing, being that they displayed his ass crack clearly, though in a way that was not particularly attractive. Next to him sat a very slender young man who was at least less than half his age. The boy was wearing a leather studded collar and a leather arm band around his right bicep. He was blonde, and somewhat cute, though it appeared he'd previously had a problem with acne, for his face was rather pitted. When I noticed that a leash was attached to the back of his collar and saw the older guy tug at it on one occasion, I surmised that they were a Dom/sub couple.

There were also plenty of people there who were decked out in full leather gear, some sporting the flat-topped leather caps, the leather jackets with no shirt underneath, the leather boots, pants or chaps, harnesses, and wrist or arm bands. Several of these patrons were paired up as couples, but there also were people who were alone, some standing in the corner eying everyone else. Perhaps they were targeting other single people that they could potentially hook up with.

Some of the people there were dressed conservatively as well. There were two men at the back of the room actually wearing business suits. Some of the people I saw were in jeans and tee shirts or Khakis, like Matt and me. As we passed through this first section of the club and headed for the double doors leading to the dance area, I felt a bit self conscious, being concerned that people were watching us. I stayed as closely behind Matt as possible, actually wishing for a few seconds that he'd attached a leash to my own collar, simply because then he could hang onto it.

When we passed through the double doors, I immediately realized that this section of the club was where all the younger set congregated. Opposite the first area, this was crowded with twenty and thirty-ish patrons. I saw lots of b-caps and saggies and sneakers. There were skaters and punks and rappers, even a few jocks. Some of the leather people were also mixed in with this crowd, but not nearly as much so as in the other section of the club.

I followed Matt up to the center of the bar, to an area that was obviously designated for ordering drinks. "Have a Bud and a diet coke," he yelled to the bar tender, having to raise his voice over the music. The bartender nodded to him, immediately filling the order. Matt paid him and handed me my cola. "What you expected?" he asked me.

I shrugged. "Sort, of, Sir," I said. "It looks so much bigger from the inside than it did before, I mean from the outside."

"Yeah, I know. Let's go over there," he pointed to a table which was surrounding one of the pillars towards the side of the room. The table was raised, having no chairs around it. Apparently it was designed this way deliberately— a stand-up table of sorts. We placed our drinks down, and I inched my way as close to Matt as possible, though being careful not to be too clingy. I did not want to annoy him at all, but I was very nervous. This was my first time in any club at all, and the fact that this one happened to be a gay bar was even a little more unsettling to me.

As I looked around the room, I was suddenly amazed. All of these people are here who apparently have attractions that are similar to my own. Most of them are fairly normal looking people, not overly effeminate or campy, just regular guys. All this time I'd felt of myself as such a loner, being so different from the majority. In this place, though, it was fairly safe to assume that pretty much everyone was into the idea of getting it on with another guy. There were literally no women present in the club, at least that I'd observed so far. Of this fact I was not disappointed, I must admit. I smiled to myself then, suddenly realizing that Matt had chosen to be with me on this, his birthday weekend, rather than with Tracy. He also had collared me and displayed me publicly as his owned property. For the first time ever, I felt far less threatened by Tracy. Maybe it was true that Matt was actually choosing me over her. It was almost too good to believe.

As we stood there, not really saying much to each other, another patron approached us. He asked if is was okay to share some space with us, using the other side of the table. Matt was polite and said sure. The guy introduced himself to Matt and they chatted between themselves. Matt finally told him that I was his boy, and introduced me to him. His name was Rob, and he appeared to be in his late twenties. From what I gathered from the conversation between them, Rob also was a dominant top. He did not currently own a boy, but had ended a relationship a few months previously. I wondered to myself what that would be like. How would you ever actually end this kind of relationship? It is not like the sub would have the option of walking away. Perhaps it has to be the Dom who makes the ultimate decision to call it quits.

But then as I reflected upon this I realized that the sub partner really did have one single shred of control in the dynamic of this unique type of relationship. He did always have a choice as to whether or not he wished to continue being owned. Of course, depending upon exactly how controlling his Master was, he might have very little or no choice whatsoever about anything other than that. So long as he chose to be owned and to obey, he was stripped of all other freedoms. This was really a sort of gift, I thought. He gave up his free will to his owner willingly. He offered the only thing that he had to give: himself and his submission. So I supposed it was actually then possible for a sub to decide to opt out of a relationship. I could not ever imagine it happening with Matt though. No matter what transpired, I don't think I'd ever have the courage or desire to break things off with him. I'd rather be dead first.

"So do you come here very much?" Rob was saying to Matt.

"Nah, this is my first time here. Do you?"

"Yeah, few times a month maybe. You check out the back room yet?"

"No, what back room?" Matt laughed.

"Over there in the corner. See the hallway? Well, that leads into the back, behind the dance floor. There is a big room back there. All kinds of shit goes on in there. Guess you could say it's where all the 'action' is."

"Sounds like it could be interesting," Matt said, grinning at Rob.

"You wanna go back there together? I mean, the three of us." He glanced over at me.

Matt shook his head. "No offense. Not looking for a third tonight."

"Worth a try," Rob shrugged. "You two are a hot couple, ya know. Hottest I've seen in a long time. Be cool to get it on with ya."

"Thanks," said Matt. "Maybe some other time."

It was only a few seconds after that when Rob disappeared. Maybe Matt's rejection had embarrassed him or something, for I did not see him again for the rest of the night. I was glad Matt had turned down his offer, though. I did not want to get it on with anyone other than my owner, ever! I did have to admit, though, that I was curious about the back room. I wondered what Rob had meant when he said "all kinds of shit."

A few minutes later Matt informed me he was gonna go get himself another beer. I looked up at him imploringly, wanting to follow him to the bar. I didn't wanna be left alone at the table without my owner. Matt dismissed my fear casually. "I'll be right back, pup. Just wait here." I kept my eyes on him as he left me and worked his way through the crowd towards the bar. I stood there fidgeting as I sipped from my drink.

Suddenly someone brushed against me, "Hey Peter! I instantly turned and saw it was someone I recognized. Ryan Harris, a kid who was in my English Comp class, stood next to me, his hand pressing against my arm. "What are you doing here?"

"Um, hi Ryan," I said, a little shocked to see anyone I knew. "Small world, huh?" We both laughed. "I'm here with...um...my friend, Matt. You know him? He goes to our school."

"Matt Porter?" he asked.

"Yeah."

"Oh my god! You're friends with him? He's totally hot. I have him in one of my classes."

Instantly I felt the jealousy rising inside me. "Yeah," I said firmly, "I *know* him." I reached my hand up to my collar, rubbing my fingers across my tag. I flipped it over with my fingers as I leaned into Ryan. "See?"

He read the tag, seeing Matt's name and address embossed on the back. "Wow," he said, "I'd have never guessed. So how'd you get so lucky to end up with a jock stud like that to own you?"

"I don't know," I said, trying to think of a catchy comeback to his slightly concealed put-down of me. Finally I said, "Yeah, I know I'm lucky."

"Lucky about what?" It was Matt, now standing behind me.

I turned to look up at him. "About you, Sir," I smiled. "This is my friend Ryan. He's in one of each of our classes at school. Did you know that?"

"No, I didn't, pup, but I do know Ryan. I remember ya." He turned to Ryan, extending his hand. "How ya doin?"

"Pretty good, thanks," he said. Ryan was about a year or two older than Matt and me, and about four inches taller than myself. He was slender, but not as scrawny as me and sported a short, stylish haircut. He did not look at all faggy to me, and in class I had never once suspected that he was gay. In hindsight though, I suppose there were a few tell-tale signs. I'd always thought of him as being shy and a bit of a loner. In fact the few words he'd said to me so far this evening were the most he'd ever really spoken to me.

I stared at Ryan as he looked up at Matt. He had big bright blue eyes, which were opened wide with sincere interest and what I perceived to be yearning. I turned to Matt, who just stood there politely looking back down at Ryan, smiling slightly. Suddenly a wave of insane jealousy mixed with fear washed over me. Ryan was trying to hit on Matt! I wanted to push him away from us instantly. I was powerless though to respond in any such manner. Matt would have been extremely upset with me were I to be disrespectful or rude like that. So I just stood there saying nothing as I looked back at Ryan. I glared at him hatefully.

"You want a drink, Ryan?" asked Matt.

"Sure! Thank you sir. "Vodka tonic?"

"Okay." Matt reached in his pocket and pulled out a ten. He handed it to me. "Run and get Ryan a drink from the bar," he said. My mouth dropped open as I took the bill from him.

"Sir—" I began to protest but stopped myself. "Yes, Sir," I said.

When I got to the bar finally, I continued to glance back over at our table. Matt and Ryan were talking with one another, both smiling and laughing occasionally. I was steaming at this point but unable to do a single thing about the situation. I presented the money and my order to the bartender who looked at me puzzled. "You sure you're old enough to be in here boy?" he asked.

"Yes...um...sir...I showed my I.D. at the door. Do you want to see it?"

He shook his head. "Nah," he said, handing me my change. I handed him back two dollars quickly, as a tip.

"Thank you!" I said, and turned to make my way back through the crowd again.

When I got back to the table with Ryan's drink, he was talking animatedly with Matt about some new CD he'd just purchased. He accepted the drink graciously, thanking Matt again but not me. "I just turned 21 a couple months ago," he said.

"Tomorrow is Matt's birthday," I blurted out. He's twenty.

"Today actually," corrected Matt. "It's after midnight."

"Are you serious?" exclaimed Ryan. "Happy birthday! Let me ask you something. Since you're a Dom, do you *give* your birthday spankings instead of receiving them?" He laughed at his own joke.

"Something like that," Matt said while smiling. "Petey's birthday is this week too. Maybe I'll just save up the spankings for then and give him both of ours together."

"Can I come watch?" asked Ryan jokingly. "You two are such a cool looking couple. You even are dressed alike."

"Thanks," said Matt. I just continued to stand there, glaring at Ryan. What a jerk, complimenting us like that even though I could tell he'd do anything to steal Matt away from me if he thought he could. I could just tell how much he wanted him. Probably he was gonna go home tonight and jack himself off thinking about Matt. I just wanted to reach right over and punch him right there!

"Come to the bathroom with me, pup," said Matt. "I gotta take a piss." He reached over and slipped his index finger under my collar, pulling me next to him. "We'll be right back," he said to Ryan.

I followed Matt into the bathroom and he stepped into a stall. He motioned for me to step inside with him but left the stall door open. "Sit down!" he ordered. I was a little concerned by his directness for he almost sounded mad. "I'm not gonna tolerate this bullshit from you, pup!" he said as he looked down at me.

I began shaking immediately, looking up at him. I felt tears forming in my eyes. "I don't understand, Sir," I said.

"You understand perfectly. You're being a shit, and I'm embarrassed to even be seen with you. You don't treat people like that, not if you're gonna be *my* pup."

"Sir, I'm sorry! I don't know what you mean!" I was crying openly.

"The way you're treating Ryan, glaring at him, interrupting him—it's not very respectful."

"I didn't mean it, sir," I hung my head shamefully. "I'm so sorry. I didn't mean to..." My voice was choking up from the tears. "I didn't mean to ...um...embarrass...you, sir."

"Look at me!" he said. I looked up at his face, seeing him standing there towering over me. "How many pups do I have?" he asked. "Huh?"

"One, sir," I said, looking at him through my tear-filled eyes.

"That's right. I have one pup, and one only. That's you."

"I know Sir," I said.

"Then what are you worried about?"

"It's just— I don't know sir. It's just that...um...well, I'm sort of jealous. I think he ...he wants you."

"So?" said Matt. "So what? Doesn't matter what he wants. Doesn't matter what you want either. All that matters is what I want. Right?"

"Yes, Sir," I said.

"And I want my pup." He reached down and wiped the tears from under my eyes. "You're gonna apologize to him."

I nodded. "Yes sir. I'm sorry."

"Not to me. To him."

"Yes sir," I repeated.

"Now open up, I gotta piss." He undid his fly then and pulled out his cock. I wrapped my lips around it obediently as he drained himself.

* * *

When we returned to the table, Ryan was waiting there just as we'd left him. I'd sort of hoped he would have moved on, allowing me simply to forget about the situation and avoid the embarrassment of an apology. I looked up at Matt as we approached, as if to indicate that I was going to obey him, and immediately I opened my mouth to speak to Ryan.

"Ryan," I said, "I'm sorry about how I was treating you. I was not...um...I mean I was kind of rude to you. Disrespectful. I'm very sorry."

He looked at me and then glanced over to Matt. Ryan smiled most graciously at that point. "Don't sweat it, man.

Everything's cool. I didn't even notice." I extended my hand to him and we shook.

"Friends?" I said.

"Friends," he reiterated. "Wanna dance?"

I shook my head violently. Matt laughed as he looked over at me. "What's the matter pup? Don't you like to dance?"

"No sir," I said.

"Would you like to dance, Matt?" asked Ryan.

"Yeah, I would." Immediately I wanted to kick myself. Had I accepted Ryan's offer to dance, no matter how humiliating it would have been, at least it would've kept him away from Matt for awhile. Now, though, they were going out on the dance floor together.

"Sir," I said, "May I get another coke while you are dancing?"

"Sure," said Matt, tossing me some cash. "Get me a Bud, and are you ready for another, Ryan?"

"Um...just a diet coke please," he said. "Hey why don't you let me buy this round?" He reached into his pocket for some money.

"We got it," said Matt. "You can get the next. How come you are stopping after one drink?"

"Lightweight," he explained. "If I drink more than one I won't be able to drive home; unless, of course someone else takes me home with him."

"Could happen," said Matt, as they turned and walked away together towards the dance floor.

Fuck. This whole situation was totally ruining my night with Matt. Drew had told me that Matt was bringing me here to show me off as his pup, but instead what was happening was that some other fag was horning in on me. The worse thing about it, though, was that I could do nothing about it. If I said anything negative at all or acted upset in any way, I knew I'd be in big trouble. So while Ryan was out on the dance floor with my man, I was resigned to just accepting it and acting as if it did not even matter to me. Maybe I should just go order myself a drink too—then I'd be more relaxed. I quickly dismissed that idea, though, cuz Matt had specifically ordered me a pop. If he had wanted me to drink alcohol he'd have given me permission.

As I turned to head towards the bar with the money, I caught someone with my peripheral vision. He was staring at me. I turned casually to glance at him, noticing that it was a thirtyish looking man, a little shorter than Matt. He looked very masculine and was dressed casually in a pair of jeans and a knit pullover. Quickly I looked away from him and continued to head to the bar. When I returned with the three drinks, the man was still standing in the same position about twenty feet from our table. He nodded to me as I set the drinks down. I quickly looked down at the floor, making sure I did not make eye contact. I turned away from him completely then, but was so worried about his presence behind me that I felt as if he were staring holes through me. I turned around a couple minutes later, and sure enough, he was still there.

I craned my neck and stood on my tiptoes to see over the people who were between me and the dance floor. Where was Matt? I wished he'd get back here. I did not like that this guy was watching me. He was not creepy looking or anything; in fact, he was rather handsome, but I was owned property and did not want him thinking that I was available or anything. My heart was pounding faster when I suddenly realized the man was standing right beside me. "Hi," he said.

"Hi," I replied, not really knowing what to do. Should I dismiss him quickly and be rude to him, or would that be wrong? Matt had just lectured me on being respectful to other people, yet I sensed that this situation may be different. If he were planning to hit on me, surely Matt would want me to avoid him. "I'm sorry," I said quietly, "I don't want to be rude or anything...um...I'm with someone."

I reached up immediately and touched my collar, trying to draw his attention to the symbol of my owned status.

Just as I said that, Matt seemed to appear out of nowhere. He was standing beside me. "Hi," he said, extending his hand. "Matt. This is our friend Ryan."

"Hi guys," said the stranger, "I'm Dave."

I sidled myself up very closely to Matt, pressing my body against his. He put his hand protectively on my shoulder. "I see you met my pup," he said.

"Well not officially," Dave said. "I was just about to introduce myself when he told me...well...he told me—"

"I heard what he told you," said Matt curtly, "and it's true. He is with someone—me."

"Oh okay, no problem. Not tryin to start anything or horn in on anyone. Just being friendly here."

"Oh yeah? Do you know what a collar symbolizes? You ought to, or else you shouldn't be in a club like this."

"Look man," said Dave, raising his hands in the air, "Like I said, I was just being friendly. Is that a crime?"

"Touch what's mine, and I'll show you what a crime is," said Matt, moving me to the side of him so he could step forward. I had not really felt this kind of anger coming from Matt since the first day that he had saved me from Devin and Kyle. He had not even seemed mad like this when he spanked me, or when he'd just reprimanded me in the bathroom. I did not say a word, but inched my way behind Matt silently.

Matt had now raised his finger and was pointing it at Dave. "I've watched you all night staring at my pup, and I'm warnin ya, get the fuck away from us! He's not available! You got it?"

"Yeah," said Dave defensively, "I got it. Christ, you can't even have a friendly conversation around here..." Matt's intense glare must have silenced him, for he turned and walked away without finishing his sentence. Matt then picked up his Budweiser and took a big swig.

"Good boy!" he said, turning to me. "What you said to him was exactly right. I'm proud of ya!"

I looked up at him, beaming. "Thank you sir," and I picked up my diet coke and drank in unison with my owner.

"Sir," I said, "Can I ask a question?"

"Go ahead...shoot," he said.

"Um...well, if you knew that guy was watching me and that he was hitting on me, why'd you shake his hand?"

Matt looked down at me soberly. "Two reasons, pup," he said, "and that's a good question, by the way. One, is because it's like I said, you have to treat people respectfully. I was giving him the benefit of the doubt until I heard what he said. Then when he lied to me and told me what I knew was not true, I got pissed. Two, I wanted to get between him and my pup, so I stepped between you to shake his hand."

"You trusted me, Sir, to leave me here next to him even when you knew he was watching me. Thank you."

"We trust each other, right pup?" he said, glancing quickly to Ryan and then back to me.

Suddenly I got the gist of what he was alluding to, and I smiled. "Yes, Sir. We do."

* * *

By the time Matt had finished his third beer, Ryan had disappeared to the dance floor. He had spotted someone who interested him, and they seemed to connect somewhat. Matt leaned in to me then and spoke into my ear. "Go to the back room. Remember where it is?" I nodded. "Wait for me there just inside the door. Don't look at or talk to anyone til I get there. Got it?"

"Yes, Sir," I said, and immediately complied with his instruction. His orders to not look at anyone were not difficult at all to obey, for it was extremely dark when I stepped inside the room. It was a very spacious room, totally open yet extremely dark. It did not appear to have any lights

at all, in fact, other than the reflection of the bathroom lights
that shone from the hallway. I could also see that some of
the people in the room were smoking, and the red glare of
their cigarette tips glowed brightly as they inhaled. I stepped
around the corner, standing quietly against the wall and
looked down at the ground. I could hear the sounds of action
around me, sucking and licking, the distinct sound of anal
penetration. Some of the guys were moaning or verbalizing
commands to one another. As I stood there I sucked in my
breath, taking in the scent of the sweat and the sex all
around me. My eyes were beginning to refocus, growing
accustomed to the dimness of the room, when someone
stepped up beside me. I was startled, moving quickly away,
when I realized suddenly that it was Matt.

"On your knees," he said, leaning his back against the
wall. I dropped down quickly as ordered, positioning myself
between his legs. "Suck!" he said. He already had his dick
out and was holding it in his hand. I moved my head
towards his crotch as he reached down, grabbing a hold of
me. He pushed my head forcefully onto his hard shaft, and I
slid my mouth around it obediently.

He moaned as he buried himself in me. He did not grip
my head real tightly at first, but instead allowed me to bob
on him for awhile. He still was holding onto me, but was not
yet taking control. I continued to service him ceaselessly,
sliding up and down, deepthroating him with each thrust. I
had placed my hands against his thighs, doing this
deliberately so he'd know where they were at all times. I
suspected that his own vision had adjusted to the light by
this time and was thankful he could look down and see me
serving him.

Finally he began to grip my head tighter. He began taking
control, pumping me on him. I relaxed myself, giving myself
completely over to his control. He rammed violently into my
throat, nearly gagging me. Repeatedly he thrust into me in
this manner, appearing to give no thought whatsoever to

whether or not I could take it. He went on like this for a good ten minutes, as the saliva and precum were dripping out of my mouth and down my chin like a faucet. Finally he tightened his grip fiercely and buried himself balls deep into me. Then he pumped! I felt it as all the times before, the cum rising up his shaft against my tongue, and I sucked with intensity. He drained himself totally into me as I knelt there serving him. I sucked out every single drop before he loosened his grip. As he pulled me off of him I looked up into his eyes. He was staring over towards the door. I moved my gaze to follow his and saw our new friend Ryan standing in the doorway . He stood there watching us.

As I knelt there, our eyes met one another, and I smiled up at him. Quickly he turned and exited the back room.

21

I was not afforded the luxury of sleeping in Sunday morning. Around 7am, Matt woke me. He had apparently awakened himself, and was sporting a rock hard erection. Saying nothing to me, he simply grabbed my head and shoved me down on himself. I was at first confused, not even awake, but once his cock impaled my throat I started to become very alert. The entire blowjob did not take more than five minutes, and when he was done draining his load into me he rolled back over and fell asleep again.

I, on the other hand, was then wide awake and hard as a rock. I knew better than to jack myself off, so I quietly slipped out of bed and headed for the kitchen. I began to rifle through the refrigerator again, digging out some items I could use to prepare breakfast. I knew Matt had specifically told me he was not much of a breakfast eater, but we had gotten breakfast together just the day before, when we were on our way to the mall and the water park. Plus, today was his birthday, and I wanted to start the day for him in a really special way by serving him breakfast in bed. I would get most of the stuff together and prepared to cook, and then when it got closer to ten o'clock, I'd start actually assembling the meal. This would allow him to sleep in. If he was not agreeable with the plan, I'd just shelve it and let him sleep longer. If I got lucky, he'd start to stir around the time I was done cooking.

There was a small television set in the kitchen which I turned on at a low volume. I watched the Sunday morning news while I diced vegetables for the omelet. Finding the news to be rather boring and dry, I picked up the remote and flipped through the stations, stopping on MTV. An episode of The Real World was replaying. I kept thinking how lame the show was—utterly stupid— while at the same time getting sucked into the reality-based drama. How could people expose themselves like that on a nationally televised program, acting childish and immature, fighting with one another as if they were in grade school? I put the knife down and rested my elbows on the counter, raising my palms up to cup and hold my chin in place as I watched the real-life soap opera.

Suddenly at the conclusion of the episode, I realized I'd wasted almost an hour of my time and I grabbed the remote quickly, flipping off the TV completely. I then finished preparing the omelet ingredients and got into the cupboard to look for something to make muffins. This also would be a good way to possibly wake Matt up. If he smelled me baking something, it may rouse him from his slumber, and then hopefully the timing would work out perfectly. Surprisingly there was a blueberry muffin mix in the cupboard, and I did not even have to prepare them from scratch. After preheating the oven and stirring the muffin batter, I poured the mixture into cupcake tins and put them in the oven. I then got out the meat from the refrigerator. I'd make him both Canadian bacon and sausage, so that he could choose—

or have both. I found some fresh fruit to dice and got that ready while the meat was frying. Finally, it was within a half hour of my target time, and I started to cook his omelet.

The muffins came out of the oven right about the same time the meat was done frying. I found a lap tray in the living room which I placed on the kitchen counter and began arranging the contents of the meal on it carefully. Matt's omelet turned out perfectly. I arranged it on the tray, garnishing it with an orange slice and parsley sprig and then poured him a large glass of orange juice. Damn it! I should have made fresh squeezed. I shrugged. I'd have had to tear the kitchen apart to try to find an orange juice strainer.

Once the meal was completely finished, I tiptoed to the bedroom door. I peeked in and saw that Matt was still sleeping soundly. What should I do? If I wake him up before he's ready, he might get upset with me, but if I don't do it, then his breakfast will be cold. What if he is pissed and says he told me before he did not like breakfast? What if I don't wake him and he gets perturbed that I wasted all that food? I paced back and forth a bit, hating myself for not having waited. Why was it that I always seemed to have good intentions but then failed in the delivery? Just as I turned to walk out of the bedroom and head back for the kitchen, I stumbled over something on the floor. It was Matt's pair of new shoes. My body lunged forward involuntarily as I reflexively extended my arms. I crashed right into the bedroom door, forcing it to slam loudly. Shit!

Matt was now awake. "What the hell was that?" he moaned.

"Nothing Sir! I'm sorry, I just tripped. I'm so sorry...I didn't mean to wake you up. I'm really, really sorry."

"Whatever!" he said groggily, "Why you up already anyways?" He was not even looking over at me, for he'd rested his head back down on the pillow, closing his eyes.

"Happy birthday, Sir," I said meekly.

"Thanks," he moaned, sounding very much uninterested.

"Um...sir?"

He did not answer right away, and I wondered if I should just leave the room and let him get more sleep.

"Yeah?" he said finally.

"I made you breakfast. If you want it, I mean. For your birthday."

He opened his eyes slowly, raising his head slightly off the pillow as he looked over to me. He smiled. "Come here," he said. I scampered over to the bed quickly and crawled up beside him, laying my head next to his on the pillow. "Thank you," he said and then kissed me.

"Want me to bring it to you, Sir?" I asked. "I made it for you to have in bed. Breakfast in bed, ya know."

"Sure," he said, still very drowsily. He rolled over onto his back and reached up to rub his eyes.

"Okay! I'll go get it." I jumped up out of bed and headed back to the kitchen, carefully avoiding his shoes on the floor this time. I was so glad he wasn't upset. Maybe it worked out after all.

When I returned to the bedroom with Matt's tray of food, he was sitting up in bed. Carefully I walked over to him, watching the tray to make sure I was holding it steadily. He reached out and took it from me when I got within his reach, setting it down over his lap on the bed. The tray had legs on each side that fit easily around either side of his legs. "I love you so much, Sir," I said, "Happy birthday."

"Come sit next to me while I eat, pup," he said, and I crawled up beside him on the bed. I lay my head down on the pillow, watching him silently. "You have fun last night?"

"Yes sir. I'm sorry I was bad, though."

"You weren't bad, silly. You just got a little jealous, that's all. Just gotta learn to control your jealousy. You know, it's not bad to feel things, pup. Usually you can't help what you feel; that's just who you are, but you have to remember that no matter what you're feeling inside, you have to be polite and respectful of other people."

"Yes, Sir," I said, "but it doesn't seem like you were too polite to that Dave guy."

"I was polite to him. I was politer than he deserved, actually. He knew what he was doing, and it wasn't until he lied to me and told me he wasn't really doing it, that I got pissed."

"I thought you were gonna punch him, Sir."

"Told you that you'd know for sure when I was mad, didn't I?"

"Sir, I have something I want to give you. Well, actually it's more than one thing."

"Oh? What is it pup?"

"Your birthday presents, Sir."

"Already gave me a present; I don't need any more." He grinned at me as he shoved a piece of bacon in his mouth.

"Please, Sir, I couldn't just only get you one gift! One isn't enough."

"Why not?" he asked, "It's the thought that counts, right?"

"Yeah, but I had lots of thoughts of you, not just one."

He laughed then, reaching over to tickle my side affectionately. "Maybe you didn't get enough tickling yesterday."

"Yes I did!" I protested, pulling away from him and jumping off the bed quickly. I hurried over to my duffle bag which was placed neatly in the corner. "Okay, I hope you like them. I really, really hope you do, sir." Kneeling down, I dug out the packages carefully from the bag, placing each of the four next to me on the floor, one at a time.

"Geesh, how many you got in there, pup?"

"Just four," I said. "Plus the lighter, which I gave you already." I scooped up the gift-wrapped packages and stood back up, turning to face him. Then I walked back over to the bed and carefully placed them next to him. "Here," I said, picking up the box containing the humidor and cigars. "Or do you want to wait until you're done eating?"

"Nah, now's fine," he said, licking off a finger before grabbing the box from me. "Want me to guess what's inside?" he toyed with me. "Maybe it's a new chastity device for my pup, or no, probably a paddle."

I giggled. "No, but if you want, I will buy those things sir."

"Messin with ya, pup," he said. Then he tore of the end of the wrapping paper carelessly and slid the box out, discarding the paper on the bedside floor beside him. "Cigars!" he exclaimed, "Cool, and these are nice ones. You fly to Cuba to get these?"

"Yeah, yesterday on my lunch break," I laughed. "They were supposed to go with the lighter, sir. I hope its not too much of a old fogy gift."

"Nah, you know I like a cigar once in awhile. Gonna share these with Alex probably. Maybe while you kiss my feet." He laughed again.

"I will!" I insisted. He smiled at me and picked up the next gift.

"Okay, what's this? Bet it's the keys to a new Mercedes. Am I right?"

"No sir," I grinned at him, "but close. Open it."

He tore off the packaging as carelessly as he'd done with the first to reveal the key chain. "Key to my heart" he read the inscription. "That's very sweet pup, come here." I walked over beside him, this time on the other side of the bed. He leaned over to kiss me. "Very true too."

I remained beside him when he picked up the third gift. He unwrapped it unceremoniously this time, offering no commentary. The package contained the boxers and b-cap wrapped together. "Silk boxers, huh? You think I'm deserving of silk?"

"More than that — much, much more than that," I said sincerely.

He put the cap on his head and left it there as he moved on to the final package. He held it to his ear as he shook it. "Can't hear anything," he said, "Nothing's ticking in there so

I guess it's safe to open." He then removed the wrapping and revealed the puppy mouse pad. "You just want me to be thinking of my pup 24/7, don't ya?" he asked. "Don't need reminders for that though."

"Really?" I asked. "Do you really think about me a lot?"

"Course I do—all the time. Think about what you might be doing, wonder if you happen to be thinking of me. I wonder if you're safe, if you're being good. Sometimes wonder if you are getting hard thinking about me."

"I can't believe—" I was instantly choked up. "I can't believe you said that, sir." My eyes filled with tears as he moved the tray off his lap and placed it on the other side of him on the bed. He slid his legs off the bed, sitting there beside me and pulled me directly in front of him so I stood facing him, standing between his legs. "I always worry so much. I always think—"

"What do you have to worry about pup?" he said gently, holding each of my arms in his hands.

"You are so much better ... than...oh sir" I was crying openly. "You are so much better than me. I don't deserve you, but you say you think about me and wonder if I'm safe."

"So why you cryin?" he asked. "That's a good thing, isn't it?"

I nodded. "Yes, Sir, I guess I am just a baby. I cry about everything."

"Nah, you're just you. Very emotional. It's cool." He pulled me close to him, turning me to sit on his knee. I leaned into him as he wrapped his arm around my shoulder. "Thank you for the presents, pup. I like every single one of them and the breakfast too. You're gonna have to finish what I didn't eat, though."

I pulled away from him slightly. "There's one more thing!" I said excitedly, wiping the tears from my cheeks quickly. "I'll be right back." I ran out of the bedroom and back to the kitchen. When I returned, I carried in my hands a big kitchen plate with a large muffin in the center. I did not

have any birthday candles but found a large, slender
emergency candle in one of the drawers of the utility room.
It was placed proudly in the center of the muffin and was lit.
I started singing "Happy Birthday" to him as he lay there on
the bed laughing.

* * *

We were in the car on the way back into the city, when
Matt looked over to me and said, "Pup, gonna tell you
something, and you're not gonna get upset by it. Okay?"

"Sure," I said, a little hesitantly, for he'd never provided
any such precursor to anything he'd previously told me.
Maybe it was bad news. "I won't be upset, Sir. I promise."

"Okay...I'm goin out tonight for my birthday. Am goin
with someone you don't particularly like."

"Tracy?" I asked.

"Yup."

"So how come you told me Sir? You know that you don't
have to. You can decide to go out with anyone you want."

"Decided to tell you cuz I wanted to. We had a great
weekend, you and me. Best birthday I've ever had in my life.
Yesterday I collared you as my pup, and I want you to know
nothing is gonna change that. Nothing. You do realize that,
right?"

"Yes, Sir. I'll miss you tonight though."

"Well, I'll tell you what. Alex is meeting up with us later
tonight, so I'm pretty sure Drew is gonna be home alone.
Why don't you call him?"

"Okay! That will be cool. Thanks Sir." He reached over
and grabbed my hand with his own, squeezing it. "You chose
to be with me the whole weekend. She just gets you for
dinner," I stated.

"Yup, cuz she's just my bitch, but you're my pup." I
laughed when he said it.

"You make it sound like a pup is better than a bitch," I said.

"Pup means more to me than a bitch does," he clarified. "Not better, just different."

"I could also just spend the evening with Kathie. She has been nagging me about never seeing me anymore."

"That's a good idea. Besides, you just spent the day with Drew yesterday. Listen, I'm gonna stop by my house before I take you home. Got something I wanna give ya."

"Okay. What is it?"

"You'll see," he said, offering no further information. As I sat there next to him quietly I reflected upon our weekend together. It seemed like an eternity had passed since yesterday morning, that so much of significance had occurred. I had learned to serve him better, was collared by him officially, and was taken out to be publicly seen as his property. The feelings that then stirred within me were so powerfully warm and fulfilling, a contentment unlike any I'd ever felt. For the first time ever I did not feel threatened by Tracy or other guys or literally anything. I felt so secure in the commitment that Matt and I had for one another. His giving me the collar was as poignant to me as a wedding ring would have been.

As for Matt spending the evening of his birthday with someone other than me, that was irrelevant. We'd spent the weekend together. We'd slept together, made love, partaken of one another in the absolutely most intimate ways possible. Although I did not fully understand Matt's desire to continue seeing Tracy, it felt to me as if she really did not mean that much to him. He never would have gone away to his cabin with me for two days if it were she he'd wanted to be with. His actions spoke far more clearly to me than any proclamations he could have made.

When he finally arrived at his driveway and told me to wait in the car, I soon was to discover he was about to perform another one of these telling "actions." I sat there patiently, resting my head against the window pane, when I finally saw him emerge from the front door, bounding down the steps casually. He was carrying a jacket— his high school letter jacket, actually. He opened the driver's side door and got back in the car, tossing the jacket onto my lap.

"Pup," he said, "I want you to wear this. I mean, when it's not eighty degrees," he laughed. "I want you to have it."

"But sir, it's your letter jacket," I protested, "I can't take this from you."

"You can't take anything from me pup. I'm giving it. I want my pup to be in my number. I want people to see you wearing it."

"Thank you sir," I said, feeling myself once again being overwhelmed with emotion. "Won't it be sorta big on me though?"

"Yeah, it'll be cute," he said. "Just roll up the sleeves."

I laughed at him then, suddenly visualizing myself in the oversized jacket. "Maybe we could get a smaller one some day, Sir. Then I could give this back to you, and we'd match."

"Yeah, that'd be cool. But you keep that one for now. I'd better get you home; it's already after six and I've gotta pick up Tracy at seven. There's one more thing though. Take off your collar and put back on this necklace. He reached into his pocket and pulled out the original beaded necklace that he'd given me. Wear the necklace in place of the collar when we are not together. I will always tell you when you need to change into your collar, or I'll change it for you."

"Should I give you the collar back then, Sir?" I asked as I reached up to the back of my neck to unfasten it.

"No, I want you to keep it with you. Put it beside your bed and look at it every night before you go to sleep, okay?"

"Yes, Sir, of course I will."

"Good boy. You've been such a good boy for me this weekend. I'm gonna lift your restrictions completely for a couple of days. You can cum as often as you want between now and Wednesday, but there is only one stipulation."

"Okay, Sir. What is it?"

"You only are allowed to cum if you are thinking of your Owner."

I laughed out loud, "Sir, that requirement is not even necessary. Who else would I think of?"

"Don't know, but there's nothing wrong with having fantasies. I just don't want you to cum to any of them other than the ones about me. Got it?"

"Yes Sir. Thank you."

"And you can see Drew whenever you want for the next couple days too, until I see you on Wednesday. Probably won't hear from me before then unless I call you on your cell. Keep it with you all times."

"Yes Sir."

He started the car and backed out of the driveway. Stopping in the road then, he leaned over and kissed me before putting the car in gear. "I love you Sir," I said.

"Love you too pup." Then he drove me home without saying another word. I bounded up the steps of my apartment building, looking back at his car as he sped off. Please don't let this ever end, I thought. It's just way too good to be true.

22

I entered the apartment carrying one of my duffle bags with the letter jacket draped over it. I had stuffed my collar inside the jacket, and I had slung the strap of the other bag around my shoulder. I stepped inside and the bag which was dangling from my shoulder slid down as I dropped the other bag on the floor. "Hi," I said to Kathie as I looked up to see her standing in front of me.

"Hey, how was your weekend?"

I smiled up at her. "It was so awesome, Kath. It was...unbelievable."

"Cool. You just missed Carter. He left about five minutes ago."

"How's it goin? I mean with you and him." I asked.

"Wonderful," she grinned. "He's amazing. Who's jacket is that?" she asked, inquiring about Matt's letter jacket.

"Oh...um...it's mine...well sorta. It's Matt's actually."

"If it belongs to Matt, then how is it 'sorta' yours?" she asked lightheartedly.

"Well he loaned it to me."

"He loaned it to you?" she asked incredulously. "Petey, it's eighty degrees outside. Why would you need to borrow a jacket?"

"Well, um, it was chilly last night."

"So? Then why do you still have it now?" She stepped over to the jacket and leaned down to pick it up by the collar. "It's an expensive jacket, too. These things cost like three hundred bucks. Are you sure he knows you have it?"

I burst out laughing. "Kathie, are you suggesting that I stole it from him? I'd cut my arm off before I stole a dime from Matt Porter." Just as I said that, my collar fell to the ground in front of us. Kathie was holding the jacket out in front of her and looked down to see the collar. Before I could lunge for it, she'd bent over to scoop it up.

"A dog collar? Is this for his dog? I thought it was just a puppy." She held it in front of her, twisting the metal tag in her fingers to read the inscription. "This has your name on it!"

"Matt named his puppy after me, remember?" I interjected, quickly snatching the collar away from her. "He must have left the collar in his jacket by mistake."

"Petey, what is going on? I know that collar does not belong to a little puppy. That thing is big enough for a frickin German Shepherd."

"I don't know, Kathie, maybe you should ask Matt about it then. Maybe he bought it for Petey to save for when he got bigger. I don't know!"

She cocked her head as she looked at me, holding the jacket out in front of her. "Petey, what is going on? Why do you have Matt's letter jacket?"

I sighed angrily, reaching out to take the jacket from her. She pulled it back, continuing to clutch it possessively. "Look," I said, "if you must know, Matt didn't want the jacket any more. He said it was from when he was in high school and it was in the past. He's moved on. He was gonna just pitch it, and so I asked him if I could have it, so he gave it to me."

She looked at me doubtfully. "Petey, stop lying to me. You know I can tell when you're lying. I've always been able to."

"Kathie!" I was getting angry now, "what is this— twenty questions? Why do you care about a stupid letter jacket? Just give it back to me!"

"Jocks don't just give away their high school letter jackets, Petey. It would be like me saying I was gonna just up and toss out my prom dress. I wasn't born yesterday." Finally she held the jacket out for me and I snatched it from her immediately.

"Thank you!" I said sarcastically. "And for your information, this jock *did* just give his jacket away. He gave it to me!" I turned from her as I snatched up one of the bags heading down the hallway to my bedroom. She picked up the other bag and immediately followed me, refusing to be dismissed.

"Petey, please talk to me about this."

I spun around angrily to face her once again. "Talk about what? There's nothing to talk about!" I then turned from her and dashed into my bedroom. She stepped in behind me, standing right in the doorway.

"I've tried to talk to you about this before. Please don't shut me out! I'm your sister, and I love you."

393

"Kathie, if you really loved me, you'd stop nagging me all the time and let me live my own life. It's not like I'm twelve any more. I'm an adult!"

She stared at me intently, making me a bit nervous actually. "Listen to me, Petey. I'm gonna say this again. I don't care what you do, I honestly don't. Please just don't shut me out of your life. I love you no matter what. Please tell me what is going on."

"Tell you what?" I snapped back at her, "There is nothing to tell."

She looked me right in the eyes, "Petey, are you gay?"

Instantly the intensity of my emotion swelled within me, and I felt myself again on the verge of tears. I cursed myself for it, wanting to be strong for once and not a big crybaby. I looked back at her, the tears beginning to obscure my vision. It was as if our stares were locked together, holding us there is stasis. I nodded.

"Petey, it's okay." She stepped towards me, her own eyes now filling with tears. "It's okay, you can say it. I've known a long time. It doesn't matter."

"I'm gay. It's true," I finally acknowledged. "And I love him."

"Oh honey," she held her arms out, and as I dropped the bag I was carrying, allowing the jacket to fall on top of it, I moved towards her embrace. I began crying openly as she held me. "Petey, why would you ever in a million years think you had to hide something like this from me? There is no one on earth that knows you better than me. No one."

I did not correct on this assumption. "I know... It's just hard sometimes," I said, burying my face into her shoulder. "It's scary, that's all. I never wanted to disappoint you."

"No sweety, I would never be disappointed in you for being who you are."

We held each other for a few moments as waves of relief and happiness swept over me. Confessing to my sister finally, as I had just now done, was like removing a big burden from my shoulders. For so long I'd wanted to confide in her, to tell her the things I really was feeling. So many times I wanted to just be honest, to stop changing pronouns, to stop making ridiculous pretenses. I'd just wanted to be me.

"I'm worried, though, Petey," she confessed, "not about you being gay. I'm worried about your friendship with Matt."

"It's not just a friendship," I said. "It is more than that."

"Petey, Matt has a girlfriend. His girlfriend is my best friend, remember? I'm not sure what his motivation is for this relationship that you have, but I'm telling you, he's not gay. Believe me, honey, I know it for a fact. I have...well...inside information."

"From Tracy," I said somewhat defensively. "Well, Matt and I have talked about Tracy. It's not like you think. He is not her boyfriend. He doesn't even love her."

Kathie got the most pitying look on her face then as she pushed me back away from her to look into my face. "Honey, Tracy thinks Matt does love her. He's told her that he does."

I pulled myself away from her quickly. "That's a lie!" I snapped. "He does *not* love her. I've even asked him myself, and he's told me. She just thinks he does."

Kathie sighed quietly, "Even if that were entirely true... even if he really never did tell her that he loves her, don't you think it's wrong that he would allow her to go on believing that he does?"

"How can you expect Matt to be responsible for what Tracy thinks? Just because she gets that in her head, it doesn't mean it's true. And it doesn't mean it's up to him to go around telling her how to think."

"Petey, do you know where Matt is right now?"

"Yes!" I snapped. "He's going out to dinner...for his birthday."

"With Tracy," Kathie added. "And then they are going up to Matt's parents' cabin for three days together. They won't be back until Wednesday morning. He's not even going to any of his classes for the first part of the week. They have had this week planned for over a month."

"You're lying!" I screamed. "That's fucking bullshit!"

"Honey, I'm not lying...Listen to me—"

"Get out of my room! Leave me alone!" At this point I was nearly hysterical, screaming at nearly the top of my lungs. "Go on!" It could not be true what she was saying. There is no way, after what Matt had just said to me moments before in the car, that he could be taking that girl — that bitch, as he called her — to *our* special place. There was no way he would spend three full days with her when he'd told me it would just be dinner. Plus he'd said he was meeting up with Alex later. I knew Kathie was mistaken.

"Calm down!" she said.

"Please leave me alone," I cried. "Please!"

She quietly stepped back. "Okay...Just calm down. Listen, I'm gonna leave you alone. I'm sorry. I—oh, Petey, please. I just don't want you to trust this guy so much. He is only using you..." She stopped her lecturing finally, perhaps realizing that the more she said, the worse she was hurting me. "I'll come back and check on you later." I did not respond to her, having turned away to stare out the bedroom window. When I finally heard the door close behind me, I ran to the bed and buried my face in the pillow and cried bitterly.

Finally I pulled myself up. I thought of something. He'd told me I could call Drew. I would do that, and he'd confirm that this was all a distortion. He'd tell me that Matt and Alex had plans together tonight, and it would prove Kathie entirely wrong. I pulled my cell phone from my duffle bag and dialed Drew's number. On the third ring he answered.

"Hello?"

"Drew? It's Peter."

"Something wrong Petey? Are you all right?"

"Where is Alex," I blurted out. "Is he with Matt tonight?"

"Yeah, sure. Didn't he tell you? They went away together for a couple of days. Matt invited Alex up to his cabin."

"Just the two of them?" I asked.

"Honey...don't go there. It doesn't matter—"

"Just the two of them?!" I demanded.

He sighed into the phone. "No. With their girlfriends."

I clicked off the phone without another word, my world suddenly crashing down around me.

Sitting on the edge of my bed, I stared straight ahead, focusing upon nothing and showing no emotion. Oddly I felt incredibly numb. I looked into my lap, seeing the phone which I'd just used to call Drew, the same phone which had been a gift to me from Matt, so that we could always stay in touch. Calmly I pressed the one button which I'd only once before used, turning the phone off completely. I looked over at my desk, and on the back of my chair Matt's letter jacket was draped. Only about an hour previously, he had given it to me, and I had accepted it, thinking it was a genuine token of his love and commitment for me. But now it seemed so phony to me. I felt so utterly betrayed and deceived.

He had lied to me. Matt had told me that he loved me. He'd stated that he thought of me constantly. He assured me that I meant so much more to him than did Tracy. He had allowed me to believe that this weekend had been as special for him as it had been for me, all the while knowing that these two days were merely a precursor to the rest of his vacation which he'd spend with his girlfriend.

I wondered at this point what it was that he told Tracy. Did he tell her that he loved her as Kathie had indicated to me? Did he quickly and dismissively brush aside the concerns that she expressed about their relationship, placating her with hollow assurances that she was the one who was really important to him? Did he take her out in public and display her as a trophy on his side the way he'd done with me on Saturday night?

I also thought about the relationship between Alex and Drew. How had they held onto each other for so long? How could Drew be strong enough (or weak enough, perhaps) to endure the humiliation and the feelings of betrayal and abandonment that he surely must experience every time Alex hooked up with some chick?

Obviously I'd misinterpreted the motivation behind Matt's actions. When he had collared me and then given me his jacket, I'd ascribed so much significance to these gestures. I'd assumed they were symbols of his commitment to me, and had mistakenly made the mental leap from commitment to exclusivity. Yet in all honesty, I had no justification in my hope for a monogamous commitment from Matt. Certainly I should have known when he told me that he was going to have dinner with Tracy that he was not reserving himself strictly for me.

How could I have allowed myself to believe the things that I'd believed? How could I have ever thought in a million years that a popular, outgoing, successful jock like Matt Porter could actually love me? Kathie's admonitions to me, her warnings that Matt was just using me, echoed in my head. She was so very correct in her assessment, although unlike her, I did not fault Matt for this reality. I faulted myself. Of course Matt would use me for his own pleasure and amusement. What else could I realistically expect? People like him did not fall in love with people like me. That would be impossible. How could I have ever believed otherwise?

Flashes of memory overtook my thoughts like projections on a movie screen. I saw how I'd met Matt at the bus stop that previous November, remembering how he'd scooped me up in his arms protectively and carried me to safety after I'd been attacked. I saw him staring down at me as I knelt in front of him for the first time on the sidewalk when he was walking his new puppy. Images of him driving in his car, relaxing in front of the television, sliding shirtless down a water ride at the park. I saw him holding me in the shower, leaning over to kiss me, cradling me in his arms after we'd just finished making love. I saw him laughing, affectionately tickling me, feeding me the scraps from his plate as I knelt beside him.

The memories were like a flood washing over me, carrying with them an intensity of emotion unlike any I'd ever felt. I could not believe this was all a lie. How could all of these things have happened between us— how could he have devoted the time to me that he had, the money, the gifts— only to be using me? I began to tremble as I thought on these things, still shedding no tears. The sadness and disappointment that I felt were beyond tears. Instead the effect was almost paralyzing to me. It felt as if blackness was suddenly surrounding me. There was no time, no purpose, no hope. Everything I'd pinned my hopes upon had been instantly snatched away from me, and I was left alone with only memories and utter emptiness.

I dropped the phone to the floor and lay back on the bed, rolling to my side to curl into my fetal-like sleeping position. I imagined what he was doing now. He and Alex surely were toasting their drinks as they dined with their girlfriends, having a good laugh together. They were undoubtedly not concerned about the fags they'd left behind, experiencing and basking in the luxury of the perks that they were entitled to by their mere existence. It was like a birthright to them. They'd never felt the agony of rejection, the fear of abandonment, the powerful and all-consuming desire to simply be loved. The only thing that mattered to them was their own pleasure, and how could I even question this? How could I even deny them this entitlement, for they were truly so superior.

I drifted into a state of mental grayness, thinking only abstract thoughts, suppressing all emotion. I did not fall asleep but was at a point where any observer would have concluded that I was in fact sleeping. This was a place I had come to often after the death of my parents. It was a safe place, free of pain and anxiety. It was a place of nothingness, seclusion, solitude. In this place I wished away my existence, for by so doing I also was wiping away all pain. How could you feel anything when you did not really exist? The thoughts of Matt seemed to morph into broader depressive images. I relived the torturous moments of my mother's passing, the feeling of abandonment I had experienced at her funeral, the surreal dreamlike state I'd wallowed in for days after the burial.

I thought of J.K. Rowling's character, Harry Potter. Had I not been so literally numb, I would have laughed aloud. Harry was a kindred spirit of mine, having suffered many of the same losses. The part I found amusing, though, was that he discovered something wonderful about himself. Unlike me, Harry was genuinely unique. He was special— gifted, heroic, brave, capable. He was everything I'd always dreamt of being myself. Facing tragic losses, insurmountable odds, and stark criticism from his peers and family, he rose to face the challenges of life. He defeated powerful enemies and took upon himself tremendous responsibility. Harry would never need a Matt as did I. Harry was his own Matt.

It felt as if I'd lost literally everything that was meaningful to myself. I'd lost my parents first, clinging desperately at that time to my sister. Now I was losing her, constantly bickering with her, disappointing her by merely being who I was. I had fallen so deeply in love with Matt then, only to discover the entire relationship to be a farce. The new friendship I'd forged with Drew was surely not secure either. If ever I were to completely walk away from Matt, I'd also be giving up Drew, for he certainly wouldn't be allowed to see me any more, not with Alex and Matt being such good friends.

I won't feel this. I won't allow myself to feel this pain. I won't cry, for if I begin crying I may never stop. I stared straight ahead as the darkness of the evening began to surround me. I did not bother to crawl under the covers or to turn on a light or to even get undressed. I just lay there curled up, willing myself into non-existence. I was so far removed from physical reality that I hardly could hear the rapping at my door. As the pounding and shouting grew louder I reeled myself back to the present, suddenly identifying the voice on the other side of the door, demanding entry. It was Drew.

When he finally pushed the door open, tiring perhaps of waiting for my answer, he stepped into the darkness very quietly. "Hey bud," he said tentatively, "I'm gonna turn on a light." Allowing the light from the hallway to illuminate the room enough for him to see, he walked over to my desk and flipped on the lamp. He then walked back and closed the door. "Petey?" he said, turning to me.

I did not move from my position when he spoke my name, but something about the gentleness of his voice tugged at my emotions. Finally I began to weep, very silently, allowing the tears to simply slide down my cheeks and onto my pillow. He stepped over to me, easing himself down on the bed beside me. "Petey," he repeated, "I'm so sorry I hurt you."

Very slightly I shook my head then, still not looking at him. "No," I whispered, "You didn't hurt me."

"Okay," he acknowledged, "You're right, I did not hurt you. I'm sorry that I was the one to tell you something that hurt you," he corrected himself.

"Why?" I stammered, "w-w-why...why would he do it?"

Drew placed his hand on my shoulder. "Honey, you're so young. This is so new to you."

"He told me tonight that he loves me. He gave me a collar." My weeping was turning to sobs, but not the kind that are violent and loud, but the kind that rack your whole body, causing you to convulse as you try to breathe.

"And I believe he does, Petey. I believe he loves you very, very much."

"No! He loves her...Kathie told me. He said it to her too. He said he loves her."

"Straight guys say a lot of shit to get laid, ya know," offered Drew, possibly realizing it was not necessarily the most helpful thing to say after he'd done so. "I mean...Petey..." he sighed. "Petey, what did he say to you? What did he say about how he feels about her?"

For the first time I turned to look up at his beautiful face. Drew was so incredibly cute; he was an absolute angel. In fact I actually thought that even through my own dark cloud of depression, *Drew looks like a cherub.* I slid my hand over to place it on his knee. "He said she is nothing to him —just a hole. He said she's his bitch."

"So what has changed then?" he asked. "If that is what he told you, then why don't you believe him?"

"Because!" I sucked in my breath as I forced myself to go on with the answer, "Because he also told her that he loves her. He told me she was nothing. He told her that he loves her. He lied ... at least to one of us."

"Or maybe she did," Drew said. "Maybe he never said that he loves her, but she just assumed it. Maybe your sister just assumed it."

"But why would he allow her to make that assumption? Why would he not tell her?"

"Why should he?" Drew asked calmly. "Why should he be concerned about what she thinks, if it's true that he doesn't care that much about her? If her belief that he loves her is going to get him laid, why wouldn't he allow her to continue to believe like that?"

"Because...because he's better than that! He doesn't just use people like that! Least I thought he didn't."

"Petey, I know you idolize Matt...God, doesn't every one? But he is not a saint. He's not perfect. He's a twenty year old college freshman jock. Up til now he has fucked girls all through high school at his own whim. You probably are the very first person he has ever really loved.

402

"He's not gonna suddenly stop being who he is just because he falls in love, Honey. You are expecting him to stop being the very person that you fell head over heals in love with."

"No I'm not, Drew...Honest I'm not! I just want him to tell me the truth. I just want him...oh god...I just want him to love me the way I love him."

"Sweety, I don't think anyone can love the way you do. You love with all your heart. You wear your feelings on your shirtsleeves."

I smiled at him then. "My mom used to say that to me...all the time."

"It's true. You're very sensitive. Doesn't make you bad. Just makes you you." He reached down to my face and wiped his finger under my eye, sweeping away the teardrops. "Come stay with me tonight, Petey. Come spend the night at my apartment. We can curl up together in my big king-sized bed, just you and me like a pajama party. Okay?"

"I can't Drew," I said, "I have class in the morning, and then I have to work tomorrow night."

"So? You can ride in with me, and then I'll take you to work in the afternoon. Please Petey. I don't want you to be alone."

I looked into his eyes. We stared at one other affectionately as he gently grabbed a hold of and squeezed my hand. "But...well...maybe."

"Okay, it's settled," he said quickly. "Now get up and get your stuff together. I'm gonna go talk to your sister. She's majorly worried about you."

"I'm sorry," I said.

"Shut up and quit being sorry for everything!" he scolded, then he bent down and kissed my forehead. "Be back in a couple minutes." He then left the room pulling the door closed quietly behind him.

* * *

Just being around Drew was helping me to feel better. On the way over to his house we stopped and loaded up on junk food. For once, I was not even worried about it being fattening. As we walked the aisles of the store we just kept picking up one thing after another and tossing it into the cart, laughing as we did so. "Oh my god, have you tried these cookies? They are sooo good!" I said to Drew. He snatched them from my hand and threw them on top of the heap of snacks we had already amassed.

"You wanna watch a movie?" asked Drew after we'd gotten over to his house. I shook my head.

"Nah, I don't think I could get into it," I confessed.

"Oh, you know what's on tonight?" Drew said, "I just remembered. Have you seen that new show called Queer As Folk?" I shook my head. "It's on Showtime. It is sort of like a gay soap opera. It's a drama. Comes on at ten. We can watch that."

"I've never even heard about it," I told him. "What's it like?"

"Oh, it's about this group of fags who live in Pittsburg. You're gonna like it, I promise. It's an awesome show, and they always have sex scenes in it."

"Gay sex?" I asked, somewhat surprised.

"Yeah, can you believe it?"

"Cool. Yeah, we can watch that," I smiled wanly.

"Cheer up!" Drew chided me. "Stop being sad about Matt. Just forget about it for a few hours and let's have fun."

"I can't forget about him, Drew," I said, looking over to see his letter jacket lying across the back of one of the living room chairs. I'd brought it with me for some reason, probably just to torture myself. "I keep thinking about what he's probably doing right now... with her."

"Well stop it. Doesn't do any good to keep dwelling on it. Besides, when Matt and Alex get back on Wednesday, they are coming back to us. No matter what happens, no matter who they fuck or don't fuck, in the end, they return to us. Shouldn't that be enough?"

"How can you say that, Drew? I mean, think about it. You are saying that even though Alex is your boyfriend, it is still okay for him to go out and sleep with other people, just so he returns home to you."

"Well, he's not just my boyfriend, Petey. You know that as well as I do. The only reason I ever refer to him as a 'boyfriend' is so that other people don't freak out. If I called him my master or my owner, I don't think a lot of people would really be hip to it."

"So because he is dominant, you are saying that it then gives him a right to cheat on you?"

"It's not cheating. The only way it would be cheating is if he promised to be monogamous with me. He never ever did that, though. I've known from the beginning that he was at liberty to have sex with whomever he wanted. I know that is pretty freaky to you Petey, but you know what's so cool with it? He is absolutely free to at any point be with anyone—anyone at all—and yet 99% of the time, he chooses to be with me. The only time he goes elsewhere is when he wants pussy."

"Or when he wants you to pimp some other fag for him."

"Yeah," he admitted, "but I'm a part of that. He's never had sex with another guy unless I've been right there with him, least not that I know of."

"But what if it were the other way around? What if you went out and had sex with some other person."

He laughed. "I'd be history," he stated matter-of-factly.

"How is that fair?" I asked. "That is totally a double standard."

"It is both fair and a double standard. There is nothing unfair about this kind of relationship. Petey, you are confusing fairness with equality. It is absolutely fair because it is huge trade-off. Sure, I have to accept some things about Alex that I don't necessarily feel comfortable with, but look

405

what I get in return. I get his guidance, his protection, his possessiveness. I know that as long as I belong to him, no one is ever gonna hurt me. I don't have to stress over big decisions...or small ones even. He has all of the responsibility. All that I have to worry about is one thing: obeying him."

"But what does all of that have to do with him having sex with women?" I asked.

"What I'm saying, guy, is that Alex is dominant and I am submissive. There is an entirely different set of rules for each of us. My role is not to question him or any of the decisions that he makes. My role is to trust him. Period. End of story. His role is to take care of me. He does whatever he wants and when he wants to do it. It is his prerogative, and I have no right to ever question him. I, on the other hand, do only what he decides I'm allowed to do. I think it's totally fair—not at all equal—but fair."

"So you don't have any problem with the fact that he has license to do whatever he wants, even if it hurts you, while at the same time you are obligated to do only what he tells you?"

"Petey, he owns me." Drew was laughing as he said this, explaining the facts to me as if he were talking to a small child. "It is not a difficult concept to understand. It's like when you own a pet. You decide literally everything that your pet is allowed to do...where he sleeps, what he eats, whether he is allowed to breed or not...everything. None of this is unfair to the pet, though. It is just that the role of an owner and pet are different. You couldn't have much of a relationship with a pet if he never obeyed you, could you?"

"But we are humans, Drew — not animals!"

"Of course we are humans. Submissive ones, though. The pet thing was just an analogy. Our role in the relationship with our dominant partners is very similar to the role of a pet to its owner. Why do you think Matt calls you his pup?"

"But it hurts me so much, Drew. It makes me so sad that he would rather be with her than with me."

"I bet if you had a puppy of your own, he would be really sad when you left him too. Every time you went away to go to work or to school or to go out with friends, I bet he would feel totally abandoned. Pups do that; they can't help it. But then when you returned to him, he'd be so happy to see you, jumping up and down, licking your face. You'd love it, I know you would. Even though you would sometimes feel sort of bad for him when you had to leave him alone, do you think his feelings would stop you from doing what you had to do or what you wanted to do?"

"No, of course not."

"Then don't expect Matt to give up what he wants to do for you. You are the pup, Petey, not the owner. You don't have any right to expect him to do what you want. If it were any other way, then you wouldn't even have the relationship to begin with."

"Unless he wanted for us to be more equal..."

"Matt Porter will never want for you to be equal with him, and Petey, be honest. Do you really want to be treated as his equal?"

I shook my head slowly. "No, cause I'm not equal to him. I confessed that to him the very first time we were together. I told him I knew he was...superior."

"You both know it, and it's not a bad thing. Your role as his sub doesn't make you a worthless person. It doesn't even mean that you are actually inferior as a person. It just means that you know your place. You each have a role. He is the leader and you the follower. He is top and you are bottom. He is owner and you are pup. It's all good, Petey." He put his arm around me.

"What if I just tell him how I feel? What if I tell him I can't go on like this cuz it hurts too much? What if I tell him I want him to end it with Tracy? I mean, if he really loves me like you say, won't he want to do that for me...for us?"

"Petey, if you start telling Matt what you expect for him to do, no matter what it is, he is gonna flip on ya. He's gonna see it as you trying to give him orders. He is gonna feel you're trying to give him ultimatums, manipulate him into doing what you want. If he at any point ever gives into a demand that you have made, it will totally change the dynamic of your relationship. It will destroy it."

"How do you know, Drew? Maybe we would be very happy by being more equal to one another. No matter what, he would always still be dominant and I would always still be submissive, but that doesn't mean he has to be a dictator to me."

Drew sighed. "Petey, sometimes you are so stubborn." He led me over to the sofa, the same one where Alex had sat comfortably that night while Drew worshipped his feet. "You have got to trust me on this, even if you don't totally agree with me. If you say to Matt, 'I can't go on like this cuz it hurts me and I want you to end it with Tracy,' he is gonna say to you, 'See ya!'"

"Well if he did that, Drew, then I guess it would mean he didn't love me all that much to begin with."

"No, it won't mean that! You've been watching way too many romantic comedies, honey. All it will mean is that he will realize that you don't want a Dom/sub relationship, and if you don't want it and can't agree to the terms of it, then there is no point in continuing. He is not going to stop being who he is, and no matter how hard you try, you will never ever change him. Even if you could change him, Petey, when it was all said and done, you'd want him to be just exactly the way he was in the beginning, when you fell in love with him. If it were some fag you wanted, you would not have started serving Matt in the first place."

"So the bottom line is that I have to accept the fact that Matt goes out and fucks pussy whenever and wherever he wants? I'm never allowed to question this, never allowed to be upset, jealous, or angry? I just have to sit back and take it like a doormat because I'm nothing but a submissive faggot?"

"Stop internalizing everything! Geesh Petey, don't you realize this is not even about you? When Matt goes out and fucks pussy he does it cuz it feels good. Period. He does it cuz it's something he likes to do, sort of like watchin a game or havin a beer. He is not doing anything to deliberately hurt you. He loves you!"

"If that is the case, then why'd he take Tracy to the cabin for three days? If he is just fucking her cuz it feels good, why's he gotta go away with her like that?"

"Four of them went together. This little vacation was as much about Alex and Matt hangin together as it was about the chicks. Who am I to say why they decided to invite the people that they did? My guess is that they just wanted some readily available pussy. Do you think I'm worried that Alex is gonna dump me for this bimbo and never come home again? No way! Just like Matt is not gonna suddenly fall in love with Tracy either just cuz he slid his dick in and out of her twat a few times."

"That's gross!" I protested.

"Sorry...too graphic, but you get the point." We both were laughing in spite of ourselves.

"Drew, what should I do?" I said seriously. "I'm afraid I won't be able to handle it. What if I get so...hurt...that I ruin everything between Matt and me?"

"You won't do that cuz I'm gonna tell you exactly what to do. You are gonna spend these next three days with me. You are not gonna go sit in your room at home being all sad and depressed about everything. You and I are gonna do exactly the same thing that Matt and Alex are doing. We're gonna have fun together. Then when they come home, we are gonna be waiting for them and you aren't gonna act like there even is anything wrong. There isn't anything wrong, actually."

"Oh my god! I'd better turn my phone back on. Matt said he might call me."

"Uh, yeah...Guess you better then. And then you and I are gonna curl up in my big bed and eat ourselves into obesity!" He busted up laughing then, hugging me once again. "Petey, I love you so much. I really do."

"I love you too, Drew...you're my best friend."

23

I could hardly believe my eyes while I watched Queer as Folk. I was totally mesmerized by the show, seeing for the first time ever people who were just like me on a regular television show. Immediately I was captivated by the character of Brian Kinney. He was so hot—so cocky and arrogant, self-assured. In some ways he seemed like an older version of Matt. The big difference was that he was 100% gay. As I watched the show I was constantly thinking of Matt. Unlike Brian, Matt did not go out and hook up with other guys constantly, and unlike me, Brian's boy Justin was extremely independent and head strong. In some ways I wanted for Matt to be more like Brian, that is, being exclusively attracted to men. I also wanted for me to be more like Justin, less wimpy and more confident in myself. But the way the two of them interacted with one another was so very similar to Matt and me. Justin idolized Brian almost exactly the same way I did Matt. Watching this show every Sunday night was definitely going to be added to my things-to-do list.

I had put on a pair of sleep pants and a sleeveless tee, and was sitting Indian style on top of the bed, wearing my glasses instead of contacts. Drew was lying next to me on his stomach, resting his chin against his palms with his arms tucked under himself. We had three different bags of chips,

Reeses Pieces, Oreo Double Stuff cookies, cheese crackers, chocolate covered raisins, and of course, Diet Coke. I kept stuffing food into my mouth, gorging myself as I became engrossed in the drama, gasping during the dramatic scenes for effect. Drew kept kicking his heel up against his butt, fidgeting as he talked back to the television set. "Kiss him!" he was yelling at one of the main characters, as if the actor was a real person who was in the room with us and who could actually hear him.

After the show was over, we surveyed the room and both busted up laughing, seeing the debauchery around us. There was food everywhere. We began scooping everything up, carrying it out to the kitchen. "Oh my god, I totally love that show, Drew," I said. "Isn't Brian like the hottest man on the planet...I mean, other than Matt?"

"You mean other than Alex," he corrected.

"Yeah, whatever. Do you think you'd cheat on Alex if it were with someone like Brian?"

He shook his head. "I wouldn't cheat on Alex for a million bucks," he said.

"Me neither," I admitted, "I mean on Matt."

"I know."

"Guess what he told me before he dropped me off?"

"What?" asked Drew.

"He said I could jack off as much as I wanted between now and Wednesday." I giggled as I said it. "Only stipulation is I have to be thinking only of him when I cum."

"Oh really? Soooo...you could whack off tonight in bed next to me, just so long as you were fantasizing about Matt?"

"Why would I do that?" I started to blush. "I mean that would be cheating, just like I said I wouldn't do for a million bucks."

"No it wouldn't! It's not like we'd even be touching one another. We could beat together. You know, like jack off buddies. Both of us fantasizing about our masters."

"I'm not sure he'd like it," I said. "Don't you think Alex would be pissed?"

"Maybe, or maybe he'd think it was cute, two fags beatin it together while thinking about their Tops."

"I don't know, Drew. I'd better wait and see if I hear from him. I don't want to be punished again."

"Okay," he said casually. "I understand."

We then went back to the bedroom and curled up next to one another in the huge bed. I rolled over close to Drew and put my arm around him. It felt so very different, totally the opposite of what it was like with Matt. Drew felt so tiny to me, so much softer. I must have felt the same to him too, for I was even littler than he was. He smelled real good though too, and was so warm. I lay there against him peacefully and gradually drifted off to sleep. Suddenly it was the next morning.

* * *

It was surprising to me how much of an adjustment it was for me to return to my day-to-day life after having just two days free from my normal routine. My weekend had been wonderful, but it seemed to me on Monday morning that it was an eternity ago that I had faced the monotony of classes and work, and I debated whether or not I even felt it was worth it to have any time off. The free time seemed to have merely heightened my awareness of the fact that real life was in essence very boring. I began reflecting on the vision that I had for my future. Certainly, my own dreams and hopes would include Matt, but my reflections were not really focused upon this area of my life. I was concerned about what I'd do career-wise, where I'd finish my education, where exactly that education would take me. For the first time ever I thought about the fact that with me being gay, I really was not likely to be a part of any sort of traditional family unit. Matt was light years away from even discussing anything like this with me, and I wondered what his personal vision was for his own future. He had already stated that eventually he'd take over his father's businesses, and I knew that with these businesses came a lot of responsibility and also a lot of money. If anyone would be able to take on a challenge like this it would be Matt; he definitely was born to be a leader.

I, on the other hand, was totally uncertain of my future in terms of career. Certainly working at a bookstore indefinitely was not a long-term goal of mine. The two things in life that I was passionate about were cooking and creative writing. I did not see myself, though, being able to work as a chef somewhere. Cooking was much more a hobby to me. If Matt ultimately did choose to spend his life with me, then perhaps I could focus upon my dreams of authorship. He could run his businesses, and I could stay at home writing books. I smiled to myself as I visualized this scenario, thinking of myself as being the good housewife, taking care of all things domestic while my man went out and made bucks, bringing home the bacon.

The mere thought of continuing in retail for much longer very much nauseated me. The bookstore was all right, for at least it put me in proximity to many of the things I loved—mainly books. Maybe some day I would own my own bookstore; this would allow me the opportunity to utilize both my passions and my experience. By incorporating Matt's business acumen, it may be the perfect blending of both our worlds.

I had also always had a certain amount of passion for civic and political causes. I considered that maybe a career choice which involved some sort of public service, perhaps working for a non-profit organization, may be quite rewarding to me. I had attended that one single gay student union meeting and had never gone back. Perhaps I should explore becoming more involved, and maybe it would lead me into a direction that I ultimately would very much enjoy. I made a mental note to bring this topic up to Drew; maybe he could advise me.

We were only two weeks away from Spring break, and I was extremely relieved. The first semester of my freshman year had flown by, but now that we were over the mid-way hurdle, these last three months seemed to drag. Even with the bashing I'd gone through first semester, and the court appearances, and the holidays, I was so caught up in the novelty of college life that time seemed to zoom by, and before I knew it, we were in a new year.

When Drew finally picked me up from the bookstore that Monday evening, it was interesting that he brought up a topic that was very much along the lines of what I myself had been thinking. "Hey Petey, how much longer are you gonna continue to live with your sister in that apartment?"

"I don't know. Guess I hadn't thought of it. I really wouldn't wanna even think of leaving her now, not after what has happened. I mean with losing our parents and stuff."

"Yeah, I understand, but still your sister probably wants to eventually get on with her own life too. I mean, you said she is pretty serious about this guy she's dating, right?"

"Um, yeah, I guess so, but I think it's kinda early to tell. They haven't been seeing one another all that long. Are you saying that, for her sake, I should start thinking about moving out?"

"No, not at all. Definitely the most important thing right now is your education. I just was wondering if you'd given any thought about what you are gonna do afterwards. See, Alex and I have talked about this. We have this huge three bedroom apartment, Christ it's more like a condo, you know. If you ever did decide that you wanted to make a move, maybe you could rent a room from us."

I smiled at him. "That's very nice of you Drew. I'd love it actually, but I wonder how Matt would feel about that. I mean, he might think it's a bit awkward that one dominant guy lives with his boy and has another boy living with them— a boy who belongs to someone else."

"Well, I guess that would be a trust issue. I know for a fact that Alex would never move in on some other Dom's property, especially when the other Dom is a friend of his. Plus, Matt would have to be able to trust you, and I think he totally does."

"I wonder if Matt ever thinks about us living together, him and me, I mean."

"Would be cool if the four of us could share a place together."

"Yeah," I smiled, "but I don't know. Matt is going to inherit all of his dad's businesses pretty soon, ya know. He probably will buy a place of his own."

"Can you imagine what it must be like to have that kind of money? I mean, to just go out and pay for a house with cash. It's beyond my comprehension."

"Yeah," I said, "When I have to scrounge up loose change in order to buy myself a Big Mac." We both laughed.

415

Drew rolled down his window and lit a cigarette. "Man, I'm down to like five cigarettes a day now. Did you notice I didn't even have any at all last night?"

"That's good, Drew, but why don't you just quit entirely. I mean, five per day is not much to give up."

He sighed, "Yeah, I know, but I just totally love the exhilaration of the first few puffs off a cigarette. You kinda have to be a smoker to know what I'm talking about. I'm just thankful that Alex allows me this one indulgence. With the price of tobacco nowadays, though, it is so stupid to even smoke. It's almost five bucks for one pack of cigarettes."

"Are you serious?" I asked. "Geesh, that's ridiculous. Why does it cost so much?"

"Taxes," he said.

"I was also gonna ask you, Drew, are you and Alex still active with the Gay Student Union?"

"Yeah, sure. In fact we have our monthly planning meeting this Thursday. We are gonna be doing a big event over Spring break. Well big for us, I should say. We are taking the entire group down to Fort Lauderdale and passing out condoms," he laughed.

"That's funny," I said, "What ever happened with that vandalism? Did they ever catch who did it?"

"Nope. I think it was high school kids actually. The good thing is that the board approved the funding to have security cameras installed in our offices, so I think our little protest may have had some effect after all."

It was already starting to get dark as Drew pulled his car into the apartment building's parking structure. "Have you talked to your sister yet today?" he asked, "She was really worried about you last night."

"Yeah, I called her from my cell phone this morning. I told her I was gonna be at your house til Wednesday. She was cool with it cuz she and Carter can then have the apartment to themselves. You might be right about her being serious about him."

"Did you eat dinner?" he asked.

"Nah. Well I had a sandwich on my break about three hours ago."

"You want pizza? It's kinda late to be cooking a big meal."

"Sure...whatever." We got out of the car and headed into the building. "Drew, let me give you some money towards it. You paid for all the junk food last night."

"Don't be a moron; you're my guest. Keep your money."

"I don't think Matt would like it if he knew I was sponging off of you, though."

"Shut up! You're not sponging. You're a college student for chrissakes. You're supposed to take handouts. It's not like Alex and I can't afford to feed you. Oh, did I tell you? Alex already has some interviews set up with some software companies. He's probably gonna have a good job lined up by the time he graduates."

"I thought he would just keep working at the same place. I mean the place where he is interning."

"Maybe, if they offer him enough money," he smiled. "I will be so glad when he starts making more money than me. It's not really even about the money, though. It totally doesn't matter that I pretty much support us right now; it's just that I think he would feel better if it were the other way around. With him being dominant, I don't think it necessarily sits well with him that he's somewhat financially dependent upon his boy."

"Yeah, that would be a little bit weird, I think. I can't imagine what it'd be like if I had more money than Matt."

"Still, a Dom's a Dom, and a sub's a sub, no matter how much money they make. I guess Alex and I are living proof of that."

Once we got inside the apartment, Drew called in the pizza order, and we sat in the living room. "I think I am gonna go change," I said. I got up and went into the spare bedroom and changed into a pair of basketball shorts and a sleeveless tee. I also took out my contacts and put on my glasses.

"You can take a shower if you want," Drew called to me from the hallway.

"Oh thanks, but I'm already dressed now," I laughed, "You're gonna just have to put up with my stench."

"Eww," he teased, "Well that's what I meant. I can hardly stand it!"

"Fuck you, Drew!" I said, "I was doing manual labor all day."

"Oh, hope you didn't hurt yourself. Better check for paper cuts on your fingers from all those books you handled." We both laughed. "I ordered vegetarian pizza for ya, bud. That cool?"

"Yeah, thanks," I emerged from the bedroom then, meeting him in the hallway.

"You look so cute," he said to me. "A little jock wannabe."

"Hey, don't make fun. My owner picked out these clothes for me."

"Probably thought you'd look cute in them while you're on your knees suckin him off."

"Duh," I said, "Of course that's what he thought." We headed back to the living room together. "I wish he'd call me," I confessed. "I've been thinking about him all day."

"Don't worry, no news is good news, ya know."

We chatted together for the next couple of hours, watching television as we ate our pizza. I was so thankful I had accepted Drew's invitation to stay at his apartment while Matt and Alex were away. Drew was becoming the best friend I had ever had. Finally, at about ten thirty, my phone did ring. I shot up off the couch like a cannonball and grabbed the phone off the dining room table. It was Matt!

"Hello!" I said, as I held the receiver to my ear.

"Hey Petey Pup," he said, "Watchya doin?"

"I'm at Drew's , Sir. We just had pizza."

"Cool. You spending the night there?"

"Yes Sir, I've been here since last night. We are staying together while you're gone."

"Oh, that's a good idea. So you know where I am, huh?"

"Yes Sir," I said quietly, "Are you having fun?"

"Yeah, 'cept you'll be happy to know, Tracy and Kelly took off."

"What do you mean?" I asked, "How did they do that?"

"Guess they got pissed at us," he laughed. "Apparently Tracy called someone for a ride. Alex and I were out on the boat, and when we got back, they had left a note. Oh well, who needs em anyhow, huh?"

I smiled broadly. "I'm sorry, Sir. That wasn't very nice of them to leave like that." I looked over at Drew excitedly, giving him a thumbs up signal. "Does that mean you are coming home early?"

"Nah," he said casually, "Not gonna let a couple of bitches ruin our vacation. Alex and I got ourselves some brew for tonight. Gonna just chill. You jack off yet, pup?"

"No Sir...but...um...I was going to ask you something about that." I stepped further into the dining room, allowing myself some privacy. I lowered my voice. "Sir?"

"Yeah, go ahead. Ask away."

"Well...um...last night Drew wanted me to...ya know...do it with him."

"Do what?" he asked sternly. "Sex?"

"Oh no...not that, Sir," I laughed nervously. "He wanted me to — you know — jack off with him." My voice was a quiet whisper.

"Speak up, I can hardly hear you."

"He wants me to masturbate with him, Sir," I said a little louder.

He busted up laughing. "So, why didn't ya do it?"

"Well, cuz I did not know if I should Sir."

"I told you that you could jack off all you want until Wednesday. You remember the stipulation, right?"

"I have to think of you when I cum, Sir."

"That's right. So don't you think that you'd be thinking of me when you jack off with Drew?"

"Of course I would Sir," I said with certainty. "Who else would I even think of?"

"True," he said, "Okay, well you can do it, that's cool. Just don't touch him, and don't let him touch you. And eat your cum when you're done. You're a good boy for telling me about it, pup."

"Thank you, Sir," I smiled. "So when are you going to be home?...I mean...um...just curious is all."

"Be home Wednesday sometime. Don't worry, we will be there for your party, pup."

"Okay...I wasn't worried. I'm glad you're having fun. Sir?"

"Yeah?"

"I miss you so much. I love you."

"Love ya too, pup. But I gotta go, got some drinkin to do."

"Okay...thank you for calling me."

"Welcome," he said, "Later." He clicked off.

The instant I clicked off my own phone, I ran back into the living room.

"You're not gonna believe this! The girls got pissed and left them!"

"Oh my god, why?" asked Drew.

"I don't know. I guess Matt and Alex were out on his boat and when they got back they found a note. They called someone for a ride. I wonder if it was Kathie."

"If so, that'll be interesting."

"Yeah, I wonder if Kathie still thinks Matt's in love Tracy now. He told me he loves me again too."

"See. Look how worried you were, and for nothing."

"I'm so glad, Drew! I mean, don't get me wrong, I don't wanna be selfish. It's not that I wanted Matt's vacation to be spoiled; I just am glad that he's not with her."

"Yeah, and I bet he won't be with her ever again either. I can't see Matt ever letting some chick get away with dissing him like that. She never even told him goodbye— just left a note."

"You think he's gonna break it off with her completely?" I asked.

"Most likely, unless there were some extenuating circumstances that we don't know about. Even then, though, I doubt he'd forgive her, unless she like came crawling back to him, begging for his forgiveness."

"Well, I've known her for a long time, and she's not the type to show any humility. She would never crawl back to him. It would be different if it were some sort of emergency or something where she had to leave suddenly, but Matt said she got pissed at him. Wonder what he did that pissed her off."

"Maybe he wanted to butt fuck her," Drew said light-heartedly, "or maybe he came in her mouth!" We both started laughing.

"Maybe she found out about me," I said more seriously.

Drew shook his head. "Not to burst your bubble or anything, but I doubt it. She probably would never in a million years think that Matt could ever have sex with a guy."

"Yeah, but maybe Kathie told her."

"Maybe, but I think that even if she had told Tracy that, Tracy wouldn't believe it. Matt's the sort of guy that people just naturally assume is totally straight. Even Alex is like that, but not quite as much as Matt. Since both the girls left together, I bet it was something that Matt and Alex both did that pissed them off. Probably they were hangin together and not paying attention to the women."

"Who cares, really? All I care about is that he called me and that he said he loves me. Guess what else he said?"

"What?"

"He said I could...um...you know...um...do what we were talkin bout last night."

"Beat off?" he asked. I smiled at him and nodded.

"So what are we waiting for? Let's go to the bedroom!"

"Okay," I said excitedly, "let me get his letter jacket. I want to be looking at it when I cum." I ran over to the other side of the room and snatched the jacket off the back of the chair, then followed Drew down the hallway and into the bedroom.

Once inside, Drew turned to me, reaching his hand down to rub my already semi-hard cock. "No!" I protested. "He said we can't touch each other."

"Oh, sorry," Drew said. He stepped back from me, still staring at me. "Okay then, take it out."

"You take yours out first. Please." My heart was beating excitedly. I'd never seen Drew naked before. Even when we changed together at the water park, I was so modest that I didn't even look at him after he'd stripped off his wet bathing suit. Smiling at me now, he reached down and slowly groped himself. I could see the outline of his cock through his shorts. He grabbed the waistband and pulled them down so that he was just in his underwear. He wore tighty-whitey briefs that fit snugly around his slender waist and buttocks. He then pulled his tee shirt up over his head, now standing in front of me wearing only his white socks and underpants. Like myself, Drew was very smooth.

I then took off my own shirt as he watched. Then I slipped down my shorts. I also was wearing briefs, but mine were blue low rise, with no fly in the front. My cock was rock hard and pressing against the fabric of the bikini-like briefs, tenting them outward. I gently rubbed my fingertips along the outline of my cock as Drew watched. There was a tiny dark wet spot near the tip of my cock head, where I was starting to ooze precum. "Take em off!" he urged me.

"Let's do it together, okay?"

We both reached down to our waistbands and pulled them down quickly, stepping out of the underwear and tossing them next to us on the floor. We returned to our upright position and continued to stare at one another. I smiled when I noticed that Drew was also completely shaved, just like me. He was rock hard. He reached under his nut sac with one hand, gently stroking it with his fingertips, while he wrapped his other palm around his cock. He was a tiny bit smaller than me and not quite as thick, but with him being shaved like that, he looked rather well endowed. He stared directly at my boner as it stuck out proudly in front of me. I did not touch myself like he was doing. I just stood there with my hands at my side.

"Let's get on the bed," I suggested. We jumped up onto the king sized bed together and knelt facing one another. "You like mine?" I asked.

"Sure," he said, "You like mine?"

I smiled at him. "Yeah. Alex makes you shave?"

"Yup. I like being smooth for him."

"Me too," I said, "I mean I like doing it for Matt." I reached down and stroked myself finally. I wrapped my small hand around my cock completely and slid it slowly back and forth while Drew stared at me intently. Not taking his eyes off me, he lay back on the bed, propping a pillow up behind him. I copied him, sliding over next to him so we were lying beside one another. I looked over to the dresser to see Matt's letter jacket displayed there prominently, and my cock throbbed in my hand as I envisioned him wearing it. I closed my eyes briefly as I stroked myself. I opened them and glanced over to Drew who was now stroking himself more quickly. "What are you thinking of?" I asked him.

"I'm thinking of how I sucked Alex off in front of you this weekend," he said. "On the cable cars."

"You thinking of how he held onto your head real tight and pumped you on him? ... Of how his cock felt in your mouth? ... Of how his cum tasted?"

"Yeah!" he squeezed his eyes shut tightly, "and what he looked like sitting there, all comfortable while I knelt to serve him, and what he smelled like."

"You like serving him in front of us?" I asked.

"Yeah! I liked it a lot...I liked...uhhh..." he was getting excited, his breathing becoming more rapid, "I liked showing you who I belonged to. I liked doing it...uhhh...doing it in public."

"Yeah, that was hot," I said, stroking myself in rhythm with him. I looked down at our legs, all four stretched out in front of us, spread slightly apart. His legs were just a few inches longer than mine. As we lay there on the huge bed, we did not come close to reaching the edge of the mattress with our socked feet. I once again looked over at Matt's jacket.

"I sucked Matt off at the bar Saturday night, in the back room."

"Cool. Did anyone see you?" he had opened his eyes and was looking over at me as he continued to jack himself.

"Yeah...this one kid we met. His name was Ryan, and I could tell he was hot for Matt. He saw Matt cum...ohh god...he saw him cum in my mouth!" I was stroking myself faster now.

"He was hot for Matt but you got to serve him? That's so hot."

"Yeah, and I was wearing Matt's collar too!"

"Cuz he owns you!"

"Yeah!...oh god, I'm getting close!"

"You're his property...his owned fag pup...and he can use you wherever he wants, in front of whoever he wants!"

"Yeah!" I said, staring right at the jacket. "Yeah, like he did one day in the laundry room at my apartment! ... In the middle of the night!"

"Yup, you're on call to serve him, twenty-four hours a day."

"And he always drains himself into me, makes me swallow every drop of his load. He feeds it to me! Oh god, I'm gonna shoot!"

"He fuckin owns you, faggot!" Drew was screaming. "He owns every part of your faggot ass. You're his property!"

"Oh god! Oh yeah!! Ahhh...Unghhh!!" I gripped my cock firmly around its base as I felt the cum load right on the verge of exploding. I held tightly to my cock, allowing myself the prolonged pleasure of the orgasm. "Yeah!!" I screamed as the first jet of cum pumped up my shaft. It shot powerfully out of me, splashing suddenly against my chest. I continued to fire jet after jet of cum, my entire body twitching as I did so. My vision blurred somewhat and I closed my eyes, trembling all over from the orgasm. I heard Drew beside me, moaning loudly himself. I opened my eyes quickly, looking over to him to watch him cum.

His toes curled as he pumped out his load. Unlike me, he continued to jack even as he was shooting, but seemed to know how to do so in an expert way, maximizing his pleasure. "Fuck yeah!" he screamed.

I lay back, exhausted, leaning my head against the wall behind me. Slowly, I scooped up droplets of my cum from my chest and abdomen, bringing my fingers up to my mouth to lick them clean. I did it slowly, at this point not really even aware of Drew's presence beside me. I was thinking of my Owner, thinking of how I was obeying him, and imagining that the cum was from his body and not my own. I had most of the big gobs of cum cleaned up by the time Drew tossed me a towel. "Wanna shower now?"

"Yeah, sure," I said, smiling up at him. "That was hot."

"Yeah, I know."

24

I woke up the following morning curled up next to Drew. I loved sleeping with him almost as much as I did with Matt, although it was entirely different. With Matt I felt so secure and protected; I felt his strength surround me and cradle me. With Drew I felt his softness, smelled the sweet aroma of his cologne, and felt very warm and cozy. I lay next to him as he continued to sleep, and I took in his beauty. He was so incredibly cute, with his short-cut blonde hair and baby face. I could see why Alex had fallen in love with him. It was interesting, the contrast between Drew and Alex. Drew was extremely slender and as blonde as could be, while Alex was tall, dark, and handsome. Alex was actually handsome in more of a pretty sort of way, whereas my Matt had a rugged, cocky kind of attractiveness to him.

My Matt. I smiled as I lie there next to Drew thinking of that phrase. How I had longed to actually be able to say it and believe it. He was mine...or I guess I was his. Regardless, we were together: Owner and pup. It did not matter to me any longer how Kathie perceived our relationship. Tracy did not matter, either. It was so clear to me now that she meant nothing to Matt. And the fact that Matt had chosen to call me last night in the midst of his chillin-and-drinkin time with his bud, was hugely significant to me. When he'd told me that he often thought of me, even when I was not around, it did not seem possible. That phone call was the definitive confirmation though.

It was only six-thirty in the morning, and I knew Drew's alarm would not sound for another forty-five minutes. I was reluctant to pull myself away from the warmth of the bed but did so nonetheless. I stood beside the bed, shirtless and wearing only my boxer briefs, yawning quietly as I stretched. I found my tee shirt on the dresser sitting next to Matt's letter jacket and pulled it over my head. Looking in the mirror, I cringed, seeing my sleepy hair sticking up in all directions. Haphazardly I splattered it down against my head, accomplishing virtually nothing as the hairs defiantly went right back to their original state of disarray. I picked up my glasses and put them on and then stumbled quietly out to the kitchen. I put on a pot of coffee and then headed for the bathroom. Unlike Matt, Drew liked his morning java. I could personally take it or leave it, being content with swigging down a pint or two of diet cola for my morning caffeine boost.

After relieving myself and returning to the kitchen, I inhaled the aroma of the brewing coffee. It always seemed to smell so much better than it actually tasted, I thought. I walked out into the living room and retrieved my backpack, bringing it back with me to the dining room table. I removed my psychology book and placed it on the table. I had a good half hour to finish reading the chapter that was assigned for today. I sat down, rubbing the sleep from my eyes, and opened the book to find the correct page. The chapter was about personality disorders and focused almost exclusively on borderline personality. As I read the symptoms of this condition, I paused to consider the possibility that I myself might have a mental condition.

Certainly I was not borderline, for I did not fit well into this description, though I had to confess that I wondered if something might be wrong with me. I constantly had slipped into these periods of horrible depression, sometimes to the point of becoming fixated upon suicide. I was often overwhelmed with grief after having lost my parents and had never seemed to fully recover from it. Almost every single day I thought of them and felt sad about their passing, and sometimes I was so overcome with emotion that I felt literally paralyzed to go on with the day-to-day functions of my life. I also wondered if it were really normal for me to be so content with being subordinate to others. Why was it that I craved domination and guidance from someone who I perceived as "superior" to myself? Perhaps I was stuck in some twisted state of pseudo-childhood. Maybe my development as an adult had somehow become arrested when I lost my parents and now I craved an authoritative influence to guide my life.

Yet, as I pondered these things, I also remembered thoughts and feelings I'd had as a small child. I really always had been a very reserved person. In grade school I'd always deferred to the wishes of the more vocal students in my class or group, particularly the males. By the time I was in the sixth grade, I was already learning who I had to be most respectful of, who I had to take orders from—like it or not. I recalled a particular incident where this classmate of mine named Todd had ordered me to go back to the classroom to retrieve his gym bag for him. We were actually already in the gym locker room preparing to change when Todd had realized that he'd forgotten his bag. I was only twelve years old at the time. Without questioning him, I ran back down the empty corridors of the hallway and found his bag in the classroom by his desk and rushed it back to him. When I returned, our teacher caught me reentering the gym and scolded me for being tardy. I did not correct her, though, and took the blame for my tardiness. She assigned me two demerits for my misbehavior. When I did hand Todd his bag, he didn't even thank me, but I never felt bad about it. It just seemed appropriate to me.

Then on another occasion back even further in my memory, I recalled another kid named Scott who was in my third grade class. Our teacher was one of the few male elementary school teachers employed by the school. His name was Mr. Matson, and he was a very skilled instructor but ruled his class with unfaltering authority. The very first thing that his students would notice as they walked through the doors of the classroom was a big wooden paddle that he had hanging from a small metal hook just inside the doorway. He was not afraid to use it, either, as we soon discovered. I remember on one particular occasion that Scott, who was an impetuous little snot at times, had gotten caught snapping rubber bands at Carrie Jennings, a tiny little blonde girl that sat in front of him. Mr. Matson made Scott clear out his desk and hand over all items within except for one pencil and the text book that was currently being used. Finally, Mr. Matson returned to his position at the chalkboard and resumed the presentation of our lesson.

Scott, being as defiant as he was, made faces at Mr. Matson behind his back. When some of the students quietly snickered, this only encouraged Scott to continue.

Finally Scott pulled out another rubber band, apparently having stashed one prior to his scolding. He positioned it expertly on his thumb and forefinger as if he were loading a gun and again pointed it at Carrie Jennings. While Mr. Matson was still at the chalkboard with his back to the class, Scott released the rubber band, nailing Carrie right in the cheek. She became instantly startled and screamed involuntarily. When Mr. Matson turned around to face the outburst, I had never before recalled witnessing such a fury of emotion. He was enraged! He dropped the chalk carelessly on the ledge and walked briskly over to Scott's desk. Scott was already beginning to protest before a word was even spoken.

"I didn't do it, Mr. Matson! Honest...It wasn't me!"

Mr. Matson grabbed Scott then by the back of his collar and jerked him out of his seat. He marched him to the front of the class, pushing him against his big wooden desk. "Hands flat on the top of the desk!" he ordered, his own masculine voice drowning out Scott's continuous yet futile protests. He used the hand with which he was already holding Scott's neck to force him down into a position where he was bent over. "Spread your feet apart!" he ordered, and Scott almost instantly assumed the servile position. As Mr. Matson then walked over to remove the paddle from the hook, Scott stood there immobile, apparently afraid to move. The entire class watched, not uttering a single sound.

Then Mr. Matson stepped into position, placing one hand on Scott's back and with the other he held the paddle. He brought his arm back almost completely, winding up, and delivered a powerful first blow to Scott's vulnerable behind. I sat there watching, my mouth surely agape as he paddled Scott's ass right there in front of this classroom of third graders. This was my first time witnessing such discipline.

I remember details about it now that you would not expect to ever recall. I remember the tight fitting trousers that Scott was wearing. They were sort of a navy blue khaki. I remember the redness in Scott's cheeks. He was completely flushed, blushing from his humiliation. I remember the sound of the paddle as it swooshed through the air, and the crack of the impact upon Scott's butt. I remember his involuntary moans which eventually became stifled screams as he endured the pain. And I remember the snickering and very subdued laughter that I heard behind me from some of the other boys in the class. I wondered if Mr. Matson heard it, or even more significantly, if Scott did.

As I sat there watching this merciless delivery of justice, I actually started to become excited. I found a peculiar sense of pleasure from seeing this cocky brat being disciplined like this. At one point I even reached my hand down into my lap and rubbed myself inconspicuously. I was sporting a tiny third-grade erection. This was my first inclination that I was aroused by authoritative-type men. After this particular incident of discipline in his classroom, Mr. Matson then became a very ominous figure to me. He was greatly respected in my eyes after this and also so very much feared. Even to this day, I still feel subordinate to him and probably always will.

I sat there at the kitchen table reflecting upon these things as I finished the chapter. I truly did not understand where my servile nature stemmed from. I suppose it had always been a part of me and maybe was not a result of a mental illness or an arrested stage of my development. It simply was a part of who I was. Maybe it was truly a variant personality type, but perhaps not a personality disorder. I was sub. Period.

I was so intent upon my thoughts that I did not even hear Drew approach me from behind. I jumped a little when he placed his hand on my shoulder. "Morning," he said. "Thanks for making coffee."

"You're welcome," I said, smiling up at him. "You look so cute when you're sleeping."

He yawned and forced a half-smile in my direction. "Thanks," he said groggily. "You get yourself some breakfast yet?"

"Um, no. I was finishing up my reading assignment for psychology. We are studying personality disorders."

He laughed. "So which one do you have?"

"Do you think I have a personality disorder?" I asked seriously.

"No," he laughed again, "It was a joke. Every student starts to wonder if they have some mental condition when they first start taking psychology. We all have a tendency to want to understand ourselves, to self-diagnose. It's normal."

"Yeah, I was worried I might be mentally ill, to be honest. I mean, don't you think it is a little bit twisted that I enjoy drinking piss?"

He busted up laughing then. "Yeah, I guess," he admitted, "but I'm not sure that makes you mentally ill. Just means you are a little kinky, and definitely sub."

I sighed. "Maybe. I just haven't really felt like a very strong person since—"

"What?" he asked.

"Since my mom died. I just feel sorta...um...sad all the time. And I feel like I am such a weak person and so...um...well, so unable to take care of myself."

"Don't be hard on yourself, Petey. I think all of that stuff is probably normal. You ever go to a grief counselor or anything?"

"No, I didn't really know there was such a thing."

"Yup. A therapist, I mean. You might need to do it. You should talk to Matt about it, see what he thinks."

"Nah, I would never bother Matt with this stuff. He'd probably dump me in a second if he thought I was crazy."

"He'd probably bend you over his knee and spank your ass just for saying that, is what he'd probably do. He would

not *dump* you just cuz you had grief issues. What kind of a
person do you think he is?"

"I'm sorry, I didn't mean it like that, Drew. Please don't
tell him I said that. I just mean...well...he already is so much
better than me. I don't want him to see any more flaws in
me." I looked over at him, feeling my emotions starting to
surface yet suppressing the urge to cry.

"Petey, shit happens. People go through stuff, and Matt
understands that. He also understands that you are a
sensitive kinda guy. Don't underestimate his love for you. He
told you last night, didn't he, that he loves you?" he stared
intently at me.

"Yeah. I know."

"Okay, then quit being down on yourself. I hate it when
my friends say bad stuff about themselves. Specially my pup
friends."

I laughed. "You have a lot of those?"

He nodded as he sipped his coffee. "A few, actually, yes.
I'll have to introduce you to some other puppy boys some
time. Some of them are so into it that they dress and act like
canine pups almost 24/7."

"Oh, geesh, well that is not what I like. I mean, um...I
don't think Matt would want that either."

"Nah, you are his pup, not his dogboy. There's a
difference."

"Really?" I asked.

"Yeah. Pups are subs who are sensitive and who crave
affection and love from their owners, just like a real puppy.
Dogboys are more like sub as in subhuman. They think of
themselves as being actual dogs who are less than their
human owners."

"Oh...wow. That seems extreme."

"See, and you thought that you were the one with the
mental illness." We laughed together. "Anyways, I'm gonna
go hop in the shower. Wanna join me?"

"Okay," I said. "Just don't try anything!"

"Aww man, never mind then!"

"Shut up!" I said teasingly and got up to follow him into the bathroom.

* * *

Tuesday night was uneventful, and Drew and I sat around the apartment watching an episode of Frasier and playing board games. He had an electronic version of Battleship, and we played three games. He beat me each time handily. I had my revenge, though, when he brought out the deluxe edition Scrabble game. I whooped him on it, earning almost triple his total point value. "Glad we're not playing for stakes," Drew confessed. "I'd be in trouble."

Before going to bed that night we decided that after school the next day I'd come back to Drew's house. I could catch a public transit bus and be dropped off only a block from the apartment complex. Then when he got home later, we could get ready to head back to my apartment for the birthday party. Drew gave me a spare key for the door so I'd be able to get in.

I called Kathie that night also, informing her of my plans. She was very sweet on the phone and concerned that I was doing okay. She made no mention of Tracy or of Matt either. Apparently Carter was going to be at the party, and other than Matt, Alex, and Drew, I did not know who else would be there. Our place was not all that big, so I could not imagine there being too extensive of a guest list.

The weather was extremely warm when I got out of class Wednesday afternoon, and I stripped off my sweater, wrapping it around my waist. I'd seen Matt do this before himself, and did so in a manner that would hopefully resemble him. It seemed the more time I spent around him, the more I tried to copy his behaviors, mimicking him in an altogether flattering kind of way. In so many ways he embodied the ideal man to me; he was the epitome. I was so

435

anxious to see him that afternoon, and wondered at what time he'd return from his vacation.

When I approached the doorway to Drew's apartment, I was surprised to hear music playing from inside. Drew could not possibly be home already. I suspected that it must be Alex. Maybe I should just not use the key at all and knock on the door instead. Pausing for a few seconds, I dismissed the idea of knocking. I did not want to bother Alex if he was there. I would just sneak in and go to the spare bedroom. I could use a nap anyways before Drew got home. I'm sure Alex wouldn't be mad because Drew had given me a key.

Quietly I turned the key in the lock and pushed the door open. I stepped into the entry hallway and set my backpack down on the floor against the wall. I then began to walk down the short hallway when I heard voices. It was Matt! Immediately I wanted to run to him, but stopped in my tracks when I overheard what he was saying. He apparently was talking to Alex and they were alone in the living room.

"Yeah, I've never had a pussy that tight...never in my life. That bitch was a fuckin barracuda. You hear the way she was screamin?"

"Fuck, that's an understatement, dude. I mean, we could hear her from the other side of the building. Don't know what you were doin to her, man, but she was fuckin wild."

Matt was laughing. "Yeah, that's not unusual."

"Fuck you, dude!" said Alex. "Yeah, you're such a fuckin stud that all the babes scream like wild animals when you're fuckin em," he said sarcastically.

"Yeah, you know it," said Matt confidently. I inched my way down the hallway then, being extremely careful to remain as quiet as I could. I crouched down into a squatting position as I approached the edge of the wall, wanting to peek around and see them but being afraid of getting caught. "Not only do I have the equipment, but I know how to use it, dude," Matt bragged to Alex.

"Shit!" said Alex, his tone again dripping with sarcasm. "You're just all that, huh?"

"I am," Matt said in a matter-of-fact manner, "and I know it. Even that frigid bitch Tracy was blown away by the way I fucked her."

"Yeah, so much that she split on ya."

"Well no bitch does that shit to me twice," he said. "She's fuckin history. I'm gonna email her my little note of disposal, just like she left me a note when she split. She fuckin doesn't deserve more than that."

Alex laughed. "That's funny, appropriate too."

"So how come we didn't hear your pussy screamin last night, since you heard us so clearly?" Matt asked. I'd never heard Matt and Alex talking like this, as one stud to another. It was totally out of context with the way I normally perceived them.

"She was more the reserved type, I guess," said Alex defensively, "but trust me, she was enjoyin it."

Matt laughed loudly, "Yeah right! She probably was sulking, pissed she didn't end up with the true stud like her pussy friend did."

"You fuckin asshole!" said Alex, though not venomously. "You really do think you're all that."

"Hey, what can I say? It's all right here." I assumed at that point that Matt was gesturing towards his groin, due to the context of his statement.

"You're all talk dude. I saw you in the locker room, and you're not all that. You ain't got any more than I do."

"Shit!" Matt said again, this time laughing harder than ever before. "You are in some major denial, dude. I got everything you got plus a few inches—say like maybe three or four— to spare."

Alex did not immediately respond to this insult to his masculinity, perhaps realizing that what Matt was saying was precisely accurate. From what I had seen of Alex the day that Drew blew him on the cable cars, Matt's assessment was

437

exactly correct. Alex's endowment was at least three inches less than Matt's. This was a no-win argument for Alex. Finally Alex spoke, "Yeah, I know you're hung pretty good," he admitted, "I shouldn't have said that."

"It's cool, dude, just chill. Don't get serious on me now, we're just messin." Matt said casually. "You know I don't care how big your cock is. We're buds."

"Yeah," said Alex, "why would it matter to me if you were bigger?"

"It wouldn't...unless..."

"What?" said Alex, again becoming defensive in his tone. "What are you sayin?"

"Not sayin anything, dude. Just there must be a reason why you're so concerned about how big my dick is."

"I'm not concerned about your dick," snapped Alex. "You're the one braggin about what a stud you are."

"Cuz of what you said about that bitch screamin," Matt added. "And then you said you said you were as big as me."

"So? What's that got to do with it? You were braggin about how much you had."

"I wasn't braggin," Matt said offhandedly, "was stating a fact. That's why she was screamin like a banshee. Plus, you are judging my size from seeing me soft at the gym. You've never seen me when I'm rock. It's fuckin huge. You'd totally know why she was screamin like that if you saw me with some major wood."

"Show it then!" Alex challenged. "Whip it out right now and show me what you've got."

"You gonna make it hard if I do?"

"Do I look like a fag to you?" asked Alex. "Do I look like I service jock cock?"

I suspected that Matt was smiling then as he did not immediately respond. "You look like you want to," he said finally. "You look like you want to real bad."

My heart was pounding in my chest as I knelt there in the hallway, disbelieving my own ears. It was unimaginable that

my owner was here now talking to this other dominant guy—
my best friend's master, no less— and was totally
emasculating him. I smiled to myself then, realizing how
much more the stud that my Matt was than was Drew's Alex.
It was funny to me that Alex was actually jealous of Matt's
big dick. It also was incredible to me that he'd allow Matt to
talk to him like this, to suggest to him that he wanted to
actually service it.

Very bravely then, I inched a little closer to the edge of
the wall, just barely poking my head out. I peered quickly
around the corner and saw that Alex had his back to me. He
was sitting in a chair across from Matt. The chair that Alex
was in was the same chair that Matt had sat comfortably in
the day I worshipped his feet. Matt was now on the sofa, the
same place where Alex had sat that same day while Drew
served him.

"Take it out," Alex finally responded, this time speaking
in a manner that sounded to me to be almost pleading.
"Please."

"I don't take out my cock, not unless it's for a good
reason," Matt said. "It only comes out to piss, to fuck, or to
get sucked."

"Okay," said Alex. "...so take it out."

Matt laughed again, this time very casually, and he
reached down to rub his crotch. He was sitting comfortably,
leaning back on the sofa with his legs spread apart. "If I take
it out, you're gonna suck it," he said confidently. "You got
it?"

Alex did not verbally respond, but merely nodded. My
heart pounded in my chest excitedly as I watched Matt then
unbutton his jeans. Slowly he unzipped himself. He was
wearing a pair of striped-print boxers. He unzipped the
jeans all the way and pulled the fly apart. Then he reached
inside the boxers and pulled his cock through their fly
opening. He was already semi hard, as he let go of his cock
and allowed it to flop up against the boxers.

"Do your job," Matt then said to Alex, offering no further instructions.

I nearly came in my pants when Alex placed his hands on the side arms of his chair to push himself up out of the comfortable seat. He smoothly slid down to the ground, moving over between Matt's legs and knelt there. I stared at Matt's cock, seeing it grow harder just from witnessing this act of submission by his dominant bud. I reached down to my own crotch then, rubbing my now hard cock impulsively. I placed my hand against the wall and stood up, wanting to get a perfect view of what was about to happen.

As I did so, Matt looked up and spotted me. Seeing me there for the first time, he offered no acknowledgment, but returned his gaze to Alex. I groped myself openly as I leaned against the wall, watching the entire scene. Alex then reached up into Matt's lap and cupped his nut sac, carefully and completely pulling it out through the fly of Matt's boxers. He tucked the flaps in around the side and rubbed his fingers gently across Matt's balls. The sensation was obviously pleasurable to Matt as his cock continued to grow. Matt thrust his hips forward, allowing Alex to grab the sides of his baggy jeans and pull them completely off. He pulled them down carefully to his ankles and removed them as any good sub would do.

Then Matt spread his legs wide, allowing Alex full access, and Alex slid dutifully in place between Matt's thighs. He bent his capped head forward then and touched Matt's cock with his lips, not yet taking it in his mouth but seeming instead to be kissing it respectfully. Oh my god! It was almost more than I could take.

Matt reached up then and placed his hands on each side of Alex's head. Alex's b-cap was positioned backwards; the bill pointed down towards his neck. Alex opened his mouth tentatively, while Matt held onto his head. Then almost as if in slow motion Matt exerted pressure with his grip, pushing Alex down on him. Alex's mouth slid around Matt's shaft, which was now fully erect, and Matt moaned pleasurably as he felt the warmth and wetness of his friend's mouth.

Now as Matt sat there, sliding his dick into the depth of Alex's throat, he finally looked up at me again, this time making full and prolonged eye contact. He smiled at me broadly and winked as I grabbed a hold of my crotch once again. I was so close to shooting in my pants that I almost could not control it. Matt seemed to realize this and shook his head slightly. I removed my hand from my groin as I watched Matt start to pump Alex on himself more rhythmically. Matt appeared to be a king as he sat there in his comfortable position of dominance. He had his legs spread apart and was holding onto Alex's head as if it were nothing more to him than a jack off toy. He was godlike, the ultimate Alpha Male. And now I knew with absolute certainty, that of the four of us—Matt, Alex, Drew, and myself—Matt ruled!

I just stood there stone-like, as I watched my owner being served. I felt no twinge of jealousy or desire to interfere in any way. I watched intently, focusing upon Matt, witnessing his pleasure. It pleased me as well, seeing him this way. I now knew how he looked when he pumped his cock in and out of my mouth. I was so thankful for this new visual.

It surprised me to see how expertly Alex sucked, actually. I would have assumed that being a Top, he would be rather inexperienced. What I did not realize was that many times Doms were previously sub. Often a Dom serves under a Master in preparation and training before assuming their own role of dominance. Alex was a few years older than Matt and me. Perhaps this had been the case with him.

When Matt approached the point where I knew that he was hedging towards orgasm, I wondered where he'd shoot. I could not imagine him pumping his load anywhere other than down the throat of his sub, although he had actually done so with me twice. My very first time serving him, he'd shot it on me and made me lick it off. The other time was when he had spanked me and had shown me that my behavior was undeserving of his cumload. Matt did not disappoint me this time though, for when he finally was about to drain himself, he forced Alex all the way down. I saw his fingers tighten around Alex's cap as he held him firmly in place. Then he moaned loudly and thrust his hips forward, pumping his load into Alex's gulping throat.

He took a good ten seconds to empty his entire load, holding Alex firmly the entire time. Then he shot his gaze over to me and nodded, mouthing the word "SHOOT." I grabbed my crotch immediately and, as commanded, fired my jizz into my own khaki trousers. I then quickly and quietly turned and dashed down the hallway into the spare bedroom to change my clothes.

Once I'd closed the door behind me I realized that I was not going to be able to get changed after all. Shit! I'd left my overnight bag in the bathroom that morning. I began pacing the floor, worried about what to do. I'd have to somehow sneak across the hall and grab my bag. I'd just need to be careful, to do it quietly enough that Matt and Alex did not hear me. It was no problem, I thought, they are preoccupied at the moment anyways, plus they have music playing. Slowly I opened the bedroom door a crack, and when I saw the coast was clear I dashed out into the hall. I turned quickly and pulled the door closed behind me. Just as I turned back around to head across the hallway, I was startled to see Alex walking down the hall directly towards me. Damn! He saw me.

I moved quickly, dashing towards the bathroom, but before I could step inside, he spoke to me. "Hey, where'd you come from?" he asked.

I was nervous at that point and starting to panic a little. I truly did not want him to know I had been here for quite some time and had witnessed him giving my owner a blowjob just moments before. If he became aware that I'd seen him, it would not only embarrass him terribly, but would also possibly affect the relationship I had with both him and his boy Drew— my best friend. "Um, hello sir," I stammered.

"When did you get here?" he repeated, "We didn't even hear you come in. You should have let Matt know you were here."

"I'm sorry sir...I ...um...I heard you guys listening to music when I got here and did not want to bother you. Right now I have to go to the bathroom...I will come out in just a minute."

Alex looked at me quizzically, most certainly aware that I was not telling the whole truth. I'd never been able to lie well, particularly not to authority figures. "You still haven't answered my question, boy. I said 'When did you get here?'"

"Oh...I'm sorry...like maybe twenty minutes ago...half hour maybe...sir." I was concerned at this point that Alex was worried I may have seen him and Matt and witnessed what they were doing.

"I don't see how we could have not heard you come in," he said.

"Well...um...you were talking about ...um...pussy, sir. And I...well...I don't feel comfortable with it, ya know. So I just...um...went into the bedroom to wait for Drew to get home."

Alex looked down at me, seeming to suddenly buy my explanation. I was turning my body away from him, trying to prevent him from getting a clear view of me. I did not want him to notice the big wet spot in my trousers. This effort on my part was not successful, unfortunately, for he suddenly did notice the spot and proceeded to grab me by the shoulders and turn me around to face him squarely. "What's this?" he asked. "Now I see why you did not tell us you were here. You were jackin off."

"No sir, no I wasn't...honest."

"You piss yourself?"

I shook my head. "Sir...I'm sorry. It was an accident."

"Wait!" Alex said, suddenly realizing something. "Matt has had this problem with you before, hasn't he? You cumming without permission and then hiding it from him. That's why he put you in chastity. You'd better come with me and face your owner!"

"No wait! It's not like that...sir, please. Matt gave me permission to cum. Honest he did. He said I could cum as often as I wanted just so I was thinking of him when I did. I could do it like that until he got back here today."

"Well, puppy boy," Alex said snottily, "Matt has been back here for hours, and if what you say is true then you already broke the rules. You were only allowed to cum until he got back. Plus, you just lied to me. You said you weren't jackin off."

"I wasn't!"

Alex then gripped my bicep very firmly and turned to begin dragging me out towards the living room. "Come on, fag, time to face the music."

"No! Stop it!" I yelled, starting to get panicked. If he dragged me out there, it surely was going to come out that I'd seen him blowing Matt, and Matt was the one who had commanded me to shoot in my pants so he'd have to tell Alex the truth. Otherwise he'd have to discipline me for something he had ordered me to do. He would never do that! I really did not want Alex to find out about me seeing him. "Let go of me!" I demanded. "Damn it! I didn't do anything wrong!"

Just then, Matt stepped into the hallway. "What's goin on?" he demanded. What is all the screamin about, and where did you come from, Petey?"

My face was flaming hot, both from anger and embarrassment. I did not like Alex seeing me with my pants all soaked with cum as they were. "This boy needs to be taught some respect!" Alex spat. "He refused to come with me, and he just fuckin swore at me! Plus, he has been jackin off again without your permission!"

Matt stood there in the archway, leaning against the wall, as he crossed his arms over his chest. He looked down at me sternly, obviously thinking about what he should do next. "Petey, get your ass outside and wait on the balcony while I talk to Alex. Now!" I pulled my arm free from Alex as he glared at me and walked briskly past them through the living room and out to the balcony. When I stepped through the sliding glass door, I turned to pull it closed behind me. Deliberately I left it open about a full inch. I wanted to see if I could hear what was being said inside. I slid down against the outside wall and sat there, leaning my head over so that my ear was as close to the opened door as possible.

Thank god! They were coming back into the living room. I'd be able to hear them. "Yeah, I heard him swear at you, Alex—" Matt was sayin. "But what were you sayin to him?"

"It doesn't fuckin matter, dude! I'm not gonna have some fagboy cussin me out. He was being defiant...totally disrespectful!"

"Just chill out, man," Matt was sayin, "I'll deal with Petey."

"That little fag has a mouth on him, Christ! Good thing he wasn't mine, I'd have slapped some respect into him."

"Alex!" Matt said sternly, sounding a little pissed himself, "careful about what you're sayin. Think about it dude. Think about what you were doin ten minutes ago and then tell me who the fuckin fag is."

Alex did not respond, at least from what I could hear. It must have been so mortifying for him to have heard this from Matt's mouth. My guess was that as soon as he'd gotten up off his knees from sucking Matt, he probably was feeling quite humbled already. Now Matt's blatant reminder did little to soothe his wounded ego. Perhaps this also was why he was trying to flex his authoritative muscle with me. He must have had to prove to himself he was still dominant.

"All right," said Matt, now calming himself, "I don't know what all was said in the hallway between you and Petey, but I

did hear him swear and am gonna deal with that. I won't
have my boy being disrespectful to anyone. But I also am
gonna tell you this. He is mine, and it's my job to discipline
him, no one else's. You got that?"

"Yeah, I got it," snapped Alex. "And you might wanna
deal with the fact that he's a liar too. He told me he wasn't
jacking off when it's obvious he was."

"Don't push it, Alex," said Matt, "I'm aware of when my
pup is lyin." Again Alex did not respond.

Shit! He was gonna discipline me again. How was it that
stuff like this kept happening to me? It wasn't even my fault
this time. I only was doing what Matt ordered me to do when
I came in my pants. Then when Alex saw me in the hall, I
had to lie; but it was merely a lie of omission. How could I
have told him the truth about why my pants really were
soaked? This was is gonna ruin everything for tonight, I
thought. Matt will refuse to come to my party now. How can
he let me have a party if I'm being punished?

I lay my head against the side of the wall and turned away
from the door. I didn't even want to hear any more of what
they were saying. God, I wish I had not come home when I
had. What I should have done was announce my presence
when I walked through the door. I should have let them see
me— both of them—and then they would not have done
what they did. I could never tell anyone about this either,
especially not Drew. He would just die if he found out his
master was sucking someone else's dick. I knew I would
have been totally devastated had it been Matt serving Alex.

Just then the patio door slid open. "Get in here." It was
Matt speaking to me. I slid up against the wall to a standing
position and looked immediately down at the ground. I
walked inside slowly, hanging my head shamefully. I knew I
was about to face punishment. Matt had moved towards the
center of the room, standing in front of the big comfortable
chair. "Look at me," he said, and I looked up into his face.
Alex was seated on the sofa.

"Petey, I'm very disappointed in you," Matt began. "The way you spoke to Alex a few moments ago was extremely disrespectful and completely unacceptable."

"Sir—" I began, but he cut me off.

"Don't interrupt me. Just keep your mouth shut til I'm finished. Just this weekend I had to discipline you for being disrespectful at the club, and now already we are back to the same lesson again. It's bullshit! You know damn well that Alex is my bud. He's my bro, and you know that you are to give him all the respect you'd give me cuz he's my equal. It's bad enough when you go around being rude to other fags and pups, but it's absolutely unbelievable when you can't even show respect to one of your superiors."

I already was crying at this point.

"What do you have to say to Alex?" he demanded.

I again looked down at the ground and then slowly turned to face Alex. He sat there comfortably, looking rather smug. "Sir, I said, as I gradually looked up at him. "I'm sorry that I was disrespectful...and disobedient. Please forgive me."

Alex did not say anything until Matt cleared his throat. "All right," Alex finally said, "apology accepted, but don't let it happen again."

"No sir," I said, "I won't."

Matt then moved over to the comfortable chair and sat down. "Get over here in front of me," he ordered. I quickly moved into position, standing directly in front of him. "Kneel," he said, and I dropped immediately to my knees. "Now what do you have to say to your Owner?" he asked.

I bowed my head humbly. "Sir, I am so sorry." Tears streamed down my face freely. "I have disappointed you again. I failed. Please forgive me. Please!" I lowered myself then, pressing my face against Matt's sneaker. He quickly moved his leg away from me, not even allowing me to touch him.

"Get up here for your punishment," he said, "bend over." I then stood up and moved close to him. He slid forward in his chair and reached up to cup his hand around the back of my neck, pulling me down over his lap. I lay draped over his knee then, like a small child who was about to be spanked. That was exactly what was going to happen, I soon discovered, as he held me there firmly in place with his left hand, forcing my head down towards the ground. He then lifted his right hand into position and brought it down forcefully against my upturned butt.

I looked up very briefly as he delivered the first blow, glancing across the room to see Alex sitting there watching. The corner of his mouth was curled into a slight smile as he watched my humiliation. He did not speak, however. Matt continued to deliver several swats to my ass, as I began to count them silently. He spanked me twelve times quickly, one-after-another, and then proceeded to deliver five far more forceful swats. My ass truly was stinging when he was finished, as he pulled me back into an upright position. "Go wait for me in the bathroom," he said, and I turned from him shamefully and did as he had ordered.

I stood there alone in the bathroom, weeping quietly as I waited for Matt to join me. I did not even know how it had been possible for me to have messed up again already. On Sunday I was so upset and despondent about the fact that Matt had gone away on a vacation with Tracy but had worked through the depressing feelings. I'd spent my time away from Matt trying so diligently to be good, anxiously awaiting the return of my owner. I'd gone to great lengths to be obedient, even asking permission before I jacked off with Drew. Never would I have dreamt that his arrival back home would be punctuated with this horrible incident of misbehavior. He should not have to constantly be reprimanding and training me, especially not for the same thing over and over. Why is it that I had not even understood the thing I'd done wrong until he just now told me before blistering my ass?

Of course it was wrong for me to talk back to Alex. What I should have done was just go willingly with him to my Owner's side. I should have trusted Matt to sort it out when I faced him. He may have had to make up an excuse for me or have simply told Alex to mind his own business, but he would not have had to then correct me for being insolent to a superior. I also understood that even though Alex had submitted to Matt and served him a few minutes before, he still was superior to me. He still was the master of this house and of my best friend Drew. He still was one of my Owner's good friends. Never should I have spoken to him in any way that appeared disrespectful. Never should I have questioned his judgment.

As I stood there, leaning against the sink and crying silently, the door to the bathroom opened. It was, of course, Matt. He stepped inside and closed the door behind him, locking it. "Come here," he said, holding his arms out to him. I lunged forward into his outstretched arms, feeling them instantly surround me. I cried aloud then, sobbing as he held onto me. He did not rebuke me for crying or even order me to stop, but allowed me to ride out my wave of emotion. When I was finished he pushed me back from him slightly, holding me at arms length to look at me. He then reached up with one hand and used his finger to wipe the tears from my eyes. "I missed ya, pup. Did you miss me?"

"Yes sir, so very much...I missed you so bad!" I was starting to cry again already.

"Yeah, well don't cry. We're together now again."

"I'm sorry Sir...I mean, I'm sorry about what I did. I should have let him bring me to you instead of fighting him. I should have trusted you to know what to do."

"Yes, very good. Didn't take you long to learn that lesson. Now, do you realize why I had to discipline you just now?"

I nodded. "Because I was bad, Sir. Because I was not respectful."

"Yeah, but more than that," he said. He seemed to be testing me to see if I fully understood some greater purpose that he obviously had. As I stared up at him, suddenly it dawned on me to what he possibly could be referring.

"You had to prove to Alex that he is still your bud—your equal?" I asked.

"Exactly," he said, "That's really impressive. I'm proud of ya."

I smiled through my tears. "I did not mean to be rude to him Sir. I just panicked. I knew he could not find out I'd seen him. It would have...well...I don't know. I just think it would have bothered him a lot. He would have been embarrassed. He would have felt like he'd been degraded in front of me or something."

"Right. You were right, pup. You did good by not telling him you saw. You just got a little over-emotional is all. If you'd have stayed calm, I'd have pulled you outta the situation, but once you yelled at Alex and swore, you left me no choice but to punish you."

I hung my head. "I know, Sir. I'm sorry."

"You're just being my pup, that's all. I know you meant him no disrespect. He had to see you punished though. Do you understand why?"

"Well, I think so, Sir."

"Why?" he asked, like a teacher in school prodding a student to come up with the right answers.

"Because if he did not see me punished, he would think that you considered me equal with him?" I asked.

"Yep," he said. "He already was feeling pretty humble after what happened."

"That was so hot!" I whispered. "Oh god, seeing him serve you like that!"

"You like that?" he smiled down at me. "You like seeing your owner getting served by another Dom guy?"

"Yeah! I liked it so much. I kept thinking how awesome you looked. I never get to see you like that when I serve you."

He laughed. "Guess we'll have to video tape it sometime, huh?"

"That would be way cool," I said excitedly.

"Take off your clothes, pup. We need to get you cleaned up. You got a birthday party to go to."

"I still get to go?" I asked with surprise.

"Course you do, silly. Why wouldn't you?"

"I thought cuz of being punished. Or I thought you would not go."

"Pup," he sighed, "Why would you think I would do something so mean to you? I'm not gonna make you miss your own party, not cuz of something like this."

"No! I don't think you're mean sir. I'm sorry! I thought...um...that you would only do that if I deserved it."

"Well you don't." He sat down on the toilet now, pulling me over to stand in front of him. He reached out and grabbed my shirt tail, pulling it up over my head as I raised my arms. He got it halfway off so that my arms were completely entangled in the shirt and then brought his hand down quickly to tickle my underarm. I immediately squirmed and laughed.

"Sir! It's tickling me!"

"No?" he said sarcastically. He pulled the shirt the rest of the way off and pulled me into him, kissing me full on the lips. "Geesh, you're getting hard again already, and you haven't even cleaned up your last mess." He was referring to my cum soaked khakis.

"Yeah, and my butt still hurts too...from the spanking."

He laughed. "You can endure a little pain for your owner, can't ya pup? You can take it."

I nodded quickly. "Yes sir! I can." He wrapped each of his big hands around my smooth sides, rubbing them gently up and down. It tickled me slightly but also felt incredibly sensual. "Sir, I love you so much."

"Love ya too pup," he said, kissing me again. "Get undressed. I wanna be inside you."

451

I then proceeded to unbutton my khakis, standing there in front of him shirtless. I smiled as I stripped for my Owner, and finally I stood there completely naked, my clothes in a heap behind me. I felt so extremely small and vulnerable, feeling almost as if on display for him. He surveyed me, smiling himself in a way that was so seductive. He knew how much he owned me; he knew that the person before him was his to have and to use as he chose. He knew that I was aware of his superiority, that I had accepted my position as his owned property. I stood there quietly, looking so very smooth and innocent...so young.

Matt reached out to me then and cupped my butt cheeks in each of his hands. He pulled me over to him so that the entire torso of my small body was pressed against his. He moved his hands slowly and very cautiously up and down my backside, easing his way down my legs and then back up. He pressed his lips against my nipple, darting his tongue out very briefly, merely to tease, I think. I squirmed and laughed as he did so, suddenly forgetting about all else in the entire world. We were the only two who now existed. There was no Alex or Drew or Tracy. There was no birthday party or school or work. There was only him and me. He was all that mattered.

I felt my own hardness as my body pressed against him. I was so aroused, even though only a few minutes before I had cum in my pants in the living room. He pushed me back away from him then, holding me out so that he could once again take in the entire sight of me. He reached down and very gently cupped my shaved nut sac in his hands. I stood as perfectly still as I possibly could, trying not to show any resistance even though the sensation of his touch was tickling me, sending shivers throughout my body. My cock

452

throbbed as he held my balls, and he looked me in the eyes. "Who do these belong to?" he asked me.

"To you Sir," I said quietly.

"That's right pup. I own every part of you—every single part—which means I own what's inside em too. It's not even your cum. It's mine. Pups cum is my cum. You understand?"

"Yes Sir," I said.

"And my cum is never wasted. My cum goes in pups mouth or pups ass...always. That's why when you shoot, you have to eat it."

"Yes Sir," I said, smiling at him.

He then turned me around, inspecting the backside of me. He cupped my ass cheeks in his hands, pulled them gently apart. "Who does this belong to?" he said.

"To you sir," I said again, this time a little louder being that I was looking away from him.

"That's right, pup. Your ass belongs to me. It is mine to use as I wish. It is what holds my cum, it's what allows me inside of you."

"Yes Sir," I said.

"You want me inside you?" he whispered to me. He was pulling me closer to him, pressing his chin against my shoulder. "You want your owner's cum inside you?"

"Yes Sir!" I cried, my voice starting to quiver. It was almost a whimper.

"Prove it. Show me how bad you want it, pup."

I turned back around, facing him eye-to-eye. With him sitting on the toilet and me standing, he was at eye level. I quickly rectified this mis-positioning by falling immediately to my knees. I stared up at him hungrily, my eyes wide as I implored him, "Sir, I beg you...please."

"Please what?" he asked, as he looked down at me. "What do you want?"

"Please Sir...please use me. Please use me for your pleasure."

"Why?" he asked. "Why should I?"

"For you, Sir. Do it to please yourself...oh please!" I knelt there staring up at him, my voice a mere whimper, high-pitched and whiney.

"For me?" he asked sarcastically, actually laughing as he said it. "I don't need you, pup. I don't need you at all. I can walk out of here right now and get my dick sucked by Alex if I want. I could even fuck him. Shit, I could just go get more pussy."

"Oh please Sir!" I cried, a tears now streaming down my cheek. "I beg you Sir. I know it's true. I know you don't need me, and I know I don't deserve you. But I'm begging you...oh please! Please let me feel you inside me! Please let me hold your cum in my body...oh please!!"

He stood up then, standing with both of his legs on either side of me. "Kiss my feet, fag," he said, "and beg to serve!" I pressed my hands on the ground in front of me and immediately slid myself backwards. I then lay prostate on the floor beneath him, my mouth pressing against his left shoe. I kissed it reverently. I then slid over on the ground, keeping my body pressed flat against the ground, and kissed his right shoe.

"I'm nothing compared to you Sir!" I whispered. "I love you so much and want to serve you. Oh please...please Sir, I beg you.

"Untie them," he ordered. I complied immediately, knowing already I was not to use my hands. I gripped his laces in my teeth and pulled them, untying his shoes humbly. I then loosened each of the laces with my teeth, carefully moving down each shoe. He then braced himself against the wall and toed off each shoe. I used my mouth to move them out of the way. "You should have your collar on, pup," he said.

"It is in my bag Sir," I said, remembering immediately that I'd left it with my clothes. He reached over to the far side of the sink and picked up the bag, dropping it carelessly on the floor in front of me.

"Get it out!" he said. I lay there then and unzipped the bag, using only my teeth. I pushed my face into the bag and pulled the collar out with my mouth, gripping it firmly in my teeth. I then slid backwards a little further and pushed myself up to a kneeling position in front of my owner. The collar dangled from my mouth as I moved my hands behind my back, gripping my left wrist with my right hand. I stared up at him, now begging only with my eyes.

Matt took the collar from me, and ceremoniously placed it around my neck, tightening it securely. Then he reached into his jean pocket and removed something. It was a rubber plug of some sort with a flat end. I knew what it was, actually, for I'd seen pictures on the internet. It was a butt plug. This particular one was about three inches long and somewhat fat. He held it in front of me. "Open up," he said, and then he shoved it into my mouth. He pushed it in all the way as if giving a baby his pacifier. I wrapped my lips around its base obediently and sucked on it. It was only natural for me to do so.

"Gonna give you your birthday present, pup," he said. "Something very special to wear to the party—Me." I looked up at him wide-eyed, with my mouth stuffed by the butt plug. "I'm gonna fuck my cum load into my cum receptacle— You. Then you're gonna wear it inside you...to your party. You understand."

I nodded rapidly as I looked up at him. He then unbuttoned his jeans and stepped out of them. He peeled his jersey over his head. "Stand at the sink!" he said. He then reached around me and lubed his finger, using some liquid soap from a dispenser on the sink. He quickly slid it inside me, twisting his finger back and forth. He pumped another squirt of soap onto his palm then and lubed his cock. He grabbed my waist with both hands as I bent over a little further. I knew he was watching himself in the mirror. As he forcefully slid into me, grabbing my hips and pulling me all the way onto him, I bit down on the butt plug. The pain shot through my rectum as I moaned and grimaced, forcing myself to endure. I remembered Matt's words to me just moments before, "You can endure a little pain for your owner, can't ya pup? You can take it." He then proceeded to fuck me savagely, not pausing for a second until he was to the point of no return. He slammed all the way into me, holding me firmly in place. I felt his cock throb as he drained himself deep inside me.

Matt then reached around my body, pulling me to an upright position. He whispered in my ear, "I'm inside ya now, pup. You're gonna wear me to the party." He pulled the plug from my mouth then and slipped his cock out of me. Quickly he slid the butt plug into position and with one smooth movement he capped me, plugging my hole to keep the entire content of his hot load in my body.

"Now get in the shower." Matt cleaned himself at the sink and then got redressed while I showered. When I was done, he toweled me dry, checking to make sure my plug was still secure. Then he dressed me in tight white briefs and a pair of baggies. He told me to go down to his car and get a jersey from his duffle bag. Shirtless and barefoot, I obeyed him without question. When I returned, he and Alex were sitting in the living room, in the same positions they'd been when I arrived ninety minutes previously. Nothing more was said about my disciple or the argument that had ensued earlier. I pulled on the over-sized jersey and went to my owner, sitting on the floor at his feet, knowing that he was also inside me.

25

When Drew got home a few minutes later, I was still sitting quietly at my owner's feet. He smiled at us sweetly and said, "That's so cute. Petey, you look like a miniature version of Matt."

"I know," I said, grinning broadly. Drew walked over and kissed Alex on the mouth, pulling back from him slowly. He then glanced over to me, puzzled.

"Matt...um, Sir.." he said, "May Petey come with me into the bedroom so he can help me pick out my clothes for tonight?"

"Sure," said Matt, tousling my hair. "Go ahead, pup." I jumped up and followed Drew into the master bedroom.

"What's wrong, Drew?" I asked, knowing immediately that something was not right due to the look he'd given me back in the living room.

"It's Alex," Drew whispered. "It was like...um...well, his kiss tasted funny. It was like he has been suckin cock or something."

I laughed nervously. "I'm sure, Drew. You already know that can't be true. Maybe it is just something he ate."

"Maybe, but I know what it tastes like when someone cums in your mouth, and what it tastes like afterwards."

"Oh...well why would a total top like Alex be suckin dick?" I asked.

"Hmm...or the more important question is, 'Who would he be sucking?'," Drew responded.

"Speaking of fucking, that's what Matt did to me when I got home. He did it in the bathroom."

Drew laughed. "Must've been pretty hot for you."

"And guess what he did afterwards?" I asked. Drew shrugged and smiled. "He plugged me!" I said. "I'm wearin a plug right now."

"Uncomfortable?" he asked.

I shook my head. "No, just feels a little weird. Plus, it keeps feeling like I've had an accident or something...in my pants."

"Must've dumped a big load into ya, huh?"

"Yeah."

"Don't worry, you'll get used to it. So how long you gotta wear it?"

"I've got to wear it all through the party, at least. It's kinda big, too. Sometimes when I move just right it makes me get hard," I laughed.

"That's the idea. Keeps you thinkin of your owner. I just can't believe that Alex would bottom for someone. That really worries me."

"Drew, stop it! You know Alex would never bottom for anyone. He's a top, and he's your owner. Probably he'd punish you just for sayin that."

"I know, you're right. I should take my own advice and stop worrying. I'm starting to sound like you now." I put my hand on his shoulder reassuringly. I knew that Drew would be freaked if he found out about Alex blowing Matt. Now, more than ever, I was determined to keep it from him. I did not want my best friend to be hurt by all of this.

"Yeah, and you don't wanna be like me, of all people," I said lightheartedly. "What are you gonna wear?" I asked.

"Oh, I got it all picked out, don't worry. Let's go out to the patio so I can have a smoke," he said. "Could that jersey be any bigger?" he asked as he tugged on the shirttail.

"It's Matt's," I said. "He ordered me to wear it."

"Cool. You look like a little boy."

"Let me get some shoes on before we go outside. I left 'em in the bathroom." I turned and headed out into the hallway. When I got to the bathroom door, Alex was inside, standing at the sink. He was brushing his teeth. Why the fuck didn't he do that before Drew got home, I wondered. I would have bet anything that Matt noticed Drew's puzzled look and told Matt to go brush.

"Excuse me, sir," I said, as I reached inside the door to grab my shoes and socks. "I really am sorry about before, sir. Please forgive me."

"No praw-lum" he said, his mouth full of toothpaste. Then he jabbed my shoulder affectionately with his fist. "You haf uh goo par-ee tu-nigh," he said.

"Thank you, sir." I turned quickly and headed back to the bedroom. "How was work?" I asked as I saw Drew was pulling some papers from his attaché case.

"Oh...same ole, same ole," he said. "I've got this whole stack of term papers to grade....ughh!" He tossed the stack on the dresser. "But I'll deal with this shit later. Need a smoke right now." I followed behind him as he walked down the hallway towards the patio. He glanced in the bathroom on his way through, seeing Alex at the sink.

"You see that?" he asked once we were outside. "Alex was brushing his teeth."

"Well, you said his mouth tasted funny. Like I said, he probably just ate something that left a bad taste."

"Yeah, right. Well, anyways, it is not for me to worry about. He's my master, and if he feels like suckin some dick, it's his prerogative. Guess it's no worse than eating pussy."

"Eww...I wonder if Matt does that." I scrunched up my nose, making an ugly face. "I hope not!"

"Well, then don't ever ask. Sometimes it's best not to know everything there is to know."

"I agree," I said, thinking just how true that statement actually was.

"You know, though, Alex has sucked cock before, but it was before I met him."

"Really?" I asked, "How do you know."

"He told me about it. He was not always dominant like he is now. I mean, well, he always knew he was dominant, but for awhile he was just sorta exploring...you know, experimenting. For some guys, they have to figure out they

461

are gay— or in his case bi — before they really understand about the Dom/sub culture."

"Yeah, I guess maybe it shouldn't surprise me so much, cuz look how he is president of the Gay Student Alliance. He must at least partially consider himself gay."

"Well, he does, yeah. I know this is gonna sound weird, but the way he feels about it is that he is 'gay' but not a fag. He makes a distinction between the two terms."

"He's like a superior gay guy then, huh?"

"Yeah, or more like a superior bi guy. Really, he doesn't do pussy that much though. Just once in awhile like this weekend."

"I know. They were talking about it when I got home, bragging about how they made these chicks scream when they fucked 'em last night."

"Christ. Well, have to say I'm not sorry I missed that conversation."

"Believe me, Drew, you should not be sorry at all." Suddenly the patio door opened behind us. It was Alex.

"Drew, get in here," he said. Drew crushed out his cigarette immediately and went inside. I followed behind, pulling the door shut behind me. "Go into the bedroom and wait for me," he said. I looked over to Matt, wondering what was goin on. Matt didn't say anything but motioned for me to come to him. I went over and stood by his chair.

"Okay, bud, we're gonna head out then," said Matt. "Petey, go grab your stuff, cuz we gotta get goin." Matt stood up and walked over to Alex. "Great times, bud," he said to Alex. "Gonna have to get together again like this, maybe take the fags next time."

"Sure," said Alex casually. "I'll see you in a couple hours, dude...at Petey's."

"See ya," said Matt. Alex turned and headed for the bedroom. I dashed into the bathroom and grabbed my bag. I picked up my backpack from the entryway as we left together. When we walked down to the car, Matt pulled me into himself, wrapping his arm around my shoulder. "We had to get outta there," he said.

"Why, Sir?" I asked, looking up to him.

"Alex needed to do some reaffirming."

"What's that mean?" I asked sincerely. "Reaffirming of what sir?"

"His status. He needs to dominate his boy...remind himself he is still top dog in his house."

"You mean after...um...what he did with you?"

"Yep. Poor Drew's gonna probably show up to your party with a sore ass and throat."

I laughed. "He won't mind."

"Nah, good for him," laughed Matt. "Let's go over to the gym before we go to your house. We got a couple hours to spare."

"Cool," I said, "and you can show me where you work. And workout."

"Uh huh," he said. "Better put your necklace on though before we get there. Not that I mind showin off my pup, but not sure they are ready to see an owned and collared puppy boy at the gym yet."

"I'll wait til we are almost there Sir. Okay? I wanna wear it for as long as possible."

"Good boy," he said

* * *

When we walked into the gym, you would have thought that God himself had entered. The entire staff made obvious attempts to cater to Matt, dropping what they were doing to greet him and to see if they could do anything for him. He brushed each of them off, though politely, telling them that he was just here showing a friend around. I smiled to myself at this description of me, all of a sudden feeling rather important.

The main gym was divided into three equal-sized rooms. The first room contained aerobic equipment—treadmills, stair masters, things like that to get your heart rate up to the acceptable level at the beginning of a workout. Matt explained this to me as we walked through the room. He led me to the second room, which had mainly just benches and floor mats. There was a rack of ankle and wrist weights and some small hand-held five and ten pound weights as well. I also noticed one of the customers using a huge rubber ball. This lady was lying on it, face down, and stretching her arms out as far as she could in front of her. I giggled quietly as I watched, and Matt explained to me that this room was mainly used for calisthenics rather than weight training.

Finally, he led me into the third room of the gym which contained all of the weight-lifting equipment. I noticed a lot of the machines were similar to the ones that Matt had in his home gym. He stopped at each one and described it to me, telling me what area of the body benefited from the use of that particular machine. On the far side of the room was a wall covered with floor-to-ceiling mirrors. About five feet back from the mirrors were old fashioned weight benches, the kind that most people used to have in their garages and basements, with those big plastic-coated weights that slid onto the barbell. The weights that were displayed here, though, were steel. To the left of us was a rather muscular man sitting on one of the benches staring at himself in the mirror. He had his arm positioned against his knee and was lifting a dumbbell which appeared to be of considerable weight. He was doing bicep curls. I watched in amazement at the sheer strength, seeing his muscles flex as he performed his workout. Matt looked down at me and smiled, "Wait til you see me work out, pup," he said and tousled my hair affectionately.

Matt then led the way into the locker room and showers. "Not much to see in here, pup," he said. "Just naked people, lot of old geezers around this time of day. But hey, everyone needs to stay in shape, huh?"

I nodded in agreement with him as he led me back into the hallway. "Let's go to the office," he said. We walked all the way back through the main gym and towards the front door. Then Matt led me up a flight of stairs which led to another hallway. I walked briskly to keep up with him as he reached in his pocket for a set of keys. He opened the door to a room clearly labeled "office" and stepped inside. The room was enormous and very plush. A huge wooden desk was at the far side of the room and behind it was a gigantic window which contained one-way glass. We stepped over to the window and looked down, seeing the entire gym below us. Literally every section of the gym except for the showers was visible from this vantage point. We could see the front desk and every employee, even the staircase which we had just ascended. "They can't see us," he reminded me. "The other side of the window is metallic. Did you notice it from below?"

"No sir," I said, shaking my head.

"Most people don't, but we can see everything that is going on from up here." He also pointed to the upper corner of the room. "And we have security cameras for inside and out of the building."

"Wow, you must feel like god up here, huh?"

"That's what I am, aren't I?" he asked, laughing to himself.

"To me you are sir," I admitted.

"How's your butt feel?" he asked. "That plug still firmly in place?"

"Yes sir, I'm totally used to it now."

"You like keeping me inside of you like that?" he asked.

"Very much!" I nodded. "I like it very, very much."

He smiled at me affectionately. "Next month we are beginning a remodel project here," he said. "Actually we aren't making many changes to the existing facility, but we are gonna add on."

"Really? It's already so big already."

465

"Yeah, but we are building classrooms. Well, actually not classrooms like in a school, but an entire wing for aerobics, yoga, personal weight training, and martial arts classes."

I laughed. "You gonna take yoga, sir?"

"Don't laugh pup, yoga is not just for wimps. Lots of jocks do it. But no, I'm not into that myself. You are gonna take a class though."

"Of yoga?" I said, surprised.

"Nah, martial arts."

"Why would I take that, sir? I mean other than that you told me to...but why?"

"So you can defend yourself. If you had known martial arts last November, you could have kicked those bullies' asses."

"Yeah, but then I might not have met you, sir."

"Maybe, but I think if two people are supposed to be together, it will happen one way or another."

"Really? So you think that we are meant to be together?" I could not believe he had just made this statement to me.

"Sure...don't you? I mean you told me that you knew from the minute you met me that you wanted to serve me, to belong to me. Right?"

"Yes, sir, it's true."

"So wouldn't you have known that even if I had not rescued you from that attack?"

"Yeah...um...yes sir, but what you did for me really made you seem like a hero, even more than you did already."

"Well we are gonna teach you to be a hero yourself, not that you need to know martial arts to do that, but won't ever hurt to learn new skills. Plus martial arts will teach you to feel better about yourself. Will make you a stronger person inside."

"Cuz I'm weak, right?"

"No, not because you are weak. I've never considered you weak, pup. Hey, if you can take my big cock all the way up your ass, you can't be too weak."

466

I laughed. "I'll never be strong like you, though, sir. I don't wanna be. I want you to protect me."

"I'll always try to protect you pup, but you also have to learn to protect yourself. I'm not with you every minute of the day, ya know."

"I know, but I wish you were."

"Way it should be," he said. "My pup should always be glad to be with his owner." He turned and scanned the room with his eyes. There was a big leather couch in the corner of the room and two chairs, all surrounding a big glass coffee table. In addition to the computer on the desk, there were two other smaller stands, each with a computer of their own. One wall had an enormous filing cabinet, all neatly labeled. The room also was immaculately clean. There was a metal statue in one corner, depicting an athlete who was about to hurl a shot put into the air. "This is all gonna be mine some day...someday soon," he said. "My dad is gonna probably retire within the next year or so, and this is only one of the many offices that he has. He does most of his work from here, though."

"Are you nervous about it, sir? I mean all the responsibility."

"No, I've been around it all my life. Have known since I was a kid that the business would be mine. Already I know how to do most of what needs to be done. I think I'm here about as much as my dad is any more."

"Maybe some day I'll end up working for you sir," I suggested.

"It's possible," he said, "but you also have to decide what you wanna do for yourself. You have to pursue the things you enjoy, find a job you are happy with."

"I'd be happy being with you sir. That would always be enough."

"What is it that you like to do, pup? Before you met me, what did you have in mind for a career?"

"Um, I don't know. It's weird, sir, cuz I was just thinking of this the other day. I think I want to do something charitable, like maybe work for a non-profit organization. Or maybe be an author, cuz I like to write."

"And you like to cook," he added.

"Yeah, but I can't see myself as a chef. I'm not bossy enough."

He laughed. "Well why don't you write me something? Write a short story for me."

"I don't know sir. I said I like to write; didn't say I was any good."

"Well you write it, and I will decide."

"I know. I'll write a story about being your pup. I'll write the story of how we met."

"Cool," he said, "but how's it gonna end?"

"Don't know yet, sir. We're still living it." I laughed.

"Well it's getting close to time for your party. Think we should motor?"

"Sure," I said, "I'm ready when you are...always."

I took one last look around the huge room before we exited. It was exciting to know that this was soon going to be Matt's personal office. I only hoped that I'd always have a place in his life. I did not want the relationship that we had to ever die, for I couldn't imagine living without him. Ever.

26

When Matt and I arrived at my apartment building I actually was reluctant to go inside. Suddenly I felt incredibly uncomfortable, not used to being the center of attention. I would have much rather been going to a party in Matt's honor or even Drew's—anyone but myself, actually. "I wish we could just skip it sir," I confided in Matt.

"Why pup? Why would you say that? This is your party, why would you want to just skip it?"

"I don't know, sir. I just don't like it. What am I supposed to do? What do I say to people?"

He laughed. "Just be yourself. Only people who are gonna be here are your friends. They like you just the way you are. Don't gotta worry about doin anything special."

"I know," I said, "just feels weird, is all."

"C'mon," he said, grabbing my wrist and pulling me up the steps behind him. "Can't be late for your own party." We stood by the door as I nervously slid my key into the lock.

"Did it look like there were extra cars in the lot?" I asked Matt. "I wonder how many people are here."

"Just go in and find out...geesh!" he sighed.

"Sorry," I said as I turned the key and pushed the door open. I stepped through the doorway cautiously and was suddenly overtaken by a room full of cheers and applause, a few people yelling "Surprise!"

I busted up laughing. "Hey, this is not a surprise party! I already knew about it!" Kathie came over to me and hugged me.

"Happy birthday, honey," she said as I again laughed. I felt my face burning up. I knew I was red from embarrassment. Quickly I scanned the small apartment and noticed the room was full of people. Actually, there were about fifteen people there, but that was a lot for our sized apartment. Two of my coworkers from the bookstore were there, one of our cousins, Kathie and Carter, Drew and Alex, a few of our neighbors, and one of my friends from high school which I had not seen in a long time. In reality, it actually was quite a surprise to me to see all of these people. I'd been expecting only Alex, Drew, Matt, and Carter. Quickly I turned to Matt, imploring him with my eyes. I did not want him to leave my side and inched my way closer to him as people gathered around us.

"Did you expect so many people?" Kathie asked excitedly.

"Um...no. Not at all," I admitted. "How did you get so many people to show up?"

"Hmm, don't know...maybe cuz...um...they like you?" she offered sarcastically.

I just laughed as I reached out to hug Carrie from the bookstore. "I'm so glad that you came. What a surprise!"

As I surveyed the guests around me, I knew I was going to have to start making some introductions. Most of these people were strangers to Matt and vice-versa. Suddenly, my pulse quickened as I realized I was going to have to decide how to introduce him. I did not want to offend him by stating that he was merely a friend, yet I also did not want to embarrass or out him in any way. I wished that I'd have thought to ask him about this previously. Quickly I looked over to Drew, who was standing about ten feet away from me. As I saw him and Alex standing together I realized that they did not necessarily even look like a couple. The average person would think of them merely as friends, just a couple of buds hangin together. Perhaps that would be the best way to handle the situation with Matt. I'd introduce him as a friend, and if he chose to reveal more, he could correct me.

"Carrie, I want you to meet my....um...best friend, Matt."

"He's your best friend and you had to think about it?" she giggled. She extended her hand to Matt, "Hi there, Mr. Best Friend, nice to meet you." He shook her hand graciously and offered no correction to my intro, so I assumed all was well and proceeded to move around the room and do the same with each of the other guests.

Kathie interrupted us briefly to offer us beverages. I elected to have a diet pop and Matt asked for a beer. Probably at some point before the party was over I'd indulge and have a wine cooler or something, but I knew that to have any alcohol now would be enough to cause me serious embarrassment later. My cousin Marc was over in the corner messing with the stereo. Obviously he had volunteered to take charge of the music. It was a good thing, actually, for he worked as a DJ for one of the local clubs, and he had tons of CD's at his disposal.

I was trying desperately to make my way to Drew, for I wanted so much to make him feel at home, yet each time I moved in his direction, someone seemed to step in the way. He did not seem to be having any problems with the mingling though, for he was conversing with another one of my coworkers whom I was sure he had not previously met. Finally when I did make my way to his side, he turned and hugged me affectionately. "I see you met Tim," I said to him, referring to my coworker. "Thank you so much for coming Tim," I said, smiling.

"Nice place you have here," Tim stated.

"Yeah, nice and small," I said jokingly, "but thanks."

I pulled Drew aside when Tim turned to talk to someone behind him. "Drew what happened after we left."

"Oh my god!" he whispered. "Alex must have really missed me while he was gone. You would not believe the way he fucked me." We both laughed together.

"Guess it's true that absence makes the heart grow fonder."

"Yeah, well you got yours from Matt too, remember?"

"Uh huh...I am wearing the evidence right now!"

"Appetizers?" offered Kathie as she approached us holding a tray.

"Wow, you really went all out, Kathie," I said. "I hope we can afford this..." I lowered my voice.

"Don't worry, we can. I received a large donation," she cocked her head in Matt's direction.

"See! He is not such a bad guy," I said to her and then turned to look over to Matt lovingly. He was talking to Marc, I think asking him about the club where he worked.

"I never said he was bad, Petey. I just said to be careful, but we don't need to talk about it now. I just want you to have a great party!"

"Thanks," I said sincerely. "Thank you for doing this. I've never had a party before."

"Look at all the gifts you got," said Drew, pointing over to a card table at the edge of the living room. "You're a popular dude."

"Oh my god!" I said excitedly. "People brought gifts?"

Drew and Kathie laughed together. "Duh! It is a birthday party," Drew said.

"If you wanna smoke, we can go out on the patio," I suggested.

"Yeah, good idea." Just as we turned to move in that direction, Kathie grabbed my arm.

"Petey, wait a second, there's someone that I want you to meet." Quickly I turned to face her.

"Okay," I said politely. Standing next to her was an attractive young man, about Matt's height. He looked to be around twenty, with wavy blonde hair, and his body was very toned and fit. He was sharply dressed and I immediately caught a scent of his cologne, Obsession for Men. He smiled at me graciously.

"Petey, this is Carter's friend Cam," she said.

"Hey Cam, nice to meet you," I said, extending my hand.

"Cameron actually...please" he said. "Don't know why, but I've never liked the abbreviation."

"Oh..." I said. "Well nice to meet you, Cameron," I corrected myself. "Thank you for coming to the party."

"Sure," he said, "Your sister has told me so much about you. I've been dying to meet you!"

"Really?" I said, turning to look at Kathie. "Funny you didn't mention anything to me about Cameron."

"Well I've hardly seen you this past week." Nervously I turned to look for Matt. He was still in the corner talking to Marc.

"Yeah, I've been kinda busy," I craned my neck to look very deliberately in Matt's direction, but was failing to catch his attention.

"Mind if I join you guys outside?" asked Cameron. "I could use a smoke myself."

"Sure, come on ahead," said Drew. "More the merrier. I shot a warning look to Drew, but it was too late. Drew and Cameron were both digging their cigarettes from their pockets and heading for the door. I lingered a second, allowing myself time to turn to Kathie.

"What's going on?" I asked.

"Nothing, honey. What do you mean? I just wanted you to meet Cam. He's such a great guy."

I squinted my eyes as I looked at her. "I know what you are trying to do," I whispered. "I don't need to be set up with anyone. I already have a boyfriend!"

She rolled her eyes, frustrated. "I'm not trying to do anything, Petey. It's just that Carter introduced me to this friend of his who happened to be gay. I told him my brother was gay and he wanted to meet you."

"Okay sorry. I just don't want him getting any of the wrong ideas."

When I joined Cameron and Drew on the patio, Cameron had already launched into some political dissertation about civil rights. "And we simply are not going to put up with it any longer. It's time that stood up and MADE them hear our voice. We will not be ignored."

"Whatcha talkin bout?" I asked, butting into their conversation.

"Gay rights," said Drew.

"*Civil* rights," corrected Cameron, "the rights of all people to be treated equally."

"Cool," I said, "Did you know Drew is an advisor for the Gay Student Union at the community college? His boyfriend is president," I added proudly. Immediately I wondered if it had been appropriate for me to reveal this personal information about my best friend, but when I looked over to Drew he did not seem bothered.

Cameron laughed heartily. "Oh, well I'm not talking about that sort of thing. These community groups and such are really just small potatoes. I'm talking about affecting some *real* change in our society— national campaigns, media blitzes, world-wide solidarity. These so-called rallies and such that the local organizations attempt are actually quite laughable. Nobody pays any attention."

I raised my eyebrows, looking to Drew and waiting for his response. He merely shrugged. "I don't know," he said casually and quite politely, "We got the administration to add security cameras." I nodded in agreement with him.

"Whatever," Cameron said flippantly. "Has your group participated in any larger campaigns? What are you doing to show support of the Gay Marriage Act?"

"I don't know, nothing, I guess," Drew answered. "Our entire membership is mainly college kids. I doubt that most of them are really concerned about marriage right now."

"See... It just goes to show you how short-sighted these groups can be. Frankly, with that kind of apathy, it's no wonder we are still so oppressed." Drew and I looked to one another and smiled, not really knowing how to respond to him. Cameron, however, did not even notice this, for he was already off on another tangent, this time railing against the 'Don't Ask, Don't Tell' policy. "I have personally met Elizabeth Birch of the Human Rights Campaign. You should hear what she has to say about Clinton." I thought to myself, how else do you meet someone if not personally? And who is

Elizabeth Birch and what's the Human Rights Campaign? I did not voice these questions though, but merely nodded in agreement with him.

Cameron's attitude and cockiness were unquestionably annoying to me as I stood there listening to him go on and on, but I definitely could not deny that he was attractive. He could have modeled for GQ, no doubt. In spite of his strong self-assurance, or perhaps because of it, I could not really pull myself away from him. Maybe it was his domineering air or his projection of self confidence. I was starting to be drawn into him. And even though he was a bit condescending, the things that he was saying made a lot of sense to me. I mean, we could try all we wanted to change some of the small things when it came to civil rights issues, but if we ignored the big picture, it would really do no good in the long run.

"—and I have this one lesbian friend named Cindy from Orlando. She is in this relationship with this super bitch Gestapo-type dyke. It drives me crazy how she lets her girlfriend boss her around. Cindy thinks she has to get permission before she even does anything. Christ, she can't even leave the house without asking for permission."

"Yeah, I've known a few people in those controlling type relationships," said Drew, turning to glance at me. He had a slight grin which probably was unnoticeable to Cameron.

"How could anyone— a lesbian no less— subject herself to that constant oppression? Aren't we beyond that sort of thinking? Didn't slavery go out in the 1800's?"

"So you think it's wrong for your friend to want to obey her girlfriend?" I asked sincerely.

"Duh!" shot back Cameron. "If two people are in a genuinely loving relationship, they are equal. Neither one of them has the right to control the other. As far as I'm concerned it's nothing but glorified slavery."

"Well personally I feel—" Drew started to say when the door behind us opened. It was Kathie and Carter.

"Hey!" said Cameron. "Come on out and join us. We were just talking about civil rights and unequal relationships."

Kathie laughed, "Yeah, I know you, Cameron. You are very passionate about the things you believe in. Actually, what I wanted was to let you know that we should get Petey back in here to open his gifts."

Carter placed his hand on my shoulder. "Happy birthday, bud. Feel any older?"

"No...but only cuz my birthday isn't really until tomorrow," I laughed.

Drew grabbed my wrist suddenly, "Come on, Petey, let's go open your gifts!" He pulled me back into the apartment, stepping around Carter and Kathie.

"Come on, Cameron," Kathie said. "Don't wanna miss the main event." He crushed out his cigarette and followed us back into the living room.

As I walked over towards the card table at the far side of the room, it felt as if all eyes were upon me, as the room got quieter. God, I hated this feeling! I reached out and grabbed Drew, this time holding his wrist. Gently he pulled himself free of my grasp and put his arm around me. "Don't be nervous, guy. Everyone here is your friend," he whispered. I made a funny face to him and felt my knees getting wobbly. Kathie had seemed to disappear all of a sudden.

Within a few seconds someone turned off the lights, and it was very dim in the room for the only illumination was from the now-silent stereo and from a couple candles that had been lit. I turned suddenly as I saw flickering lights coming from the kitchen area. It was Kathie, and she was carrying a cake covered with nineteen birthday candles. All of a sudden Cameron burst into song, leading the others in a chorus of "Happy Birthday." I instantly felt myself blushing. They continued to sing as Kathie approached me, holding the cake out in front of me. It was awesome, decorated expertly with a remarkable likeness of Harry Potter flying

476

around on a his Nimbus 2000. "Wow!" I said. "That's a cool cake."

Once they had finished singing, Drew urged me on, demanding that I make a wish. "Make a wish now, Petey, but don't say it aloud. Then blow out your candles." I closed my eyes tightly, thinking hard about what my wish should be, then slowly I opened them and looked up. Matt was standing directly in front of me, on the other side of the cake. I smiled at him, knowing instantly what my wish would be, and inhaled a deep breath before blowing with all my might to extinguish the burning candles. Everyone cheered loudly.

"That was quite a blowjob," Drew said to me quietly. "I knew you were skilled, but geesh!" We laughed together as I looked directly into Matt's eyes. He was everything to me, my whole world, and my wish had been that he'd feel the same about me. I did not know that I wanted an 'equal' relationship as Cameron had described; all that mattered is that it was one with Matt. God I wished I could have kissed him right then.

"Get the lights!" Kathie yelled, and instantly the room was re-illuminated. "Okay, Petey, now it's time to open your presents. Which one do you want first?" She had placed the cake down on a nearby coffee table and stepped over in front of the stack of gifts. "How about this one?" She picked up a big, bulky package that was expertly wrapped and tied with a gigantic red bow. She handed it to me.

"May I sit down?" I asked shyly, as several people laughed. Then I turned and sat myself on the edge of the sofa, holding the gift in my lap. "It's too pretty to open," I admired.

"Who's it from?" asked Drew loudly. I carefully tore off the card, and removed it from the envelope.

"It's from you guys, silly!" I said to Drew, holding up the card and laughing. "This one is from Drew and Alex," I said loudly to the crowd of people who were gathered around me. Carefully, I removed the tape amidst demands from the onlookers that I just tear into it. I let out a gasp when I finally revealed what it was. There sitting on my lap and staring at me was the most adorable over-sized stuffed puppy that I'd ever seen. He had huge brown eyes and floppy ears and was wearing a tag that simply said 'Pup.' I squealed with excitement. "Oh my god! I love it so much. He's so cute!" People around me were laughing, responding to my own over-zealous excitement. "Thank you so much Drew! And Alex. Where's Alex?" I scanned the room for him and suddenly his head popped out behind Matt. "Thank you Alex. Thank you so much!"

I placed the pup down on the couch beside me as Kathie handed me another gift. It appeared to be a book of some sort. Carefully I removed the card and opened it. It was a rather generic card as if from someone I did not know real well. When I got to the bottom of the verse and saw the signature, I knew why. It was from Cameron. "Oh Cameron, you did not need to buy me a gift! You hadn't even met me yet." He shrugged, brushing the hair from his eyes.

"Can't show up for a party without a gift for the guest of honor," he explained.

Again I carefully unwrapped my gift, and sure enough I was right, it was a book. It was a book about gay athletes, titled *Coming Out of the Locker Room*. I looked at it inquisitively, turning the book over to read the back. "This is very nice, Cameron. Thank you." I placed the book beside me and moved on to my next gift.

I continued to open my gifts, one after the other, amazed and moved to tears by the generosity of the party guests. I had never before been showered with all of this attention and was feeling absolutely astounded that this group of people would come together to honor me this way. It was odd, for I'd attended birthday parties before, plenty of them, but had always been too reserved to request one for myself. My mom would offer to throw me a party every single year, but always I refused, saying "Nah, but thanks anyways." A couple of the gifts were not actually gifts at all but instead cards containing money. Even my aunt— Marc's mother— sent a card containing a twenty dollar bill. I also received a thirty dollar gift certificate from the bookstore where I worked. It was given to me by a coworker actually. Perhaps it was "last-minute."

Carter surprised me by presenting me with two tickets to the opening game of the Marlins. Although I was not big into watching athletic events, it excited me to receive the gift. I would simply give it to Matt. He could either take me with him to the game, or perhaps he'd want Alex to go with him instead. "Carter, this is an awesome present! Thanks so much!" I reached up and held the tickets out to Matt. "Would you hold these please?" I asked him.

"They're yours, Petey," Matt said. I was a bit taken aback by the fact that he did not call me "pup," but I understood, being that there were all of these other people present.

"I know, S—, um...Matt, but I want you to hold onto them for me so they don't get lost."

He laughed. "Okay...we can go to the game together." He winked at me.

I moved on to the next gift which Kathie had just set down in front of me. It was a thin rectangular package. Couldn't be a book. Not a CD or cassette. "What is it?" I asked curiously, holding it up to my ear to gently shake it.

"Open it," she said, urging me on. "Go on, open it and see." It was cool to see my sister's excitement as she watched me. I found it peculiar that I'd never before noticed that gift-giving could be as rewarding to the giver as it was the recipient. Finally, I could delay no longer, and tore open the package hurriedly. My mouth dropped open when I saw what was inside: a beautifully framed portrait of my parents and me. My mind was instantly transported to this memory, the unforgettable moment in my life which I had actually disallowed myself to recall prior to this moment. It was three years ago, but suddenly felt as if only yesterday. Kathie was there too; she was the photographer. She had stopped the three of us, forcing us to pose for the picture.

"This was the day that—" I began, but could not finish the sentence, my voice escaping me as I choked up with emotion.

"That you received your award," Kathie finished for me.

Drew squatted down beside me, resting his hand gently on my arm. "What award was that?" he asked, looking up to Kathie.

"Petey received an award from the National Honor Society for an essay he had submitted. It was a contest, and Petey's essay was selected and featured in their quarterly newsletter. He was presented this award the same night that my father...that he ...um...suffered his heart attack."

"Wow," said Drew quietly. "What was the essay about Petey?" he said to me.

I shrugged. "It doesn't matter," I said, almost to myself.

"It was beautiful," Kathie answered for me. "It was about the importance of family relationships. It was so beautifully and masterfully written that I could not even adequately describe it. Anyways, I took this picture of our parents and Petey that night after Petey was presented with the award. They were so proud of him. Later in the evening, after we had gotten home, our dad had his heart attack. I'd completely forgotten about the picture. It was in a roll of film which I had never remembered to develop. I was so surprised it even turned out after all this time."

"They looked so happy," I said as I stared at that picture. "How could this have been only hours before—"

"They were proud of you," Kathie said. "Look at how proud Dad looks, standing there with his arm around you."

Tears streamed down my face freely now. "Kathie, thank you for this gift. Thank you so much." I stood up, handing the picture to Drew to hold for me, and stepped over to Kathie to hug her. We embraced as I cried silently in her arms. "It is such a beautiful picture. Thank you."

"I love you Petey," she whispered in my ear, "I love you so much."

When I returned to my seated position on the sofa, wiping my eyes one last time, Kathie informed me that this was my last gift. I smiled up at her, "I can't believe all of these presents," I said. As she handed me the present I knew immediately that it was from Matt. I could tell by the handwriting on the envelope. He had labeled it simply "Pup".

"It's from Matt," I said quietly yet excitedly. Quickly I looked up to find him. He was still standing directly in front of me. "Thank you," I said, before even opening the card.

"Don't thank me yet," he laughed. "Maybe you won't like it."

"I'd like anything from you, S—, um...Matt," I said. Carefully I opened the card, revealing an adorable picture of a puppy wearing a cone-shaped birthday hat. I laughed aloud. "How cute!" I said, holding up the card for the others close by to admire.

I then opened the card to read the very simple verse, "Have a doggone good birthday!" it said. Again I laughed. Underneath it Matt had written, "Pup, yer the coolest! Have a great B-day. M." I handed the card to Drew to read as I looked up into Matt's eyes.

"No...you're the coolest." I smiled at him broadly. Then I returned my attention to the gift. The package was not big and felt as if it weighed nothing. For a second I thought Matt had given me an empty box. Even when I shook it, I could hear nothing inside. Carefully though, I unwrapped the package and uncovered a plain cardboard box with no markings on the outside whatsoever. I looked up at Matt, smiling, but was rather puzzled. "Go on, pup...open it!" he urged me. He now was calling me his pup, perhaps not thinking in the heat of the moment.

I dug my fingers under the lid of the box, pulling it free from the transparent tape that held it closed. I opened the

lid completely and stared inside. There were papers—
brochures of some sort—inside the box. I reached in and
pulled them out. Amongst the paperwork was a small folder.
I saw that it was labeled "Passageway Travel" on the front
cover. Matt had gotten me a trip!

"You got me a trip!" I screamed delightedly. Kathie stood
watching me intently, her mouth agape. I opened the folder
quickly. It contained two tickets for a cruise, a Caribbean
cruise! "Matt! Oh my god! You got us a Caribbean cruise!"
He smiled at me proudly, nodding. "Oh thank you so much!"
I jumped up from my seat, papers flying everywhere as I
lunged towards him. "Oh thank you , Sir! Thank you so
much!" He grabbed a hold of me, laughing and hugging me
as I squirmed delightedly in his arms.

He leaned into me, pressing his mouth right next to my
ear, so that no one but me could hear him. "I love you, pup.
Happy birthday."

"I love you, too!" I said sincerely, making no effort to
quiet my own excitement. "Sir, I love you with my whole
heart!"

As he pushed me back from him, holding me at arms
length, I stared up into his eyes. "Thank you. Thank you so
much." I then spun around and backed into him, feeling him
wrap his arms around me, holding me in front of him. As I
turned to face the crowd of onlookers, our new friend
Cameron was standing next to Kathie. I smiled at them,
wanting them to share in my excitement. "Can you believe it
Kathie? A Caribbean cruise!"

"That's very nice," she said calmly. She reached down to
the sofa, turning her gaze from me, and gathered the papers
that were strewn everywhere. She then stepped towards me,
handing me them. "So when are you going?"

"During Spring break," Matt answered.

"Sorry Drew," I said, as I turned to him. "I won't be able
to go to Fort Lauderdale with you."

"No problem, kiddo," he said, smiling sweetly at me. "Maybe next year."

"Oh I can't believe this! This is my best birthday ever!" I said.

Cameron stepped towards us then. "May I see the brochure?" he asked.

"Sure," I said, and handed him the flyer, though I still clung tightly to the folder containing the tickets.

"Hmm, I had a friend who went on one of these cruises. He was rather disappointed, I'm sad to say." I felt the smile on my face starting to drop as I looked at Cameron intently. "The food was lousy. The entertainment was atrocious. Most of the other passengers were old, disgusting trolls. I really hope you are not disappointed by this. I wish I'd have known you sooner. I could have hooked you up with a truly exceptional package with RSVP, a gay cruise line—"

"We are happy with the 'package' that we have," Matt interrupted him. "Show a little respect, will ya. It's Petey's birthday!" Matt gently moved me to his side as he addressed Cameron, stepping towards him.

"Oh no...I'm sorry, I did not mean to offend you or anything. I just get carried away sometimes. Please... I meant no disrespect."

"Apology accepted...Cam," Matt said, staring him directly in the eye.

"That's Cameron, if you please," he corrected Matt.

"All right, Cam," Matt repeated, stepping even closer. At this point Kathie stepped up, moving between Matt and Cameron.

"Hey, is everyone ready for some cake?" she asked.

"Come on, Petey!" called Drew. "You have to cut the cake. You're the birthday boy." I looked up quickly to Matt and he nodded, so I stepped behind him and went to Drew. I held out my travel package to him, and he took it excitedly. "This is so awesome, Petey. What a wonderful gift. I'm so happy for you!" He hugged me affectionately. "Let's go to the kitchen and cut the cake."

Soon the music was playing again as Drew and I began cutting and serving the birthday cake. I lost track of Matt momentarily, though I was concerned, after witnessing the little confrontation only moments before. "Drew, have you seen Matt?" I asked. "Where did he go?"

"He is probably in the bathroom or something, don't worry," Drew assured me.

Politely I excused myself as I made my way around several people and headed towards the hallway. Once out of the living room, I quickened my pace as I headed towards the bathroom. I got to the door and pushed it open. Empty. Then I turned and stepped down the hall further, down to my bedroom door. I pushed it open, peering inside. There he was, whew! "Sir, what are you doing?" Matt was seated at my desk chair, using my computer. "Don't you want some cake?" I asked.

"Sure, pup, in a minute. Come in here, though, for a second. Close the door." I obeyed immediately, rushing over to him. Immediately I dropped down to a sitting position on the floor beside his chair. I did not like standing where I was taller than him, not even briefly.

"What are you doing, Sir?" I repeated.

"I'm downloading something that I emailed to ya," he said. "I emailed it from my laptop this weekend. Geesh, you gotta check your mail more often, pup. You got like a zillion messages. Surprised your box will hold all these."

I laughed. "I've had over nine hundred messages at one time, sir. Most of that stuff is just spam. That's why I don't check it often enough."

"Well delete all this shit, okay?" he said, "and start checkin your mail every day, cuz sometimes I'm gonna be sendin you stuff."

"Yes sir," I said.

"Okay, the download is done. Here look at this."

He clicked on the icon to open the file he had just downloaded, and a picture appeared on the screen. It was an illustration of some kind. As the graphics got sharper, I started to be able to make it out. "It's a bone...like on my collar," I said.

"Yup, it's exactly like that. In fact, I had your tag scanned, and then an illustrator who works down at one of the mall shops drew me a replica of it. It's going to be your other birthday present from me."

"But sir," I said, "Why would I need a replica when I have the real thing?"

"Cuz you are gonna take this drawing with you, pup, when you go with me tomorrow. We are going to go get you a tattoo."

"You mean you are gonna have this tattooed on me?" I asked excitedly. "Like, permanently?"

"Yup," he said matter-of-factly. Just as he said this I turned to see someone standing in my bedroom door. It was Kathie.

"Hey," I said, smiling up at her. It was not like her to enter my room without knocking first, but I was too excited to care. "This is a wonderful party, Kathie. Thanks for everything."

It was as if she had not heard me, as if I was not even there. She was looking directly at Matt. "Petey is *not* getting a tattoo," she informed him calmly. "Especially not one like that!"

Matt turned in his chair, swiveling to face her. I backed up slightly so as not to be bumped by the chair leg. I looked up into Matt's face, concerned about what he was going to say. "I guess that would be up to Petey to decide," he answered her. "He has a right to get a tattoo if he wants."

"He doesn't want! Petey would never in a million years get a tattoo. I know him. I know my brother. The only reason he'd do something like that is if someone was forcing him to do it."

485

Matt then looked at me, still remaining very calm. "Petey," he said, directing his full attention to me, "have I ever forced you to do anything?"

I quickly shook my head. "No, never...Sir."

"Sir?!" Kathie raised her voice as she looked over to us. "Why do you keep calling him that? He is the same age as you!" Kathie stepped completely inside the doorway, pushing the door closed behind her. "Petey," she said, calming herself as she spoke to me, "this is your birthday party. I don't want to argue with you. We can talk about the ... tattoo...tomorrow."

"I call him 'Sir' because I love him, and because he owns me!" I screamed at her, placing my hand against Matt's leg, clinging to it. I was now in a kneeling position as I looked up at her. "I love him and I want to belong to him...forever!"

"Oh my god," Kathie said, rolling her eyes. "Petey, nobody owns you! Think of what you are saying!" She turned away from us quickly, raising her hand to her head, rubbing her temples. "God, I cannot even believe I'm hearing this stuff." She turned back around slowly to look at me. "Petey," she said again, "how can you be so much of a ...um...oh god...how can you let him do this to you? You do not have to go around taking orders from other people. You don't have to allow other people to control you. Didn't you learn anything from Mom and Dad? Didn't you learn how important it is to have an equal relationship where both partners respect one another?"

This time Matt spoke. "If there is one thing that Petey knows about, it is respect," he said. "Petey has respect for all people, even if they don't believe exactly the way he does." He placed his hand on my shoulder as I knelt beside him. "Look, I've never forced Petey to do anything...never will, either. He can walk away from me at any time; it's always his choice."

"You make me sick, you know that?" Kathie spat back at him. "You are nothing but a fucking user. I know about what you did to Tracy. You were having sex with her, telling her that you loved her...all the while letting Petey think you were in love with him. You think because you have money and can afford Caribbean cruises and weekend retreats at your private cabin, that it gives you the right to take anything you want...from anyone!"

"Shut up!" I screamed, "Don't ever talk to him like that!" I had jumped to my feet. "He doesn't use me. He's never used me!"

Suddenly there was a knock on the bedroom door. "Hey, what's goin on in there? Everything all right?" It was Carter's voice. Kathie stepped back over to the door, opening it. Carter stood there with Cameron at his side. "What's going on? What's all the screaming about?" He looked at Kathie, seeing the tears streaming down her cheeks.

Matt had stood up, and I scrambled to rise from my kneeling position to stand beside him. "Everything's cool," he said, "I was about to get goin." He then turned to me. "Pup, you have a great party; you deserve it."

"No!" I yelled. "Please don't go, sir!...Please!" He placed his hands on my shoulders then, holding me in front of him and looking down into my eyes.

"It's okay, pup. It's best I split right now, before this whole thing explodes. You stay and enjoy the rest of your party. Drew is still gonna be here."

"I want to go with you...please!"

At this point, Kathie spoke up, "Let him go." Her words were directed at me. "Petey, let him leave."

I was now crying as I turned to her. "Why do you have to be like this, Kathie? Why do you have to say such mean things? Why can't you be happy for me for once? Can't you see that we love each other?"

"Pup," Matt said calmly, again turning me to face him, "maybe she is right...at least partially. Maybe I have used you. I want you to think about it. I want you to think about it hard, okay? I don't want you to see me again until you know

487

for sure that this is totally what you want. I never want to force you...never."

"I don't have to think about it," I cried. "I already know what I want. I only want one thing...to be with you!"

He then turned to Kathie, as if he had not even heard my declaration to him. "Kathie," he said, "neither one of us can tell Petey what to do with his life, or who to love. He has to decide the kind of relationship that he wants for himself. I've never once told him that he had to do anything he didn't want to do. He does things for me because it's what he wants.

"As for me, I love Petey. I love him more than anything or anyone ... ever." He looked down at me affectionately. "He's my pup. I would never do anything to hurt him. And I never meant to hurt Tracy either, not that I owe you or anyone an explanation. She assumed things about us that simply were not true. I had no control over that."

Cameron then spoke up, "If you love him so much, then why do you treat him like such a subordinate?" I thought Matt might reach over and deck him at this point.

"Mind your own business, Cam," Matt said, completely ignoring his question.

"Hey," said Carter, "You guys, this was an awesome party so far. Why are we in here arguing and not out in the living room enjoying ourselves? I don't think anyone should leave. Kathie, if Petey wants to have Matt at his party, I say he should stay."

"If he goes, I go," I said confidently. "I'm not going to let you drive him away from me."

"Petey," Matt said firmly, "if I go, it will be my own choice. Remember to be respectful. Your sister threw this party for you."

Kathie sighed dramatically. "You are so noble," she said with sarcasm. "You're doing this on purpose, making yourself into some martyr or something, sacrificing yourself for Petey's sake. It's a bunch of bullshit! Stay if you wanna stay. Go if you wanna go! I don't give a shit.

"Petey, I only am concerned because I love you. I see the way that he treats you. I see the way that you've changed since you've known him. Cameron is right. If he does truly love you, he would not treat you like you are inferior to him. But it's your call. You do what you want. If you want to go through the rest of your life being someone else's lackey, someone else's slave— then go right ahead." She turned from me and exited the room dramatically.

Carter raised his eyebrows as he looked over to us. "Anyone want a beer?" he asked. Cameron had already turned and swept out of the room, following Kathie. We both shook our heads. "Well, come on back out...both of you, and Matt, please don't go because of this. Kathie just gets a little over-excited."

"Thanks, man," he said to Carter. "We'll be out in a minute."

"Sir, I don't want you to go," I said as Matt closed the door behind Carter. "You already have made my birthday wish come true, you know. You already have made me happier than any pup could ever be."

He smiled at me. "How's that?" he asked, stepping over to me.

"You told them. You told them you loved me."

"Well, it's true. I don't say things that aren't so."

"You know, I think that I should consider taking Drew up on his offer, sir."

"What did he offer, pup?" Matt asked as he pulled me into his chest.

"He said I could come and live with them, rent a room from them. I think it might be best."

"That what you wanna do?" he asked. I nodded.

"I love Kathie so much, but I don't think she ever is gonna be able to understand...about you and me. I don't think she even wants to."

"She cares about you, doesn't want you hurt. Nothin wrong with that, pup. She's your sister. She thinks I might hurt you, and she is tryin to protect you. That's all."

"Well, you are the one person I don't need protection from. You're the one who protects me."

He kissed me then, saying no more. No other words were necessary as we fell backwards on my bed, rolling on top of one another, pressing ourselves as close to one another as possible. He pressed his hand against my butt, pressing the plug with his finger. He knew exactly where to find it, and he reminded me with his touch that it was he who had placed it there.

"You're inside me," I whispered, and he kissed me again.

27

When I woke up that Thursday morning, a feeling of euphoria swept over me. I could hardly believe the events that had transpired the previous evening. My sister Kathie had thrown me the absolute best birthday party that anyone could ask for. I was overwhelmed and truly amazed by the outpouring of attention I'd received, and the gifts were incredible. How could I have ever even dreamt of receiving a Caribbean cruise and tickets to a Marlins' game? I looked up to my dresser, squinting for I did not have on my glasses or contacts, to see the beautifully framed picture my sister had given me. I would always cherish that photograph—my parents and me.

After the confrontation in my bedroom, when Matt had openly declared his love for me, things calmed down a bit. No further discussion of the controversial topics of my tattoo or my ownership were again broached. Instead, Matt and I had quietly returned to the party. Some people were doing Jell-O shots by this time, and the volume of the music had been cranked up a few notches. Matt had a couple of beers with Carter as I clung insistently to his side. We were joined by Alex as well, and I stood listening intently as they discussed things which I barely understood. Most of their conversation was related to sports, with an occasional reference to chicks. I scanned the room and noticed that Cameron once again had Drew cornered. Undoubtedly they were again discussing some political issue. I watched them as Cameron lifted his arm to place it against the wall above his head. I could see the outline of his bicep through his dress shirt. He truly maintained a well-toned body, obviously being very diligent with his workout schedule.

Finally, I broke away from the circle that I was in, not wanting to leave Matt's side, but also finding myself very hungry. I loaded up a plate with the appetizers that my sister had prepared and headed for the patio. When I stepped outside I noticed that Carrie and Tim were on the patio as well. "Hey there," I said, "Are you enjoying the party?"

"Sure," said Tim. "It's cool. That was an incredible gift that your friend gave you. The Caribbean cruise, I mean."

"Yeah, isn't that unbelievable?" I said. "I like all my gifts, though, every single one."

"Cool," said Carrie. "Wish I were going on a cruise for spring break," she laughed. "I'll get stuck working even more hours than usual since you'll be gone, you schmuck!" She affectionately shoved me as we both laughed. "You're a lucky guy to have a friend like that."

"Yeah, I know. Believe me, I totally know how lucky I am." Just as I said this, Drew and Cameron stepped out onto the patio. "Hey you guys, did you get something to eat? I was starving."

"Yeah," said Cameron, "I had a plate earlier." He and Drew stepped over to the side of patio by the railing and lit their cigarettes. "Hope the smoke doesn't bother you," he said. I shook my head and smiled. "So Petey, you just a full time student right now, or do you work somewhere?"

"I work down at Worlds' Gate Press, the bookstore down on Division Street," I said. "These are my coworkers, Tim and Carrie." The three nodded to one another and smiled. "And this is my friend Drew," I said to them, "—not sure that you met him yet. Yeah I just work three or four days a week, plus school."

"That's a nice bookstore," he said politely. "They have an impressive gay-interest section."

"Yeah, we do," said Carrie. "Seems like that section is really popular in our store."

"Yup. You have a good location to attract that clientele. You are right in the center of the gay district."

"Really?" I asked. "I never realized there was a gay district."

"Well originally there were a lot of gay businesses down there. Lot of the bars have gone straight though."

"Yeah," interjected Drew. "That was where Alex and I first met, at a bar down there. It was called the Copa. That was only four years ago, and now you'd never know it had even been there. They've totally changed that whole area. I think that bar now is a flower shop or something."

"So Alex was only twenty when you first met him?" I asked. "Wow, that is like mine and Matt's age — almost."

"Yeah, I know. I lucked out there, getting myself such a hot young stud," he raised his eyebrows at the two straight people in our presence. "But speaking of Alex, I'd better put out this cigarette and get back inside. Don't wanna be away from him too long," he laughed as he flicked the cigarette over the railing onto the pavement below.

"I'll be in after I'm done eating," I said. "Okay?" He nodded and returned into the apartment.

"Peter, this was a great party, but we really should get goin," said Tim. "Thanks for inviting us. We should hang out sometime."

"I'd like that. Thanks for coming!" I smiled at them again, not really sure what else to say. "Thanks again for the gifts, you guys. They were awesome." When they left the patio, it left just Cameron and me. Hesitantly, I looked up at him, then quickly turned to look through the patio window, spotting Matt right where I'd left him. He had his back to us. "Um...and what do you do, Cameron?" I said.

"For a living, you mean?"

"Yes sir...um...I mean, yes."

He laughed at me. "You don't have to call me sir; in fact, please don't. Makes me feel old, like my father. I work for a non-profit organization. It's called Gay and Lesbians United for Equality...or GLUE." I laughed at the acronym, and he looked at me puzzled as if he didn't understand what I found so funny.

"I was thinking of doing that myself. Working for a non-profit organization, that is. I also like to write, so I might try to eventually get some things published."

"Oh yeah? That's right, I remember what your sister said about your essay. I'd love to read some of your stuff sometime. Have you ever posted anything on the internet?"

"No, nothing like that. I'm not that good yet. I would not wanna do that until I get a degree or something."

"Well if you have a talent for writing, it's not like you need a degree to prove it, Petey. Is it okay for me to call you Petey, or do you prefer Peter?"

"Petey's fine," I said warmly. "Unless you are uncomfortable with nicknames." I laughed, remembering how he'd corrected me earlier about his own name.

"Nah, I just don't like my own nickname. When people call me 'Cam' it sounds like an abbreviation for camera. I just think it's sorta weird, ya know. Hope you don't think it's snobbish or anything."

"No, of course not," I shook my head. I then bit a piece of meat off the chicken leg I was holding. "These are so good, even though I don't usually eat very much meat."

"Really?" he said, "I don't either. In fact, I'm pretty much vegetarian. Lot of meat isn't good for you, especially red meat."

"I know. Do you like to cook?" I asked.

"Love to. I love to throw elaborate dinner parties too. I'll invite you to one sometime."

"That would be great. I love cooking myself. I even was thinking of becoming a chef. I don't think I'd like working in a restaurant, though."

"Nah, me neither. Man, if I'd have known, I'd have gotten you a great cookbook, instead of the sports book I gave you." He shrugged.

"Oh, I think I'm gonna love that book. I love jocks!" I giggled. "Can't you tell by my boyfriend?"

"How long you guys been together?" Cameron asked.

"Well, that's kinda hard to say. We first met each other...officially, I mean...back in November. I was getting beaten up at the time actually, and he saved me. Well, he took me to the hospital and stuff. These two guys were kicking and punching me. It was terrible."

"Wow, what a story! Did you press charges against the guys?"

I nodded. "Yeah, Matt insisted on it. Well anyways, after that whole incident was over, we didn't see each other for almost two months. Then one day I was walking home and ran into him on the sidewalk. He had this little dog with him. It was so adorable! It reminded me of the Little Rascals dog Petey. You know who I'm talkin about?" He nodded and smiled. "Then we were talking and he told me how he had just gotten the dog and he'd named it after me. I was so shocked by it, and it made me feel so awesome.

"Well then he invited me to come over to his house, and I did. Then we fell in love, and that's that."

"Wow, what a beautiful story. He saved you and then fell in love with you, huh?"

"Yup," I beamed. "I love him so much."

"Your sister was talking to me about you and Matt. She told me some things about your relationship."

"Well, she doesn't really like Matt that much. I wish she did though; she just doesn't know him that well, that's all. She thinks he's just using me or something. I think that's so crazy!"

"Why would she think that?" he asked, taking a drag off his cigarette.

"Well I think she just doesn't understand about the kind of relationship we have. She thinks it's unfair or something."

"Is it?" he asked.

"No, it's not unfair at all. I mean, she thinks that because Matt makes more of the decisions about things than I do, that he is being too controlling. What she doesn't realize though is that I want him to decide things. I want for him to kinda be the leader in our relationship. You see what I'm saying?"

"You like him to make decisions for you because you don't feel capable of deciding things for yourself; you are indecisive?" he asked, though it seemed more like a statement to me.

"Yeah, I guess so. Well, I don't know. The decision-making thing doesn't really matter to me, actually. He makes the decisions because it just seems right for him to do it. I don't see anything wrong with that if it's what we both want, do you?"

"No, I guess not, but I would have to wonder if it is really what you want. Maybe you go along with this arrangement because you love Matt so much and are so infatuated by him that you'd do anything to make him happy, but have you ever stopped to ask yourself what will make you happy?"

I was getting a little bit perturbed by him at this point. "He makes me happy," I said confidently.

He raised his hands in the air, palms facing me. "Hey, didn't mean any offense, Petey. I just want you to know that there are many kinds of relationship available to you. You don't have to be controlled by another person. You can find all of the qualities that you have in Matt in a guy who is not gonna want to control your every move and tell you what to do all the time. There are plenty of gay guys out there who have all that Matt's got and more, and who are looking for a guy just like you."

I was starting to blush. "Well, I doubt that," I said, "but even if it were true, I'm not looking for anyone besides Matt. I don't think that he is overly controlling of me. I like him just the way he is, and wouldn't trade him for anyone."

"Okay, well that's cool then, but listen to me, if you ever need to talk to anyone about this, I want you to feel free to give me a call, okay? Here, this is my business card. Call me any time, all right?"

"Sure, but I promise you, I won't call you to complain about Matt. I'd love to keep being your friend though...if you want." I smiled at him again, licking some barbeque sauce from my finger.

"Yeah, exactly. I'd like that very much."

I remembered this conversation as I lay there in bed that morning. I remembered how confidently Cameron had sounded when he assured me that there were guys out there who were everything that Matt was, but not controlling. Was it true that Matt was too controlling of me? That was the only way I'd ever known him to be though. From the minute I was first alone with him, I knew that it was the right thing for him to tell me what to do and for me to obey him. It never seemed wrong to me. In fact it felt like the most incredibly right thing I'd ever experienced.

I lay there thinking of the contrasts between Matt and Cameron. Matt had short medium brown hair and dark eyes. He was so very masculine and handsome, the perfect all-American jock. Cameron was a jock himself, but was fair haired with deep blue eyes. Cameron also had a nicely-built body, very similar to Matt's in fact. I wondered for a few seconds what he would have looked like with his shirt off—or naked. I felt myself becoming aroused as I lay there. I reached down under the covers to touch myself, not sure if I was aroused by the visions in my mind of Matt or of Cameron, or of both.

Quickly, I pulled my hand free, not being entirely sure I even had permission to touch myself that way. I then thought more about Cameron. Unlike Matt, I doubted that Cameron would ever give me an order not to touch myself. If Cameron were my boyfriend and he caught me doing this sort of thing, what would he do? I bet he'd wanna watch. I bet he'd wanna join me maybe, possibly even touch me so that I didn't have to touch myself. Matt wouldn't though. If Matt caught me doing this, he'd punish me. He'd put me in that chastity thing again, maybe even spank me.

Then I remembered Matt's words to me from the night before, "Maybe I have used you. I want you to think about it. I want you to think about it hard, okay? I don't want you to see me again until you know for sure that this is totally what you want. I never want to force you...never." It had not completely registered in my mind what he'd been saying, not until right now at this minute. He was saying that he wasn't going to see me any more until I decided what I wanted. He wanted to make sure that I did not feel he was just using me. Wait, though, I'd answered him. I'd said to him no, I did not need to think about it. I already knew the answer. He was all that I wanted; I'd made that clear. Hadn't I?

He had brushed me off, though. He ignored my declaration to him and to the others in that room. When I'd said to him that I knew with certainty, it was as if he'd pretended not to hear me. Then why did he kiss me afterwards? Why did he tell me that he loved me? Why did he touch me so tenderly?

Before Matt left me that evening, he had come to me. His demeanor was very casual, and he reminded me to think about things. I was too excited to understand what he meant. I had all the gifts around me, all the guests saying goodbye, all of the chaos. He had said, "Think about what I said, pup." I guess it had not registered. Maybe I'd thought he meant to think about the tattoo, or to think about our upcoming cruise. No, it was clear now. He was reminding me to think about *us*. He wanted me to make sure he was what I really wanted.

Yet all this time I was the one who had been so very worried about what he really wanted. His encounters with Tracy had driven me nearly out of my mind. I still became

insane with jealousy when I thought about him being with
another person, male or female. It had not been until that
moment in my bedroom in front of my sister and Carter,
that moment when Matt declared openly to them that I was
his pup and that he loved me, that I realized he truly did
want me. Now he was forcing me to decide for myself what I
wanted. Did I want him, or did I want someone who was
more my equal?

Even when I thought of Cameron, though, I did not
consider myself to be equal with him. He was successful,
affluent, masculine and athletic. In his presence, I felt
subordinate to him, yet his demeanor did not convey to me
that I was less than him. He shared common interests with
me and believed in many of the same things that I did. He
insisted that I call him by his first name rather than "sir." He
did not tell me what to do. Even in the way he spoke to me
about Matt, never once did he say that I should do one thing
or another. He merely urged me to look closely at what I
really wanted.

All of this talk about being indecisive seemed to ring truer
than ever just then. I found it ironic that Cameron had
suggested to me that perhaps I did not really want a
relationship where I was not included in the decision-
making, when now already I was unable to decide even how
I felt about it all. I loved Matt so very much, and I knew that
he would make me so happy simply by being with me, yet
now this other new possibility had emerged. I possibly could
have someone who possessed all of the qualities about Matt
that I admired and worshiped, yet who also treated me as an
equal. Wasn't that like having the best of both worlds?

No! I couldn't think like this. Matt had meant everything
to me these past months. He'd been the one who had saved
me. He'd showered me with presents, bought me new
clothing, a cell phone, a fuckin' Caribbean cruise. Just the
evening before, he'd taken me with him to his gym, and we'd
discussed our future together. He was sharing the intimacies

of his life with me—his true feelings. It was true that I submitted myself to his authority and strove to obey his every command, but this had never been something that was forced. It just came naturally. When I knelt before him that first time, it was I who declared my intention to him. I was the one who had known in my heart that I was the way that I am...submissive, perhaps. I wasn't even sure what it was, or why it was. It just was me.

Cameron simply did not understand what it meant to be an owner or a boy. He did not know what it meant to me when Matt called me his pup and put his collar on me. He did not even begin to comprehend the feeling of completeness I experienced every time I knelt before my owner and received his blessing. He had no way of knowing about my sincere need to worship Matt. Of course, Cameron and Kathie would not fully understand; it was not supposed to be that they understood everything I was feeling. Matt understood, though, and that was where the connection we shared became so powerful. He and I were fused together emotionally as well as physically. I had given myself over to him entirely, and he knew me in ways that nobody else ever had before or probably ever would thereafter.

How could I even question these feelings? How could I ever even compare what Cameron was presenting to me with what I already genuinely had with Matt? I needed to see him, to see Matt. I needed him to hold me and reassure me he was all I ever needed. I needed for his arms to engulf me as they had the night before. I needed his touch, his soothing reassurance that he loved me. These were the only things I wanted. This security and this all consuming love were transcendent; they went far above and beyond any hopes of self-fulfillment that I might have with an equal partner.

As for my own hopes and dreams, my own vision of the future, Matt had not held me back. Just moments before the party, he and I had discussed what I wanted for my life. Instead of dictating to me that I must remain always in his shadow, he had urged me to think for myself. He had told me to explore what I felt, to pursue the things that made me happy. Even when I suggested that I come work for him, he was dismissive of this possibility. He was not wanting me to sacrifice my individuality in order to serve him. He wanted me to be everything that I dreamt of being, not just a miniature carbon copy of himself.

After Matt had left last night, I had thought of him as I removed the plug he'd placed inside me. His instructions to me when he last spoke to me were to take it out; he did not want me sleeping with it. I did as he had told me, and felt him still inside me. Even after all of those hours, it was as if we had just been intimate with one another. That was how I fell asleep that evening, and now here I was the following morning questioning that very feeling of contentment which had for so long sustained me. I prayed that I'd see him this day. Today was actually my real birthday. I was actually nineteen now for real. I hoped we could be together, just him and me, and make love the way we had the very first time.

* * *

My class load that Thursday was light, no major tests or exams, and I was anxious for the day to conclude. I knew that I did not have to work that evening. I had requested it off, for it just seemed right to give myself a bit of a break on my birthday. When I got out of my last class I headed for the parking lot on foot. I had ridden the bus that morning instead of my bike, hoping to catch up with Matt and maybe give him an excuse to drive me. As I looked around the parking lot, I spotted his car parked close to where he normally tried to park. I briskly walked over to it, relieved that I had not missed him.

Placing my backpack on the ground beside me, I leaned against his car and waited for him, feeling fairly certain that he'd be along soon. I stood there watching the passers-by, amused by some of the antics of college frat boys and their buds. Many of the students were paired up, either with same-gender friends or with their significant others. Everybody needed someone, it seemed. I needed Matt, and I thought that he must need me too.

After waiting about five minutes, I almost was about to walk away, realizing that if I did not get to the bus stop soon I'd end up having to walk home. Just then I heard Matt's voice and excitedly swung around to greet him. As I did so, I was somewhat taken aback, for he was not alone. By his side was a college-aged blonde female, one I'd never seen before. "Hey pup," he said as he approached me. "What ya doin?"

"Um... I was just hangin out, waitin for ya."

"Cool. Petey, this is my friend Kim. We are in a few classes together. You gotta work this afternoon?"

I shook my head. "Nope, took my birthday off," I smiled. "What are you doin?"

"Kim's goin with me back to my house. We have a big exam coming up, and we're gonna study. Then tonight I'm working at the gym. You need a ride somewhere?"

I shook my head, suddenly feeling crestfallen. "No...um, no, thank you. I should get goin though before I miss the bus."

"Well, you want me to just drop you off at home?"

"No!... I mean, no, I don't wanna bother you. Thanks for everything, Matt. I mean the gift and stuff, and for the—"

"Hey, everything's cool. You been thinking about the things I told you?"

I nodded. "Very much. I have thought about them a lot."

"Good. Well maybe we can get together tomorrow or Saturday. How's that?"

"Okay...well, I gotta run. Nice meeting you, Kim." I picked up my backpack and dashed off towards the bus stop.

I glanced back at Matt one last time before rounding the corner out of his sight. My eyes were stinging from the tears, as I willed myself to suppress the emotion. I did not want him to see me like this. I truly had no right to cry. It just was that I had been thinking of him all morning, wanting desperately to talk to him about the feelings I had. I wanted to tell him how I had concluded that I could not be happy with anyone but him, for he made me feel complete and satisfied. I was bursting to tell him that I did not need equality or even want it. All I wanted was to be his, to be by his side as his pup. That was enough.

I had not been able to tell him any of these things, though, for he was not alone. He was with a female classmate, a "study partner." I couldn't help but wonder if this was just a euphemism for another one of his "bitches." Maybe they were going over to his house to study, or maybe they had other plans entirely. When Matt had first invited me to his place, the friendly visit I had planned on turned into something much more. I bet that was his intention with this Kim as well. She was merely a replacement for Tracy, another pussy to fuck.

I wiped my eyes as I approached the bus stop, trying desperately to think of anything but Matt. Quickly, I shoved my hand into my pocket to retrieve my bus fair, and along with the wadded up dollar bills that I pulled out was a small card—a business card. It was from Cameron. I had shoved the card in my jean pocket the night before, and then when I was hurriedly transferring my money into my khakis this morning I must have grabbed the card as well. I looked down at it and remembered his invitation. He had encouraged me to "call at any time" that I needed to talk to someone about my situation. I looked the card over pensively, debating whether or not to even keep it. As I boarded the bus I pushed it back down into my pants' pocket and found a seat. The bus began to pull away, and I hesitantly reached back into my pocket again for the card. I brought it up to examine it more closely, studying the rainbow colors in his company monogram.

Finally, I reached into my backpack and removed my cell phone. It was the phone that Matt had given me—the phone I had barely ever used. I began to dial Cameron's number, but then stopped. After a few seconds I heard the recording, "If you'd like to make a call, please hang up...." I pressed the cancel button and put the phone back in the backpack pocket. I sat there quietly, my mind churning, the emotion rising within me again, and once more pulled out the phone. This time I was quicker, dialing all ten digits. I waited a couple seconds, on the verge of disconnecting the line a second time, when I heard that familiar voice, "Cameron Fields," he said. "...Hello?...Hello?"

"Um...Cameron..."

"Petey?"

"Yeah...it's Petey," I said meekly.

"What's wrong, bud? Are you all right?"

I then began to cry. "I'm...uh...I'm on the bus, on my way home..."

"Is someone threatening you? Are you in danger?" he said rapidly, suddenly concerned and excited.

"No...no, nothing like that. Can I talk to you? Can I come talk to you?"

"Sure, Petey! Sure you can. Where are you at right now? Where's the next stop that you can get off the bus?"

"On Eighth and Woodmere," I said, "We're about three blocks from there."

"Okay, cool, not far from my office. I'll pick you up at the bus stop there in ten minutes. Okay? You gonna be okay til I get there?"

"Yeah," I said. "Um...thank you."

"Any time. Just don't worry, I'm on my way...okay?"

"Okay," I hung up the phone, feeling suddenly worried that I may have done the wrong thing. I should have called Drew instead of Cameron. I couldn't have reached Drew though; he would still be working. I should have just waited. Why did I call Cameron? Why did I let myself get so upset like this? I debated for a couple minutes about not even getting off the bus. I had to though. It would be so rude of me to call him and then just stand him up, leaving him to wait at the bus stop for nothing. Matt would punish me for something like that, for sure, even if the person who I stood up was Cameron.

We hit two red lights in between the place where I'd called Cameron and the bus stop where he was to meet me, so with this delay he'd had time to get there before the bus even arrived. I stepped off the bus and saw him standing there. I couldn't believe how he'd dropped everything to come to me. I couldn't believe he'd be so nice to me. "Hi," I said sheepishly, looking down at my shoes. "I'm so sorry to call you."

"Don't even think of apologizing. I told you to call me any time, didn't I?" he reassured me. "I'm glad you called. Come on, let's go over and get some lunch. Have you eaten yet?" I shook my head. "Okay, good, me neither. There's an awesome deli just a block from here—walking distance. You cool with that?"

"Sure" I said, looking up to him. I smiled as we made eye contact. "You're a really nice guy, you know," I told him.

"I try," he shrugged, and then he put his arm around my shoulder as we walked together up the street.

* * *

Once seated in the café, I began to pour my heart out to Cameron. "You see Matt's not like you...or me. He is not just attracted to guys. He likes pussy...ur, um....girls too."

"But he's with you, Petey. It's fine that Matt is bisexual. There's nothing wrong with that, but since he is with you and is your boyfriend, then he shouldn't be seeing girls on the side."

"But he never promised me that he wouldn't see girls. He never said that he wanted only me...you know, like

505

monogamy. He never said that, so how can I expect him to keep a promise he never made?"

"Don't you think that you deserve to have that promise made to you, Petey?" he asked, reaching over the table to place his hand on top of mine. "Don't you think that if you are being faithful to him that he should do the same for you?"

"I don't know! I'm so confused about it. He owns me; it's his right to decide who he sees. It's not up to me to say. It's only up to him to say."

"Who has been telling you this stuff?" Cameron sighed. "Petey, Matt only owns you if you allow him to. Don't you see what a double standard there is here? Matt gets to go out and screw anyone and everyone that he pleases, while you sit at home and wait for him. You, on the other hand are completely monogamous and wouldn't dream of ever being with anyone else."

I looked into his eyes, "Well, maybe I might dream of it, but I wouldn't do it."

"Exactly! There's nothing wrong with looking...or fantasizing. What I'm saying, though, is that he has one set of rules for you and another for himself. How is that fair?"

"I don't think it's supposed to be fair, Cameron. Okay, let me explain how I see it, okay?" He nodded as he leaned into me. "I see that Matt is this awesome, perfect-looking jock. He can be with anyone he chooses, male or female. He can pick up chicks when he wants pussy, or he can get other fags— um, gay guys to give him blowjobs, he can do whatever he wants with whoever he wants. But instead, he chooses me."

"So you think that because Matt is this hot stud, you have to take what you can get. You have to settle for whatever he chooses to dole out to you, huh?"

"Yeah, sorta," I nodded. "He likes chicks and guys both. I can't change that no matter how hard I try. He is just the way that he is. Period. If I love him, don't I have to accept him for who he is?"

"Sure you do, Petey, but what you are talking about is not who Matt is. You are talking about his behavior, what he chooses to do. He may be bisexual by nature, but he's not a slut by nature. He makes that decision all on his own."

"Please don't call him names, Cameron. I don't want you to say things like that about him."

"I'm sorry, you're right. I'm truly sorry. It's just that it pisses me off to see him hurt you like this. You know what, it pisses your sister off too. She is very concerned about how Matt's using you."

"Why do you keep saying that?" I asked defensively. "Didn't you hear what he said last night? He has never forced me into anything."

"Petey, I personally think that what Matt is doing to you is worse than physically forcing you into anything. What he is doing is playing mind games with you. He knew from the beginning that you were vulnerable, easily impressionable. Then he moved in and started to take over your life. I think it's nothing but a power trip to him. It's a game. I don't wanna hurt you by telling you this, kiddo, but it's so obvious. You deserve so much more than that; you really do!"

"How do you know it was him that moved in on me? How do you know that I didn't *want* him to treat me the way he has?" I felt my temper starting to rise, feeling the need to defend the one single person that I loved with my whole heart.

"If that is the case, then why did you call me today? How come you were crying when you saw him with his new girlfriend? It hurt you...of course it did! I know that deep inside you don't want to be treated this way. Maybe it is that in some twisted way you feel you deserve it."

"Cameron, do you have any idea how much Matt has done for me?" I snapped back. "He rescued me like I told you last night. He bought me new contact lenses, haircuts, brand new clothes. He got me a whole new wardrobe! Plus, he takes me places with him and pays for everything. You saw what he gave me for my birthday present last night! How can you say that he is treating me bad?"

"Listen to me, Petey," he said, trying to calm me, "Matt has a lot of money. His family does. It is no big deal for him to buy you a cruise or a new wardrobe of clothes. It's not like he had to go out and earn that money, ya know. It is there for him to use...he's spoiled."

"Well, he could be just using it on himself, but instead he chooses to buy things for me. Plus, he doesn't even like it when I get him gifts in return. He tells me I should not be spending all my money on him."

"You shouldn't Petey. That's one thing I agree with him on. He has the disposable income to spend. You don't!"

"Maybe this was a mistake...to talk to you like this." I pushed my chair back and immediately stood up.

"No wait! Wait Petey, I'm sorry. I'm not trying to hurt you."

"You're not hurting me! You're making me mad! I can't believe the things you are saying about Matt. You don't know anything about him. You don't know what he is like!" I was yelling at this point.

Cameron looked around us quickly, reminding me that we were not alone by his worried expression. "Please..." he said calmly, "Please sit down. I'm sorry. I did not mean anything bad about Matt. I was not trying to diss him in any way. Will you please sit down and let me explain myself? Please?" He looked up at me with the most imploring expression upon his face. I took a deep breath then and slowly sat back down.

"I never was attracted to guys who were like myself, Cameron. I'm still not, and probably never will be. I'm attracted to dominant guys like Matt. I want to feel protected and cared for and loved, and I want to be owned. I don't want to be the one who makes the decisions and has the burden of all the responsibilities and who has to worry about everything. I don't want to have to tell other people what to do. That sort of stuff just is not who I am. I don't want to be in charge.

"What I get out of my relationship with Matt is something that you probably won't ever understand. Maybe I shouldn't even waste my time explaining it to you, but I'm gonna try. When I first met him I knew in my heart he was all I ever wanted. I knew instantly that he was the person I wanted to spend my whole entire life with. I just knew. Never had I felt so contented and so fulfilled than I did when I was with him."

"But he doesn't have to treat you like—"

"Please let me finish!" I took a deep breath. "You think that our relationship is unfair and unequal. I guess there is no denying that everything about our situation is not perfectly equal, but then I really wouldn't want it to be. You see, there is a trade off...something that most people just don't understand. Matt does have control over me. He does have the right to make the decisions and to tell me what to do. But along with this privilege, he also has great responsibility.

"Matt is the one single person who is ultimately responsible for my well being. He takes care of me by protecting me, teaching me, guiding me. He also has to deal with the consequences of all his decisions. It's not like he is just given this blanket privilege to do whatever he wants. He sometimes makes tremendous sacrifices for me to keep me happy and safe and protected."

"Petey, when has Matt ever sacrificed for you?"

"The fact that I'm even sitting here talking to you shows that Matt is willing to sacrifice for me. He knows that he could have just pulled me out of that party last night and banned me from seeing any of you guys ever again. Instead, he allowed me to make my own choice. He allowed me to keep the relationship that I have with my sister, who I love immensely, even though she doesn't like him. He allowed me to decide for myself what will really make me happy, and you know what? I've decided!"

"But you still are not dealing with the real issue that got you here to begin with, Petey," he said to me. "You still know in your heart it is wrong for him to have sex with other people."

"Maybe. I don't know, really. I have heard of people having open relationships before, where they are not just monogamous with each other. I don't judge them because it's not my business, so why are you judging us?"

"I'm not judging you. You're the one who called and said you wanted to talk to me. I'm just giving you my objective opinion."

"Well, remember that it just that—your opinion. Cameron, I don't mean to show disrespect to you...really, but you claim to be this ultra liberal person who is so extremely tolerant; yet you are being so judgmental of our relationship simply because it is different from what you are comfortable with."

"Now wait a second..." he was getting defensive this time. "That is not the reason that I have problems with your relationship. It isn't because of it being different. I have concerns about it because it is hurtful to you."

"But who are you to decide what hurts me or what doesn't? Shouldn't I be the one to decide that?"

"Then why did you call me?"

"I think I called you because you approached me when I was vulnerable, just like you accused Matt of doing. You knew that I was going through a time that was confusing for me, and so you specifically made yourself available to me. If you had not given me that card last night, I'd have waited after seeing Matt with that girl and would have called my friend Drew when he got out of work. We'd have talked it through, and he'd have helped me come to the same conclusions that I have reached now...on my own."

510

"I can't believe how you are twisting this whole thing around, Petey. You are making me out to be the bad guy. All I've done is try to help you. I promised your sister I'd do what I could, but I see now it's useless."

I then leaned back in my chair, feeling a sudden surge of confidence. So this was what Matt felt like every day of his life, huh? I almost laughed aloud. "I love him. You can't change that and neither can Kathie. No one can."

"You know, I think I probably should get going," he said curtly. "I'm sorry I was not more help to you Petey."

"Oh, you were extremely helpful to me, Cam," I smiled at him. "You helped me see things from a whole new perspective."

28

I was beaming when I stepped out of the café. It was twelve city blocks to the college and at least the same distance to Matt's house. I didn't care, though; I'd have walked a thousand miles for him without even thinking. I turned briskly and slung my backpack over my shoulder as I headed for Matt. With each step my pace quickened, and I smiled a little more broadly at each passer-by that I encountered. I didn't even feel like walking, actually; I felt like skipping or leaping or jumping. I wanted to shout to then entire world how much I loved him. At this moment nothing was going to stop me from telling him so either...nothing.

Halfway along my trek, I could not wait any longer and broke into a run. I ran as fast as I could, dodging people along the way, jumping over curbs, and crossing intersections against the light. My heart pounded in my chest excitedly as I turned down the street where he lived. When I spotted his house, I began to run even faster. Leaping across the lawn and up the steps, I grabbed the railing and leaned into it, panting and gasping for breath. I waited less than five seconds before lunging towards the door, and I lay on the bell, ringing it over and over. I did not stop pressing the bell after the first few rings, but continued to trigger the doorbell over and over, waiting impatiently for my hero to hear me.

Finally the door flung open and I stood face-to-face with a somewhat astonished and rather perturbed looking Matt. I smiled up at him broadly and lunged myself towards him, stretching my arms out wide as I yelled, "I love you with all my heart! I want you...only you!" Out of pure reflex he extended his own arms, allowing me to fall into him. I hugged him tightly, wrapping my small arms around his torso. "I want the tattoo! I want to be yours completely, and I want everyone to know...the whole world! I've thought about it enough, sir. It's what I want. You're all I want, for now and forever!"

Matt laughed aloud as he wrapped his arms around me, allowing himself to be pushed backwards by my overly-zealous gestures of affection. He stumbled backwards a bit and began to lose his footing as I pressed against him. Before we knew it, we were in a heap on the floor, me lying on top of him. We laughed giddily as we rolled around in each others' arms. His hands moved down my body as he dug his fingers into my side, and I laughed uncontrollably. He then leaned in to kiss me square on the lips. At first his lips met mine with a powerful passion as he grabbed my head and held me against himself; then the kisses turned to tender and romantic expressions of affection.

"How did you decide?" he said as he pulled my face away from his. "How did you know I was the one you wanted?"

"Cam convinced me," I said seriously, looking him right in the eye. Then we both laughed. As we rolled around together on the floor, Petey the pup came scampering in, licking our faces and wagging his tail excitedly. I reached up to pet him as he barked playfully, and I could do nothing but laugh. Amidst all of our excitement, we barely heard the door close behind us.

"Must be Kim," Matt said. "Guess she figured out I wasn't in the mood for studying."

"What are you in the mood for, sir?" I asked him as I lay my head on his shoulder.

He pulled his other arm up to clasp his hand behind his head and looked down at me. "Hmm," he said thoughtfully, "How about you and me study together, pup? We can study each other."

"Oh, you wanna be my study partner, sir?"

"Forever," he said. "I think this could be the beginning of a beautiful relationship." I looked into his eyes and smiled.

TO BE CONTINUED in book two

www.ingramcontent.com/pod-product-compliance
Lightning Source LLC
Chambersburg PA
CBHW010436100726
47904CB00008B/2371